The ASTRAL

ALSO BY KATE CHRISTENSEN

In the Drink

Jeremy Thrane

The Epicure's Lament

The Great Man

Trouble

The ASTRAL

A NOVEL

KATE CHRISTENSEN

DOUBLEDAY

NEW YORK LONDON TORONTO SYDNEY AUCKLAND

www.doubleday.com

Portions of this work were originally published in slightly different form in *Open City Magazine.*

Grateful acknowledgment is made to the following for permission to reprint previously published material:

City Lights Books: Excerpt from "Malagueña," from *Poem of the Deep Song/Poema del Cante Jondo* by Federico García Lorca, translated by Carlos Bauer, copyright © 1991 by Carlos Bauer. Reprinted by permission of City Lights Books.

Random House, Inc., and the Wylie Agency LLC: Excerpt from "Funeral Blues," from *Collected Poems of W. H. Auden* by W. H. Auden, copyright © 1940, copyright renewed 1968 by W. H. Auden. Reprinted by permission of Random House, Inc., and the Wylie Agency LLC.

Jacket design by Emily Mahon.
Jacket illustration © Susan Wides. Courtesy of Kim Foster Gallery.

LIBRARY OF CONGRESS CATALOGING-IN-PUBLICATION DATA
Christensen, Kate
The Astral : a novel / Kate Christensen. — 1st ed.
p. cm.
1. Middle-aged men—Fiction. 2. Adultery—Fiction. 3. Parent and child—Fiction.
4. City and town life—New York (State)—New York—Fiction. 5. Domestic fiction.
I. Title.
PS3553.H716A9 2011
813'.54—dc22

2010049794

ISBN 978-0-385-53091-0

PRINTED IN THE UNITED STATES OF AMERICA

10 9 8 7 6 5 4 3 2 1

First Edition

For Brendan

Bring me an axe and spade,
Bring me a winding-sheet;
When I my grave have made,
Let winds and tempest beat:
Then down I'll lie, as cold as clay.
True love doth pass away!

—WILLIAM BLAKE, FRAGMENT FROM "SONG"

Though thou loved her as thyself,
As a self of purer clay,
Though her parting dims the day,
Stealing grace from all alive;
Heartily know,
When half-gods go,
The gods arrive.

—RALPH WALDO EMERSON, "GIVE ALL TO LOVE"

Part ONE

Chapter One

Toxic water streamed with gold like the belly of a turning fish: sunset over Newtown Creek. Tattered pinkish-black clouds blew overhead in the March wind. The water below me rippled with tendons and cowlicks. Just across the brief waterway were the low mute banks of Hunters Point, church spire, low-slung old warehouses. An empty barge made its way down the creek toward the East River and the long glittering skyscrapery isle. I stood behind the chain-link fence the city had slapped up to keep the likes of me from jumping in.

I was hungry and in need of a bath and a drink. At my back thronged the dark ghosts of Greenpoint, feeding silently off the underwater lake of spilled oil that lay under it all, the polyfluorocarbons from the industrial warehouses. I had named this place the End of the World years ago, when it was an even more polluted, hopeless wasteland, but it still fit.

As I stood staring out through the webbing of fence, my mind cast itself through the rivulets of my own lost verse. I netted little flashes of lines and phrases I'd been reworking, "Held spellbound, your mollusk voice / Quietly swathing my cochlea / In tentacles of damask cloth" and "Slow-weathered verdigris of our once bronzed thighs," but they sounded dead to me now. All I could really hear was *Luz, Luz, Luz* like the feeble pulsing signals of a dying heart. Heartache was a physical thing, a pain in my chest, a sort of recoiling tension with an ache like a bruise. There was a withheld quality to my breathing lately, as if I had been sucker punched and was waiting to get my wind back, but no wind came. I could remember whole published poems, but if these new, destroyed verses still existed in my brain, they fled from the webbing of my memory like darting schools of tiny fish, scooching away the instant before capture.

I turned away from this butt end of waterfront warehouses and walked back the way I'd come, along Manhattan Avenue, past the flophouse where I lived now, bare mattresses piled in the front window. I passed junk shops full of old radios, used dolls, and cowboy shirts, Goldsholle and Garfinkel Inc., Mexican bodegas, liquor stores, the abandoned hulk of JK Restaurant Supply with its twisted metal grate, small markets with root vegetables in boxes along the sidewalk, butchers' shops festooned with loops of kielbasy. I went through the intersection at Greenpoint Avenue, the dingy McDonald's, defeated Starbucks, opposing Arab newsstands, and on to the old Associated Supermarket with its sexy Polish girls pouting at nothing as they rang up your groceries. The outdoor clock at the Smolenski Funeral Home was permanently stopped at 6:30, both hands pointing straight down to hell.

I hung a right off Manhattan Avenue and aimed myself toward the glowing neon sign in the window of Marlene's, one of the last local old-man bars. Was I an old man yet, at fifty-seven? I'd been going there for years. The place had rusty tin ceilings, original wainscoting, two-dollar drafts in small, icy mugs, and moose antlers. The one concession to the new millennium was a flat-screen the size of a small car.

"Hello there, Harry," said George as I came in. The most deadpan voice I have ever heard. If he has any feelings that cause him to lie awake wracked with turmoil in the small hours of the morning, he's not telling. What he'll do is pour you a grudging whiskey finger for three bucks. Never a double; that's not the way they do things at Marlene's.

George has a pocked face the color of gray chalk, a thin colorless wavelet of hair pasted to his scalp, and small protruding eyes. He has a day job at the Acme Smoked Fish warehouse on Gem Street, but he moonlights, so to speak, at Marlene's, for the social life it affords him; otherwise he would have none, he once confided in me with endearing frankness. Marlene is his sister.

I parked myself on a stool midway down the empty bar. George handed me a whiskey and I swallowed it whole and felt a little warmer. My mother was Irish, my father English, but whiskey unites my opposing factions; I like the smokier, pricier, older single malts, but the cheap blended brands do the job just the same.

"How are things, George?" I asked as he set my second whiskey before me.

"Never better," he said. "Yourself, Harry?"

I looked him in the eye. "Never better."

Marlene's opens every day before noon and closes in the very early morning and is almost always populated by its regulars, most notably several local women who park themselves in a row at the bar and settle in for the duration like birds on a wire, smoking and kibitzing and getting shitfaced. But here George and I were tonight with the place to ourselves, separated by a barrier of scuffed wood, he serving, me drinking, a scenario that plays itself out everywhere, all the time, two lonely men doing some manner of business together, not quite making eye contact.

"Couldn't find the remote the other night," said George. "Looked for it everywhere, all over my apartment. High and low. Even tried the freezer."

"What were you watching?"

"One of my programs," he said. "The one with the doctors. So I'm looking for it and the phone rings. I go to pick up the phone and press the remote and say, Hello? So there was the remote. Then I couldn't find the phone. Finally found it on top of the fridge where

I left it when I was looking for the remote. Sometimes it seems like the world is playing a joke."

"And it's not always funny," I said. "By the way, Luz threw me out."

"What? She did? When was this?" He looked truly shocked. Long-term marriages apparently appear as permanent to others as geographical formations; when one dissolves, it's as if Fuji or Fiji had disappeared overnight.

"Not too long ago," I said.

"Well," he said, "that's tough. That's just tough. So where you living now?"

"I'm renting a room in the hotel down by Newtown Creek."

He cocked his head and set another whiskey in front of me. "This one's on me."

"Thanks, George." I lifted my glass. "'Blindly we lurch through life like crones / Plying high heels on the cobblestones.'" That was from one of my old poems, the ones that were as accessible to my memory as my own name.

"Sure," he said. He was used to my delusions that I was the neighborhood bard. He folded his arms and looked down at the scuffed surface of the bar. "Those cobblestone bricks down on West Street are made of wood, not clay, did you know that?"

"Near Noble Street," I said. "You can see the tree rings in them if you look closely. I wrote a poem about it. 'Frets, concentric, fraught with letters from old clouds.'"

"I was afraid they'd catch fire when the Terminal Market went up a few years back."

"Me too," I said. "I kept thinking, if the wind were blowing inland, the whole neighborhood would catch. It would have happened so fast—a piece of burning ash falling just so."

I had watched the grand old warehouse burn with Luz beside me, both of our faces pressed to the same windowpane.

George shot me a look. “Right, you live in the Astral,” he said. “That must have been scary.”

“Used to.”

“That’s right,” said George, the tip of his tongue swiping at his upper lip. “Maybe you’re better off out of that place. I hear there’s mushrooms growing in the bathrooms and bedbugs living in the furniture. I hear the super has a photo studio in the basement where he takes pictures of young Asian girls.” He said this last without a whiff of salaciousness. George seems to have excised the sexual part of his brain as a way of keeping his life simple. Smart man.

The door opened, and Karina entered and charged down the bar toward me. “Hi, Dad!” she said. “I thought you’d be here. I wish you would get a cell phone.”

“Why do I need one?” I asked as she kissed me on the cheek. “You know where to find me.”

“I’ll have a draft, please,” she told George, then said to me, “I’ve been worried about you. How are you?”

“Never better,” I said hopefully, but I already knew she wasn’t having any of it, and anyway, I was flattered by her concern. My daughter had just turned twenty-five, but unlike other girls her age, she was totally uninterested in anything beyond a narrow range of severely ascetic passions, the most intense of these being Dumpster diving, colloquially known as freeganism. She regularly foraged for and redistributed quantities of garbage, or rather “perfectly good food and clothing,” to “the poor,” of which I was now, come to think of it, one. In addition to trying to save the world from its proliferation of waste and to save the poor from deprivation, she has never been able to shake the notion that she’s solely responsible for the well-being of her family.

Karina’s coloring is like mine, pure English/Irish, reddish-haired, fair-skinned, blue-eyed, rather than her olive-skinned, black-haired, dark-eyed Mexican mother’s, but her face looks so much like

Luz's—oval shape, large eyes, blunt nose, a quiveringly focused expression like an alert animal's—it pierced my heart just then to look at her.

"Come on," she said. "Tell the truth."

"The truth," I told her as she took a swig of bitter foam, "is that life goes on, like it or not, till you croak."

"Oh Dad," she said without appearing to have heard me, "I wish you would come and live at my place. That hotel is a death trap. Guys knife each other in the hallway."

"Thank you," I said with a brief internal quailing. Had it come to this, that my own daughter thought I was incapable of taking care of myself? Of course it had; she had thought that since the day she was born, and she was right. "Thank you, Karina, but really, I'm all right."

"I have that extra little room," she said, bossy and insistent.

"When is the last time you heard from your brother?"

"Hector? He never calls me."

"I haven't been able to contact him for a while. The only number I have for him is some sort of public telephone, and no one seems to be willing to go and fetch him when I call. He's always in some sort of meeting or working or asleep."

"Why are you trying to call him? You never call me."

"Because I'm worried about him, and I'm not worried about you."

"You can't call just to say hi? Look, I came all the way over to Greenpoint to track you down. And Hector can't even bother to come to the friggin' phone."

"I'm worried about him," I repeated, "and I'm not worried about you."

She laughed. "Okay, okay. But come on! He's probably just busy." She took another sip of beer. "Dad, please come and stay at my place. Please. You're living with junkies and vagrants and lunatics. It's dangerous."

"I like it there," I said. "It suits my purposes for now. I don't want to move all the way to Crown Heights. That's not my neighborhood. I don't know anyone there, and it's too far from Marlene's, but thanks for the offer."

"Then please get a cell phone. I have a heap of cast-off phones in a drawer, so all you need is a cheap monthly plan. Or pay as you go."

"I don't have any money," I said. "Have you seen your mother lately?"

"I just came from there. She needed help getting rid of some things."

"My things," I said without inflection.

"Well, she says you don't want them."

"I want them," I said, "to stay right where they are, waiting for me to live among them again."

This put an end to our conversation for a moment. Behind me on the enormous flat-screen, a coiffed Latina in a blue jacket looked directly into the camera and with plush red lips intoned the goings-on of today's world with cool, sultry authority. She reminded me of Luz. But everything reminded me of Luz right now, even the moose antlers above the bar. They made me think of our twentieth-anniversary trip; there had been moose antlers over our bed in the Adirondacks cabin we'd rented for a week. Luz had asked me to take them down and put them in a closet, or better yet, outside where they belonged. They were disgusting, she said; they were cruel. That I hadn't done so, on the grounds that it was not my place to redecorate property belonging to others, was ranked thereafter in her hypothetical marital black book as one of my offenses. At least, I had always assumed it was hypothetical. Maybe she had written it all down somewhere. If so, I wondered what she would do with her compendium now that it was all over. Sell it at a stoop sale? Publish it as an antimarriage manifesto?

"Oh, well," I said, "never mind about that. Will you come with me to visit Hector tomorrow?"

Karina lifted up her glass and looked into her beer as if it were piss, then set it down again. "I have a lot to do tomorrow."

"Come with me," I said. "The garbage will wait."

"It's not that. I have a deadline. I'm writing an article for an online magazine. It's going to take all day because I spent this afternoon tracking my parents down and making sure they were all right."

I said before I could stop myself, "So your mother is all right."

"Of course she is," said my daughter. "She'd be all right in a nuclear war. But underneath, you know."

"I know," I said. I was too sad to say any more.

George had moved down to the far end of the bar and was concentrating on the TV news, or seeming to, while he busied himself with a pinkie fingertip, pulling wax from his ear. I motioned to him, caught his eye, pointed to my whiskey glass. He nodded and made his way down the bar with the bottle.

"Dad, I think this whole thing is horrible," said Karina. "I'm not taking sides, I swear, I love you both, and it's none of my business. But is it true you're involved with Marion? No, don't tell me. I don't want to know."

"Is that what your mother told you?"

"Well, it's classic. Men usually have affairs with the women they're closest to. Their female friends, their wives' sisters or best friends, their co-workers, their friends' wives . . ."

To mask my horror that Luz would tell our daughter this, I grinned at Karina. "How do you know so much about men's extramarital affairs? You're a lesbian. And you're not married."

She shook her head at me and waited for my answer.

"No," I said clearly, nodding my thanks at George for pouring me a generous shot, at least three drops more than usual, "I am not having an affair. Not with anyone. And definitely not with Marion." Looking up to stare with half-tipsy self-righteousness into the middle distance, I caught George's eye. He was gazing at me, poker-faced, but I thought I caught a glimmer of amused sympathy somewhere in his left cheek, which twitched slightly.

"George," I said, "my wife has gone completely batshit. She ripped up my poetry notebooks and threw my computer out the window and kicked me out of our apartment."

"She said you were writing love poems," said Karina, "and they weren't to her."

"They weren't written to anyone," I said. "Not anyone real."

"She seems to think they were written to Marion. She said it was obvious you've been in love with her forever. She said, also, that she knew it already, she's known it for years; the poems just confirmed it."

"Those were my private notebooks," I said. "I've been falsely accused by someone who trespassed in my personal property. She spied on me. She came to a false conclusion and will not let me explain."

"She told me she's through. She doesn't want to hear your excuses and lies. I can't believe she's doing this to you now, after she threw Hector out."

"And she destroyed my work," I said. "Completely wrecked it. It's poetry, Karina. It's invented. All the women I was writing to are imaginary. None of them is Marion."

"I believe you," said Karina. "But she said she's worried that when the book is published she'll be publicly shamed."

"No one is going to publish them, probably."

"You don't know that!" said Karina, always my defender.

"This is all just nuts. Oh damn it all to hell."

"Don't cry, Dad. I'm sure she'll come around, she's just a little crazy right now."

"I am not crying," I said. I cried all the time lately.

"I think you should wait a week or two, let her cool off."

"I hope she hasn't said anything to Marion," I said, rubbing my eyes.

"They had a long talk yesterday. She went over to Marion's. She was there for like an hour and a half. Marion told her there's nothing going on."

My heart thudded with hope. "And?"

"Mom didn't buy a word of it. She told me that Marion's behavior start to finish was completely disingenuous. Marion denied everything and tried to comfort Mom, which of course only pissed her off more."

"Oh, Jesus," I said. "I have to go." I pulled some bills out of my pocket. I was too flummoxed to see how much it was. Karina covered my hand with her own and handed George a twenty.

"Keep the change," she said to him.

"Thank you very much," said George. I put on my wool pea jacket and watch cap.

"You take care, Harry," George called after my receding back.

Karina walked with me along the dark, windy sidewalk. She is as tiny and sparrow boned as Luz, and I am as spindly, tall, and long legged as Ichabod Crane, so she practically had to hold on to my flapping coattails to keep up, but my girl has always been tenacious, like a burr.

"Go home," I said. "Work on your article. Don't waste any more time on your crazy old parents."

"I am going home," she panted. "I'm heading for my car. I wish Mom would believe you."

"Well, she won't."

"She must have some reason to think such a thing."

"Don't get into the middle of this," I said.

"You won't come with me? My place is warm and the room is free."

We stopped to face each other on the corner of Norman Avenue.

I bent down, took Karina's face in both my hands, and kissed her on her icy little nose. "Good luck with the article," I said. "Let me know when you can visit Hector with me. Leave a message at my hotel, they might give it to me, you never know."

"You call me," she said.

Chapter Two

I flapped my way through the windy evening, past deserted industrial streets slanting away to my right, low warehouses with the isle of Manhattan glittering off across the river, a baroque concoction of lights and metal, like an enormous, gaudy brooch. Marion lived in a house on Berry Street on the south side of Williamsburg, a building she had bought back when this neighborhood looked like a Wild West pioneer town of low buildings, big sky, and wide, spookily quiet streets. I often expected to see tumbleweeds blowing along while a stranger in black rode into town on his horse. This was back in the eighties; not so long ago, really. Now it was a tapas place here, vintage boutique there, wine bar here, upscale baby clothing emporium there.

And kids everywhere, stylish, artfully coiffed kids, walking around shooting off at the mouth about God knew what. Kids the same age as my own two, but nothing like them at all except they came conceivably from the same species.

Karina didn't know a bacon-wrapped date from a pig in a blanket; she knew that some people threw useful things away that other people might want. She also knew how to renovate an old house with revamped, recycled, and free materials, condense her political and social concerns into effective talk-radio sound bites, run a meeting of like-minded eco-conservatives, and fret about others' emotional well-being, but never her own. From the time she could talk, my daughter had been selfless and earnest, outraged by waste and pollution, hell-bent on doing whatever she could to ease the earth's burdens.

As for Hector, as far as I could tell, he was aware of little else besides the fact that Jesus Christ was supposed to be coming back at some point. He'd been excited about this since his sudden epiphanic conversion at the tail end of his adolescence. After spending several shy, gawky, antisocial years playing video games, avoiding girls, and trying all the drugs available to the average New York City teenager, he emerged from his room at seventeen, a virginal, naïve, wild-eyed believer. Jesus bloomed in his heart, but not, to Luz's deep disappointment, with the formal, ritualistic trappings of Catholicism. Hector's faith was fundamental, elemental, intuitive, and bare-bones. Jesus lived in Hector's heart, and Hector sought to imitate him, to adhere to what he saw as the primary Christian imperatives: faith, chastity, poverty, obedience, sobriety, and humility. The Messiah was going to return, and Hector wanted his soul to be clean and prepared, wanted his mind to be free of any illusions and thoughts that might prevent his recognition of the savior's return.

He was now twenty-seven and showing no signs of outgrowing his anticipation. On the contrary, he had found a whole group of people who shared his feelings, who'd invited him to come and live with them on their farm out on Long Island, where they swanned around all day through the sea grass in white robes, looking at their old-fashioned pocket watches and counting down the hours, or so I imagined; I'd never actually been there.

I climbed the steep steps of Marion's stoop and rang her doorbell, which resounded on the other side of the thick wooden door. I waited with my back to the door, tapping my foot, looking down deserted, seedy South Eighth Street, far-off sky-high windows winking dully from the projects, plastic bags swimming in midair, windblown cans scuttling along the sidewalk. In the air high above me, the iron girders of the Williamsburg Bridge alternately whined and hummed with tires. The long, fast walk had warmed me, but I felt wracked with hunger and emotional panic. I wanted the door to open quickly, and at the same time, I hoped Marion was far away and not home.

The door opened. I turned to face her. Her long silver-black hair was loose instead of pinned up, and she clutched the collar of a dark red bathrobe to her throat. She looked even paler than usual. I was aging right along with her, of course, but I had been frequently startled, since her husband had died, to see how much older she looked.

"Marion!" I said. "Are you sick?"

"Harry," she said. "I was wondering when you would turn up. Come on in."

She shut and locked the door behind me and followed me through the entryway, past the staircase, back to the kitchen. I took off my coat and hung it on the shoulders of a chair and seized my cap in both hands and ripped it from my head in a frenzy. "Karina told me Luz was here yesterday," I said.

She leaned in the doorway, her hand still clutching the bathrobe at her throat, and nodded, looking at me with skepticism, amusement, sympathy, and irritation. Marion has always had a knack for these dramatic, multilayered expressions.

"Oh hell," I said. "Are you sick?"

"No," she said, "I just didn't bother getting dressed today. I decided to stay in bed reading and drinking tea. It's cold and windy out; I didn't have to be anywhere."

Marion Delahunt and I first met in 1975, the good-bad old days. When I first saw her, she was in the corner of an East Village dive bar with a Leica, photographing transvestites and drag queens. I was sitting on a bar stool sipping a draft beer, gawping and wide-eyed and fresh from the Midwest, soaking up the ambience. It was two in the morning. She started photographing me, which thrilled me, because I had aspirations to some sort of stardom in those days, as do most kids who come to New York. I wondered who she was, this dark-haired, tall, confident girl; maybe she was a professional photographer, maybe she had connections. I offered to buy her a drink. She asked for a Bloody Mary, explaining with high-handed, slightly affected nonchalance that it was a breakfast cocktail, and she had just rolled out of bed. I didn't know enough yet to see through her carefully manufactured persona; it took me a while to catch on to the fact that she was as young and naïve as I was. It turned out that she was not a professional anything, she was an art-school student working on a long-term project, documenting downtown nightlife. "Yeah, me and every other MFA hopeful," she said. From then on, Marion brought me along on her homework junkets, to loft parties and clubs and other fascinating scenes. We stood together in the glamorous, drugged, dolled-up crowds, thrilled to be part of it all. We were partners, in cahoots, both pretending we already belonged, both dying to make a name for ourselves here. We were never, manifestly and explicitly, lovers. When it was time to call it a night, we always gave each other a chaste but urbane kiss on the cheek and went off in separate directions, me to the East Village where I lived with two other guys, Marion to Chinatown to her dumpy walk-up studio.

I might as well have been gay, or a eunuch, or a woman as far as she was concerned, and as far as I was concerned, we were the best of pals, and I didn't want to try to mess with that. And, in the long run, Marion wasn't the person I was looking for; she was too much like me. I didn't want a twin, a *semblable,* I wanted a muse, a challenge. Marion was a witness at Luz's and my wedding in 1980, and we were hers and Ike's three years later. Hector and Karina were Marion and Ike's godchildren.

Marion and I had known each other for thirty-five years and had never once kissed on the lips, never even come close.

"What a mess," I said.

"She seemed totally convinced," said Marion. "Where the hell did she get that idea?"

"Apparently we were seeing more of each other than usual this year."

"Well, Ike just died," she said.

"Another reason she's suspicious," I said.

"She's threatened by me now, after all these years? Look at me, I can't even get out of bed and get dressed, let alone conduct an affair!" She laughed. "Although of course the two are not mutually exclusive."

"Can I have a drink?"

She handed me the whiskey bottle and a glass. I was evidently the only person who drank Marion's whiskey, or else the current bottle was always coincidentally at the exact same level as the last time I'd come. She kept a bottle of Bowmore on the counter for me; it was one of my favorites, very good but not overpriced.

"Sit down," she said. She poured herself a glass of red wine and joined me at the kitchen table. Marion had a crackpot's kitchen: the walls were jammed with bright, grotesque little paintings, most of them her own, most of them portraits; she was not really a painter, but she liked to do it as a hobby. A red 1950s Chambers gas stove sat between the doorway to the mudroom and the back window, which was steamed up from the huge, hissing beast of a radiator underneath it. The refrigerator was tarted up to look like a cartoon woman's upper body with a big red mouth, full boobs, a beauty mark, and a curl of auburn hair pasted to her forehead. Marion hated countertop appliances and had almost none; she made coffee in a battered old aluminum drip pot and toast in the broiler. On the black-and-green linoleum floor sprawled a squinting, disreputable tabby cat whose basketball of a stomach was probably bigger than the rest of him put together. He had the personality of a prosperous burgher: suspicious, xenophobic, and expansive when drunk. This was old Blancmange, nicknamed Mange, at least by me.

"I told Luz to see a therapist," said Marion.

"What did she say?"

"She took it in. I hope she'll do it. She told me she can't sleep, she's having a nervous breakdown, this betrayal is more than she can take, and so on."

"I haven't betrayed her."

"Not with me, you haven't." She looked shrewdly at me. "And I haven't betrayed her at all, ever."

I glared at the old cat Mange. They were ganging up on me, these harpies. "Marion, this time I'm innocent. That was twelve years ago, and this is now."

It was true: twelve years before, I had sneaked off a few times to the apartment of an acolyte of mine during the long, glorious, ill-advised, tawdry summer when I taught a poetry workshop at the Right Bank, back when there was a Right Bank, a bohemian-type bar on the river under the Williamsburg Bridge. I turned forty-five that summer, and therefore it was the prime time for such behavior. Samantha Green was a lost, needy, thirty-year-old sylph of a would-be poet. Our several furtive couplings were intensely erotic for me, pornographic and thrilling. I could do things with her that Luz had no interest in. Samantha was eager and willing to let me act out my adolescent sexual daydreams on her. I fucked her from behind at her kitchen sink, in the shower, on the living room couch. As I sneaked out of her building and walked back to the Astral through the hot, familiar streets, I felt guilty, light-headed, and terrific.

Of course Luz found out, because Samantha called her up and told her, out of spite, after I ended it with her. Then there was hell to pay, hell that was in my opinion far, far out of proportion to my crime, but in the interests of preserving my marriage, I took it all. Luz threw things and screeched and excoriated me and interrogated me and demanded the emotional equivalent of a pound of flesh, but it all finally simmered down except for those rare times when Luz's path crossed Samantha's somewhere in the neighborhood, and then she'd come home hissing and spitting and I would have to straighten her out and soothe her all over again. "Yes, I love only you. No, Samantha didn't mean a thing to me. Yes, I swear on everyone's mother's dead body, you are my love, my wife, my muse, my heart, the light of my life, my Luz." Often it would be a day or two before she could see straight again. And I always heaped presents and flowers on her, especially on Valentine's Day. The things a guilty husband has to do; it was one peccadillo in thirty years, but ever since then, I might as well have slapped a scarlet P on my forehead—for Philanderer, alas, not Pimpernel.

That whole long-ago rotten tamale and its horrible fallout had been bad enough, but this time, it was much, much worse. And I hadn't even had the intense pleasure of an illicit affair. And I couldn't soothe her, because I had nothing to apologize for. I knew that Luz simply wanted me to confirm her suspicions so the two of us could engage in another lengthy round of psychodramatic, Catholic wrangling—interrogation, purging, groveling, punishment, more groveling, more punishment, which then would lead, finally, to hard-won atonement, eventual (grudging and provisional) forgiveness—so of course my recent claim of innocence had only maddened her more. My denials got neither of us anywhere. A guilty confession would have saved us, but I could not lie. So out I was thrown on my ass, and all my new work was shredded. I wasn't sure which was worse, my fate or that of my book. Actually, my book had it worse. I was still here and would probably survive; my book was dead.

"She told me you haven't been yourself lately," said Marion, but she said it mildly, as a question.

"And what is that supposed to mean?"

"It means she thinks there's something going on with you, but she doesn't know what."

"You live with someone for thirty years, raise kids side by side, sleep on the next pillow every night, break the same bread at the same table. And you find in the end that you don't know this person really, not at all. Maybe I knew her at the beginning. I don't know. If so, then at some point in all those years she turned into a stranger. I don't know when or how, but there it is."

"Since Ike died," said Marion, "I've been going through his papers. He kept journals, did you know that? I didn't. I found all of them in a box in the closet under the stairs. It took me weeks to open the first one, but once I did, I couldn't stop reading."

I gazed at her with keen interest. Anything to do with the topic of wives reading their husbands' private papers secretly, without permission, was a matter of grave urgency to me at this moment. "You violated his privacy," I said. "And he can't defend himself."

"The thing is," she said, rolling her eyes at my dramatic defense of Ike and ignoring it. "The thing is, it's so odd, I don't know what he's even talking about half the time; he hardly refers to me at all, as if I were some sort of pet or object. I suppose I went looking for proof that he had loved me . . . signs of my own existence. But I found someone else instead. I don't know what to make of it. And he's gone now, you're right. I can't ask him." She reached into her bathrobe pocket and pulled out a pack of cigarettes. She lit one with a purple lighter, then offered the whole caboodle to me.

I hesitated; I had quit twenty years before. Then I took one and said, "Oh well, what the hell." I lit it, inhaled with confidence as I recalled doing in my youth, coughed and choked and hacked, and stubbed it out in the ashtray. "I don't know what's happened," I said. "They must make them stronger than they used to."

"Well, not exactly," she said, smiling, smoking.

"What did he write about then, if not you?"

"Some interesting things about politics and music and reactions to movies and plays, but mostly boring things. His aches and pains, especially as he got sicker. Minor irritations, things he saw on his walks. Some observations about people, but not me. Never me. The point is, the man who wrote those journals isn't Ike, not the Ike I was married to all those years. I don't know who the hell that guy is."

"Surely he was allowed to have a private life that didn't include you," I said. "Surely he was allowed to write about whatever he wanted."

"Surely he was," she said. "Of course he was. But surely I'm allowed to make whatever I will of those writings."

"But there's nothing in the marriage vows that precludes recording one's private thoughts!" I said. "Nothing, as far as I can recall, although I took them so long ago, it's a blur. But 'I swear to write only about my all-consuming obsessive love for you' doesn't seem to have been one of them."

Marion laughed and leaned back in her chair with her lanky legs stretched out. Her bare feet were pale and bony and almost translucent. The silver in her hair sparkled metallically in the light of the chandelier behind her in the hallway. "But you don't know for sure."

"I'm almost certain."

"Marriage is so odd," she said. "You owe each other so much, but nothing at all."

"It's like performing in a theater sometimes, you're playing a role," I said. "You go through the motions night after night and it all adds up to commitment and longevity and the appearance of intimacy. I feel like I've just come offstage." I thought about Ike's death for a moment, the suddenness of it, his funeral and memorial, Marion living here without him. "You have, too."

"And here we are in the dressing room," said Marion. "All out of costume, just ourselves."

There was a brief silence. My head buzzed as if there were a gigantic rotating fan somewhere nearby, but I knew there wasn't, it was coming from inside my own skull. Marion's face looked ravaged and drawn, lit by the stark whiteness of the back porch light coming in through the window.

"Thank God you're my friend," I said.

"Harry!"

I wiped snot and tears away.

She leaned forward and eased my whiskey glass from my grasp, peering at me. "How much have you had to drink? Never mind, I'd better feed you."

"I could eat a sandwich," I said.

She leapt up and pulled things from the fridge: I noted with dog-like interest a package of ham, a block of cheese, half a baguette, jars of mustard and mayonnaise. She piled it all in front of me, handed me a knife and plate, and sat down again. I mashed a lot of everything into the bread and wolfed it down.

"Where are you living now?"

"Flophouse," I said, my mouth crammed full.

"You can stay here, you know," she said, lighting another cigarette.

"That's one way to drive her around the bend."

"Well, it's a bit cramped, with the upstairs rented. But I do have a couch."

"She would buy a submachine gun and mow us both down."

"Chips?"

"Please."

She reached behind her and unearthed a bag of potato chips and handed it over. One thing about Marion, she always had food.

"Your new book," she said. "She destroyed it?"

"Every leaf and molecule."

We pondered this.

Marion poured herself more wine, then released my whiskey glass to my own recognizance. I took a slug, or a draught, as the poets used to say, the real ones. "Was your impression that there was no chance in hell of my being let back in?"

She didn't answer right away.

"That means yes?"

"I was under the impression," she said carefully, "that what you did or did not do is not the point. Want to know what I really think? Honestly, Harry, there's not a thing you can say. She's not rational.

This goes beyond that. She wants to think you're evil and I'm evil. Maybe it's like a kid hearing a fairy tale, so she can be safe. Or not. Really I have no idea. It shocks me, a little. She's perfectly intelligent."

"Intelligence doesn't preclude madness or irrationality."

"I was afraid of her when she was here. She sat across from me and watched me and asked leading questions like a trial lawyer." She mock shivered, laughed, and was serious again. "She seemed icily insane."

I knit my eyebrows together. "Luz isn't entirely crazy," I said. "I did have an affair, once."

"Twelve years ago!" She laughed.

"Which feels like five minutes."

"Harry."

"She knows me."

"What? Come on."

"I mean she knows what I'm capable of." I remembered Luz's electric, weeping fury as she'd uprooted me from our home, her dark, outraged, heartbroken face. "I might as well be guilty."

Marion laughed, a short, dry scoff.

"I wish I were guilty," I said.

There was a long silence. Between us the air vibrated with that sound I'd heard before, the one I had thought came from my skull.

She slashed at the air with her arm. "Oh, to hell with it," she said. "This is a private drama you two are playing out that no one can talk you out of. There's nothing I can say to you. You don't want advice. You're trapped in this thing with her, and you don't want to get out."

"Well, maybe, but only because—"

"Go on." She flapped her hands at me. "This has nothing to do with me at all. Go on, go off to your flophouse like the criminal you are. Put on your hair shirt and flagellate yourself all night."

Before I knew it, my coat and cap were on, and I was outside in the cold night, heading up Berry Street with my head down.

Chapter Three

Lying awake just after dawn, I heard a grunting, coughing racket in a nearby room, one of my neighbors having some kind of fit. I jumped out of my fly-stained little bed and pulled on my shoes, corduroy trousers, and jacket and clattered downstairs and out the door. I walked with my head down toward Greenpoint Avenue. It was slightly warmer out here than it had been the night before, and the wind had died away to nothing. A bird chirped from God knew what tree. A cat slunk through the gutter past me, intent on breakfast. Bird and cat and I were alone out here, greeting the day together. Just ahead was a bodega with its metal grate up. I went in and got myself a cup of burnt-smelling coffee in a paper cup.

My funds were small and dwindling. Luz was the breadwinner in our family. I was too proud, now that she had falsely accused me, to use any of her hard-earned money and was relying instead on the meager contents of the bank account I'd opened shortly after I had first arrived in New York and augmented with my paltry poetry earnings through the years. My small local original bank had been bought and sold and bought and sold several times over, so now, through no doing of my own, my wee little bit of money was held in the monster fist of one of the conglomerates. I was amazed to have any left at all. I'd recently done a bit of adding and figuring, and I was fairly confident that if I lived frugally and adopted some of Karina's more practical habits, I might make it till summer. On the other hand, I might have to get a job. I had no idea who would hire me, given my limited skills and experience. I was keeping the idea at bay for now, but occasionally a glimmer struck me—the most obviously expedient of these was bartending at Marlene's on the nights when George stayed home to watch his programs. I could rustle up a few students for poetry workshop, teach English to immigrants, collect cans from recycling bags on curbs and cash them in at the Associated. I had plans lined up, just in case.

The coffee was so hot it scalded my teeth, but I kept on nipping at it. I had some species of a hangover, an ache in my temples and a roiling in my gut and a terrible feeling that my dearest friend was now angry at me in addition to my dearest wife. I have never been able to tolerate having anyone angry at me unless there was a clear, specific course of action I could take to make everything all right again.

The morning sun lit the aluminum siding on the low frame houses so the street glowed with bilious industrial colors, dried-blood red and pus yellow and abscess green. Overhead was a sky as big and wild as a sky in a spaghetti western. Clouds piled and massed in a streaky, inconstant blue of various depths and intensities. A panel truck careered along the avenue and jounced by me, its bones rattling in the potholes. Then came the B43, empty, lit up inside like a diner in a Hopper painting, lumbering toward the end of its route at Newtown Creek.

When I was a wet-eyed boy starting out in the poetry racket, I pledged my lights to metered, rhymed verse. My models were old-fashioned, and so was I. Through the decades, I kept quiet company with a disparate, brilliant fellowship of my own assemblage: Blake, Crane, Auden, Pound, Yeats, Chesterton, and a few others. As a youth, I plunked out traditional songs while all around me roared honking street jazz. My stiff little formal lyrics gradually attenuated through the decades into the easy human pulse of a beating heart, my doggedly perfect rhymes gave way to a visceral, practiced conversation, and my tight-assed jejune ideas about love and the world melted into raw emotional stuff poured into a mold and held there, barely.

Poets rarely earn a dime to rub against another dime, but I got published in literary journals and magazines. I won little prizes here and there, attained a following, mostly of fellow poets. Then, in 1987, an editor named Glenda Savage at a small new Brooklyn press took me under her wing and published a collection of my work, *The Fourth Bell*, and then she published another, and then another, every three or four years, and I also published individual poems in actual glossy magazines that paid for it. In 1995, *Poets & Writers* ran a pretty little puff piece about me. I was asked to judge contests and teach at workshops and sit on panels with other poets to discuss the terrible state of contemporary poetry. I taught at the New School for a while until they phased me out. I contributed a nice little portion of the family income. Who could ask for anything more?

But then, around the turn of the millennium, it all dried up and blew away. Glenda Savage left Halcyon Press to move to London with her husband and three kids, and with her went my champion and protector. Halcyon stopped publishing me, and I couldn't find anyone else who was willing to take up the task. In short, I fell out of favor. Who knows why these things happen? It was as if I had died, but I hadn't died. I was still writing, a ghost ship icebound in a frozen sea. Or at least I had been writing until recently.

I had been working on a book of crown sonnets that had been almost finished when Luz destroyed it: ten corona sonnets, ten crowns on ten beautiful, made-up heads, ten merry-go-rounds of seven sonnets each, each one beginning with the last line of the one before it until the circle closed, the last poem ending with the first line of the first. I was hoping to be able to reconstruct them all by memory. If I had been many years younger and fresher brained,

I would have been confident of my ability to do so. Now I wasn't so sure. Luz seemed to have destroyed my memory along with everything else.

All my life I'd willingly set my poetics into predetermined molds, shaped language according to external dictates. I had surrendered up much of my volition, harnessed my imagination in service to strict poetic rules. Perhaps I needed someone else's external, imposed will, because internally, I had none. My father shambled around the house after my mother died like a dry drunk with his pants unzipped. My mother was a devout Catholic and registered nurse who raised me, her only child, with loving but distant sternness, absolute religious conviction, and unswerving ideas about my potential genius, and then she died in a car accident when I was eleven and left me to the chaos of my pathetic, lost father's downfall. I had spent the rest of my childhood reading, daydreaming, and waiting to escape from Iowa and never come back.

. . .

Of course I'd married someone so much like my mother, a woman I could never fully possess, who believed in my genius and supported but controlled me. And of course I likewise shackled myself to the most ironclad poetic forms. Inside, my viscera were unsupported by spine. In my brain, nuanced flickering dim lights illuminated shades and variegations; there was no certainty in me, no absolutes, no belief in anything but the essential mystery and unknowability of the universe. I needed to be propped up. I needed my muse, my wife, to withhold her deepest self from me, to judge me and find me wanting, so I could excoriate myself and win her and convince us both of my worth by writing these insanely disciplined, convolutedly accomplished poems. This allowed me the freedom, or so I had thought, to invent, and write love sonnets to, imaginary women. The whole system had been carefully calibrated and cantilevered, and self-perpetuating. And I wanted it back.

I discovered as I turned into India Street that I was aiming my steps homeward.

. . .

I wasn't surprised to find this. I had evidently decided to overlook something essential about Luz: she was impossible to convince of anything she had decided was untrue. She could not and would not ever admit she was wrong on any point. I knew these things, but my rational self had given up and was going along for the ride, curious to see what would happen.

And as I walked, bits of my own verse came back to me, lines about one imaginary woman's naked, tender inner arm, another's pink-red lower lip shining with saliva, the arch of another's bare foot as fretted and taut as fire-glazed glass, and I wanted to hit myself in the forehead with a baseball bat. Of course, it was possible that I had written these poems and left the notebooks lying on the kitchen table so she'd read them and throw me over the parapets, so that I'd be free to go off in search of the tender, the taut, the arched, the pink-red. Maybe I had wanted her to eject me.

But assuming I hadn't, then I was a blithering nimrod. Luz has a cold, impeccable exterior inside which beats a soul as fragile and silken and easily crushed as a baby mouse. The contradiction is lethal, maddening, and lovely. Her exterior defends her interior with hawk-talon rabidity. She is quick to judge and pounce, as black and white in her moralistic reasoning as the average eleven-year-old. She knows not nuance, she recognizes neither grays nor subtlety. Her mind is a swift, keen, cold, unbending scalpel that cuts through malignant uncertainty, penetrates rotten inconsistencies, slices through defensive skin to extract what she takes to be absolute truth. When she is wounded, she goes for the kill. She is implacably resolute to the point of insanity: Her pride is paramount, and it will not admit to folly. She twists any idea until it matches her need to be right.

As she ripped my offending poems to shreds she called me a hack. She called me washed-up, overrated, pretentious, and sentimental. She told me she couldn't believe any other woman would ever want me. It went on. I was old; I was flabby; I was useless and a coward. Her eyes sparked black flames of scorching poison. Even as I tried and failed to plead my own case, to save my own life, I had to admit to myself that she was in some way rather scarily magnificent. She was vengeance incarnate. She was a piece of something eternal and elemental. She would have made a brilliant banana-republic dictator or medieval religious despot.

"You are my love," I had told her. "These women are nothing but inventions."

"You liar," she said, with venom. "You lying coward."

The ongoing tedium of thirty years' cohabitation hadn't dimmed or slaked my feelings for her, only my ability to reassure her of them as often as she needed, or (to be honest) ever, really. She was justified in thinking I was lying, based on the affection I'd shown her in recent years. We had never stopped making love, but we had long ago stopped being romantic, which I know is much worse for women.

Then I stopped on the sidewalk, and my heart almost stopped, too. Coming up India Street toward me through the bright, clear morning air was my wife. She hadn't seen me yet. She walked with eyes downcast, not quickly but with a clear sense of purpose. She was going toward the bus stop and thus to the subway at Bedford Avenue; her hair was in a neat bun and she wore sneakers, which meant that she carried her nurse shoes in her bag.

The shock of her familiar, beloved self coming toward me rendered me as still and speechless as if I had been electrically shocked. She didn't notice me until she was several yards away, and there I was, blocking her path. She ground to a slow halt and idled there, waiting for me to let her by, staring at me as if I were a bum. Her eyes glittered.

"Excuse me," she said when she saw I wasn't budging.

"Just talk to me for five minutes."

We did a little sidewalk dance, back and forth.

"I'll be late for work."

"You have never been late for work, and you never will be."

"Let me by."

"Please listen to me."

"I don't want to hear it."

We were speaking softly, normally.

"I'm not a liar. I'm not a cheat. I'm a knucklehead, yes, but I'm not having an affair with Marion or anyone else."

"Liar," she said.

"You upset her the other day. Her husband just died. She's all alone. She needs your friendship now and she needs mine, too."

"Go and be with her then," said Luz to my chest as we do-si-doed. "Go and be with your *friend*."

"This is ridiculous."

"Yes."

We came to a stop, finally. I looked down at her. She looked up at me.

"Can I come home?"

"No."

"Have you heard from Hector?"

She looked at me sharply. "No," she said. Luz had strong ideas about the ways to worship God. Before Hector had left to join the group, he and Luz had had a terrible fight about what she took to be his rebellious defection from the devout Catholicism she had inculcated in him from birth. She had told him that if he joined, she would cut him off. Apparently, as always, Luz had made good on her threat in the most literal way.

"Karina and I are going to drive out to Long Island and visit him. Will you come with us?"

She wavered; I saw it in her face. She was remembering that the four of us were a solid family, independently of what happened between her and me: she and I had kids together, kids we had loved and raised together, grown kids whose parents we still were.

But the tidal pull of our past wasn't strong enough. She shook her head. "I'll never go there," she said, her lips tight.

"We'll miss you."

She stared at me, breathing through her nose. Her nostrils vibrated. "I want a divorce, Harry. I'm going to file."

When she said this, all my internal organs shrank like salted slugs. "No," I almost shouted.

"I hate you," she said.

"I know you do. But you're wrong."

She stared hard at a spot just beyond my head. I watched her carefully, knowing that with the slightest sign of softening from her, I had a chance to make her listen to reason. I waited for a small, brief window of neutrality that could either be widened or made to snap shut. Her lips twitched slightly. I pounced.

"I saw Karina last night."

She squinted at me. "So did I."

"I know," I said. "After she saw you, she came to find me at Marlene's. She told me you were convinced I was having an affair with Marion and that you had talked to her about it, so I went to see Marion to find out what was going on. I hadn't seen her in weeks. She said you had already made up your mind and wouldn't listen to a word she said. She was hurt and angry. She has been a good friend to us both through the years, and this is coming out of nowhere, Luz."

Luz made a noncommittal sound in the back of her throat.

"She said she felt like she was on trial," I added. "Why did you do that to her?"

"You always got so happy and excited when she called," she said. "If you and I were talking, and she called, you interrupted me to answer the phone, and your whole expression changed. When you had dinner with her, you came home looking like you were in love and you just got out of bed. And since Ike died, she was predatory. She was enticing you and trying to take you over. Like a lone wolf trying to steal another wolf's mate. I could see it, Harry. I trusted her and let her into our family. She had no children of her own, and I let her be a godmother to ours, and this is what she did."

We had been round and round on this pony ride many times already, but once we got on, we couldn't get off. And, as always at this point in the roundabout, I felt a rising and uneasy sense of guilt: she had forced me, in her accusations, to admit something to myself that I had never before allowed to surface. It was partially true, what she said. I loved being with Marion. She understood me and knew me deeply, she asked me for nothing, and she made me laugh. And of course there had always existed a certain potential well of attraction between us. I had always enjoyed the possibility, had always appreciated that it was there and could exist without any of the mess.

And after Ike's death, it was true, I had spent more time with Marion. Since Ike died, we had gone out together every week or two to a local pub for hamburgers and drafts, and each time, although I had as a matter of course invited Luz along, she had stayed home, giving no reason except that she was tired. Of course, now I knew she'd felt intense, mounting paranoia about Marion and me. But how would I have known that? She had never said a word to me about it, and all along she was watching us with suspicion, resenting my closeness with Marion, her brain ticking, looking for clues by eavesdropping on our phone calls, reading our letters and e-mails. Of course the specter of my long-ago affair was haunting her. That, I understood.

And maybe Marion and I had become a bit more overtly affectionate. Yes, we had. Maybe Luz was sensing a sudden and real shift in the decades-old balance between Marion and me, an upset that caused our untapped feelings to bubble a little, harmlessly but palpably. I had been feeling lost and alone in recent years, like a failure, a has-been. Marion had just lost her husband. We were pals, comrades, drinking buddies in our hour of mutual need and sadness. But I had not touched her, nor she me, except for the usual hug and kiss hello and good-bye. And that was the only thing that mattered right now. Luz could accuse me of loving Marion, of feeling a certain attraction to her, of occasionally preferring Marion's company to hers, all of which I could readily admit, but her sole grounds for throwing me out had been that we had slept together. And we had not.

"I have never slept with Marion," I heard myself saying; it was the next line, right on cue. "Nor have I ever wanted to. I love her. That's different. I'm not in love with her; she's my friend. I'm always happy to talk to my friend."

But Luz had seen the flicker of guilt in my face while I was thinking, had tracked my thoughts and, as always, read into them without any allowance for nuance or degree. An eye-shift of guilt was all the proof she needed.

"You're lying," she said. "You two have cooked up some kind of story and expect me to believe it just because you both tell me the same thing. What did you do, rehearse it? Marion is as full of shit as you are. Just tell me the truth, Harry, give me that one sign of respect. I know you've slept with her. I know it here." She punched herself in the stomach. "Just admit it, and we can go from there."

All the horrible memories of the aftermath of my affair twelve years before resurged and made me want to vomit. It didn't matter that this time I was innocent, didn't matter what I had or hadn't done. It was the same thing all over again. The half of me that was Irish Catholic wanted to confess and be done with it. But I couldn't lie to Luz. The English Protestant half of me told me I couldn't.

"*Dios mio*," she said, watching me.

For an instant she let me see how much intolerable pain she was in, and then her face snapped shut again.

Well, she had created it for herself. Maybe she wanted it. What a fierce little wackadoo, this person I was married to.

"Just because your stomach thinks it's true doesn't mean it's true," I said. "Your stomach doesn't know everything."

"Every time you deny it, I get angrier. It makes it worse. First you betray me, then you lie to me. That's insult added to injury."

"Has it occurred to you that I'm not lying?"

"Of course you're lying. You fucked around on me once, and now you've done it again."

"But consider for one minute the possibility that I haven't. One minute. That's all I ask."

Her face was shut and blank. "I know it here," she said, punching her own stomach again.

I was dizzy with the surreal feeling of existing in an entirely different universe from my wife. "You destroyed a year of my work," I said. "For no reason. I'm completely innocent." Suddenly I wanted to punch her in the stomach right where she had punched herself, but harder. Lethally hard.

"You deserved it." She poked me on the shoulder, her finger like a talon. "I hope you never write another word. I hope you rot in hell on earth."

"Fuck you," I said. "You're pigheaded and wrong and you're acting like a lunatic."

She managed to slither around me only because I was reluctant to restrain her forcibly. But she wasn't getting away that easily. I turned and kept pace with her on the sidewalk, managing to walk beside her even as she did her best to shepherd me into the gutter.

"An entire year of work, gone," I said. "Gone."

We walked along angrily together. Our paces had always matched despite the near foot disparity in our heights. We walked half a block in tight silence.

And then I wasn't angry anymore. Poor Luz, believing I had wronged her so cruelly with our trusted friend.

It was much easier to be angry. The alternative was crushing sadness.

"Luz," I said to the top of her head, "I love you, I want to come back. If you'll believe me, I'll forgive you. Clean slate, start over, everything forgotten. I'll write another book, it doesn't matter. This is no good. I miss you every second. I need you, Luz. There just isn't anyone else. You're the only woman I want."

Her head was down, so I couldn't see her expression. Something about the contained way she was crying, the almost furtive, intense secrecy of it, gave me a small explosion of fear that her mental state was more shaky than I'd suspected. The words *nervous breakdown* and *hormonal changes* surfaced in my brain.

"Is it menopause?" I asked her. I couldn't help myself. "Is that what this is about?"

She made a livid, startled, choking sound, as well she should have, and darted away from me. I let her go. Our futile ritual conversation was over. I watched her disappear along the sidewalk like a small retreating crow in her long black coat.

When she was out of sight, I threw my coffee cup into someone's garbage can and trudged down toward the Astral.

I had told her I loved her over and over these past few days, but I didn't know what this meant anymore. When we were young and new, I loved her with the pure intensity of early romance, and when our babies were little, I loved her with the urgent loss of the new father supplanted by his young. But through the decades, things had gotten dirty between us, corrupted by familiarity, the pain we caused each other on purpose and by accident, our blind spots, all the things we couldn't say or see. By now, I felt so many complicated, ancient, powerful things for and about Luz, a mish-mash of memories and associations and anger and irritation and physical knowledge and attachment and blind habit and nostalgia and dependency and intertwined roots, I wasn't sure it could all be lumped together as love or any other one word. Love was a word for the young and hopeful. I wanted to get old and die with the woman I'd come through so much with, my fellow grizzled veteran of the same wars. I wanted my memories all in one place until the end. It didn't matter what either of us had said or done. But maybe that was a kind of love. And maybe it was more than that; maybe Luz and I had achieved love in its highest form between a man and a woman. Not that it did me any good now.

Chapter Four

Midway down the block, the Astral Apartments came into view, an enormous, six-story redbrick tenement castle-fortress that spanned a whole block of Franklin between India and Java. The place was compelling to look at from without, blighted from within. Great rock-face brownstone arches curved over the entryways; above them, windows were set into recessed arches that rose to the fifth floor of the facade, and above these were crenellated decorative rooftop embellishments. Three-sided bay windows were festooned ghettolike with webbed metal gates, stubbled with air conditioners, made fancy looking with decorative brickwork and lintels. The building's huge corners were rounded and towerlike. No opportunity to decorate had been wasted; even the structural steel storefronts on the first floor, housing a café and a Laundromat, were gussied up by their own rivets. The place had been built by Charles Pratt in the late 1880s to house his Astral Oil kerosene factory workers; Astral Oil's slogan had been "The holy lamps of Tibet are primed with Astral Oil." To which they might have appended "And the refineries of Astral Oil are primed with cheap labor." Some claimed that Mae West had been born in this building; I didn't see why that couldn't have been so.

As soon as I saw the place, I changed my mind about going home. In order to get into my own apartment, I would have had to bribe the super, since my wife had no doubt changed the locks on me, and I couldn't afford to bribe anyone. And I had lost interest in sneaking into my longtime home to look into my own refrigerator and rustle up some breakfast and sit in my old chair and take a shower, which had been my original, if vague, intent. Seeing Luz walk away from me in tears like that had filled me with a furious itch to do something worthy of her disapprobation and mistrust. My anger was tempered with the kind of nausea that demanded palliative action. If she was going to vilify me, then I would goddamned well give her a reason to. No reason to be all sad-sack about things. I needed to find a woman, any woman, to justify all of this.

I walked back up to Manhattan Avenue, where all the public clocks were stopped at some arbitrary hour. I stomped along until I came to the doughnut shop and saw their window full of freshly made doughnuts, real doughnuts, and saw the Polish girls behind the counter, handing waxed-paper bags and change to customers.

I went in and took a seat at the counter. "Chocolate cake doughnut and a cruller," I said to the luscious, sultry lass who approached me inquisitively. "Coffee with milk and sugar." She brought it all without expression. I ogled her as she refilled the cup of the guy next to me, a beefy Polish gentleman who smelled of last night's vodka binge and who had a head like a boulder. His eyes were of a blue so pale they had almost no color at all; his hair, so blond it was likewise almost colorless, was buzzed over his scalp. His big round head was set into bricklayer's shoulders, a torso like the back of an armchair. I knew all this because I turned to look at him to ascertain why he was looking at me. He did not appear to like what he saw. We had a brief silent staredown.

"Beautiful day," I said, biting into my cruller.

He didn't answer. I turned my attention back to the girl, who was now slouching by the cash register, looking at nothing. She wore the expression so many of the Polski lasses wore, that contemptuous, flat, blasé look that warned all comers that she had heard it before and hadn't cared for it much the first twenty-seven times. An old photographer friend of Marion's and mine had once boasted to me that he frequently hired these doughnut-shop girls to pose for him.

He'd always offered to show me the pictures he'd taken, but he never seemed to get around to it. I could only assume he was fibbing wishfully, or else he'd shoved all the photos into a shoebox he kept under his bed and took out to drool over on rainy nights.

And who could blame him? Polish girls managed to ooze and withhold sex simultaneously. They dressed for Mass and grocery shopping alike in slippery little cleavagey minidresses, sheer hose, and stilettos. They smelled of some pheromonal perfume only they seemed to have access to. Their bodies were at once soft and tight, breasty and rumpy but willow waisted and slender armed and long legged, like some idealized doll. They seemed totally removed from the effect they had on men. They didn't flirt, didn't acknowledge or encourage our stares. In fact, they seemed to be unaware of us, as if they'd put that dress on by accident, as if they looked and smelled like that through no effort or design of their own. And they wore their disdainful expressions on faces as comically gorgeous as cartoon vixens', with peachy skin, curved lips, ski-jump noses, and heavy-lidded eyes of a dizzying, mad blue.

The guy next to me was muttering under his breath, something in Polish I didn't catch but that was not, I was guessing, his mother's recipe for stuffed cabbage. And he was shifting on his stool in a way that made my hackles rise. If he had taken a dislike to me, he was welcome to it, as long as he kept it to himself.

Feeling a little better than I had fifteen minutes before, cheered by the doughnut girl and sugar and grease and the warmth of this little place and the rumbling, incipient violence to my left, I finished my cruller and began on my chocolate doughnut. I motioned to the girl and then to my coffee cup. Without appearing to exert the slightest effort, she was before me in a flash with the pot, pouring. I looked up at her and smiled.

"Thank you," I said. "You are incredibly beautiful."

The man on my left gave a volcanic shudder. The girl looked at him, then went back to the cash register. Then everything happened very fast. The man said something to me in Polish, something brief and savage, a snarl on a hot gust of vodka fumes. I turned to tell him I didn't speak Polish, but as my neck swiveled, he punched me in the ear. I dropped my doughnut. The girl shrieked and clapped her hands to her cheeks. Her counterpart in the back of the room called to someone in the kitchen. I rubbed my ear, puzzled and slow to understand. My fingers came away without any blood on them, but there was a high ringing sound in there. The Polish drunk, seeing that I needed elucidation, punched me again, this time in the side of the head, missing my ear. My vision went black and then cleared. I stood up and launched myself at him and got his thick bricklayer's neck in a choke hold and squeezed my thumbs against his Adam's apple. "Bastard," I said between clenched teeth. I stared into his ice-hot-blue little eyes. Then I spat at him.

I was a malnourished string bean of a poet eligible for AARP membership. He was a youngish man who looked as if he spent half his time at the OTOM Gym on Calyer Street pumping iron and the other half drinking lethal-grade hooch in McCarren Park on a bench. It was not going to be a fair fight, but it felt good to pretend to myself, as he gathered his forces to kill me, that I was impressing the doughnut girls.

Then he struck. One meaty hand squeezed both of my bony ones, convincing me to release my grip on his windpipe. The other meaty hand punched me full in the face and picked up the metal napkin dispenser and slammed it into my eye. I was pulled off him by someone very firm and purposeful, and then my enemy and I were both in handcuffs being led out of the doughnut shop by two cops who clearly would have preferred to stay there all day. My nose was streaming blood. My eye throbbed. Adrenaline and pride prevented anything from hurting yet, but this was going to be a bitch.

The Polish drunk must have been the doughnut girl's much-older boyfriend, I surmised, or her uncle or father, or a friend of her uncle or father, or a friend of her boyfriend's. Whoever he was, he hadn't liked the way I looked at her and had felt entitled to wipe that look off my face. Well, it was gone.

The 94th Precinct house was just a couple of blocks away on Meserole, but the cops put us into two separate squad cars and drove us there. This turned into a somewhat roundabout, laborious route because all the east-west streets in Greenpoint run one way. I sat in the backseat watching the cop drive. He was a terrible driver, the kind who sent me into a frenzy of corrective urges. He had a jerky accelerator foot and bad steering technique, at once too sudden and too indecisive. I had never had a driver's license, myself, but I knew bad driving when I saw it.

My attacker and I were led out of the cars and into the building through the paper-strewn foyer into a warren of desks and filing cabinets and made to sit quietly several yards apart while two cops officially charged us with public misconduct and fingerprinted us and did all the bureaucratic hoopla required to make us feel like fifth graders who'd thrown spitballs and set off the fire alarm. When it was all over, I asked what was going to happen next.

"We keep you here for a while. Then maybe we take you to Queens."

"I want my phone call," I said.

I was led into the hallway where there was a dinosaur of a pay phone and then the cop put some coins in the slot and handed me the receiver. He was not a bad sort, as they go. I'd seen him around the neighborhood with his partner. He was a tall redheaded Irish-looking lad, rawboned, as they used to say; his partner was a chubby little Latino guy with a mustache. They always looked like a pair of comically mismatched dogs forced to walk along together.

I called Marion, of course.

"Harry," she said. "Are you all right? You sound terrible. Did you make it home okay last night?"

"I'm in jail," I said. It was hard to talk with my lip so swollen.

She was quiet just long enough to register her simultaneous amusement and alarm. "You're what?"

"I'm only in a holding pen for now, at the station at Lorimer and Meserole. But it sounds like they're going to take me to Queens and throw me into the real clink."

"What did you do?"

"Got hit in the ear by a meathead and had the bad luck to fight back."

"Then you're innocent! Do you have a lawyer?"

"They'll give me one, I guess."

"Have they set bail?"

"So far they've just read me the Miranda, fingerprinted me, and told me I was not welcome to disturb the peace any further."

"I think that's just a misdemeanor," she said. "Are you sure they're not going to just book you and release you?"

"They might," I said. "As crimes go, this was pretty low on the totem pole."

"I'll be right there," she said.

"No need," I said. "I can walk from here if they let me go."

"Please," she said. "See you soon."

We hung up.

Then I was thrown into the holding cell with the Polish guy, whose name as it turned out was to my private amusement Boleslaw Grabowski. There we were, alone together at last. Boleslaw stayed put on his bench, slumping a bit. I likewise slumped on my bench and pressed to my raw nose, lip, and eye the wad of Kleenex some nice lady cop had handed me. It was turning a lurid pink from a combination of drool and blood. Boleslaw seemed mildly pained by my continued existence, but on the whole quiescent.

"This is perfect," I said out loud.

He cleared his throat with a strained, glottal quack, looking down at his shoes, which were as flat and shiny and red-brown as roaches.

"It's good to have things go from bad to ludicrous," I said. Violence beat in my veins to the rhythm of the throbbing in my head.

He was watching me now, wary, his eyes shifting from side to side.

"When things go wrong, it's easy to feel that there's a conspiracy against you, that some force is causing things to go badly for you through no fault of your own, or maybe through some fault of your own that you can't recognize. Like a bad dog being punished."

I spoke in a pleasant, easy voice, but his small eyes were narrowed as if he understood the meaning rather than the tone of what I was saying. I almost expected him to reply in perfect English, but things like that only happened in movies and books.

"You're probably a Catholic," I informed him. "And you probably believe, because you've been told since you were a wee pierogi by the guys who run the church, that there's some father figure in the sky who made you punch me. Some dark part of yourself, of course, made you punch me, but you're a puppet in your own mind. That is how you see yourself: a puppet of fate. Or destiny if you prefer, or whatever the word is in Polish. With your strings being pulled by that god up there."

I looked at him with all the compassion I could muster, given the fact that my face was hamburger.

"But there's no dignity in that way of thinking. Character lies in irony. That's where the real story is. I went in search of a woman. And found the doughnut girl. And allowed myself to dream of what I wanted to do to her. And then wham boom, I got socked in the head and arrested. It would make me laugh if my lip wasn't fucked up. It makes me laugh anyway."

I tried and failed to laugh and noted that the effort hurt quite a bit, as did talking, but my teeth were chattering from the delayed shock and pain, so it was either gabble away or go catatonic.

"Maybe this sounds a bit simplistic to you. Maybe you think I'm being too hard on Catholicism and religious faith in general. Well, maybe I am, but I prefer the hard bedrock of ludicrous chance to the suffocating pillow of belief."

I could tell Boleslaw was silently considering punching me in the head again.

"I have to confess, Boleslaw," I said, pronouncing his name to rhyme with "coleslaw." "I believe in rhyme and rhythm. But my adherence to form is loony. I make it much harder for myself than it has to be. I follow arcane rules that went out of business a hundred years ago. No one is making me. There's no one there. I do it only because it strikes me as beautiful and difficult and interesting. The forms are just there to be used. They're not God given. People invented them, people follow them. Adhering to the most beautiful poetic forms is as human as getting drunk on plonk on a park bench and pissing yourself. And that's the ultimate irony, our dual nature."

I felt a queer onrush of fellowship toward Boleslaw then. I stood up and paced around, shivering.

"So it's hilarious, the way you hit me in the head. Irony is a gel that colors things a certain way. It doesn't exist independently of the beholder. Two people can apprehend it together, which is always fun, and which I anticipate will happen when I see my friend Marion soon and tell her what happened."

I sat down again and was silent. Boleslaw fell asleep, snoring with a drunk's unconcern, habituated as he was to sleeping on hard benches. My face hurt like hell. I separated the pain into two opponents, broken nose vs. split eye, and allowed them to compete for Most Unbearable. First the nose pulled ahead with a slow, sharp throb. Then the eye came up the backstretch. Then they settled into a pulsing gallop together, neck and neck.

About two hours later, the police let me go with a slip of paper stating that, on a date in the not-too-distant future, I was expected to show up in court to plead my case and accept my punishment. For now, I was free. I left Boleslaw sleeping there without saying good-bye. I hoped never to see him again.

Marion had been waiting all this time in the station house, drinking coffee and chatting with the cops and tapping her foot. When she saw me, she leapt up and strode right toward me, shaking her head. She wore a fitted dark red pantsuit, motorcycle boots, and a long black fake-fur coat. A big heavy-looking camera was slung around her neck. Her loose hair glinted. Her face was very pale. She looked shocked to see the condition I was in.

"Marion," I began.

"I'm taking you to my doctor," she said, cutting off my thanks. "We'll go up there right now. This is an emergency; he'll see you."

I tried to say something, but my mouth had frozen.

"I'm paying, so shut up."

"I have insurance," I said, or thought I said.

"In return, I get to take your picture. Holy shit, Harry, you look like a grenade exploded on your face. Hold still. Right here. It'll just take two seconds."

She posed me in front of the admitting desk with cops moving around in the penned-in desk area behind me and snapped me from several angles. I tried to look as gruesome as I could, which wasn't hard.

"All right," she said. "Let's go."

The doctor was three blocks away, on Norman. Marion worked some magic, or else they were having a slow morning, and I was ushered in right away. The kindly doctor shot me full of novocaine and stitched up my eye and adjusted my nose and swabbed around my swollen, bloody lip with some sort of numbing, soothing agent.

Afterward, I felt much better but couldn't talk. Marion helped me walk to her car, loaded me in, and drove me to her own house. She helped me up the steps and deposited me on her couch like the big baby I had become. She covered me with an afghan and brought me a glass of water to wash down my pain pills, then went away and let me sleep until dark.

I woke up so hungry I was nauseated. My eye throbbed gently

but on the whole didn't feel too bad. My nose felt pretty awful, but that was another story. I threw off the afghan and walked stiff legged into Marion's kitchen. She sat in her red bathrobe with her feet up on the table, reading a book by lamplight, drinking a glass of wine.

"How do you feel?" she asked when she saw me. "I made some soup. It's on the stove."

"I can't ever thank you enough," I said.

"Your wife called me while you were asleep."

"Did you tell her what happened?"

"She said in the nastiest imaginable tone, 'I bet he's at your house, isn't he,' and I'm sure as hell not going to lie to her or anyone about you or anything, so I told her you were here, and why. And then she told me what she thinks of me. Apparently she has hated me or at least been threatened by and jealous of me for a very long time. I should have known, I see now, but somehow I didn't."

I helped myself to some chicken noodle soup and sat at the table and looked into my bowl, remembering Luz's many ongoing leading questions about Marion through the years, questions I had always chosen to ignore, being innocent. "What did she say?"

"That she has been watching us for years. She's eavesdropped on our phone conversations. She said she did this because she knew all along and wanted evidence. She claims she's got all the evidence she needs. She said my manner with you is predatory and yours with me is flirtatious. She thinks I am a sleazebag without a conscience. I am also a liar and a narcissist and a mediocre artist. We both are all those things, actually. Good God, Harry, if it weren't so shocking and insane, I would think it was hilarious. But I'm afraid she's really crazy. She is obsessed with the idea of us together. Almost like she wants us to be having an affair, and she can't accept that we're not no matter what we say. There is absolutely nothing either one of us can say to her."

I looked up from my soup, which I was now slurping. "I have to try," I said.

"Please. You still wish you could confess your guilt? You still want to give any weight to these ridiculous accusations?"

"She's my wife," I said. "I don't want my marriage to end like this. I want to make it right. I'm innocent, and she's wrong. I have to make her see. I can't just let her think these things. She's making herself sick. I want to go back to her and put all this behind us."

"So you'll go back again, and again, and keep trying to explain," said Marion. She sounded weary. "And she will bait you and accuse you and seem to believe you and then she'll go psycho all over again when she realizes she doesn't have what she wants, which is evidence of our affair, of your guilt, and therefore of her own justification in behaving this outrageously. It's so clear. It will never happen, Harry. She can't possibly accept our innocence now. She can never accept it because then she'll have to admit that she behaved like an out-of-control lunatic. As long as she thinks we're guilty, she feels justified and sane. She would rather that than to take you back and admit she was wrong and forgive us both for what we didn't do. Honestly, as your friend, I think you should let her deal with this by herself. Don't address any of this. Don't engage with it. You'll just fan the flames."

"What did you say to her on the phone just now?"

"I cut her off. I told her I didn't want to hear it. I wished her well and said that I hoped she'd get some real help. Then I asked her please not to contact me again, ever, in any way, and then I hung up."

"You hung up on Luz?"

"Yes, I hung up on Luz."

I got up for another bowl of soup. "Well," I said.

Luz was not the sort of person people hung up on; most people were intimidated by and respectful of her cold, aloof, self-protective dignity. Of course, all her dignity had exploded. Her armor was shredded, and her weakness was exposed. I knew how terrified this must make her feel. No matter how right Marion was, and I knew she was right, and no matter how furious I was at my wife for treating both me and my old friend this way, I couldn't shake a certain compassion for what she was experiencing right now, picturing Marion and me all cozy together in Marion's kitchen, which was in fact the case.

"This soup is good," I said. "Thank you for taking me in."

"The couch is yours, and to hell with what Luz or anyone thinks. Of course the news is probably all over the neighborhood by now that you and I are shacked up."

Marion was, in her way, as proud as Luz. She was trying to pretend for both our sakes that she wasn't bothered by any of it, but I could tell how upset she was by all of this. She was as deeply angry and horrified as I was.

"Tell who?" I said. "Who is there for Luz to tell? Why would she do that?"

"Because, Harry. Not to be overly dramatic here, but she wants vengeance. No doubt she's put the news out far and wide that I've stolen you away from her, James and Lisa and Phil and Suzie, everyone who knows us."

I looked at her.

"Well," she went on firmly, "our real friends are our real friends, and anyone who wants to judge something they know nothing about, and which is none of anyone's fucking business, can go right to fucking hell."

"I hope she's not talking to anyone," I said.

"Of course she is."

"Then let's have a real affair!" I laughed angrily. "Let's do it, then! Why not? If everyone is going to think we did anyway, why not?"

Marion gave me a look and handed me the whiskey bottle and a glass.

I poured myself some whiskey, took a gulp, set my glass down, and said, "None of it's funny, I know."

"No," said Marion.

"Sorry to joke," I said.

"Ah come on," she said, "we need all the humor we can get right now."

We looked together at the lamp as if some genie might pop out of the lightbulb and return Luz to sanity and composure. None did, so we drank more, and then we went to bed, separately, but united in shared pained outrage.

Chapter Five

I lay on Marion's couch, wide awake. Since I couldn't bite my right thumb with my lip all split, I worried its cuticle with my left index and middle fingers, scraping the skin until I could peel off a bit, then starting over. It distracted me from my face. My relationship with this thumb was lifelong and complex. Sucking it deep into my mouth and allowing the ridges of my rooftop and the folds of my tongue to create a rhythmic vacuum of adhesive flesh had been my infant solace, probably from the womb, and then, after my mother died, I stopped thumb-sucking cold turkey, even in the privacy of my bed at night, and started chewing it. It stopped being a pacifying tool and turned instead into the victim of my self-mutilating aggression, the catchall scapegoat of my inchoate fears, secret woes, and unspoken furies. I started ripping the skin off around the nail, cuticle and all. Years went by during which I transformed the skin around my thumbnail into a shiny coat of scar tissue. By the time I graduated from college, the nail itself had stopped growing normally; it was ridged and misshapen, lumpy on its nail bed.

After I moved to New York, I tried to leave it alone. But I couldn't stop. On the subway, alone in a bar waiting for a friend, after a shower in front of my little black-and-white TV set, I ripped the scar tissue off and made more scar tissue. Then, one drunken night in 1979, just after I'd turned twenty-seven, I was in a bar and did something stupid, I can't remember what, but the result was that I chipped one of my lower front teeth. This had the unexpected side benefit of turning that tooth's edge into a miniature knife blade that made my thumb-ripping even more efficient, so efficient that, several months later, nipping off what I thought was a hunk of previously undiscovered cuticle from my poor tortured thumb, I dislodged and excised a tiny half-moon of thumbnail, exposing a sliver of naked nail bed underneath the cuticle itself.

Vaguely repentant and scared, like an addict who had finally gone too far, I slapped some antibiotic cream and a Band-Aid on it and went to sleep. In the morning, when I ripped the Band-Aid off to find out what had transpired in the night, I saw that the sliver of naked nail bed had sprouted a pink, spongy, porous, highly sensitive muffin of flesh that puffed above the nail. It was evidently full of nerve endings, because it hurt like hell whenever I bumped it accidentally or even brushed it on a towel, a sweater. It was oozing, wet, weird, a cellular, blood-vessel-filled swollen tissue unlike anything else on my body. I decided not to put another Band-Aid on it; being so spongy and moist, it looked like it wanted air.

In Muscatine, on my childhood friend Gabriel's horse farm, when a horse's wound sprouted this kind of puffy, extra-sensitized skin, Gabe's father called it "proud flesh." As far as I could recall, the vet threw lime powder on this proud flesh and brushed it hard to remove it. I had no access to lime powder and the idea of putting anything so caustic on it and abrading it with a brush made me scream inwardly with intolerable imagined pain. I waited for it to go away on its own. Instead, it got more infected and oozed more and throbbed with pain so sharp I couldn't sleep.

In those days, I was working as a teacher of English as a second language to adult immigrants, a job that gave me lots of time off and a good per-hour wage but no health insurance. I shared an apartment with two other guys in the East Village and lived as frugally as I could, and it was still hard to save a dime at the end of every month. I was mad at myself for causing this injury, and mad at my thumb for betraying me, finally, after all these years of our quasi-sexual, quasi-abusive relationship. I felt like a molester who'd finally been ratted on: guilty, embarrassed, perversely furious.

Finally, after about a week of pain no amount of alcohol or aspirins could alleviate, I caved and went to the emergency room at St. Vincent's. It was a Monday afternoon; I'd figured this was the best time of the week to go, because it wouldn't be crowded then with the bread-and-butter dramatis personae of the ER: overdosing suburban kids who'd been sold stepped-on, shitty drugs, stab victims of hotheaded ghetto family members, and drunks with broken noses and bleeding eyes.

I was right. After a short wait with several calm, ordinary-seeming people who all appeared, as I no doubt did, to have nothing wrong with them whatsoever, a female voice called "Harry Quirk" over a loudspeaker, and I went into the little office and sat down.

"So what brings you here today?" asked the triage nurse, a sweet-faced, lithe Hispanic girl who looked too young to be working anywhere at all, let alone at a real job like this.

I showed her my thumb. "Proud flesh," I told her.

"Proud what?" She laughed. She had big white front teeth. She was wholesome looking, chipmunky, with dark straight hair and no makeup, a blunt little nose, dark eyes. What kept her face from outright plainness were those eyes: they flashed, cool and intelligent, and their alluring gleam was half hidden by heavy lids, thick short lashes. Her arms in their navy blue short-sleeved uniform shirt were muscled, slender, long, and I could see the shape of her thighs under the navy blue trousers.

"In Iowa, the horse vet called it 'proud flesh,'" I said. "I know it just looks like it's swollen, but it's actually a thing, it's full of nerve endings, and it bleeds easily, and it's infected."

She looked from my proud-flesh muffin into my anxious face. She was still laughing. "Proud flesh," she repeated.

“Yes, so it’s not just a simple thing, it feels like it’s got roots or tentacles or something under the nail bed, it’s really in there, so I don’t want someone just slicing it off. It hurts like a bitch.”

“Harry Quirk,” she said, looking at my chart. “It’s not up to me to diagnose that thing, all I’m doing is sending you to the right place. But I can tell you that ‘proud flesh’ is not what the doctor who sees you is going to call it.” She leaned in a little closer. I could smell the subtle warmth of her skin, her sweet young breath. I hoped I smelled all right, but I doubted it. She took my hand in both of hers and turned my thumb toward the light so she could see it better. No other person had ever looked so closely and intimately at my poor old mistreated thumb. Her clinical, unsurprised, nonjudgmental gaze dissipated some of my self-loathing. “Off the cuff, I’d say granuloma.”

“It looks like proud flesh,” I said. “Doesn’t it? The way it stands up like that, inflamed and aggrieved.”

She laughed at me again. “What do you do, Harry?”

“I’m a poet. To earn money, I teach English as a second language.”

“To immigrants,” she said.

“That’s right.”

“And you write poetry,” she said. She considered me. “I read poetry, but mostly in Spanish. I started doing it to help me with the language. My parents came from Veracruz, in Mexico, but I was born here. I grew up speaking Spanish at home but then I switched to English when I got older. I love Neruda, do you?”

She was flirting with me. I couldn’t believe my luck. “Yes,” I said, although I hadn’t read much Neruda.

“What kind of stuff do you write?”

“Rhyming metered stuff. Old-fashioned. In English.”

“You’re from Iowa? Your parents are farmers?”

“My father owns a restaurant,” I said. “It’s a diner-type place where the farmers go. And my mother was a nurse. Like you.”

She looked at me with her cool silent laugh, and I looked back at her.

There was a long pause.

"Go get your paperwork from the desk," she said, breaking the spell, I thought on purpose, I hoped because she was as rattled by our chemistry as I was. "Tell them you're supposed to go to fast track."

I kept my eyes on her face, waiting to see whether I was right.

She dropped her eyes. Instantly, I was hard.

"When I'm done here," I said, "I'm going to come back and get you. Let's go take a walk."

Her face was businesslike and vulnerable in equal parts, as if she were taking me in, assessing me, understanding all the things she would be sacrificing if she fell in love with me: financial security, cultural similarity, a traditional husband who knew how to fix things and hold his own in the world. What she was offered instead by my unprepossessingly lanky, fresh-faced self, I have never fully understood. All I knew then and know now was that, from the instant I met her, I had to have her: she was silky and cool, dusky and exotic but a true-blue good girl, an industrious little gopher. And she must have sensed, whatever else she felt about me from the outset, that I wanted her and wouldn't take no for an answer.

"I get off at five thirty," she said.

When she got off work, I met her at the door to the emergency room and we walked briskly together down to Chinatown, to Wo Hop, a humble little place in a basement on Mott Street. We sat at a grease-stained booth by the mirror in the back and shared platters of sautéed Chinese broccoli, pork dumplings, and mu shu pork with extra pancakes. Luz chose these things quickly and snapped the big menu shut without another glance and handed it over to the smiling waiter. I was impressed by her decisiveness and precision with the lengthy, complicated menu. She showed absolutely no interest in what I might have wanted. This should have struck me as ominous, I now suppose, but I was so smitten, I found myself charmed by her frank, untrammeled need for control. This insistence on doing what she wanted would play itself out in ten thousand ways over the next three decades plus. I always capitulated to it. In fact, I craved it.

We navigated our disposable wooden chopsticks and swilled Chinese beers from the bottle. The Tsing Tao was cold and pungent; the food was hot and salty. Soon the back of my neck was burning and my scalp prickled from an MSG overdose. I was pleasantly buzzed, and my gums were nicely stimulated by the soft wood of the chopsticks. I felt easy and relaxed and excited with this bossy, focused, hard-assed girl.

"Thanks for ordering," I said.

"Most guys get annoyed when I do that," she said. "It's just that I have to have what I have to have."

"I don't mind," I said. "I like it when you say what you want. It's soothing."

She gave me a skeptical look.

"My mother was the same way," I said by way of convincing her that I meant it. "She was the boss, she ran the house. It was me, my father, and her, and from the minute we woke up, she told us what to do. She picked out my clothes for me every morning, I ate what she put in front of me. We gave her no trouble, and the house ran like a navy ship. She was the admiral, my father was the cabin boy, and I was the ship's monkey; that was basically the hierarchy. She dragged us to Mass, and then she made us wait in the car while she visited her aunt after church because her aunt didn't like men, and we were compliant and meek about this, as we were about everything. Sometimes we'd sit in that car for an hour or more in the dead of winter. We kept the heat on and played Twenty Questions. Finally, my mother would come running back to the car through the cold blue air, her coat around her, to land in the passenger's seat, breathless and half laughing. 'I thought I'd never get out of there!' she would say to us." I imitated my mother's high, fluted voice. "'Sorry, boys, but you know Aunt Mathilda, you two are such gangsters, and she's so *refained.*' We always laughed, and we were always so happy to see her again. Dad was all right, a sweet man, really, and he adored her. My mother died when I was eleven, killed by a drunk driver when she was coming home from the market with our week's groceries. After that, we totally fell apart . . ."

Luz looked keenly at me. "My father left when I was eleven," she said. "That's a coincidence, isn't it? Then it was me, my mother, and my sisters. All girls. We didn't fall apart, though, we were relieved, because he was a mean drunk. It was a lot calmer after he left. But we all loved him so much. When he wasn't drunk, he was the most amazing man in the world. He met my mother when they were both only fifteen, in Veracruz, and after they got married, when they were twenty, they came to New York together and managed to make their lives here. But then he started drinking, and when he drank, he'd hit my mother and yell at us and pass out for twelve hours and wake up like a half-drowned dog, all apologetic and crying. He was so pathetic. Finally, after no more than five nights like this, my mother threw him out. You don't mess with her. She was madly in love with him, but she just can't be treated like that by anyone. It broke her heart though. She has never looked at another man, but she also never spoke to my father again. After he left, he would call us girls up out of the blue and say he was coming to get us to take us to the Jersey Shore or, like, to Radio City Music Hall to see the Rockettes at Christmastime. We'd get dressed up and wait in a row on the couch not saying a word. We'd sit there and sit there. Sometimes I would get so excited I threw up. My mother tried to tell us, but we never listened."

"Let me guess," I said.

"Yeah," she said. "You know how that story always goes. But we fell for it, every time."

"Is he still alive?"

"He died eight years ago," she said.

For some wholly irrational, brutally self-serving reason, I was relieved. This meant that I would have no competition for Luz's love, not in this world, anyway. And Luz and I were even: she had lost her most beloved parent, I had lost mine. We would be free to be alone together, man and wife, without parental rivals. This struck me as a boon.

"I can't believe you're glad he's dead," she said, her eyes glinting, narrowed.

"What?" I said, shocked. How had she read my mind?

"Admit it."

"Luz," I said, "why would I be glad your father is dead? I just met you, I never met him, I lost my own mother—"

"I saw it in your face," she said. "Don't argue."

I stared at her, my chopsticks suspended with a piece of Chinese broccoli dangling from their pincers. She was right, of course, but this was the sort of thing most people would have let go, would have overlooked in the interest of lighthearted flirting, especially on a first date.

"Right," I said. I ate the piece of broccoli and chewed and swallowed. "You're insane, you know that?"

"I am not insane," she said. Her voice was soft but piercing. "Apologize for that, too."

"Wow," I said.

She didn't move her eyes from mine. Her face was a stubborn, slitty-eyed mask, fixed with a cold smile. She looked like a small olive-skinned raptor with rabbit teeth.

Because she was right, and because I wanted her, in fact I wanted her more than ever, because I needed her, or someone like her, I said, "All right then, if that's what will make you happy." I leaned back in the booth and took another swig of beer. "I admit it, and I am sorry." A tongue of lust licked at my groin. I ate a dumpling.

"Good," she said, flinty voiced, eyes pinpoints, "but I need to know why you would even think such a thing. It's disturbing, Harry."

I laughed. There was nothing else I could do.

Luz paused a moment, surprised, and then laughed too, raucous, unrestrained. Her laughter from then on was the source of her greatest power over me, whether or not she ever knew it.

Or rather, her laughter was the source of one of her greatest powers over me. We went to bed that night, the night we met. Luz brought me with her, without discussion, back to the Astral. We climbed the stairs to her third-floor one-bedroom, laughing and excited. In bed, naked, with me, she was kittenish, sinuous, carnal, darling, ravenous, generous, selfish, laughing, violent, intimate, cooing, and soft. And from that night on, I was in her thrall. No matter what she said or did out of bed, and no matter how needy, bossy, or crazy I knew she was from the outset, I was hers.

Luz agreed to marry me after my first proposal, barely a year later, even though I was a penniless teacher, even though I was not a practicing Catholic. We both knew exactly what we were getting into, what the deal was. Luz would inspire and control me, and, when she had to, support me and our kids. And, although for the most part I would disappoint and infuriate her, would always be wrong, always fall short, I did have one thing to offer, or rather, two: she announced, early on, after reading some of my poems, that I was a literary genius, and that therefore I would write great poetry and give her brilliant children who were half white and had a better chance of acceptance and success than she had had.

She asked the super at the Astral to give us a bigger place on a higher floor. We moved in together just before our City Hall wedding. Our two witnesses were Marion and Luz's older sister, Carmen. Luz's mother had wanted her to marry a Mexican, or at least a Catholic. Her sisters warned her that I wasn't successful or professionally promising enough. Luckily, I didn't have to deal with any male relatives, and by the time Karina and Hector were born, the Izquierdos seemed to have collectively resigned themselves to my presence in the family, and might have even decided they liked me well enough after all. What they thought of me now that Luz had kicked me out, I could only guess.

Chapter Six

Traffic," said Karina, stopping behind a gas tanker. At the point of tension, I had an unbidden but startlingly beautiful image of us hitting the thing, making it explode into a lethal fire embracing the expressway, the entire wall of stopped cars, with a quick blast that would liquefy us all. "There's always traffic now. Everywhere. Too many cars and not enough roads." Karina tapped the steering wheel with her thumbs, exactly the same thing her mother did when she drove.

We had been driving for quite a while, and she had not yet mentioned the mess of pulp that was now my face. She had come to pick me up at Marion's and had reacted silently but strongly when Marion had come down the steps behind me and leaned in the driver's side window to say hello to her. Karina had said a cool hello, but other than that had succeeded in ignoring Marion, whom she had known since she was three days old. Then we drove off, leaving Marion behind, and Karina's cool manner had continued in the car with me. I assumed from this suppressed reaction and subsequent silence that she was keeping her judgment to herself, but was in no way reserving it. Something had changed in her attitude since the other night at Marlene's. The air in the car was thick with unspoken things. I found myself in the grip of an irrational resentment of Marion. I had been remembering lately certain things she had said about and to Luz through the years, things that had seemed unimportant at the time, but which in retrospect had taken on a condescending tone, as if she had never taken Luz entirely seriously.

Although she was quite intelligent, Luz wasn't artistic or especially well educated, and she was a practicing Catholic. It occurred to me now for the first time that maybe Marion had always looked down on her because of all this; maybe this had had some part in causing this terrible seismic rift in my family.

Just as irrationally, I also found myself annoyed at Karina. My private life was my own damned business, as her own private life was hers. I owed her no explanation whatsoever. And yet there she sat, simmering and brooding.

"Don't you wonder what happened to my face?" I asked her in a louder voice than necessary.

Karina glanced over at me. "Mom told me. You got in a fight and got thrown in jail."

"I got attacked out of nowhere by a drunk while minding my own business in the doughnut shop, and the cops let me go."

"But you have to go to court."

"Maybe not," I said. "The case will very likely get thrown out."

Her face was implacably unsympathetic. She was on her mother's side, all of a sudden. Of course she was. Her character is made up of some contradictory combination of Luz's proud, cerebral righteousness and my own well-intentioned foolhardiness. She is eager to be loved by one and all, eager to do the right thing, whatever that may be, just like her father, but will also rapidly and efficiently turn her mother's swift rapier judgment on anyone who fails to live up to her standards. Clearly, Luz had made her believe all the terrible things about Marion and me that she was also, no doubt, making others believe as well. There was no refuting any unspoken accusation, I knew, but it was typical of my quixotic doggedness that I was determined to try.

"As for Marion and me," I told my daughter, "we're not sleeping together."

The car gave a slight lurch; we leapt forward and sped up as the traffic eased suddenly.

"But you're staying there," said Karina. "I offered you the spare room at my place."

So that's what this was about.

"I can't mooch off my daughter," I said. "I refuse to be a burden on you in any way. An old friend, that's different. That's what friends are for."

"That's what family is for. And Mom is going even more off her rocker now that you're living together. It's just adding fuel to her fire. She's throwing things. She's beyond enraged. Last night I was afraid I would have to take her to the emergency room for a sedative or tranquilizer or something, it was that bad. Like a full-blown panic attack. You should find somewhere else to live or I'm afraid she'll go totally berserk, Dad. Whether or not you guys are having an affair, it doesn't matter at all."

"You should not be involved in this," I said.

"How can I not be?" Karina was suddenly near tears. "Mom calls me and starts ranting and I feel like if I don't go over right away and keep her company she'll . . . I feel like I'm all she has."

Our car shuddered in the thermonuclear backwash from several eighteen-wheelers in a row exploding by us. Karina kept us on course, looking straight ahead at the expressway, which was so thick with traffic it was hard to believe we were moving at all.

I decided to change the subject. "How are you doing these days?" I said abruptly. "How's the freegan business going?"

As always, Karina recovered her aplomb quickly. "Okay," she said. "I've been invited to be interviewed for a talk show on WBAI next week. Listen, Dad, I have to say, I think this group of Hector's sounds weird. I've thought so since he joined. I think maybe . . ." She tapped her thumbs against the wheel.

"You think maybe what?"

"That it's some kind of cult."

I snorted. "Everything's some kind of cult," I said, "if you scratch it hard enough. Hell, look at Catholicism."

"I took a class in college on cults and religions, Dad. Cults are distinguishable from religions in very crucial ways, and it's not hard to tell the difference: in a cult, there's a hidden doctrine and there's mind control. Catholicism has no hidden doctrine: what you see up front is what you get. And there's no mind control, either, despite all the guilt and pressure and catechism. Mind control is a very specific thing."

"Tell that to the Vatican."

"I will," she said, laughing. "I'll get them on the blower right away."

"How's your new girlfriend?" I asked.

"We broke up," she said.

"I'm sorry," I said.

"I'm not," said Karina.

"Take this exit, the next one coming up," I said, squinting at the directions, which Karina had printed from the Internet. Hector's group's place was near Sag Harbor. Apparently they lived communally in a manor house on a big property that one of the members had inherited. It all sounded very grand to me, hardly in keeping with their purported aims, which were to live humbly and simply, sharing everything as the first-century Christians had, not that this mattered at all to me one way or another. In fact, if anything, it was a good thing for me if these kids lived well. Hector had invited us for dinner and had told Karina, when she'd called to confirm that we were coming, that tonight was the celebration of a couple's engagement, so we were in for a party, with wine, dancing, music, and a feast. I was looking forward to this feast. Since Luz had booted me, I was constantly hungry and never seemed to be able to feed myself properly. I'd had to tighten my belt a notch already. My trousers were sagging in the butt even more than usual. I looked forward to eating a lot of whatever they were cooking. I hoped they weren't vegetarians.

The roads were winding and narrow but empty. My chest

throbbed; all the blood in my body felt as if it were expanding in my veins and skull, heating up, trying to burst free. As I directed us to the house, clutching the directions as if they held the answer to some or even many of my current problems, I allowed the thought to penetrate me that Luz might not take me back, soon or ever. I needed a job and a place to live. The brown shingled beach houses of the rich and privileged sat humped amid bare woods and dunes like big harmless cartoon bears. I stared at them through choleric eyes, imagining the ills, pains, struggles, and heartaches of the souls who would come to live in them in the warmer months. I would have bet that most of them would be no happier than I was now, and some even less so. Envy of the rich was something I had ever felt a whiff of. If anything, having nothing tangible to struggle against caused them to notice the emptiness of time without purpose. Just like the rest of us, they were bored and tired and full of yearning. Those big houses were illusory. No one could occupy more than three rooms. The rest of their houses mocked them, empty and unused, dark, shadowy places they tracked through on their way to the kitchen, the den, the bedroom.

I began to cheer up a little. It might be nice to get some dull menial job, if I could, and stop wracking my brains to remember all that lost poetry. I could just let all of that go, maybe earn a paycheck at the Hasidic lumberyard carrying plywood and restocking the nail bins, and then put myself to sleep at night with a can of baked beans and a beer or two in front of the television. The lonely middle-aged men who haunted Greenpoint, those hard-faced solitaries drifting along the sidewalks with their hard-luck slouches, had always struck me as the loneliest people on earth, but maybe there was a particular coziness, too, in their lives. Maybe life without Luz wouldn't be so bad, really, once I got used to it. As George the bartender had put it, no one moved your stuff when you were out.

"Left here," I said, "at this driveway."

We drove through an open gate and back along a crackling little lane through a meadow of dry brown grass. Karina parked on the shoulder, and we got out and stepped onto a driveway paved with crushed oyster shells. We walked toward the house, hugging our coats to our bodies in the wind. The sea air was sharply clean and tangy and cold. The house was a gigantic old gingerbready place with a wraparound veranda, a widow's walk, dormers and bay windows, balconies, and a tower. Beyond it a dark, chilled ocean stretched away under a dense slate sky. I could feel a storm coming.

"I'm nervous," said Karina.

"Why?"

"Who are these people?"

"Hector's friends, I guess."

We climbed the steps of the wide porch. Immediately, the front door opened, and a woman stuck her head out.

"Is Hector here?" asked Karina.

"Welcome!" the woman said. "Please come in!"

She was tall and thin and alight with some sort of joy whose cause was not immediately apparent. She wore a plain long-sleeved navy blue dress with an apron over it, and her hair was in a bun. I wondered whether she was the maid.

"I'm Mantle," she said. She reached for our coats; we eased out of them and let them go. The house was bright and clean. Fresh roses in vases stood on tables, and there was a smell of food, a babble of voices elsewhere. I started to feel festive.

She stowed our coats in a capacious closet and shut the door, then turned and said, "You must be Hector's family. We call him Bard, just so you know. I hope that won't be too confusing for you."

I laughed. "Because he dropped out of Bard, or because his father is one?"

"Are you going to give us new names, too?" said Karina.

"Only if you want to come and live with us," she answered. "I'll tell Bard you're here."

Karina cleared her throat. "What was your name, before?"

Mantle stopped midflight with a startled expression. "I was Teresa," she said after a very brief instant of apparent reckoning, then she flew away.

Karina stared at me. "A cult," she whispered.

"Dad, Karina," said Hector, and there he was, decked out in a white shirt and dark blue trousers, both made of some kind of Indian cotton and cut loose and flowing like girls' clothes. Last time I'd seen him had been eight months before. Back then, he had been a strung-out string bean hopped up on zealous anxiety and sparking like a whipping wire with no grounding, lost and angry, but now he looked plumper and calmer. His black hair was longer, tied against the back of his neck in a little ponytail. His sweet, round Mexican face was sprouting a mangy beard. I hugged him hard. I fought back unexpected tears. We had never been close. I'd always had a certain amount of tension with him, or maybe it was that he had always, since he was about six or seven, pushed me away with self-generated competitiveness, trying to beat me out for things I had absolutely no interest in fighting him for: Luz's love, supremacy, power. I had endured with sympathy and secret amusement his carefully mounted assaults on my atheism, my very existence as his older simulacrum. My tolerance of his one-sided battle had only infuriated him, I knew. He wanted to weaken me, to put me in some place that would allow him to rest his foot on my neck. I had always understood that the growth of his ego was predicated on his ability to prove my ultimate inferiority to him and my incipient demise. I was aware that he had always loved and hated me equally, with a necessary and probably healthy force, but no matter what, he was my boy, and I was glad to see him.

"You look great," I said through a choked-up throat.

"Yeah, but you're fat," said his younger sister.

Hector laughed. "The food here," he said, patting his little belly with endearing pride. "You'll see. What happened to your face, Dad?"

"Long story," I said. "Nothing serious."

"How's Mom?"

"Another long story," I said. "More serious."

He seemed too buoyant to be curious. "Wow, it's so good you're here. Come and meet everyone."

He took us into a small hallway, then through open French doors into a huge, formal dining room filled with about forty people. I had a sudden sense of surreal displacement; at first I thought they were all identical clones, then at second glance I realized it was because all of them were white, able-bodied, good-looking, and apparently under thirty-five, and they were all wearing the same outfits, everything crisp white and navy blue cotton: for the women, dresses and aprons, their hair in buns, and for the men, the same loose garb as Hector's, all of them with ponytails at the napes of their necks and varying successes with facial hair, some with full beards and others, like Hector, with whatever they could muster. It was odd to see such deliberate uniformity. The room was big enough to accommodate five long tables set with white tablecloths and linen napkins, water and wineglasses, white plates and bowls and several layers of cutlery. Each had a vase of flowers in its center and candlesticks with tall white tapers. On a sideboard were bottles of wine, trivets, and bowls. I felt as if I were in some sort of elite postgraduate boarding school. There were no children present, which strongly added to this impression.

"Can I offer you a glass of wine?" my son asked Karina and me.

"Yes," I said. "Please."

"God yes," said Karina. "Hector, what's the deal with this place?"

Hector smiled at her. "There's no deal," he said.

"You all live here?"

"Yes," he said. "Isn't it beautiful?"

"Sure," she said. "What do you do all day?"

Hector looked as if he were about to burst out of his skin with happiness. "We men work on a construction crew together," he said as if he were telling me he'd been nominated for a Nobel Peace

Prize, "and we set up portable cafés at events around Long Island, but that's mostly in the warm months. In the winter, we do a lot of praying, talking, that kind of thing. Look, you'll see, I'll give you a tour and describe the whole thing. But for now, relax, meet everyone, it's a great night. Lark and Mesquite are engaged. This is a truly ordained union. I'll be right back."

"Truly ordained union," Karina said to me. "I want some freaking wine."

As if she'd heard this, a woman who could have been Mantle's sister arrived with two glasses of red wine and delivered them to Karina and me with a smile so warm it seemed a bit psychotic, given that we had never met her before.

"I'm Plum," she said. "You must be Bard's family. We've all heard so much about you! Welcome."

"I'm Karina. Who is the leader here?"

A cloud passed in front of the beaming intensity of Plum's face. "The what?"

"I'm just wondering who's in charge here, of you all, of this group. So far, it's hard to tell."

Plum's eyes were an intense shade of blue; I realized that they were the same shade as Mantle's and surmised that they must have been wearing the same color of tinted contacts. "Oh, you must mean Christa, but she's not really a leader, she's more like a guide. She'll arrive very soon. I'm sure you're excited to meet her."

Karina's arm and my arm were informing each other that this whole place and everyone in it and everything they wore, said, and did smacked of cultness, it reeked and stank to high heaven. Plum turned to say something to another eerie-blue-eyed clone of herself and I muttered to Karina, "You are right."

"I know!" she said. She gulped some wine. "Hey, this is good wine."

I took a gulp and felt it warm my chest and spread out to my whole torso like a mild flame. "Let's take him home with us," I said.

She snorted. "He'll never come. This is his dream come true. Ever since he was like twelve I've predicted that he'd end up in a place like this."

Three bearded young men approached us then with those intense, seemingly self-willed smiles of warm, loving welcome I was beginning to expect from everyone in this bunch. The men's eyes were not the eerie blue of the women's: two of them had normal brown eyes, and the other guy's were a nondescript hazel. They introduced themselves as Track, Wing, and Umber. I was beginning to enjoy the faux-Chippewa prophetic-shamanistic quality of these names. The underlying humor I found in them made me think this whole way of life was just being made up as it went along, and that allowed me to relax and imagine that this place was like an ongoing children's game, with a similar kind of collective imagined reality that bordered on hypnosis but essentially did no harm.

"We're so thankful you came to join us for tonight's feast," said Track. He had a Long Island accent and looked Italian.

"We're so thankful that you invited us," said Karina.

"I'm looking forward to this feast," I said.

"It's such a tremendous occasion," said Wing, who was blond and slightly frat-boyish, with a snub nose and ruddy complexion. "I'm so glad to meet you both. Bard is a beloved brother of ours. It must seem strange, our style of living, how we dress and talk, and all of it. If you have any questions, please feel free to ask. We love to talk about our way of life. Nothing makes us happier."

"Can I sit with you guys at dinner?" Karina asked. "I have a lot of questions."

All three of them regarded her with interest and, I thought, speculation, as if they were scoping her out as wife material. There was a strong atmosphere of mating fever in this place. The absence of babies was no doubt temporary and something they were all seeking to rectify.

I was tempted to inform these fellows that my girl was queer as a lopsided fish and had her own strong, unshakable ideas about how to live that most likely would not dovetail with theirs in any meaningful way, but I forbore. Instead I said, "I'll join you, as well."

"Great," said Wing with a gleam in his eye.

Just then, all the air in the room seemed to flow toward the French doors, along with everyone's gaze and attention. The room went silent. A woman who must have been Christa, the nonleader guide-type person, entered without flourish or fanfare. She was dressed all in white and her blond hair was loose around her shoulders. Her eyes blazed blue. She raised one arm in greeting to the room at large and said, "Let's celebrate! Here's to the loving couple!" The room erupted into applause and laughter. Someone handed Christa a glass of wine. Hector appeared at her side.

Wing said in a low voice to Karina and me, "You've probably heard that she and Bard might be making an engagement announcement of their own soon! We're all praying that it will be ordained. We would be so thankful. Bard is such a blessing to us."

I heard Karina suck in her breath. When Christa took Hector's arm as if she had already married him, I felt a pugilistic lurch of fatherly protectiveness.

"Everyone, sit and eat!" called Mantle, or someone who looked like her, and in the chair-scraping hubbub that ensued, we all sat down.

Chapter Seven

Several more Mantle lookalikes whisked forth from some unseen kitchen and distributed to each table platters of sliced roast beef and baked potatoes, a bowl of green beans and a bowl of peas, a gravy pitcher, a basket of bread and plate of butter, more wine, a water carafe, and a wooden bowl of green salad. Christa sat at the head of our table. I had been placed at her left, Hector at her right. Karina sat next to him, and going down and around the table were the three bearded henchmen Track, Wing, and Umber, and the handmaidens Mantle and Plum, and another blue-eyed woman with her hair in a bun and bearded man in a ponytail whose names I didn't know yet.

When the food steamed on each table and the serving wenches had seated themselves, Christa stood up.

"I would like to welcome our guests," she said in a confident, husky, California-surfer-inflected voice. "Harry and Karina, our brother Bard's father and sister. Please make them welcome if you haven't done so already. It is a blessing to have them with us for this occasion!"

There was a rustle and general murmur of what sounded like agreement. I tried to look interested. I was about to pass out from hunger.

"We are gathered here tonight to celebrate the coming together of a beloved sister and brother. Lark and Mesquite have known for quite some time that Hashem means for them to be joined in his name. So they came to me and told me that this was on their hearts, that they both had been called to each other by the divine will of Hashem and that they said that they wanted me to make it manifest in the community. They want to marry each other as soon as possible. Praise Hashem! Thanks be to Yashua!" She raised her wineglass; we all did the same. A clinking hubbub ensued. The couple at the foot of the table bowed their heads, smiling.

"Now let us eat," said Christa, and sat down.

As the platters and bowls migrated by me, I heaped onto my plate as much food as it would hold and began shoveling it into my mouth as quickly as the outer limits of decorum would allow. Across from me, Karina ignored her food. Her eyes were narrowed and glittery; she was paying close, potentially combative attention to everything around her. Hector looked from his sister to Christa to me, smiling with what I could only call beatific joy.

"Why do you call them Yashua and Hashem?" Karina said.

"Those are their names," said Hector. "Their real names."

"Why do you all live together like this?"

"We want to share everything communally and live in harmony together with like-minded believers."

"So what do you all believe? Do you all believe exactly the same thing?"

"We believe Yashua will return," said one of the other ponytailed guys, Lark maybe. "He may even be here now."

"A lot of people believe that," said Karina. "My mother, for example. But she doesn't need to live with other people who think so, she's happy to think so all on her own."

There was a silence among the group members, a condescending, smug withholding. Karina felt it as much as I did. I saw her eyes glitter as she looked at her brother.

"Why not just go to church with Mom?" she said to him. "Nothing would make her happier. I've never understood why you wouldn't. You're both Christians."

Hector smiled. "I've always known that the Catholic script is deficient in certain understandings," he said. Next to him, Christa nodded, barely. "They don't go far enough. It's a corrupt and false doctrine. Coming here, I found others who share this knowledge. Our belief is pure. We believe in the teachings of Yashua himself, without intermediary."

"Then what about her?" Karina asked, jerking her thumb at Christa. "Isn't she your leader?"

They all laughed. Underlying their laughter was the same joyful smugness that had permeated their shared silence.

"Well," said Hector, "she isn't a leader in the usual sense, are you, Christa? Yashua is our leader. Christa's a prophet, and we listen to her divinations because they're helpful revelations that further our understanding of his will, but no one leads anyone else here. That's the point. We're all equals in the eyes of Hashem, our creator."

Karina made a sound in the back of her throat.

"It does seem strange at first," said Christa. "I know."

Karina stared at me as if she was waiting for me to say something. I raised my eyebrows and smiled at her and the table at large with pleasant acceptance. I had just been thinking about the shower I'd taken earlier that day in Marion's cozy claw-foot tub, which had a circular shower curtain and lots of different soaps and shampoos, all of which I enjoyed sampling. Standing naked under the hot water, I'd taken an inventory of my flesh as it now was, surveyed the territory south of my head. Was this what my years on earth had amounted to, this skinny sack of bones and guts, those stovepipe arms and the bloated little goatskin of a stomach, these sagging man-dugs and mushroom-white shanks crosshatched with rust-colored hairs? Without this body, I was nothing. I had taken poor care of the thing over the decades; I'd never exercised much, I'd smoked for twenty years before quitting one day, suddenly through with the whole enterprise, and I still drank too much and didn't feed myself adequately. Standing there, I suddenly envied those who scorned the flesh and sustained a faith in some kind of life beyond it. How felicitous their outlook must be! They could look at the wreckage of a half century or more of living and see it as a temporary aberration, a withering cage they'd soon escape.

But, as usual, this envy stayed with me only briefly before it turned to boredom, and I got out and dried myself off and forgot the whole thing. Now, sitting here, warm and drowsy and sated with nourishing food, listening to the stilted claptrap these clean-scrubbed dressed-alike kids were reciting as if from memory, I wanted to give them all big hugs, get the hell out of here, and escape to a big festive party where everyone was drunk and behaving outrageously and inappropriately.

I had been studying Christa throughout the dinner as covertly as possible, mostly as a potential wife for my son, if recent rumor was to be believed, but also as the possible leader of this purported cult, if Karina was to be believed. She was a common blue-eyed blonde of a type I'd never found appealing, self-serious but not intelligent, self-possessed but not noble, charismatic but not profound. She had the unnatural smoothness of a former beauty queen or cheerleader, the kind of woman determined to preserve herself by any means possible. Because it was impossible to guess her age, due to lack of motility in brow and around eyes, preternatural plumpness of lips, and perfectly gold-streaked blondness of hair, I decided she was well over forty. This in itself was no big deal; an older woman might be just the thing for a lost, searching, arrogant, sensitive mama's boy like Hector. And if she did indeed have this bunch under some kind of mind control, so what? I didn't share Karina's belief that this was necessarily a bad thing. Hector had been an odd duck from birth, a wild child given to violent fevers, then an abstracted, moody teenager who tried every drug there was, then a sudden overnight convert to Jesus-freakdom who seemed likely to take up a placard and go about Times Square. This group seemed like the perfect place for him. I couldn't muster up a head of steam about it, although I could tell from Karina's darting glances at me all through dinner that she wished I'd back her up.

In the car on the way home, more than two hours later, she drove with borderline-reckless grimness. She had drunk a lot of wine at dinner. Afterward, the tour of the place Hector had given us seemed to upset her; there were eight bedrooms, the four largest of which were filled with bunk beds, the other four of which contained one double bed each. The rooms were all neat, simple, airy, and seemed comfortable enough, but something about the sleeping arrangements had put her into a funk.

I would have offered to drive, but I had never managed to get my driver's license.

"It's like the army or boarding school," she was saying. "My older brother is sleeping in a bunk bed in a room with seven other guys like a stupid cabin at sleepaway camp. And who gets the rooms with the double beds?"

"The three married couples and Christa, probably," I said, "and Hector will no doubt move in with her after they get married, so then he'll be living like a grown-up, in a room with his wife."

"And that's another thing! He can't seriously be going to marry that bimbo."

I smiled at the dim reflection of myself in the passenger-side window. "Why not?"

"Because she's a bimbo."

"Hector doesn't question the way you live, does he?"

"Of course he does. I'm a godless heathen who's doomed to burn in the lake of fire when the Messiah comes. So are you, by the way, and so is Mom, which is the most incredible thing of all. That's what they believe; that's what they said in their little prayer circle after dinner, before the droning Yashua singing and boring Israeli folk dancing, don't you remember? That they're thankful they're not among the homeowners, professionals, and godless makers of faithless art who will be condemned to the hot oil bath when Yashua the Second comes back. In case you missed it, that was a pointed reference to us, and Mom. I own a house, Mom's a nurse, you're an atheist and you write poetry . . ."

"Oh well," I said, "if it makes them feel better about themselves to imagine us burning in hot oil, what harm is it doing?"

"They're a cult, Dad," she said. "That means they're all under mind control. I just know Christa manipulated one of them into giving her that house. I tried to worm it out of Hector, and he said one of his brothers gave it to the group as part of his worldly goods when he joined. Meanwhile, she's marrying Hector, and why? He doesn't have a dime. When I asked him, he said he has extraordinary visionary power because of his virginity. I bet you anything she's using him for his purity. If she marries a virgin, it obscures the fact that she is obviously not one."

"How do you know she's not a virgin?"

"She's got 'tramp' written all over her."

I laughed. We drove along in silence for a while. Karina calmed down a little, and so did her driving.

"How old do you think she is?" Karina asked.

"Older than Hector," I said, "but he's a grown-up. He can marry whomever he wants."

"It doesn't bother you, that place?"

"I wouldn't want to live there," I said. "I could hardly stand to be there for just an evening. But Hector isn't me. I always felt the best I could do for you kids was not to be a hypocrite. I wouldn't want anyone telling me how to live. As long as you're not serial murderers or Nazis, as long as you're doing what makes you happy, that's all I care about. Honestly. You're both grown-ups now. You don't need parents anymore."

"Sometimes," said Karina in a voice so quiet I could hardly hear her, "I do."

"Yeah," I said, "me too. But it's better not to have them anymore after a certain age, on the whole. And on that note, please don't think you have to take care of your mother and me, or Hector either, for that matter. You don't have to take care of any of us. Write articles, write a book. Find a fantastic girlfriend. Rescue stuff from Dumpsters and give it to the needy. Look, if you want to do something for me, go out and have some fun once in a while. You're so serious."

"Life is serious."

I smiled at her and patted her shoulder and let my arm lie against her seat back.

"So I'm dropping you at Marion's?" she asked as we neared the city.

"That's where I'm staying for now."

"For how long?"

"Until I can find a job and a place to live."

"You moved out of that fleabag hotel?"

"It was a bracing adventure before I got my face bashed in, and then it just seemed sordid. And," I added, forestalling her from saying what I knew she was about to say, "thank you for offering me your spare room, but I need to stay in North Brooklyn. I have to stay close to home. And I am not having an affair with Marion."

"So you keep saying."

"And I'll keep saying it as long as it takes until you believe me."

She sighed. "Dad, I believe you, I just think it's cruel to Mom that you're living with her, of all people. What about staying with James and Lisa? What about Phil and Suzie?"

"They haven't invited me. I think they're on your mother's side in all this. Karina, I don't see how she and I are going to get through this. All I want is to make it right with her somehow and save the ship. She needs help."

"I've been telling her to go to therapy," said Karina.

"As long as she doesn't go to Helen," I said. I had never met Helen, myself, but I had heard enough about her through the years to know that she was a power-mad fake.

"I think she made an appointment with Helen today," said Karina. "Look, it's better than nothing."

"Helen's worse than nothing," I said with alarm and rage.

"Well, she needs help," said Karina, "and she's heard about Helen from her friends, so she trusts her. She's going to freak out when she realizes what Hector is doing there in that weird place, marrying a woman she's never met. She's going to have to be hospitalized."

She stopped in front of Marion's building and idled there, looking at me in the glimmering darkness. "Take care of yourself, Dad," she said.

"You too," I said. "Thanks for the ride. Thanks for coming with me."

I kissed Karina's cheek and hopped out of the car.

Marion wasn't home, I knew; she'd said she was meeting a friend for dinner and wouldn't be back till very late. I let myself in and lay on the couch and stared at the patterns made by the light from the streetlamp on the plaster ceiling. I hadn't wanted to admit this to Karina, but the visit to my son's new house, the thought of him marrying that manifestly unworthy woman, had left me with an uneasy, mildly depressed feeling that was enriched and augmented by the idea of my wife becoming the client of that horrible therapist and my daughter going home alone to her little house in the ghetto. My poor family was in shambles.

It had not always been thus. Ten years before, we'd been a solid nuclear unit, dollhouse style, mother, father, boy, and girl. The kids went off to high school every day, Luz to work, and I stayed home to write.

Well. Two years before the supposedly solidly nuclear time I was remembering, I'd had that affair. I was not on the whole as much of a slouch around the house as other husbands I had heard about. I frequently shopped and cooked and cleaned, and I always paid all the bills and took out the trash. However, on more days than I cared to recall, Luz came home from her shift, climbed the stairs to the top floor of the Astral, and unlocked our door bearing the groceries she'd bought with the money she had earned, to find me at our dining room table, surrounded by crumpled-up paper, blinking and muttering, "Oh, is it that time already?" After giving me a surprisingly affectionate kiss, she would carry the groceries to the kitchen, where she cooked supper with Karina, the two of them yakking away, and sometime during the meal Hector would wander in late from wherever the hell he'd been and join us and fill his plate, and no one would have much to say, really, and after the meal I washed the dishes while everyone else dispersed to solitary escapes, the kids to their computers and Luz to the telephone to talk one by one to her mother and sisters, who all lived in Queens and were therefore essentially on another planet. When the kitchen was clean, I crawled into a hot bath with a book to alternately read and stare unseeingly at my bony knees rising from the gently steaming water, rewriting poetry in my head. I crawled into the bed I shared with Luz in our tiny bedroom to find her already asleep. Sometimes she would grunt in her sleep by way of greeting. Sometimes she would awaken enough to spoon herself around me. Once in a great while, we would cleave to each other in sex that was more fondly reminiscent than passionate, but no matter, I always felt, sex was sex. In the morning, she was gone before I awoke, and so were the kids.

It hadn't been perfect, but we had been a family once, and now, it seemed, we were four separate people flung asunder to our various, unrelated fates. This made me feel lonelier than I had ever been in my life. Maybe Karina was right. Maybe Christa was no good, maybe this whole place, this group, this belief system or whatever it was, was a festering bunch of damaging hooey. If that turned out to be the case, then I had to exert whatever influence I had to try to persuade Hector to leave. I wanted this for the good of my son, of course, as any parent would have.

But secondarily, I wanted it for Luz. She loved Hector more than she loved anyone else on earth, with the kind of passion that set my teeth on edge because it was not aimed at me. I had never objected overtly to this all-encompassing adoration of her firstborn, her boy, but I had felt at times with uneasy premonition that it was out of proportion, that there was something Oedipal and potentially tragic about it. Hector looked a lot like Luz's dead father, after whom he was named. I had often wondered whether Luz's grasping, smothering fixation on him had driven Hector away, first into strange, violent medieval fantasies as a boy, then into video games and drugs as an adolescent, and finally to fundamentalist religiosity, the perfect instrument to break his Catholic mother's heart. Hector had dropped out of Bard College at twenty and gone out West, to Missoula, then Santa Fe, and finally Mexico, where he'd lived in a sort of commune outside of San Cristóbal de las Casas for five years with a little band of Christian hippies. The last time the four of us had been together as a family was last summer, when Hector was home for a few days on his way from Mexico to live in the community in Sag Harbor. He didn't tell us how or why he'd been invited to live there, only that he was going.

"It sounds like the perfect place for me," he told Luz, Karina, and me. He had rolled in that afternoon with a smoke-smelling backpack, a fuzzy little beard, and a woven bracelet around his wrist. He'd taken a Greyhound bus all the way from Santa Fe, where he'd spent a week with friends en route from Mexico. We hadn't seen him in more than a year and a half. We were all sitting around the kitchen table, eating the feast Luz had made in honor of the prodigal son's return.

"Perfect why?" Luz asked. She had missed Hector desperately the years he'd been gone, mourning him as if he were dead and sobbing to me that she'd lost her baby, her boy. But she wasn't showing any of this tender maternal longing now. "You're a Catholic, *mi hijo.* These people don't sound legitimate to me, this group. They sound like hippies, or worse."

"What's worse than hippies, Mom?" Hector asked.

She flashed her eyes at him. "What will you do all day there? What kind of life is that for you?"

"What have I been doing all day for years? I'll live with people who believe the same things I do, and I'll work to support myself. You should be glad I went to Mexico. I learned about my heritage, I speak fluent Spanish, I lived among my people. Why aren't you happy about that either? Would you rather I went off and robbed convenience stores and fathered illegitimate children and took drugs?"

"I'd rather you stayed close," said Luz. "Then I wouldn't have to worry about you all the time."

"The red snapper is great," said Karina, "and this is crazy. I don't go to Mass, Mom. You seem fine with that. Why does Hector have to be Catholic when I'm not?"

"Thanks," said Hector to Karina. "Good point."

"Hector," said Luz, "is a Catholic and he has been since he was a little boy. I'm trying to help him remember that. You never had any interest in church, Karina, you're an atheist like your father. But Hector is like me, he believes in the Eucharist, the Holy Trinity, going to confession. I know him better than he knows himself. It's my job as his mother to say these things. I can't let him ruin his life."

"Please," said Hector. "Spare me the sanctimonious dogma. I'm an adult, I can make my own decisions about where to live and what to believe."

"Really," said Luz, so worked up she was spitting fire. "What exactly do you believe, then?"

"I believe in the word of Jesus Christ. I'm sorry, I don't have much patience for priests and rosaries and confession. The Vatican is a place of hypocrisy and power mongering. The Catholic Church controls belief and dictates faith. I have a direct relationship with God. I don't need anyone to watch me when I talk to him. I don't need to stare at Christ nailed to a cross while I pray."

Luz put her hand to her breastbone. I could see how much agony she was in. "Harry," she said to me.

"What does it matter, Luz?" I said, trying to comfort her. "He's a Christian, at least. You should be glad of that and let him go his own way."

Luz turned to Hector and said with clinical chill, "If you go and live with those people, I'll cut you off."

Hector laughed. "What is this, a vaudeville melodrama?"

"I mean it," said Luz.

"I have no doubt," said Hector, "and okay, that's your choice. If you can't accept the way I am, then stop speaking to me, go ahead."

"I can't accept this," said Luz. "You're breaking my heart."

"That's ridiculous," said Karina. "In case you haven't noticed, I'm gay, and I don't believe in God at all, and you see me every week, Mom. I really don't understand what the big deal is here."

Luz looked askance at Karina, as if she had nearly forgotten what she was doing there. "You're a good girl," she said, waving her away. "You treat me with respect, you're a loving, sweet person, what you do is your own business. But Hector." Her face glinted with hardness. Her tears were suppressed with every muscle in her jaw, their pressure mounting in her lymph nodes.

"Right," said Hector. "You hold me to totally different standards. You've made it clear all my life that you wanted me to become a priest. Sorry to disappoint you, but I want to live as an equal in a community of friends, I want to worship as I choose and answer to no one, and someday I want to get married, not to give you a heart attack or anything."

"I didn't expect you to be a priest," said Luz. "I don't know where you got that. All I ask is that you stay true to the way we do things and respect the church you were raised in."

"I hate the church I was raised in," said Hector. "I reject it absolutely. I'll never go back. You have to stop trying to control me. It might work on Dad, but it doesn't work on me."

Luz pointed toward the front door of the apartment. "Go," she said. "Right now. You can't sit there and speak to me like that, you can't treat your mother with such disrespect, and I will never accept this choice of yours."

Hector left shortly thereafter. I tried to console her, but Luz was pale and resolute. She refused to discuss Hector. She refused to admit that she was devastated.

So now she had banished both husband and son.

Karina was right; marrying that bimbo, which was exactly what Christa was, would be the final twist of the knife. It would cause Luz as much pain as anything I had ever done, or not done.

I could not squelch a foretaste of the heroic sense of accomplishment I would enjoy, the possibility of presenting myself to my estranged wife as the savior of her baby. In this beautiful scenario, she would then have no choice but to take me back, and in the end, that would be good for us all. It was the one thing I could do to make things right again, short of procuring evidence of my nonaffair with Marion, which was of course impossible.

I must have fallen asleep, because suddenly Marion was turning lights on and clattering around in the kitchen.

Chapter Eight

"What a night," Marion said when I lurched into the kitchen, clumsy with sleep, to join her at the table. "I offended Amy so badly she'll never speak to me again. How was your night?"

"My son is in a cult," I said, yawning widely and rubbing my face between my hands.

"Oh great," she said. "Sounds like we're even." She looked even paler than usual, maybe because she was wearing makeup, which didn't especially become her.

I finished yawning and reached over for the whiskey bottle and glass and poured some for myself while Marion poured herself some wine.

"How did you offend Amy?" I asked. Amy was Marion's younger sister. She and her husband were both biochemists. They had two overachieving sons, both currently getting PhDs at Harvard. I had met Amy a few times and had found her humorless, sexless, and challengingly, frighteningly bright.

"I told her about this whole thing with Luz," said Marion. "She told me she's felt my friendship with you was inappropriate for years but never said anything. She said she didn't blame Luz a bit for being suspicious and upset, she would be too if Joe had a friend like me. And she was shocked when I told her you were staying here. I mean horrified. She told me I'm risking public shunning. Like this is a Tolstoy novel." She laughed. "As if I'll be forced to wear a scarlet A."

"I think you mean Hawthorne," I said.

She rolled her eyes.

"How did you offend her? She'll speak to you again. She's your sister."

"I told her she's living in the nineteenth century. She told me to wait and see, and to be very careful. I told her . . . whatever, she is so fucking annoying when she gets judgmental."

"So you told her what?"

"That obviously *she's* the one who's judging me. As usual. I was furious. Thinking those things about our friendship all those years, that's bad enough, but never saying anything? And then after my affair with James, she practically tried to commit me to a mental institution. Not literally, but you know. Amy has always made it clear that she thinks I act in sexually inappropriate ways, even while Ike and I were married. That's probably because Joe is a lump of clay and Amy is about as sexy as a car battery. And she seems to think I'm some kind of famous photographer and I need taking down a peg because I'm full of myself. In fact, I barely eke out a living and I have to hustle for work. But she's got this idea about me, she's had it all our lives. Thinking she has to take me down."

"Was she offended when you called her judgmental?"

"No, she was offended when I called her a sanctimonious, narrow-minded cunt and stomped out of the restaurant."

I tried not to laugh and on the whole succeeded. "Oh," I said.

"It's not funny."

"No," I said. "But you were right."

She snorted. "I love you, Harry. So I went to a bar down the street from the restaurant she'd picked, which of course was vegan and overpriced, and I left her to pay the bill. I sat at the bar and drank two glasses of wine by myself and flirted with the bartender, the two guys at the bar, and the delivery guy who brought me my cheeseburger and fries. One of the men sitting at the bar asked me for my number and asked me out for dinner next week. He was extremely cute, but much too young, of course, and I'm sure he was just being nice."

"He wasn't just being nice," I said. "He's going to call you."

"Amy's not going to speak to me for a very long time." Marion put her feet, which were encased in thick red socks, on the table. She twisted her hair up with her hands and secured it on top of her head without the benefit of any tool that I could see. I'd always wondered how women did that, but had never asked.

"How do you make your hair stay up like that?"

"I tie it in a knot," she said, as if that explained anything. "Anyway, what about Hector? Tell me about this horrible cult."

"It's not that horrible," I said. "They're a bunch of nice white kids living in a beach manor. It's idyllic, except that they're under the thumb of a cheesy blonde in her late forties who calls herself Christa and apparently talks a lot about the end times."

"End times," said Marion. "That gives me dire thoughts of Kool-Aid."

"She's planning to marry Hector, the token brown person, and the virgin, and the mystical savant, so I'm told."

"Is Hector really still a virgin? At twenty-seven?"

"Well, I don't have ironclad proof. But he became deadly serious about chastity when he found Jesus. And as far as I could tell, he wasn't getting any action in high school. He spent almost his entire adolescence in front of the computer."

"Do you think he's in any danger in this place?"

"It all looked fine on the surface to me, but Karina was not so sanguine. She thinks he's been hypnotized."

"He's marrying some woman he just met," said Marion.

"Apparently," I said. "Well, he's old enough to do whatever he wants."

"He has no idea what he's doing! He's a baby! He needs guidance!"

I tilted my glass of whiskey and gazed into it and sloshed the whiskey around until it whizzed about the glass in a maelstrom. "Maybe," I said. "But I'm not in the habit of telling my children what to do. That's Luz's department, and she's distracted right now."

"So you step in," she said. "I mean it, you can't let poor Hector get trapped in something he might not be able to get out of easily. You know how passive he is, how sensitive and malleable. He might disappear into this cult or whatever it is and never come back. I've heard stories of people lost to cults. It's tragic."

"Well," I said, "it's not 'tragic' in the classical sense, it's just extremely sad. But I take your point."

She rolled her eyes at me again. "Harry."

"Actually, I was thinking before I fell asleep that I have to get him out of there."

"How would you do that?"

"Hire a thug to kidnap him. Handcuff him in a cheap hotel room by an airport. Disconnect the phone. Torture him until he agrees never to go back."

"That's what I thought."

"In other news," I said, "apparently Luz is going to see Helen next week."

"Oh my fucking God," said Marion. She poured herself more wine and took a deep gulp. "Oh my fucking God," she said again.

"Exactly," I said. We stared at each other.

Almost everyone we knew went to Helen Vollmann for therapy, including our friends James and Lisa Lee, who both saw her separately and together, as well as our friends Phil and Suzie Michaels, as well as another friend, Tracy Scudder. But more to the point, Marion's late husband, Ike, had seen her, and so had Samantha, the aspiring poet I'd had my brief, ill-advised, long-ago affair with. To make the plot even thicker, about three years before Ike died, Marion had had a very brief but apparently intense affair with

James Lee, and so it had come to pass that in that affair's painful, complicated aftermath, Helen had been the individual therapist for three of the four parties involved: Ike as well as both James and Lisa. Marion, the lone holdout, had stayed away because she was as suspicious of Helen as I was.

And with good reason. What therapist with a shred of ethical spine would agree to individually treat both members of a married couple, let alone an entire group of friends? The unhelpful lack of boundaries of this was clear even to me, who had never set foot in a therapist's office. Who knew what Helen would say to Luz when she got hold of her? If Luz went to see Helen, it would be a disaster. Helen had never met Marion or me. But she knew that we had both already had affairs with other people from Ike, Samantha, James, and Lisa, and all four of them had certainly told her. Given her lack of ethical boundaries, Helen might very well decide that Marion and I, being prior cheaters, were therefore definitely sleeping together. She would proceed accordingly in her treatment of Luz, which would mean the certain death of my marriage and the end of any hope of ever convincing Luz of the truth and thereby saving her sanity and my own life.

"I'm going back to sleep," I said. "I'm depressed as hell."

"Same here," she said. "I'm going to stay up for a while and stew. Sweet dreams."

I went back to the couch and tossed around on the lumpy cushions with my brain in a spiderwebbed jumble until just after dawn, then got up, got dressed, and went out into the cold fresh morning. The sky over the bridge and river was a clean, pale, wind-scoured blue with banks of salmon-pink clouds floating just over the bridge's struts. The rhythmic sound of tires on the expansion joints overhead was like high throaty animal cries in a swamp. I hiked up and over to the entrance and climbed the steep ramp, high up onto the bridge, and strode fast along the walkway over the road, hunched in my coat, the tips of my ears tingling, my nose going numb. I had for company various joggers, Hasidim, and kids on bikes. I stopped halfway across the bridge and looked downriver at the wide, streaming blue water just beginning to catch glints of light, the old piers and massive freight ships of the Navy Yard. Even Shaefer Landing, that monstrous bit of residential development squatting on the waterfront, gleamed a dreamlike, underwater green in the clear sunlight. At dawn, everything was new made. It was a poem, and in the old days I would have been inspired to write a good one. Now I conjured nothing but doggerel: "The sun-cudgeled copse of cars on the Billyburg Bridge / Sits stuck still in the morning arm of some god's law . . ."

When the sun had risen high enough to begin to warm things up a bit, I turned back and came off the bridge and went down toward the river, hung a left on Wythe and walked its just-awakening length. I passed the old empty diner that had once been revamped into an upscale Italian place, now closed and boarded up, where Phil and Suzie had had their wedding about eighteen years before. The party had been held in the fenced-in garden with tables, with a little stage for a band, a bar, flower beds, vines, potted trees. It had rained in a hard, brief cloudburst that night, but we didn't mind getting wet. We were all there, Luz and me, Ike and Marion, James and Lisa, Wendy and Giovanni, Debra MacDougal, Dan Levy and his wife, whose name I could never remember, Sylvia and John, Mick and Terry. Hector and Karina were there, too, at a table with everyone else's kids. Luz wore a black strapless dress and the dangling sparkly chandelier earrings I'd given her for our tenth anniversary, and her shoulders were bare, her hair up. I remembered with a pang of loss how beautiful she had been that night, laughing and open and comfortable in her own skin, a rare mood for her.

It was a good night, a great party. Phil and Suzie had been together for more than eight years and had a five-year-old daughter and another kid on the way; she had finally gotten her divorce from her first husband, and so they were getting married. There was a lot of affectionate joking in the wedding toasts about Suzie making an honest man of Phil, the barn door being closed long after the cows had escaped, Suzie's checkered past being laid to rest, the long-delayed shotgun wedding. We were a closely knit group of old friends back then. Five of them had gone to college together—Phil, Debra, James, Sylvia, and Giovanni—and most of us had met and coalesced into a group shortly after we'd all moved to New York in our early twenties. Phil and Giovanni and I had shared an East Village apartment during my first years in the city, until I married Luz and moved to the Astral. Dan and I had a long-standing, mostly friendly poetic rivalry. I'd of course known Marion for many years, and Ike and Luz had both been folded in when they'd married Marion and me. We had all known one another, it seemed, forever.

This was long before we were splintered into isolated factions by circumstances that ended friendships and tore the circle apart: a vicious fight between Sylvia and Lisa, former best friends who became sworn enemies after an unbreachable misunderstanding; a joint real-estate venture gone awry between Phil and Suzie, Sylvia and John; the public fallout of my affair with Samantha and Marion's with James; and most recently, this terrible mess with Luz and Marion and me. These days, all remaining friendships were conducted on an individual basis, according to who took whose side in a given dispute, who believed whose side of any given story, whose loyalties ultimately lay where. But back then, and for years, we were a big, loose, easy flock of trusted pals, a de facto family of neighbors, fellow artists.

That night, at the wedding party, Luz and I sat at a table with Ike and Marion. We four were especially close in those days. We had frequent dinners together at each other's house, they were our kids' godparents. Ike and I had a warm if small-scale friendship; he was a good guy, I was a good guy. We didn't have a lot in common, but we both loved Marion, and we respected each other. And although

Marion and Luz had some degree of ongoing tension because they were so different and because Marion had been my friend before Luz came along, and so had a prior claim on me that Luz had to accept, they had always been amiable enough and even became affectionate after they'd had several drinks.

I recall that Marion drank even more than usual that night and seemed slightly unhinged, wild. I sensed that her attention was elsewhere, that she was flying off from us, but I wasn't sure where or to whom. When Ike suggested with mild concern that she might have had enough to drink, Marion told him to back off. I laughed, Luz didn't. I could sense Luz there next to me, offended by what she took to be Marion's disrespect for her husband. She had never been amused by Marion's teasing disparagements of Ike. He was a mensch, Ike, an ambitious, dapper, charming guy who had allowed Marion unlimited autonomy and freedom, supported her when sales of her work were down, understood her need for solitude, brought her coffee in the morning before he left for work. As always, Luz chose to keep her thoughts about Marion's unseemly wifely behavior to herself, but I knew I'd hear them later, on the way home, and I'd be in the wearying position of having to choose between defending my friend, thus annoying my wife, or keeping my mouth shut and feeling disloyal to Marion, whose side I saw.

Marion had always made the mistake, if it could be called that, of talking to Luz and me as if we were in agreement about all matters. Luz's cool responses and silences had never fazed her. Luz was my wife, so therefore Marion was as frank and easy with her as she was with me. It was Marion's nature to be open, to assume that her friends wouldn't judge her, the way she, out of loyalty and open-mindedness, and as a matter of principle, did not judge them.

A little later on, Marion and Ike had some sort of marital altercation and walked off together still arguing long before the rest of us were ready to go. After they left, Luz and I danced shoulder to shoulder with everyone. Hector and Karina were nearby with a flock of all the other midsized kids. The band was good, a retro jazz ensemble with a terrific girl singer. There my wife and I were, dancing with our friends, their kids, our kids. I remember that we all sang along, kids and grown-ups, to "Somewhere over the Rainbow," half laughing at the sentiment but giving it our throaty all. That was the band's last number of the night. Passing the old restaurant, I saw our ghosts there, held in time like a stuck thought burned into the air, although back then we had taken that happy night for granted.

I threaded through a thin smattering of early young workgoers, past dogs on leashes attached to humans. I stopped in at a deli on Manhattan Avenue and got myself a paper cup of hot coffee, which I sipped as I walked almost all the way to the End of the World. As I passed India Street, I glanced down its length reflexively and was half relieved, half disappointed to see no sign of Luz, who was probably on the bus to work already; she was always on time. As the saying used to go back in olden times when people wore watches, you could set your watch by her. The empty street taunted me with decades of lingering memories. It looked slightly darker and more shadowy than the rest of the world, as if nostalgia had given it a sepia, long-ago cast. I turned my face away and tottered on into the wind that became stronger the closer I got to Newtown Creek, as if the water had unleashed some icy, toxic sprite of air that was funneled by the chute of the avenue right into my face.

Mazatlán had just opened. I went in and sat at the counter. It was warm and lively in there, with a melodramatic Latino pop video full of half-naked glistening women in heat on the overhead TV screen, the smell of hot grease and coffee, and a lit-up 1970s Corona sign on the far wall. My toes curled in my shoes with relief at getting out of that cold wind.

Every table was already taken, and even the counter was well populated. As was appropriate for this hour on a weekday, the clientele was either older working class or young, hungover hipster.

"*Hola,*" I said to Juana, who kissed me on the forehead as she went by and sloshed some hot coffee into a cup for me.

"Airy," she said, "*cómo estás*?"

Before I could answer, she was off. I waited to catch the eye of my brother-in-law, Jaime, who wielded a single spatula in the execution of various tasks involving eggs, tortillas, bacon, home fries, and sausages. Jaime had been married to Luz's older sister, Carmen, since they were just out of high school. Carmen and Jaime had four grown daughters and three grandchildren, and they both worked harder and with more dedication and forbearance than almost anyone else I knew except Luz herself. Nevertheless, Jaime somehow always managed to look like a rockabilly punk with a bad attitude who was just one wrong step short of getting suspended from high school. He wore checked cowboy shirts with the sleeves rolled up and flashy boots with appliquéd lizards on the toes. His hair stood straight up like a three-inch black bristle brush, and he had equally brushy sideburns. Why he took such stylish pains I had no idea; he was in no band, and he pursued no women. It was no doubt his one means of self-expression in a tame, obedient life, the equivalent of my poetry writing.

"*Hermano,*" he called to me over his shoulder, "want some breakfast?"

"No thanks, Jaime," I said. "I'm looking for a job, actually."

He turned. "What happened to your face, man?"

"Got into a fight with a drunk guy."

He gave me a look, long enough for me to understand that he knew every detail of my recent behavior according to his wife as told to by mine, but not so long that I would read any judgment or disapprobation into it, if only because that wasn't his style, and then he turned back to his grill. "You okay?"

"No," I said. I had always liked Jaime. He was entertaining to talk to at Izquierdo family gatherings, the kind of man who never said anything objectionable but always seemed to be about to. Under his carefully honed veneer of offhanded cool-cat levity, he was thoughtful, decent, and kind, and his wife and daughters and grandkids walked all over him.

"Yeah, didn't think so," he said. "I'm really sorry, bro. We're not really hiring, but I will definitely put in a word for you. How's your cooking?"

"I'd be happy to wash dishes," I said. "That's more what I had in mind. My cooking is not good. But I think I can get dishes clean pretty well."

"It pays shit," he said. "But you get to eat before and after your shifts, so there's that benefit."

"Shit is better than what I'm making now. Especially with food."

"How do I reach you?" He set a plate of fried eggs, tortillas, and potatoes in front of me, then slid the hot sauce and ketchup within my reach. I could have kissed him. My second good meal in twelve hours.

"Through Karina," I said. I couldn't give him Marion's number, couldn't have her picking up when Jaime called, it wasn't right somehow. "I don't have a phone at the moment."

"Okay, then," he said. "I'll ask the boss. You never know."

I finished my food and said good-bye and left as big a tip as I could risk, given my low funds, and hightailed it out of there feeling shamefaced and angry at myself for not having been a more productive person all these years. As I made my way back along Manhattan Avenue, I remembered my dream from the night before. I was lying in Luz's and my bed with the flu and a high fever and Luz kept bringing me bowls of delicious-smelling soups and stews, pozole, *sopa de lima* with fried tortilla strips, the oxtail soup with the thick, bright green broth she only made on special occasions like Christmas and birthdays, spicy black bean soup with sour cream and toasted cumin seeds. They all looked and smelled like the essence of life-giving restoratives. I was very hungry and kept trying to sit up and eat them as she offered them to me one by one, but I was too weak, too sickly, and each time I fell back onto the pillows while she looked hurt and disappointed.

I stepped on this line of thinking before it could take over my brain, since it did no one any good, least of all me. I dwelled instead on Jaime's brotherly kindness, the fact that thanks to him, I had just eaten a big, solid breakfast and might have found a job somewhere where I could stand to be for eight or more hours at a stretch.

I ducked my head into my coat and was swamped with a memory of Christmas past: the year Karina was twelve, Hector fourteen, it was our turn, as it was every four years, to have the Izquierdo family over for Christmas dinner. We four had gone to midnight Mass the night before. It was something we had always done, and I didn't mind. I liked the holiday masses well enough, it was the regular Mass I couldn't stomach; it reminded me too much of my childhood, that snow-bright midwestern winter light refracted in the church, a stark shaft of sun illuminating the bloody Christ on the crucifix. My mother whispered to me during the service, and the sound of her papery, dry voice in my ear made me shrivel inside to the size of a closed fist. It was overwhelming, the cryptlike vaults and apses, the cold breath of the air in the church, Father Mahoney's reedy, undertaker's voice, the dusty incense that smelled like perfume on a woman's corpse, the wafer that turned to fleshlike paste on my tongue.

But the crowded Christmas Mass at St. Cecilia's was always a cheery, neighborly affair, even festive, and we four walked home through the quiet, cold streets of Greenpoint together afterward, Karina and I up ahead, walking fast and mangling Christmas carols with made-up lyrics mocking the crass materialism of the holiday ("Deck the halls with lots of presents" and "Silent night, give me some loot, all is calm, give me some gifts"), Luz and Hector lagging behind, earnestly discussing Catholic doctrine. When we got home, it was very late, but Luz always let the kids open their presents before bed. That way, we could sleep late the next morning while they played with their new toys, which were now all computer games and digital gadgets, sadly for their midwestern-raised poet father who had come of age in the fifties and wanted his own children to read the classics and play with chemistry sets and sleds as he had. That morning, we lolled in our bed and made love, fairly passionately for a long-married couple. We were still okay then; I hadn't had my stupid affair yet, that wasn't until the following summer. We were still intact.

The Izquierdos arrived from Queens at two o'clock on Christmas afternoon bearing food and presents. Luz had spent Christmas Eve day making the green oxtail soup and the pork in spicy sauce that her family always ate on Christmas. Her sister Carmen brought cinnamon chocolate cake with whipped cream, her sister Pilar brought a bottle of rum, peanuts, and cans of guava juice and condensed milk to make the traditional family blender cocktail, and their mother, Natividad, brought homemade tamales. The Izquierdo women were a look-alike bunch, all of them fierce, glossy, tiny, and preternaturally talkative. I always enjoyed seeing them in the aggregate.

After dinner, all the cousins went into Hector's and Karina's rooms. Carmen, Luz, and Pilar sat with their mother in the living room, jabbering away about their jobs and kids and, as a no-doubt distant afterthought, their husbands. After we husbands had washed and dried and put away all the dishes, we stood in the kitchen leaning against the counters drinking beer, joking with a funny kind of pride about how demanding and bossy our wives were, how in thrall we were to the domestic tyranny of children and schedules and Izquierdo sisters. Pilar's husband, Roberto, a round-faced, unflappable courthouse clerk, was as genial, devoted, and secretly subversive as Jaime and I were; in other words, we were the perfect husbands for the Izquierdo sisters, who all, even as grown adults, constantly jostled for dominance amongst themselves and competed for their mother's attention. I sensed among us three husbands a shared undercurrent of potential rebellious mischief held in check out of inertia, self-discipline, and a strong preference for harmony and fidelity. We were a convivial threesome; our wives were distracted, so we were free to idle, making conversation.

As the sky outside darkened so that our slouching reflections appeared in the kitchen windows with a collection of empty beer bottles behind us on the countertops, I could hear the women's voices in the living room. Luz sounded especially wrought up. Every so often, the topic of their dead father came up, and it was always painful and contentious. Luz defended him, Pilar reviled him, and Carmen, the oldest sister, tried to analyze and understand him, while Natividad sat silently, sometimes fanning herself with one hand.

Finally, when the rum was gone and they were all talked out, the Izquierdo women, as one force, gathered up their children, empty dishes, new presents, bags, and husbands, and out they swept, calling good-byes and kissing all of us and thanking Luz for dinner. Their sudden absence was deafening, a reverse thunderclap on our eardrums. Luz and I stood looking at each other, marooned and tipsy amidst the wrapping paper and fallen pine needles and blinking tree lights and cake crumbs. I was pleasantly buzzed and sleepy, but I could see from my wife's pinched, distraught face that it was by no means bedtime yet. She sat next to me on the couch and, because Hector and Karina were in their rooms and couldn't see or hear, she gave herself over to the tears that she'd held back all day out of pride. "I'm the only one who loved him," she said. "I feel so sad for him, he was so lonely, my mother never let him back, she banished him, he tried to come back but she never let him . . ."

Now that Luz had done the same thing to me that her mother had done to her father, these words struck me in hindsight as ironic at best and inescapably prophetic at paranoid worst. At the time, though, I leapt at the chance to assuage her vulnerability. She was usually so pent up and fierce. She cried like a little girl, a little girl who had had too much rum, and I soothed her, rubbed her back, kissed her teary cheeks, feeling fatherly and reassuring.

"You have to promise me," she said, wiping her face, fixing me with her gimlet stare. "Harry, I mean it, promise me you'll stay with me forever, you'll never leave me."

"Of course I promise," I said, a bit puzzled by her fear that I would ever think of doing anything else. "I promised when I married you, and it's still true."

"Never leave me," she said coldly. Her eyes were wet and bloodshot, but they were stone hard, untrusting, angry. "Say it."

"I'll never leave you," I said. "I promise. Never, never, never."

Ah, Luz. So much for that. I let the headwind blow me to Marlene's, which was, of course, closed. I idled there in front anyway in case Marlene took it into her head to open up this early for the first time in the ninety-odd years she'd been running the place. I blew on my fists to warm them and watched a comically squat middle-aged hausfrau with an enormous head of curly salt-and-pepper hair and bulbous eyes walk her beagle. She was very gentle with the leash, unhurried, indulgent, allowing the little animal to piss wherever he wanted and to sniff every molecule in the pavement.

"Hello," she said quizzically as she passed by me, probably thinking I was one of the neighborhood drunks waiting for my morning fix.

"Hello," I said back. "Cold morning."

"Well, it's March, what do you expect," she said like a nun reprimanding a sinner, and the brief warmth she'd inspired in me by her treatment of her pet curdled into antipathy. What a bitch. I watched her waddle on her way, glad to see her go. What made some people so unaccountably mean-spirited when others were so instinctively generous? I had never been able to fathom it.

I wandered down and over to Gem Street and stopped in at the

Acme Smoked Fish office to find out whether they were hiring; I had a nice little fantasy of manning the loading docks with George the bartender. I made my way through the hosed-down, fish-smelling warehouse with a drain in the middle of the concrete floor, past the freezers and stainless-steel tables with nozzled hoses dangling overhead and galvanized trash-can-sized buckets. I went into the little office and filled out the application that was summarily handed me by the brusque walrus-shaped man at the desk, and although it contained nothing but evidence of my woeful unemployability, he put it into an important-looking file as if it might come in handy someday and thanked me for stopping by. I half hoped they would hire me; unlike many people, I liked the smell of fish, fresh, smoked, day old, and otherwise. I wished I could have written that on the application, since it was my best qualification for the job.

Then I walked along the riverfront. At the foot of North Seventh Street was a corporate, manicured waterfront park, just a lawn with some hideous cast-iron sculptures and benches scattered here and there and a big sign on a fence listing all things verboten, dogs and booze and other things that used to be allowed everywhere as a matter of course. This was the place where not so long ago local hipster kids used to climb through the fence and have wild parties on the heaving weed-wrecked concrete pads with ashcan fires and hibachis and jugglers throwing burning sticks, flames in the night leaping and giving off sparks. An entire ragtag marching band had rehearsed here every Sunday afternoon in warm weather. To give Luz some solitude and breathing room, I used to come down with Karina and Hector and a sack of deli sandwiches, potato chips, cookies, and soda. We'd sit on the concrete by the water and eat lunch and listen to their rough-hewn renditions of Balkan songs. I enjoyed eavesdropping on their fights, which were as heated and intense as a group-sized lover's quarrel and were often set off by the shouts and hectoring of the band's de facto leader, a good-looking, cocky, loudmouthed trombonist, muscular in his wife-beater and falling-down old-man pants and straw boater hat, a guy everyone seemed to love even as he pissed them off. My kids, who were teenagers by this time, thought the band was the coolest thing they'd ever seen. Those picnics had been a high point for all of us, until the Towers fell, and then we'd stopped going.

Chapter Nine

I walked on toward the Williamsburg Bridge, which looked in this uncertain light like a gray-purple dragon-serpent hybrid spanning the river on massive haunches. To my right was the new ghost town, the unfinished, uninhabited, unsold boom-time developers' hubristic folly of forty-story waterfront towers. They served no purpose but to blight the view of the river and Manhattan, which had in days past been achieved by looking out across a beautiful, bleak, flat landscape of rubbled lots and rotting piers and torn chain-link fences. I scuttled under the bridge along Kent, past the old Domsey's Warehouse, where, back in bygone days, you could buy cheap, good used clothes, the old Domino factory with its glowing, blue-green-white glass sugar-cube tower, soon to be torn down to be made into condos, the antiseptically corporate entrance to Schaefer Landing, and to my left, the dull gray factory building where fashion designers and "turntablists" and video artists lived in overpriced, squalid lofts with astounding views. Then I was at the entrance to the lumberyard where my one Hasidic acquaintance, a crackhead accordion player named Yanti, had told me they might hire me someday if I ever needed a job.

J & B Lumber was housed in a corrugated-tin warehouse on a fenced-in lot on the river. Trucks drove in and out; Hasidic guys in wool scarves and work gloves bustled around looking important and busy and white-faced with cold, side curls flying, eyes blinking myopically, shouting the harsh gibberish that was their mysterious language. Having lived in this neighborhood for so many years,

I had had enough experience with this medieval Jewish sect to know that in the aggregate, they could be unpleasant to deal with, but I was willing to work for them if they paid me what Yanti had said the going rate was. At this point, I was willing to work for anyone for anything. The first thing to do was find Yanti, who always worked on weekday mornings and so would certainly be here now.

We had met back in the late eighties in a long-gone bar on Berry Street called the Ship's Mast, back when they used to host local bands there and serve chafing dishes of free, not-bad macaroni and cheese, hot dogs, baked beans, and chili. They had cheap beer, which was nice and cold. I was there that night for supper, but the music was not optional, so I listened. They turned out to be surprisingly good; Yanti was playing the accordion with his group, a motley bunch of Hasidim in their shirtsleeves playing what sounded like half rap, half klezmer. By pure happenstance, when they'd finished, he and I struck up a conversation at the bar, and then a couple of weeks later ran into each other in line buying cigarettes at Amjed's deli on Bedford Avenue and walked out conversing some more, lighting up as we went. Of course, being the hustler that he was, Yanti handed me a flyer for his group's next gig, and, having nothing better to do when the night rolled around, I went, and brought Luz with me, and three meetings made a friendship of sorts. Luz didn't like him, instinctively, on sight, or ever. Given this, and the fact that I was not a Hasid, the development of my friendship with Yanti was limited in terms of things like dinners at each other's house and whatnot, but within our constraints, we were always affectionate and frank and unguarded with each other when we met in the street or talked on the phone.

He was the exception that proved the Hasid rule. He was something of a black sheep among them, I gathered. His wife had understandably fled with their five kids back to her family in Toronto, so he had rented a room from his boss and was sending his family every cent he didn't put into his pipe. Most Hasids apparently spent their fun money on blow jobs from crack hos, but Yanti just went straight for the crack and cut out the middlewoman.

I wandered around through a whirling ballet of hand trucks full of bags of cement, men carrying stacks of two-by-fours, and forklifts laden with drywall. Finally I found Yanti behind a counter with two other Hasids, with a stubby pencil behind his ear and a scowl on his face as he totted up a line of figures with another stubby pencil. He wore Dickens-urchin gloves, the kind with the fingertips cut off.

"They recently invented things called calculators," I told him. "Also adding machines. Or so I hear."

He looked up at me, about to tell me to go fuck myself, then he saw who I was. "Harry! Go fuck yourself!"

"Yanti! I will!" I said. He came out from behind the counter and gave me a boisterous hug. He was fatter and pastier than he'd been the last time I'd seen him, about five or six months before, but other than that, he looked the same. And he still smelled faintly of chicken fat and mustiness.

"So what can I get for you today, my friend?" he asked urgently, clapping his arm around my shoulders and leading me back into the stacks of lumber. "You finally fixing up that place you live in for your beautiful wife?"

"Used to live in until she threw me out," I said. "No, I'm here to ask for a job."

He stared at me. He had always had a puppy-dog crush on Luz and made no secret of it, which was probably why she didn't like him. "Threw you out," he repeated.

"That's right," I said. "I'm homeless at the moment and broke and I was hoping you'd put in a word for me here, even though I'm not Hasidic, and I probably have a rabbit's chance in—"

"Of course," he said, but he was still obviously stuck on the fact that Luz had pitched me out.

"I can load things or something," I said. "I promise I'll earn my keep."

"Yeah yeah," he said, and wiped his mouth on the back of his hand, then his nose on the back of his thumb, then his eyes on the back of his wrist, an odd, possibly diagnosable tic he had. "Yeah. So how you been? What have you been writing these days?"

"Oh," I said. "Luz wrecked my new book. So I have nothing to show. I can't remember any of it, either. I think she erased my brain's hard drive on top of everything else."

He laughed. Being dumped by one's wife was old news to him, and if anything, it was also probably good news, because now we were on equal footing. Back when I'd lived in my warm little nest with my own wife, he'd felt, probably, in a one-down position with me. Now we were two bachelors, two womanless guys, shooting the shit together by the racks of four-by-sixes and whatever those other boards were.

"Shit," he said. His lower teeth were uneven and tobacco stained, but his upper teeth were spanking white and even as a picket fence. I guessed he'd run out of money to pay the dentist, but maybe he liked the effect. It was certainly arresting. "She's a nice girl, your wife. Eh, what are you gonna do. So what else you been up to?"

"Looking for a job," I said.

"Yeah?" he said. "Where are you gonna work?"

"I hope here," I said.

"Here," he said. "This place is a death trap. Last week someone cut his finger off."

"I'll take my chances," I said.

"You work here, you're taking your chances all right."

"I'd be happy to," I said.

"What are we talking about?"

"I want to work here," I said. "I want a job."

"You don't. Believe me. This death trap? Forget it."

"If you can find me anything at all, I'll take it."

"Yeah, and cut your finger off."

"I'll be careful."

"It's great to see you, Harry!"

"You too, Yanti."

"It's been what, a year?"

"More like eight months."

"Too long!"

Yanti's brain had a natural tendency to short-circuit. He had explained to me that since childhood, his skull had been full of static, like a radio tuned to no station with the volume turned up. This was why he needed the drugs, to quiet the buzzing roar. Nothing else worked for him. If he didn't have them, he went a little nuts trying to focus. Just walking to the corner to buy milk and the paper became an Olympic-scale trial of concentration. As a result, conversations with him were always like this, circular and exploratory. I sometimes felt as if I were walking an intelligent dog. And, as with a dog, I found I had to tug on the leash to get us to go in a straight line.

"Are there any openings here right now?"

His mouth twitched in the patchy nest of his beard. "Yah." He scratched his head under his navy blue watch cap. "What can you do?"

"Anything," I said. "Within reason. I can lift things and add numbers and answer the phone. I can put screws in little paper bags. I can order things from a sheet. Anything except drive a truck. No license."

"I'll talk to Shmuley," he said. "We might need someone in the office. An office job, that's better for you. You're no macho guy. You're no Rambo." He laughed so hard he wheezed.

I smiled and waited for his mirth to die down. "Thank you," I said. "An office job would be fine. I need it. But I'll do macho work, I don't mind. I'm flat broke. If you get me anything, I'll owe you a big one, Yanti, I mean it. Let me give you the number where I'm staying." I reached up and took the pencil from behind his ear and scrounged up a piece of paper in my pocket and gave him Marion's house number. Then I put the pencil back in its slot, kissed him on both hairy cheeks, shook his hand, and let him get back to his totting up.

I threaded the streets up to Berry and went back under the bridge, to the Mullet, the bar nearest Marion's house, which I knew would be open, even at this hour. The Mullet's motto, emblazoned on a shingle under the bar name, was "Business in the front, party in the back," and the décor was some urban northerner's idea of vintage, authentic trailer-trash: hubcaps, beer signs, laminated paneling, linoleum in the front room, shag rug in the back. The bar top was Formica; the curtains were polyester zebra print. I sat at the bar and ordered a Moonshine Fizz, which came in a miniature tin bucket and tasted cheerful and deadly in about equal parts, which was exactly what I needed at the moment.

I began to work my way through it, inspired by the barmaid's shirt, which ended at her sternum to show off her bare midriff, and was sleeveless, to show off her muscled biceps, as well as tight, to show off her cute breasts. I also loved her jailbait braids tied with twine. I would have sweet-talked her, but that would have accomplished nothing but getting myself thrown out of there, since girls like that invariably turned out to be lesbians with chips on their shoulders. Occasionally, I liked the daytime drinking of hard liquor. It made the daylight seem artificial and the air extra oxygenated and gave me an adrenaline rush, like being in a casino.

I was about halfway through my drink when I heard a voice above and behind me saying, "Well, if it isn't Harry Quirk." I turned to behold my auld acquaintance Dan Levy, a small, wiry fellow in a down coat and jeans. Dan lived around the corner from here. No doubt he had come to the Mullet for the same reasons I had: proximity to home, a desire to blur the edges, and, not least of all, the girl behind the bar.

I thumped the bar stool next to my own. Dan sat, ordered what I was having, and when it arrived, we hit our miniature buckets together. He took a big swallow and said, without preamble and not without sympathy, "I hear you've been having some personal troubles."

"My God," I said. "Quite a grapevine in this small town. Aren't we too old to care what we all do anymore?"

He had the grace to look chagrined. "I guess we are," he said. He looked into his glass. "What's in this drink, anyway?"

"Tastes like bourbon and lemon soda," I said. "And a little extra something. Sweat, maybe."

He tasted his drink again. "I hope it's hers," he said with a flick of his head.

The bartender pretended not to hear him. So did I; it made me uneasy to see Dan Levy still playing the cocksman. Marion had always thought he was a blowhard, a troll, but as far as I could tell, this view had not been shared by most other women. Dan had left many parties over the years with many lovely lasses. Eventually, he married a girl, or rather a woman, named something like Terry or Tina, one of the loveliest of the lasses, and they had kids, and the decades went by, and now he looked as hangdog and restless as anyone else. This disappointed me, for some reason. We'd been tacitly rivalrous once, Dan and I, back when we were young and it all mattered. Dan was a language poet. His work was cerebral and experimental and, to my tastes, cold. In the olden days, he had frequented poetry slams and sported an ostentatious Jewfro and affected a kind of literary street diction that went straight up my spine. Sometimes he read his work accompanied by a black free-jazz sax player. Meanwhile, I was, in Dan's estimation anyway, a throwback, a nonentity, a noncontender, writing my defunct lyrical, visceral rhymed verse in my corduroy trousers and Irish sweaters. But now here we were, two hoary practitioners of a skill as useless as bloodletting or butter churning, sitting side by side on a cold late-winter noon in a hipster bar.

"It's true," I said. What the hell. "I'm having some personal troubles."

"Right," he said. "It's never fun."

The silence that ensued was difficult for me. I wanted to defend myself, but my pride prevented it. I owed no explanation to Dan or anyone. But I wasn't cheating on my wife. He hadn't said so outright, but he'd obviously heard I was. Anyway, somehow I had thought my long years of neighborliness and fellowship with everyone around here would give me a pass, a benefit-of-the-doubt card, while Luz and I sorted all this out. But it hadn't, I could tell from Dan's expression, which was half sympathetic, half rapacious predatory zoo animal. Of course no restraint or loyalty kicked in when something scandalous was being thrown around; gossip was a drug no one could turn down, raw, bloody meat to caged cheetahs. My suspicion that everyone would believe the worst without question had just been confirmed.

"Funny day," I said after several pulses of silence went by. "I was just remembering old times, walking through the streets."

"Which ones?"

"Which streets?"

"Times."

"The ones when we were young and no one cared what we did."

"So we thought." He said it scornfully.

"No one cared," I said, trying not to bristle.

"I guess you have reason to be nostalgic these days."

He did not say it with any particular judgment, but still, I quelled a volcanic eruption of anger in my stomach. Two weeks ago, I might have told him to go fuck himself up the ass. Now that I was marked as a pariah of sorts, I needed his fellowship. "Yes," I said. "I guess I do."

"So," he said, scooching closer to me, breathing on my face, "what's it like to be with Marion Delahunt? I always thought she was hot, as a matter of fact, and I never got a taste of that. But I bet her shit is correct."

His drink was already almost half gone.

"You're such a fucking tool," I said before I could stop myself.

He put both hands up. "Just asking, man."

I shook my head. "I'm not sleeping with her."

"Sure, sure."

I stared at him hard, unsmiling, trying in some cockamamie way to defend Marion's honor.

"Hey, I believe you." He leaned in even closer. I could smell his musky skin. "But if you were," he said with silky intimacy, "then good on you."

I harrumphed on a burst of exhaled air. "You fuckhead, you know Marion wouldn't touch either of us with a cattle prod."

"Yeah! That's an image. Marion Delahunt with a cattle prod. Now I'm getting turned on." He laughed at his own incorrigible horndoggedness, and then I laughed too, and then we both backed down.

"You asshole," I said, still laughing.

"Hey, someone's got to be an asshole around here."

"How's Tina? How are your kids?"

"They're all still around here somewhere, I think. Well, the kids are in college now, but Tina stuck around, I'm pretty sure. So what were you thinking, about the old days?"

"How much fun they were. They probably weren't really. But in retrospect, it does seem that we enjoyed ourselves a lot."

"You? You had a stick up your ass even then. I fucking cannot believe you never tapped Marion, seriously, man. Jesus fucking Christ, you spent every minute together. And then you married someone else. Not that she's not a tremendous person, Luz, she's a lovely person, but now Marion. That is a girl. I used to dream about that girl back when I had dreams."

"She's my friend," I said. Here was my chance to defend myself, but I wasn't relishing it as much as I'd thought I would. "Like brother and sister. I have never touched her. It's not like that."

Dan leaned his head on one hand and rested it there and gazed at me with melancholy skepticism. His face had not aged much through the years, but his skin had darkened with time, his schnozz had become wider and flatter, so now he almost looked like the hip black dude he'd once aspired to be. His hairline had receded far back on his skull; his longish, once-black hair was now mostly silver. The effect was wizardy and comical. He looked like a swarthy elf.

"Yeah, the old days," he said. "We were no happier then."

"Are you sure?"

"Think about it."

"I'm sure I was," I said. "Look at me."

"You really aren't fucking Marion? And your wife threw you out anyway?"

"That's right."

"Harsh," he said. "That's unfortunate, Harry, I'm sorry. At the very least you could actually be, you know, getting some."

"I appreciate your delicacy and tact," I said.

He sat up straight and put one didactic finger in the air. "Chicanery. Tomfoolery. Skullduggery," he said with suggestive challenge and then waited for me to take my turn.

"Quackery," I said after a moment of consideration; I wasn't in the mood for this old game. Anyway, I was out of practice. "Treachery, humbuggery."

"Hey now," he said. He drank from his little bucket. "Roguery, robbery, forgery."

I drank from mine. "Buggery, which is different from humbuggery and therefore counts, pettifoggery, brigandry."

He slapped the bar and knit his bristly silver-black brows together. "Perjury, usury, savagery."

"How's your work going, really?" I said.

"Fuck you," he said.

"I thought so."

"How's yours?"

"Lingerie," I said with tipsy vehemence, and he laughed.

"I'm gonna let that one slide."

"Hackery, gimcrackery."

"Jiggery-pokery, rookery . . . cuckoldry."

"Diablerie. Harlotry. Flimflammery."

We toasted each other with our silly drinks and together studied the pulchritudinous bartendress with thoughtful attention.

"Buffoonery, japery," she said, coming toward us to inspect our drinks. "Ready for more, gentlemen?"

"Japery," said Dan. "Good one."

She rolled her eyes, but not in an unfriendly way.

"No more for me," I said. "My budget won't allow it."

"It's on the house," she said, busying herself with ice, bourbon, and mixers. "Slow day; I'd rather have company than stand here alone. The regular crowd doesn't show up till late afternoon. I'm Lexy, by the way."

"I'm Harry," I said, "and this is Dan. We're the early bird special crowd."

"He means we're too old to be in here," said Dan.

"Pish tosh," she said, setting fresh Moonshine Fizzes in front of us. "Poppycock. Balderdash."

Neither Dan nor I had a comeback. We stared at her with slack-jawed interest.

"The poets crap out," I said.

"We're a dying breed," said Dan.

"Oh, don't be such a drama queen," I said.

Lexy tapped the bar with her fingernail. "The obvious one is moonshine," she said. "Anyway, what the fuck? I know a lot of poets, and they're like half your age."

"Claptrap, malarkey, flummery!" said Dan.

"That's the spirit," said Lexy, whose name had now revealed itself to be comically apt and possibly made up.

"Rot," I said. "Tripe, twaddle. Is that your real name?"

"Short for Lexicographer," she said. Her face was so pretty, it confounded the eyes: creamy-skinned, brown-eyed, aquiline-nosed, luscious-lipped. Her bare upper arms glistened with dewy, muscular, supple youth. Her neck was a pearly stalk made of lily petals. "My last name is Verbiage."

"Wow," said Dan in that calculatedly hipstery, testosterone-infused breathiness that women had once found incomprehensibly seductive. "Your parents must be out of their fucking minds."

"Or I must," she said. "No, I'm kidding, it's short for Alexis, last name's Levy."

"Get the fuck out, Levy, mine is too," said Dan.

"Get the fuck out, Levy," she said, laughing. "I guess we're distant cousins."

"I hope not," said Dan.

She laughed again. When she laughed, her mouth gleamed, her teeth shone. She was perfect, like a sex android. She was a wet-dream wish fulfillment. Years of conditioning by the prevailing social winds, not to mention my wife and daughter, almost forced me to back away from my carnivorous attitude toward this intelligent, autonomous young woman, but I was drunk and attracted enough to let it prevail.

"You're a poet, Lexy Levy?" Dan asked in his nasal hip-hop coo.

"Nah," she said, "I'm a playwright. But I really am friends with a lot of poets. They're everywhere. It is not a dying art, not at all."

"Where do the kids read, these days?"

"'The kids,' as you call them, read all over the place. There's a bar on Grand Street, there's another one on North Sixth, all over the place. So, Dan Levy." She squinted at him. "Should I know your name?"

"Not unless you follow obscure old zines and chapbooks," he said. "Harry here, you might have heard of him. He has a legitimate publisher."

"Had," I said. "She moved to London."

"What's your last name, Harry?"

"Quirk," I said. "As in eyebrow. As in idiosyncrasy."

"Harry Quirk!" she said. Her lit-up, excited expression was quite possibly the best thing that had ever happened to me in my entire life, besides the birth of my kids and maybe my wedding day. But maybe not. "I can't believe it! Harry Quirk! One of my friends, like, worships you. She owns all your books. She thinks you're like an unsung genius. Oh my God, I can't believe this, I have to text her, hold on."

She got out her cell phone and began punching buttons on it.

I watched her with apprehensive disbelief. The day had reached its zenith, its apogee, along with the sun. From here, it would be all downhill: the friend would show up, I would invariably have another Moonshine Fizz and, in my state of flattered excitement, behave like the knucklehead I was and thereby greatly disappoint my alleged fan, who was no doubt Lexy Levy's equal in wit and beauty, and then I would wind up feeling queasily, stupidly, pointlessly drunk.

I slipped from my bar stool and waved good-bye to the Levys, who watched me go with some consternation and surprise. Back in the cold, bright day, I made my way to Marion's empty house, where I lay in lordly supine bliss like an emperor on the couch and surfed a fresh wave of hope and joy into a long, restorative nap.

Part TWO

Chapter Ten

One night in mid-May, as I slept alone in my tiny apartment on the second floor of the Astral, my body lost a battle with an interloping virus, and by the time I awoke, the battlefield had long been conceded.

I had moved back into the Astral only recently and hadn't yet accustomed myself to this lower elevation, difference in air pressure, and strange new neighbors. I was back, but I wasn't exactly back. It might have been the stress of the move and the strangeness of being only half here that caused me to succumb to the late-spring virus that had been felling the general populace.

On awakening, I noticed first a strange taste in my mouth, metallic and foul. Next I noticed that my skin was crackling and hot, then I became aware that my head was full of sharp stabs, and finally, as I came fully awake, I felt the dull pressure of phlegm in my chest and throat. I fell back into bed. I had no time or patience for influenza. I had fallen asleep determined to do many things in the coming days, but now none of these things could happen until my immune system had killed the intruder. I was forced to cooperate by spending the morning in fetal position under the covers, then panting hotly on top of them, then shivering under them again, then sweating and clawing at my shirt to get it off and throwing the blankets from my burning near-carcass, then collapsing into my wracked chilled flesh and clinging to the bed as if it were pitching on a stormy, cold sea. My entire body hurt, or rather, its surfaces did, as if my entire skin from scalp to tiptoe had been sprayed with a corrosive, tenderizing chemical, or as if I had dipped myself in Newtown Creek.

I had no phone and was too sick to go down the hall and borrow my neighbor's; I was on my own. I couldn't call the lumberyard to let them know I wouldn't be in, couldn't call Karina. At noon, I got up and with great effort and concentration made myself some coffee to help with my powerful headache. I drank most of a cup before I fell back to violent sleep. In the midafternoon, I forced myself awake again and urinated a weak, unconvincing, dark yellow puddle into the skanky toilet, then filled a smudged glass with lukewarm water from the tap and drank it with greed. As the setting sun bounced its secondhand glow onto nearby buildings and thereby through my north-facing window, I awoke to find myself drenched in sweat that was both hot and cold at once. I changed my shirt and U-trou, as my prep-school-educated friend Chip used to call his briefs, tried and failed to eat a banana, and drank another glass of water, then fell into bed.

I bleated a little, thinking of Luz coming home from work, walking past my window without knowing I was in here, walking right by me as I shivered and mewled. And if she had known I was sick, she might have walked by anyway. I was sure of it, the more I thought about it; she would walk by and enjoy it. She was probably cooking her supper now up on the top floor, alone in our apartment. I wondered what she was making. I felt as vulnerable as a newly hatched insect, rickety and wet and easily squashed, confused by this sudden change. My fever caused a mirage in my perceptions, my internal landscape and physical surroundings alike distorted by shimmering heat waves. My body heaved and gasped and shuddered with pain, and my psyche created a concomitant reaction by summoning all the regret it possessed, at the immediate forefront of which, ahead of my ruined marriage, lost poetry, my son in a cult, my daughter a lovelorn trash collector, my parents forgotten corpses in the fields of Muscatine, Iowa, my former dreams of flaming literary glory a small burning heap of charred rags, I regretted having been forced, two weeks ago, to leave the wholesome safety of my hideout in Bushwick, the easygoing, sane company of Zeldah Speck, and the comforting daily contact with a pack of dogs.

For six weeks, I had lived in a room in Zeldah's basement. She was a zaftig, caustically wry, unassuming, deeply religious black woman of about my own age who owned a tidy, bare-bones little Section 8 house just off Broadway in the heart of Bushwick. I'd moved in with her in mid-March, right after I started working in the waterfront lumberyard office with Yanti and got my own set of stubby pencils and fingerless gloves. She was a friend of Karina's, or rather, she was a fellow do-gooder who knew Karina from do-gooder circles. Instead of Dumpster diving and giving things to needy people, Zeldah took in abandoned dogs and tried to find them devoted, stellar owners, so in a sense, she was also in the recycling and redistributing business.

She had an extra bedroom, Karina had told me, and she needed someone to walk the dogs morning and night and keep an eye on them on the weekends while she was making the rounds of the city in her Chevy van, picking up and delivering dogs and incidentally preaching the gospel to anyone who was available to hear it.

"I'll go and see her," I told my daughter. "Go today," she said. So after work I rode up Broadway on the sturdy blue one-speed that had been rescued for me by Karina from a Dumpster in Bed-Stuy. I rang the doorbell, and when Zeldah peered at me from behind the chain on the door, I said, "I'm Karina Quirk's father, and I've come to take care of your dogs." She unlocked the door and let me in without a word. She was barely five feet tall and about the same in circumference and black as coffee; I am, of course, an unnaturally pale, tall, and skinny person. We made a striking pair. She marched me down to the basement and into the backyard, a fenced enclosure of torn-up lawn containing a muscular, writhing, haunchy mass of musky-smelling, panting, slavering beasts. They bugged their eyes at me, and I offered them a hand to sniff. "They like you," said Zeldah with more hopefulness than truth. "You'll be fine." Then she showed me my basement bedroom, a little windowless cubicle next to the laundry room furnished with a single bed, a small bureau, and a chair, just like a prison cell except without a sink or toilet. "Yes, I'll be fine," I said. Zeldah told me to settle in and that we were having rice and beans and chicken for supper and to come upstairs in a little bit, and I was installed, just like that.

The next morning, I took the dogs out for a walk. It was almost, but not entirely, a disaster. We came back, and I took them downstairs through the basement and put them out in the yard and came back upstairs for breakfast. Zeldah was decked out in her pink smock and loose-fitting white pants, ready for a day at the beauty parlor, coiffing heads. We ate in silence at the table. In all the time I lived there, we were never chatty in the morning. We saved our thoughts and gossip and business for evenings after work, which I found very restful and easy.

Zeldah finished loading the dishwasher and picked up her purse. I went to the coat closet and hauled out the gigantic bag of kibble, which Zeldah bought in bulk at Costco every few weeks, and poured the morning's rations into a bucket. After I fed the dogs, I rode my bike all the way down Broadway and turned left onto Kent. At the end of the workday, I rode back up Broadway, went through the house and down to the dog yard, put leashes on Spike, King, Serena, Jeeves, Tom Thumb, and Mickey, collected a huge wad of plastic bags, and out we went. It went better the second time. They tried to knock me down and trip me. I picked up a staggering amount of dog do without getting any on my hands, and I managed to keep them from knocking anyone down or bolting or humping me.

We went back home, where Zeldah was making stew, and I opened a beer and, feeling shy, went downstairs and sat in my room until she called down that it was ready. After dinner, we sat reading quietly together, I with a poetry book, Zeldah with her Bible, which quickly became a routine: me on the brown fake-leather couch, Zeldah nearby in her matching brown fake-leather swivel easy chair, sitting with one foot tucked under her, the other planted on the floor, turning the chair to and fro. She always put on the ten o'clock news. For the entire half hour of its duration, she kept her eyes on the screen, rapt and attentive, arguing nonstop with newscasters and advertisements alike in a stream of genteelly euphemistic, Christian-lady hotheadedness. "About that Afghanistan situation, you go in somewhere like that you better clean up your mess before you come home. Don't you be telling me that stuff works, I tried it once when I had a sleepless night and I had nightmares. Look at that sad meal, I wouldn't eat that if you paid me a hundred dollars. If you want good food, you have to make it yourself."

Every morning before work, I walked the dogs along Broadway past closed fried-chicken palaces and cheap clothes emporia, dark behind their pulled-down grates, while the train came to a high, metallic, drawn-out stop on the elevated tracks overhead. The dogs jostled and snuffled for crumbs on the ground. When King was adopted by someone who seemed worthy enough to pass muster, we were down to five dogs. Zeldah was careful about the people she gave her animals to; if she got a whiff of violence or neglectfulness, the person was given the heave-ho. She took tremendous pleasure in telling people they were unworthy of one of her dogs. Dogs, she loved; people, not.

As the weeks went on, with experience and slightly warmer weather, my mornings and evenings with the dogs had become easier. The dogs got to know me; I got to know them; we all knew the route and the routine: down Broadway, over past the projects, and back again the roundabout way through a network of funny, crooked little streets, and home. Picking up all their shit no longer fazed me; I carried at least twelve bags with me whenever we went out and had memorized the locations of all the garbage cans. And the mechanics of all of us sidewinding along, joined together by six-foot leather thongs like a gigantic, unwieldy sea creature trying to walk on land, wasn't quite the comedy show it had been. I had begun to train them to heel, to stop at the crosswalks, and to walk in an orderly fashion without bumping or nipping at one another. They turned out to have pretty good characters, these dogs. The only problem had been King, who was touched, easily spooked, extremely stupid, and intolerant of the other dogs, but he had gone to Connecticut and was giving someone else a migraine.

Simply by virtue of staying away from the old haunts and working too hard to dwell on anything, my regret, loneliness, and heartache lessened. And on one particular morning, the day Zeldah threw me out, I was feeling unusually chipper, although I was trying not to admit to myself or think too hard about the reason why: Zeldah's daughter Camille was due to arrive back home tonight after spending a month in Georgia, looking after Zeldah's sickly older sister. Camille was a wicked beauty, sharp-tongued and lustrous at the same time, the daughter of the redoubtable Zeldah and the sweet, beautiful Rastafarian dude Zeldah had been married to for a brief time before he'd died of lung cancer. She was thirty, which of course meant she was far too young for me, which naturally added to her allure. She was also my landlady's most precious thing in the world. I could not dream of sullying her or even look at her funny, and I had no intention of ever doing so except in the privacy of my imagination in my little monk's cell in the basement at night, and then, only with the utmost respect and consideration, since my balls were only just regenerating from the crushing they'd gotten from Luz and I had little power, onanistic or otherwise, these days.

As I left for work that morning, Zeldah called after me, "I'm praying today for God to bring my baby back home tonight and for her safety always."

I was used to other people's prayers; Luz had prayed for me for years. Her requests had generally taken the form of hoping I would become a Catholic for the good of my own mortal soul. I found having someone pray for something I actually wanted surprisingly invigorating. "Amen," I called back up to Zeldah.

But it wasn't a simple prayer. Her tone had held a warning. I hadn't sensed it.

Zeldah was in the kitchen when I got home from work, stirring things in pots and peering into cupboards. The house smelled of garlic and spices. I took a bottle of beer from the refrigerator and headed down to the basement. For an hour I sat in my straight-backed chair at the small, crappy table I'd found in the street. I worked on the epic poem I'd been trying to write, which was entitled, fittingly enough, *The Astral*. I envisioned it as the story of Adam banished by Eve, sent from the marital Edenic nest to live alone in the cold wilderness. It was intended to be a sort of modern-day, secular, personal *Paradise Lost* or *Inferno,* but it wasn't going well. Adam's voice was too bathetic; there was something false and self-exculpatory about the whole enterprise, or maybe the problem was that I didn't believe in God. I wrote in a notebook I'd bought in the ninety-nine-cent store with pictures of fluffy ducks on the cover; I had no laptop anymore and couldn't afford a new one.

Well past the cusp of midlife, in the dark and the cold,
I am suddenly alone and cannot see my way ahead.
Behind me, the lights and warmth of our garden lie,
Our garden where my dark and vengeful wife will lie
Down to sleep tonight without me, and all the trivial
Testaments to her being I took as given—
Her hair on the pillows, in the drains, in my food,
Her reading glasses, her glass of water,
The splayed book by her side of the bed,
Our bed, our old bed in our old apartment
Where we lived high above the street like gods,
All of it is gone.

At six thirty, I leashed the dogs and took them upstairs, quivering with nervous anticipation at the thought that Camille might have arrived for dinner. I found Zeldah sitting at the table, smoking a cigarette with slow, careful dreaminess. She smoked one cigarette a day, right before she cooked dinner, because, according to her, it stimulated the appetite. I would never have thought this was something she needed help with, but of course I would never have said so.

After our walk, the dogs and I arrived back home and bounded together up the steps and into Zeldah's living room. And there was Camille, perched on the couch, looking radiant and amused. I felt exactly like one of the dogs, panting and openmouthed and unable to hide my joy at the sight of her. I wanted to leap at her and lick her entire face with big swipes of my tongue and sneak in a few furtive humps of her leg.

The dogs did all of that. She suffered their enthusiasm and smiled at me.

"Welcome back, Camille," I said.

"Well, hello there, Harry," she said in her laughing, honeyed voice.

"Okay," called Zeldah from the kitchen. "It's about ready."

We gathered at the table. Zeldah had lit candles and put out place mats, something she never did when it was just her and me. I looked at the feast Zeldah had made after a long day on her feet ministering to other people's hair: catfish dipped in cornmeal and fried, caramelized chunks of baked butternut squash, boiled greens, black-eyed peas, and corn bread. I sighed with happiness.

We bowed our heads. Zeldah said, "Dear Jesus, we thank you for bringing my girl back, and for the food we are about to eat. Amen."

Camille and I murmured "Amen" in unison, and I could feel the word leaving our lips simultaneously, which was nothing like kissing, but felt intimate nonetheless.

When Zeldah asked me to move out the next day, I was caught unawares. I had intended nothing. She looked directly at me, told me she liked me fine, nothing personal, a man would be a man, but she had to protect her girl.

For the second time in recent history, a woman was asking me to get out of her house because of some imagined sexual infraction I hadn't committed. The irony, rich and cosmically hilarious though it may have been, afforded me a wild, itching grief and very little humor at all.

I felt as if a rare chance for freedom and salvation had been snatched away from me unexpectedly, as if a kind of innocent, happy second childhood had come my way like an unexpected blessing, saved me for a while, and then ended with an unspoken but harsh and half-true accusation. I'd scrambled to pack my things, glad I owned so little. I loaded myself onto my bike, weighted down with my bag of clothes and books, and pointed myself toward the old flophouse near the End of the World. After one unhappy, uncomfortable night there, I went to see the super of the Astral.

My decision to move back in there was instantaneous. It was the homing instinct, the bracing, comforting realization that I could live there if I wanted to. My loneliness now was so keen and all-encompassing, I couldn't imagine going to live in a different building, a place I didn't know at all, among strangers. I yearned to go home.

The super gave me the cheapest, smallest unit in the building, for almost as much rent as Luz paid for the place upstairs. It was on the second floor just off the entryway, a studio with a tiny kitchenette in the foyer, a chintzy bathroom a whole step up from the rest of the place because the plumbing had been put in as an afterthought, pipes run along the baseboards, and a painted plywood floor. The toilet ran all the time and wobbled when I sat on it. The sides of the hard plastic shower stall were festooned with splotches of bile-green mold that resisted cleanser and scrubber. The room itself was irregularly shaped; it narrowed from the entryway to the window as if whoever had partitioned it couldn't have been bothered to use a level or a measure when he slapped up the drywall. But there was indeed a window, which was good, and it looked out onto the street, which was also good, and my upstairs neighbor didn't stomp around too much, so all was far from lost.

Still, this minuscule dump was a big comedown from the sunlit, spacious aerie on the top floor with its three bedrooms and comfortable living room, the butter-colored cozy kitchen with the Formica table and chairs, the earthy smell of well-watered houseplants in the windows. I tried not to think too much about my old marital bed, a sublimely comfortable king-sized pillow-top mattress, as I lay down here on my hard single futon on its wooden frame, looking up at the spiderwebs in the ceiling corners, the dingy off-white paint, the sepia stain over my armchair. Well, here I was, and it was home, for now. There were no bedbugs or roaches in 2-C, so that was a start.

But it was a terrible place to be sick. Late that night, when the pain was bad and my fever was very high and my pulse was weak, I became aware of how easy it might be to die. The process presented itself to me as a simple bodily function, as elemental and uncomplicated as breathing. I could feel the membrane there, felt myself go up to it and press the top of my head against it the way a newborn crests before emerging. I tested it with curiosity and some real intent. It was tougher than I'd thought, the portal out of life. It resisted me, and I lacked the strength to push through, so I merely slept instead.

The following early afternoon, I awoke in high spirits. My fever had broken. I felt a lot better, I discovered as I stood upright.

I heated up a can of chicken broth and drank the whole savory, salty potful, then finished the banana I had abandoned. I dressed, tottering a bit, and made my shaky, purblind way out the door and down the hall to my neighbor's little den. He was a lively gaunt Irish fellow of roughly my vintage who enjoyed hosting wild parties in his tiny place, the more the merrier, the later the better. I found him awake, barely, with his hair askew and his face dented by the sheets.

I imagined I looked like his mirror image, for different, less enviable reasons. I could see, behind him in his bed, tawny limbs, a swath of flossy hair, cigarette smoke rising in a burst from a sweet mouth. He leaned against his door frame and fished around in his pants pocket and handed me his cell phone with a bleary smile. I took it with an equally bleary smile.

They weren't happy to hear from me at the lumberyard, but apparently by some miracle I still had a job; when I'd failed to show up, Yanti had covered for me. Not knowing where I was, he had made up some story about me being sick with the flu, and so, because my story matched his, all was saved. I promised to be in tomorrow. Moishe somewhat indifferently told me I'd better be. "I will," I said, and clapped shut the flat shiny beetle.

"Thanks, Brian," I said to my neighbor, and he dismissed the dollar bill I tried to give him for letting me make the call.

"Put it toward your own phone," he said, as he always did.

Back in my room, I stripped the bed and gathered up my discarded sick clothes and carried them all to the Laundromat in the building. I sat in a chair and watched the suds go round and round. There was a dim ringing in my ears, the echo of fever's weird rhythms. Everything looked too big, too hard-edged, too bright. My papery skin registered every current of air passing over it with the sense-memory of pain.

In due time, I transferred the wet cloth wad to a dryer and sat slack-jawed and lulled, watching it tumble through hot air for the better part of an hour. When the machine stopped, I came out of my trance and carried the hot tangle back to my room and sorted it out and made the bed, folded the clothes and stowed them in their rickety dresser. I washed the dirty dishes in my tiny sink, dried them with my newly clean dish towel, and put them into the metal overhead cupboard. I turned the shower on full heat, full blast, and stood under it soaping and shampooing myself as long as I could stand it. Dry, in clean clothes, I swept and dusted and mopped my little room, opened the window to let clean air in, tidied up a few papers and books and magazines, drank a pint of orange juice I found in the mini-fridge, took two pain relievers, ate a baloney sandwich and half an apple, then crawled back into bed.

It had never occurred to me to wonder, during my smugly domesticated thirty years with my nurse wife, what solitary people did—how they coped when they got very sick. Now I knew very well what they did. What good it did me, I wasn't sure.

Chapter Eleven

The next morning I clawed my way out of bed, drank coffee, dressed, and locked my door behind me. The Astral had several lobbies, all bleak little featureless foyers that were little more than stairwells lined with mailboxes with signs that said NO LOITERING. I disobeyed the sign and hung around my own lobby, my face pressed to the smeared, greasy glass door, watching the sidewalk on India Street until I caught sight of Luz in a crisp white blouse, carrying her nurse shoes in a bag to keep them pristine until she got to the hospital.

I went out and easily fell into step beside her. "Luz," I said. "Good morning."

She didn't look at me or answer, but I could feel her start of surprise at my sudden appearance.

I felt everything I had to say to her rise in my throat. "I know you don't want to talk to me. I know you're angry. But I'm here. I won't go anywhere."

I turned to look down at her, to address the rest of what I had to say to the top of her head, but she had disappeared. I whirled around. She had made a full stop, suddenly, so I had been left striding along talking to no one. I watched her duck across the street and continue along without me, her head down.

Some poison slid its way into her bloodstream,
Deranged her, siphoned off her fear into a pool
Of molten hate from which a black and terrible goddess

Sprang and pulled my ribs apart and crafted straw Eves
Out of a snake-pit of caprice and held them up as evidence,
These writhing lies, and nailed them over our bed.

I went back to the Astral and unlocked my bike. I wheeled it along the heaving sidewalk to Franklin, mounted it, and rolled southward along the neatly painted bike lane, relieved to be alive on this heavy morning with fat warm droplets from low swollen clouds flying splat into my face. Much younger, speedier bicyclists went by me, their silky hair whipping around behind them, wheels whirring. I took my stately, convalescing time. As I pedaled along, I recited to myself a poem I had memorized years ago and had recently read again, Czeslaw Milosz's "On Parting with My Wife, Janina." For the last ten years of her life, Janina had apparently been incapacitated by a severe illness, which one, I didn't know, and then she died and was cremated. Czeslaw nursed his wife through this difficult decade, and then, after she died, wrote a raw, self-castigating poem describing her corpse's consecration to the flames and the terrible guilt, sorrow, grief this caused in him—"I loved her, without knowing who she really was . . . I inflicted pain on her . . . I betrayed her . . ."

At the end of the poem came a hot outrush of what I had always taken to be a good way of removing himself from this unbearable sense of having failed her, by crying out for the fire to come and get us all. I had once thought it made a kind of sense, metaphorically, but my recent fever had taught me otherwise. A fire had raged through my own living body and left it weak and battered, not purged, not transformed, just more fragile. The closeness to death I'd felt the other night had been a breath of something friendly and familiar and inviting. Now it seemed to me that Janina Milosz had shuffled off her diseased body and vanished, and Czeslaw was left on this side of things to mutter to himself and expose his own failings, probably born of ten years' worth of suppressed resentment and horror at nursing the decaying, dying, diseased woman who had been his lover and mate. All of this I fully understood and empathized with, but then he leapt from grief and guilt into a yearning for some incandescent, wholly imagined transcendent immolation. As I recited the poem to myself now, I was with him all the way up till the end. I found myself wishing that he had cast his imagination back to his wife instead and re-created her somehow, attempted to know her through the poem meant to honor her.

This stubborn need and desire for the concrete and emotionally direct was my own failing, I knew. These guys who took the big leaps—Yeats, Blake, Milosz—I loved them all, but I could never go with them in any way but verbally. Reading, I felt them fly into the celestial light, to fairyland, up to the divine embrace. And my own family knew how to do this. Luz believed in the resurrection, in confession and Communion. She didn't go to St. Cecilia's every Sunday to Mass, but she went often enough, and she got something out of all that incense, prayer, the eating of the wafer, the drinking of the Thunderbird or Manischewitz or whatever was in the carafe that day. And Hector had inherited from his mother this ability to live among the deities in exaltation and exploded it into exponential fundamentalism. His life was so outside my ken, I couldn't imagine what propelled him through his days. Although Karina was like me, practical and earthbound, she had strong ethical and political structures and strictures, and her life approached religiosity in her adherence to them. All I had was poetry, and these days, my faith in its forms had left me high and dry. I could not write anymore, it seemed. *The Astral*, my epic poem of loss and displacement, was going no better now than it had at Zeldah's, although I'd returned to the place of inspiration. If anything, I was more stuck than ever. Starting over from scratch with a new book of poems after the destruction of that other, almost-finished book required a strength of character I knew I possessed but was having a lot of trouble mustering and making manifest.

Right now, mourning my living wife and wrecked book of poetry and ability to write at all, I envied all those romantically inclined types who had the means—poetic, religious, or otherwise—of ecstatic transcendence. Mired to the end, I'd be, and then I'd die and cast it all off and go away, but until then, I was stuck on the ground, scratching my ass or whatever else itched. It had always been thus. I was not an ecstatic or a mystic. I had not one cell of that. When the time came, I'd find out where it all went by going there, but until then, I had nowhere to go but here, nothing to write about, when I could write, but dull, brute experience itself.

This frame of mind lasted long enough to get me to the lumberyard, where it immediately evaporated under the whirling press of exigencies, flapping side curls, scraps of paper with numbers written on them. After a couple of missed days, my vivid vacation in the foreign country of illness, the lumberyard struck me on returning as more strange and wondrous than ever before, these pasty fundamentalist Jews running around in their eighteenth-century stockings and fantastical hats, their glasses fogged with urgency having to do with drywall. I turned on my computer and kept my head down and did my work and told Yanti I was feeling much better, thanks. Today's task was preparing vendor checks. As lowest man on the totem pole in Accounts Payable, most of the data-entry drudgery fell to me. I didn't mind this. I had a heretofore untapped proficiency with a spreadsheet. I liked inserting numbers in boxes. The careful recording of monetary information soothed and interested me.

What I disliked was when I was interrupted by the ringing of the telephone at my elbow, which was never for me, but which I was expected to answer with the words, "J and B, Accounts Payable." I was no receptionist. I had no "people skills." But answer it I must, through gritted teeth. Today, it rang more than seemed possible. A glitch while I was out had caused a general grumbling and grousing among certain of our suppliers that I was expected to explain and fix. No sooner had I placated one unhappy vendor than another decided to tax my reserves of goodwill. Soon it would be time to do the payroll; I looked forward to payroll every two weeks the way Santa Claus must have looked forward to Christmas, if he'd existed. I loved preparing paychecks, loved the intimacy of everyone's machine-punched time sheets, knowing everyone's hourly wage. I enjoyed the secret warm feeling in my chest I got, making sure everyone was paid what he'd earned. But these vendors were another story. I secretly resented them with childish superstition, sure they were bilking the lumberyard, sure they were overcharging or rooking us. With quiet, steely efficiency, I dispatched their phone calls, thinking to myself as I did so, You rooster, you crook, you shyster, you nogoodnik, you shameless cheater.

At noon, I realized I had forgotten to bring a lunch. Getting sick, I had fallen out of the rhythms of my workaday life so easily. I left the lumberyard and headed for Marion's house like a hungry homing pigeon who knows where to find some birdseed. I skidded up to her stoop, locked my bike to a street sign, and rang the bell, looking forward to seeing my old friend and eating her ever-present deli meats and cheeses on a baguette.

The door opened. Marion looked out. I almost didn't recognize her. She wore eye makeup and no lipstick; she had had her hair cut shoulder length and dyed its former glossy chestnut. She wore something very flattering, I didn't inspect it closely enough to determine what it was, but I had the overall impression that she'd gained a little weight and that she looked many years younger than the last time I'd seen her. Two months ago, she had been gorgeously wrecked, battered by Ike's death, honed and lean and slightly mad looking. Now she looked smooth, and she even smelled different, more citrusy. I had a strong, sudden impression that she went out a lot these days; she was put together in that easy way of women who have a lot of dates and appointments.

When she saw me on her stoop, her expression changed, only slightly, but I caught it.

"Marion," I said. "Hello, I haven't seen you in so long."

"I know," she said. She neither smiled nor invited me in.

"Well," I said, caught off guard. I had anticipated a sandwich, a chat, a cup of coffee. Marion had never once looked at me with such an expression before in all the years I'd known her. It felt like a dark, cold wind coming off a beloved tropical island. "I came by to say hello. How are you? You look great."

"I'm on my way out," she said. "I have an appointment in the city."

I stood there staring at her for a moment. "Wait," I said, "you're angry at me."

"No, I'm not," she said.

"Because I haven't been in touch."

She didn't answer. Instead, she looked at me as if I were simple-minded and daft. We stood there, Marion impatient to be off and not trying very hard to hide it, and me, feeling guilty without knowing precisely why, as I seemed to do so often of late.

"Because of this mess with Luz?" I said. "I am sorry beyond words. It's a nightmare."

"I have to go," she said. Her whole body hummed with gathering energy like a plane before it starts down the runway.

"Let's meet later then. Tell me a time."

She looked sideways up at the sky and clucked her tongue against the roof of her mouth. "Listen, walk me to the L. We can talk on the way."

She shut and locked her door and started down the stairs. I left my bike where it was and fell into step beside her on the sidewalk. Neither of us spoke for a time.

"I'm sorry," I said again after almost a block of this strange, tense silence.

"Why are you sorry? For what?" said this new, glamorous, voluptuous version of Marion without looking directly at me.

"I'm sure I did something," I said. "You wouldn't be angry otherwise."

"No," she said. "The thing is, I'm not angry at you. You haven't done anything. You've been through hell. You're still going through hell."

"Well, I haven't called you in a long time," I said. "Maybe you feel I abandoned you."

"You owe me nothing," she said. "Friendship is a strange animal. It only thrives in voluntary enjoyment of each other's company, in the pleasure of nonobligatory connection. I repeat: you owe me nothing. I mean it."

"Still," I said. "Let me apologize. I need to."

We were dodging beautiful, intent kids with artful haircuts and either too-tight or too-baggy clothing, or both, going about their inscrutable business, kids who looked past us as if we weren't there.

"It's nothing you did," said Marion. "In fact, it's been a slight relief to have fallen out of touch with you for a couple of months. I'm weirdly traumatized by the whole thing with Luz. She's told all our mutual friends about our supposed affair. Not one person has asked me whether or not Luz is telling the truth. Not one. So that's what they all think of me. Good to know."

I watched her face and said nothing. The added weight, or something, had smoothed her skin, made her look refreshed and dewy. Her hair fell around her cheeks. She had looked just like this about fifteen years before. I would have suspected a face-lift or other artificial measures, but I knew Marion too well to ever think she'd resort to expensive trickery to look young. She couldn't afford it, and she'd never cared that much about aging.

Of course. She had a lover. That was it. I quailed a little at the thought. But I couldn't be jealous; I didn't feel that way about her. Maybe I was jealous *of* her, for having found someone new.

As we crossed Grand Street, I avoided stepping in a pile of dog shit. "I'm the one who brought this on you," I said.

She laughed. "Harry! Stop with the hair shirt."

"It's grafted onto my torso."

She turned toward me and looked at me for what felt like the first time in this entire conversation. "Maybe I should have been more careful about my claims on our friendship when Luz came along. Maybe I should have backed off a lot more than I did. I just assumed she knew it was pure friendship between you and me. I gave her too much credit for sanity. But I should have known better . . . I've been feeling guilty about it, like I brought it on us all somehow. Maybe my sister was right. I just kept right on acting the same toward you after you and Luz got married, same as always."

"That's nothing to feel guilty about," I said. "I did the same thing, I didn't change at all toward you when you and Ike got married, why should I? You and I are like family to each other."

"It's been so hard, these past months," she said. "I mean it's really been a kind of relief, not talking to you, although I've missed you and wondered how you were. But in those weeks after Luz lost it, every time I talked to you, I started having a small panic attack. Afterward, it would take me days to calm down. And I would walk through the streets, completely paranoid, expecting to be ignored or judged by people I had not long ago considered my friends and felt perfectly comfortable with. My dreams started turning dark and twisted. I felt like a pariah for something that wasn't based in any kind of reality at all. Talking to you, even though it was very comforting on one level, somehow fueled all that and made it worse. I started questioning my actions, started feeling really terrible."

"I'm so sorry," I said.

She pulled a cigarette and lighter from the outer pocket of her bag, lit up, and took a drag. "What a lot of silly melodrama. We're all just a bunch of aging bohemians."

I laughed. "Meet me later," I said. "Let's get a burger."

"See you at Tom's at seven," she said.

I left Marion at the L stop and turned back toward the south side. I was tired, from leftover fatigue from the flu, stress, general unhappiness. I stopped in at a deli and bought a ham and cheese sandwich. I ate as I walked. The sun shone. The air glittered with surges of life renewing itself. Walking through the neighborhood I had lived in for more than three decades, I felt as if I were in a primitive imitation of a landscape almost recalled, in a spell of déjà vu, a neighborhood with near-semblance to a known place. But instead of giving way with a snap back to real time, the eerie almost-remembrance persisted. I was sure I had been here before.

Chapter Twelve

Tom's Alehouse was a down-home neighborhood joint on Bedford near McCarren Park, low ceilinged, dark, and generous with the food portions. Marion was in a two-seater booth in the back room when I got there. She already had a pint in front of her. I slid onto the high bench opposite her and eyed her beer with envy.

"How was your date?" I asked her, helping myself to a gulp. It was good to be back at Tom's with Marion. It had been months.

"What date?" said Marion. "I had a shrink appointment."

I set her glass back down with a thunk. "With Helen?"

"Harry!"

The dark-haired, Aussie-accented waitress appeared; I asked for a pint and a burger. Marion seconded the order.

"So you're not seeing Helen?" I asked. "You promise?"

"Am I completely insane? Have I lost all reason? No and no. Therefore, I'm not seeing Helen. When Ike was seeing her during our troubles all those years ago, she demanded that I come in with him for a few sessions. Not for couples counseling, mind you. So she could set me straight about some things that I clearly didn't understand. She had an agenda! I went nowhere near her, of course."

"I know," I said. "By the way, Luz is seeing her once a week."

Our fresh beers arrived just as we collectively finished the first one. Marion lifted hers, stared at the foam on top, and set it back down again.

"So Luz is seeing Helen," she said with unhappy resignation.

"I think so, yes," I said. "Also, I've moved back into the Astral."

"What?" She looked shocked. "Are you two back together, then?"

"I'm in a shitty little studio many floors down. She isn't speaking to me. So no, we're not back together. But I figure I'm showing her something she needs to know."

"Harry! Maybe you have lost all reason. Why did you go back?"

"Because I got thrown out of where I was before." I told her about Zeldah, Camille, and my supposed potential transgression.

"Oh, that's too bad," she said. "So many people are so scared of other people's desires and lusts. Right before I had the affair with James, I think, in retrospect, I wanted to leave Ike, but I didn't know it, I couldn't face it. So I started drinking too much and flirting with everyone. I think I was directing all my frustrations outward to avoid admitting that to myself. So I slept with James, who was just as lonely and unhappy as I was. We were a match and dry kindling. The affair was inevitable, looking back. Stupid, but inevitable. And afterward, Ike was perfectly sane and rational about the entire thing. It made me love and respect him even more. Lisa, on the other hand, was a screeching harpy."

"She forgave James easily enough," I said. "It was you she couldn't tolerate."

Marion gave me an impatient look. "The point is, when someone is thinking of leaving a marriage, sometimes they have to create a huge disturbance in the fabric, behave destructively, run amok in some way, to rip open an escape hatch. No one seems to understand this but those of us who have been through it. Anyway, I was talking about Luz today with my entirely legitimate therapist, thinking about why she threw you out."

"She didn't drink too much or flirt with anyone."

"No, not at all," said Marion. "She imploded, I exploded. It's much less socially damaging in the long run to implode, but it's harder to identify when it's happening, so it's potentially more dangerous. It's like she had a tumor growing somewhere deep and hidden, whereas with me, it was all on the surface, like a violent allergic rash. Less toxic and deadly in the long run, but much more unsightly, short-term."

"She watches and waits," I said.

"And judges and concludes," said Marion. "And persecutes you for thought crimes."

"Exactly." I laughed. "My marriage was like a court of law in which I was always guilty, but I didn't exactly know why. A court of law in a Kafka novel."

"I never liked Luz," Marion said. "That's not something I ever admitted to anyone before now, even myself, but I can admit it now, because of all this. I never liked her. It's a horrible thing to say, it sounds so snobbish and superior, but I never considered her my equal, or yours, frankly. Not because she's not smart, she is smart, but she's not at all . . . imaginative or interesting. Or maybe it's that she has no capacity for joy or wildness. It's not snobbery, I assure you. I just don't like her, in my gut. I always thought she was a cold bitch, and worst of all, untrustworthy—"

"Luz?" I said, amazed.

"Let's leave aside for now the fact that she eavesdropped on our conversations and read your private work and our correspondence," she said.

"All's fair in love and war," I said. "She thought I was cheating on her."

"I disagree!" said Marion. "No one has the right to spy on another person. No one. I never would have spied on Ike, no matter what. Maybe it's just that I had too much pride, and too much respect for him and myself and our marriage. I would have asked him directly. No, it's more than that with Luz. The crux of it is, I don't trust someone with such a misleading, carefully controlled exterior who's volcanically angry inside, totally lacking in self-knowledge, and compensating for her blindness toward herself with wacky suspicions and theories. Which ought to make me feel sorry for her, but

I hate her guts as much as she apparently hates mine. Which is not fun. I don't enjoy hating anyone. I feel like this was forced on me. Or something. Am I ranting?"

"Yes," I said. "I love Luz. She's my wife. No matter how right you may be about a lot of this, you're missing how vulnerable she is, and how these things come out of self-protectiveness. She's been badly hurt, by her father when she was little, and by me when I slept with Samantha."

"Luz and Lisa," said Marion, as if she were listing species of household vermin. "They try to achieve power they don't otherwise have by terrorizing their husbands, vilifying other women as evil predators, and portraying themselves as the innocent, wronged victims of their spineless husband and some femme fatale."

"Spineless," I said. I couldn't help smiling. No matter what she was going on about, Marion amused me with her hotheaded rants; I never paid strict attention to the thrust of them. She was always half right. "Thanks a lot."

"I walked by Lisa on the street the other day," said Marion. "After all these years, she still stares at me all bug-eyed and moonfaced and tragic as if I had killed her puppy, as if I had strangled her newborn baby in its sleep. And what did I do? I slept with her poor, sex-starved husband, and then I sent him back to her and walked away without another word. Meanwhile, she had an affair herself. How can she be so hypocritical?"

"I think most people would prefer to keep their spouses to themselves, Marion," I said. "To play devil's advocate for one moment, I think most people take umbrage when someone else borrows their husband for sexual purposes. And it's only human to want vengeance when someone wrongs you, isn't it? To tell everyone about it."

"Vengeance, victimization, wronging, it's all psychodrama," said Marion.

"Very human emotions, some might say," I said, knowing this would only egg her on.

"If someone has an affair," Marion shot back, "either the marriage is over and the person wants out, or there's a big problem in the marriage that needs to be addressed. Either way, it's between the two or three or four people involved and no one else. Lisa shamed Ike by telling everyone. He was the one she really punished. If she hadn't said anything, we could have all moved on in private."

"So what would you have done if Ike had had an affair?" I asked.

"I would have been wildly hurt and sad, of course, because I loved him, maybe even heartbroken if I thought he loved her. But I would have understood, or at least, I would have tried to. I would have tried to figure out my own part in it all. That's what you do when you truly love someone, not beat your chest and rend your garments and accuse and demand retribution. The woman he was involved with would have been beside the point, whether or not I knew her, whoever the hell she was. The other woman is always beside the point. And this notion that I'm predatory is so fucking childish, like I'm the big bad wolf in a fairy tale. Ridiculous. Lisa is a redheaded troll."

"Wait a minute," I said. "'Redheaded' is a pejorative?"

"Your hair is white."

"It was not always thus," I said. "And I also tend to bristle at the phrase 'spineless husband.' No matter what you may think, I moved back to the Astral with every good intention in the world. My part in this is voluntary and conscious. No matter how crazy she seems, I'm choosing to engage with Luz in all of this. I want to try to convince her to let me come back. This isn't passivity or resignation, Marion, it's what I want to do. It feels like the only course of action I can take."

"Good luck with that," she said with wry skepticism.

"I need it," I said.

We addressed ourselves with enthusiasm and focus to our hamburgers when they arrived.

As I ate, I remembered a hot, bright early Saturday evening last

July. Marion had invited Luz and me over for dinner in her backyard. She and Luz hadn't seen each other in almost two months. As Luz and I walked from the Astral along the waterfront to the south side, we were mostly silent. I felt as if she was lording something over me, something I didn't know I'd done, and my instant reaction, wrongly or rightly, was resentment. So I clammed up. We didn't say much as we stumped along. No doubt my silence fed into her idea that I didn't care about her, that I was a selfish lout who took her for granted and ignored her.

When we got to Marion's, I let Luz go up the stairs first and came up behind her. Luz rang the bell and stood looking off down the street. The hardness of her expression, so set, so stony and implacable, infuriated me; I fully believed I had done nothing to deserve it. I felt innocent and beleaguered and righteously nettled.

Marion answered the door looking pale and thin. "Hello!" she said.

"Hello," said Luz with cool formality.

Marion was an old, close family friend who'd just been widowed; was this the best my wife could do?

As a sort of well-intentioned corrective, I embraced Marion with all the affection Luz had withheld from her. "Marion, hello," I said with exactly as much warmth as I felt. "You look beautiful."

"I look half dead," she said. "Come on in, you two, it's so good to see you. Especially you, Luz! It's been so long, I've missed you."

We sat on Marion's patio and drank wine while she fiddled with her gas grill.

"Ike used to grill," she said. "It was his thing, I was never allowed to. So this summer, I've taken it upon myself to master the damned thing, sort of in homage to his memory, sort of in bereaved defiance. It's amazing how grief can be subsumed by grievance if I let it."

I laughed, Luz didn't. I could feel her bridling in defense of poor dead Ike.

"How's work, Luz?" Marion asked with oblivious cheer.

"Lots of trouble," said Luz. "I don't mean the patients. There's a doctor we think is stealing Dilaudid because he's addicted to it, and we have to report him. One of the orderlies tried to commit suicide the other night and was brought into the ER by his wife. My friend was on that night, she knows him well, she said he was completely out of it, he didn't recognize her. They pumped his stomach and sent him to psychiatric and he's under observation."

"Good lord," said Marion. "That's awful."

"It's terrible," said Luz. "For one thing, it makes me so frustrated when things aren't going right. I want to correct it all, but I can't, and I find that more stressful than anything really."

"I know you do," said Marion. "You hate things you can't control."

"And it's not just those things," said Luz. "There are other random things that add up to even more stress in an already stressful job. I wonder what's going on."

"Mercury in retrograde?" said Marion, smiling.

Luz didn't answer. She thought belief in astrology was a heathen superstition. To Marion, it was a playfully ironic lark. There was nothing I could say to solve this, short of revealing to both of them the extent of their misunderstanding, which I had no interest in doing.

I stood up and excused myself and went inside to the bathroom. I concluded my business and loitered there as the toilet tank refilled, reluctant to go back outside, but not sure why. The toilet tank topped up and fell silent, and then I heard voices. The open bathroom window looked out into the yard.

"Really, Luz, I had no idea," Marion was saying. "It's been so long, I figured everything was okay."

"I've never really gotten over it," Luz said. "I'm still so angry! Sometimes I think, what am I still doing with Harry?"

"Really?" Marion sounded surprised. "But you two are—"

"Maybe," Luz said, "we could have lunch sometime and talk about it."

"Maybe," said Marion without conviction.

At the time, that night, I was surprised that Luz would turn to Marion, my oldest and closest friend, who had had an affair of her own, to talk to about her lingering resentment of my own affair. Now that I knew that she had already thought Marion and I were involved, I could only think that her obsessively intense envy of Marion had made her want to insert herself into our supposed affair and hijack it. I could understand this if I squinted and looked at it a certain way.

But back then, I knew nothing at all. When I went back outside, the salmon was on a platter and the grill was off. We sat at the table on the patio and helped ourselves to the grilled fish and passed bowls of cold salads, platters of grilled peppers and portobello mushroom caps. We opened a third bottle of wine; things had become almost pleasantly hazy. The night was warm, the food was good, and we all knew one another well, no matter what was going on under the surface. In my usual confrontation-loathing way, I decided to believe that everything was all right. Luz had mouthed off to Marion about me just now, but she said such things all the time to her sisters, and they to her. There was no heat behind any of it. Women liked to bond by complaining about their husbands. We weren't perfect; they had a lot to complain about. So be it. I let it go and stretched my legs out under the table.

The night air was tinged with a fuzzy electric-yellow light from streetlamps and smelled of starter fluid from hibachis in nearby yards, wet earth and grass from Marion's yard, and grilled fish. The air itself had dimension and depth. I began tinkering with my newest crown sonnet in my mind as I watched that acid-ochre light play on the faces of the two real women I loved most, Marion's fair-skinned, bony face fretted with fine wrinkles, her long, swooping nose, deep-set eyes, and slightly craggy brow, Luz's olive-skinned face, dotted with velvety moles, her blunt rounded nose and black eyes under a smooth, rounded brow. They were as different looking as two women could be. I appreciated the contrasts between them.

But I wasn't writing a poem about either one of them. I'd fashioned its subject out of whole cloth. Like the other women I was purportedly writing to and about, she didn't exist anywhere but my imagination. I was wrestling with the final couplet of the sonnet, which now went, "And so your body holds not one life, but two: / That of your past, and that of my love for you." I knew it was bad. I knew, in fact, that it was embarrassingly puerile, but I couldn't think of another way to get at what I was trying to say about the imagined sexual love of the speaker for his middle-aged mistress. I pictured him as a long-married man, like me; all of the narrators in these poems were imaginary, as well. I imagined their love affair as long-standing, clandestine, fraught with urgency. She seemed to be falling out of love with him, and he wrote the poem to try to woo her back, to convince her that ending the affair would cause more harm than good, and anyway, she was bound to him because he loved her so much. He was writing, in effect, a profane, erotic ode to her aging and beloved body.

When Luz went inside to use the toilet, I knew that she would be able to hear everything Marion and I said. She would immediately put together the fact that I had likewise overheard what she and Marion had said earlier while I was in there. This would be useful to me on the way home. I was planning to tell her what I'd overheard, and then she'd have to admit that my affair was still bothering her, and then I could reassure her, and then all would be well.

"Harry," said Marion when Luz had gone inside. "Is everything all right with you two?"

"I don't know," I said. "Why do you ask?"

"Because Luz seems out of sorts. It could be the trouble at work.

But I thought I'd check with you. It's none of my business, but I'm concerned."

I could sense Luz inside Marion's house, sitting there on the toilet, listening.

"She's barely speaking to me, if that's what you mean," I said.

"Yeah, that was kind of what I meant."

"She goes through these times," I said. "I can't do anything if she won't tell me what's pissing her off. So I wait."

"Maybe you should take some sort of action," said Marion.

I was too mellow, too hazy with wine and food to feel alarmed by any of it. I was amused; what could Marion possibly know about what was going on with Luz when she almost never saw her? I lived with Luz every day. I would know if something was seriously amiss. "Marion, she's not acting any differently from how's she's acted for almost thirty years. She'll come around, she always does. I think you're projecting."

"Maybe," said Marion. "Maybe not. I wouldn't say anything, but you're my best friend, Harry."

"I'm not at all offended," I said.

"Good," said Marion. "I also wanted to say that—"

Just then, Luz came back outside and sat in her chair and took a sip of wine. "Sorry," she said into the abrupt silence. "Am I interrupting a conversation?"

"Not at all," I said. "Marion's worried about us. She's worried that you're really angry at me this time."

"This time," said Luz. "This time?"

"Of course," said Marion, standing up and beginning to clear plates, "it's really none of my beeswax. Wait here, I'll get dessert." She went in.

"I overheard everything you two said just now," said Luz.

"Likewise, when I was inside," I said. "Every word."

"Oh," she said. "Then you knew I could hear you!"

She laughed. The sound of her laughter, so rare and refreshing, gave me a warm internal detonation.

"I can't believe you missed a trick," I said.

She laughed again and put down her weapons. And so, once again, things failed to come to a head, to burst out into the open air between us. For the rest of the night—during dessert, then a nightcap—we seemed to be friends again, my wife and I. She seemed warmer toward Marion, too. Something in what she had overheard had made her so, but I had no idea what it was.

On the long walk home, I said, "So why haven't you been speaking to me? What have I done?"

"Forget it," she said, yawning. "I'm too tired, let's just go home."

"And so to bed," I said. I shouldn't have let it go. Two blocks passed as we walked along. Instead of drawing my wife out, instead of adamantly refusing to collude in her silent condemnation of me anymore, I was still thinking about that damned final couplet. I had mentally thrown out the old one during dinner and was suddenly alight with an idea for something much better. He had nothing to give her but his body and their long history together; nothing to offer but more clandestine sex, but that had to be enough, or a part of him would die.

"Harry," said Luz in that clipped way she had when she felt neglected, "what are you thinking about?"

"The poem I'm working on."

"When can I read your new book?"

"When it's finished," I said.

"So," she said. "What are the new poems about?"

"They're dramatic monologues," I said. "Men speaking to the women they love. Everyone is imaginary."

"Ah," she said, but I could tell she wasn't really listening.

Out of a long-standing reluctance to discuss my work in progress with my wife, I then failed to repeat and impress on her the absolutely, purely imaginary nature of the women in my poems.

This was the only time I talked to her about it. When she opened and read the book months later without my knowledge or consent, she immediately leapt to the wrong conclusion, possibly understandably, possibly not. And so, the next time we talked about my book of sonnets to imaginary women, it had already been destroyed, and Luz had thrown my computer from our window onto the sidewalk below. She told me I was having an affair with Marion and demanded that I move out.

It was too late then to tell her what I could have told her, simply and directly, that night. And if I had, everything might have turned out very differently. I would never know.

"Remember that night last summer?" I said now to Marion as she dredged a french fry in a puddle of ketchup. "When Luz and I came over for dinner? Luz asked you to lunch while I was in the bathroom. I overheard her. She wanted to talk about our problems. She said something like, 'Sometimes I wonder what I'm still doing with Harry.'"

"I remember that night well," said Marion. "I tried to warn you there was something going on with her."

"Did you ever have that lunch?"

"We never did," said Marion. "She called me the following week, and I said I was busy and couldn't. It didn't seem loyal to you. I was never friends with Luz like that, one-on-one. I didn't understand why she wanted to start that, suddenly. And to be frank, I had no interest."

"Why do you think she asked you?"

"Why? It's obvious. She wanted to discuss your marriage with me so that I'd somehow accidentally reveal in some way that you and I were involved."

"I should have been more attentive to her," I said. "I should have tried harder to tell her things. I wasn't the most forthcoming person, either."

"Harry! Stop it. I mean it. Anything you'd said to her would have been used against you. Maybe it's nothing you did. Maybe she simply knew that you didn't love her anymore, and that's what drove her around the bend. She trumped up this whole melodrama about you and me to forklift you out. Instead of being direct, she had to create a big mess."

"But I do still love Luz," I said. "You know I do."

Marion didn't answer, just gave me a look I knew well, a wiseass combination of empathy, condescension, and ironic amusement.

"I just remembered one of my sonnets," I said. "The whole thing just came back to me, while I was eating."

"Recite it," she said, "right now. I'll write it down so you don't forget it again."

"It doesn't matter," I said.

"Yes," she said, taking a pen out of her bag and aligning an unused napkin in front of her as if it were a piece of paper. "Come on, Harry."

With self-conscious impatience, I said the thing out loud while Marion scribbled it down.

The quickening years have late outdistanced you,
And now they bring your ripened flesh to bear
On all that would arouse us, once taboo,
Now seems to you a futureless affair.
Under every tree that bears sick fruit,
In every paradise whose walls exclude,
Desire will plant a parched and furtive root
No matter how our sanctioned lives intrude.
How true it is—we're softer and more wrinkled:
Every body bears the marks of age.
Love only knows the stars have always twinkled,
And all the rest is commonplace outrage.
My love, I have nothing more to give.
Return to our old bed so I may live.

"Good lord," said Marion as she wrote the final line, "no wonder she threw you out! 'Return to our old bed so I may live' indeed."

"I know," I said. "It's pretty damned incriminating if you don't know the woman isn't real."

"If she thought it was me you wrote it to, no wonder she believes we've been having an affair for years." She looked down at what she'd written. "I like this," she said. "It's good. I like the 'sick fruit' and the twisted Garden of Eden theme."

"It's funny," I said, "I'm using that in this new thing I'm writing. The Garden of Eden is the Astral. Luz is Eve, and the apple is this book of sonnets."

"Who is the snake?" Marion asked with a sidelong gleam of laughter. "Me?"

I laughed too. "Not at all," I said. "The snake is figurative. The snake is Luz's insecurity and fear. The snake is the obsessive suspicion that made her spy on us, that tempted her to read my book without permission."

"And destroy it," said Marion. "God damn her. Can you remember the other sonnets and reconstruct the book?"

"No," I said. "I can't. The book is gone."

The waitress came and took away our empty plates and an order for another round. One old, maudlin country and western song after another had been playing on the jukebox, tingeing our entire conversation like a heart-wrenching, tear-stained movie sound track. I hadn't realized this, but when an old punk standard came on, the Ramones in fine fettle, I perked up and sat up a bit straighter on the hard wooden banquette.

"Were you really in love with James?" I asked her.

She cocked her head at me. "I was indeed, for about two weeks back there during a strange, dark, and terrible time in my marriage. Why do you ask?"

"James," I said. "I don't know. He doesn't strike me as your type."

She was watching me closely. "Why not?"

"He just doesn't."

"Maybe," she said, "but I don't know why I have to have a type. What's the matter, Harry, are you jealous?"

This flirtatious question seemed to come out of nowhere, shot like an arrow from darkness to pierce the ancient scrim of our friendship. It startled me. "Jealous of whom?" I said. "I'm not possessive of James. I can share him."

She was still watching me. She didn't laugh. "Come on, let's just say it," she said. "Just once, and then we walk out of here and never bring it up again or even think about it. Let's clear the air, though. We need it after all this nonsense, Harry. Luz is crazy, yes, because we have never once breached her trust, but I think she's put her finger on something that's always been there, and it wouldn't kill us, or our famously platonic multidecade friendship, to pick it up and look at it, just once."

My heart did a slow thudding thing and I was suddenly in a cold sweat. "Okay," I said. "Fine. All those years ago when we were young and single and ready to fall in love, what kept us from it?"

"I'll go even further," said Marion. "Why did we not marry each other? We're so compatible, so much alike, and so well suited to each other's habits and ways of seeing the world. Why did we marry two people so different from us? Would we have been happier together?"

"We'll never know," I said. "We might have made each other miserable."

"I wonder," she said. "I've never let myself wonder before. There's an almost familial taboo in my mind where you're concerned, there always has been, a serious NO TRESPASSING sign on the door marked 'Harry.' "

"Me too," I said. "So much so that I've never even thought of you that way."

"You mean sexually."

"Right," I said. "And it's not that I don't think you're beautiful.

Somehow . . . I have always been so comfortable being your friend. I've never had that curiosity about you that I had when I met Luz, the burning urge to uncover her. You and I are open books to each other."

"We are," she said. "Indeed. I knew you immediately when I met you. I mean you and I are . . . we're like birds of a feather, we're allies, our souls are fraternal. But some people marry their soul mates. Some people aren't afraid to be so known and seen and understood by their spouse."

"You think we were afraid of each other?"

"We were afraid of ourselves."

"Who's writing this dialogue?" I said. Neither of us laughed. Our new pints of foamy beer arrived. We each took a good pull and set them back down at the same identical instant. "Have we talked enough about this?" I said.

"Not quite," she said. "There's just a little more to say. Part of me is disappointed in us, that we shied away from the one person we might have been fulfilled by if we'd both had the balls. And part of me is relieved. I know it's too late now, and that's a relief, too. I wanted to hide in plain view with Ike. I wanted to be adored, a bit blindly. It made me lonely but it also made me feel very safe. I wanted to be the star with him, and if I'd married you, I would have had competition."

"I know," I said. "I know, I know."

"But we might have challenged each other even more as mates than we ever did as friends. We might have been better artists and people because of our rivalry, our shared need to be great. We might have pushed each other to our limits, and we might have achieved tremendous things. The saying goes, you should marry your best friend, and I always thought that was silly, but now I don't know."

"We'll never know," I said. I was clutched with regret suddenly.

"Nope," she said. "And now we never talk about this again as long as we live."

"Are you seeing someone new?" I asked. "You have that air about you."

"Not yet." She smiled. "That very young guy called me. The one I met in the bar back in March, the night I was so mad at Amy. He's called me a few times, but I've put him off. I've just felt it was too soon after Ike's death. He wouldn't give up, so I gave in and agreed to have dinner next week."

"Ah," I said, allowing myself to feel, just this once, a bracing thump of jealousy. "And so it begins."

"The widow ventures forth from her shrouded mourning chamber," she said. "I have to take the black veil off sooner or later. It's been a year."

"I'll toast to that," I said.

We finished our beers, paid up, left a generous tip, and went out into the warm spring night, making our way through the usual flock of smokers clustered on the sidewalk around the front door. We kissed each other on the cheek and went off in opposite directions, me to my house, she to hers, as always, as ever.

Chapter Thirteen

The next morning dawned in Greenpoint as it did everywhere else in the world, but maybe not as poignantly or as fleetingly. The low sun splashed a silky tenderness onto the grimy building facades and over the trash-heaped, rubbled empty lots along Franklin and then Kent. In the early morning stillness, the air was almost fresh, almost breathable, as if strong nighttime winds had magically scoured it. I rode my bicycle along the riverfront. I glided to the lumberyard with my raggedy hair streaming behind me, my shirt pressing against my bony chest. The river glittered and pulsed in the sunlight. The air blowing across the lumberyard lot smelled of new life, gentle promise.

But the morning was a wretched stretch of scrambling and shame. An invoice had been lost, possibly in the mail, possibly by me, possibly at the hand of Yahweh. I, being the suspect at hand, struck my boss as the likeliest culprit and was subjected to a dressing-down in Yiddish, which he had evidently forgotten I didn't fully understand, except for the common invectives every New Yorker knew as a matter of course. I blinked with ersatz apology (ersatz because I strongly suspected the hand of Yahweh, who, I joked to myself silently through my teeth, would hear from me later). As Moishe yelled, I noted the curious fact that the edges of his beard were the same shade of yellow as his dog teeth and the whites of his eyes. The corners of his teeth, the corners of his beard, the corners of his eyes; there was something about it that smacked of the Torah. It reminded me of the biblical injunction "Do not reap the corners of your field," or something like that, the reason they all wore those side curls. The rest of Moishe's head was a pasty, dramatic off-white: skin, teeth, hair, beard, all except those feral, symbolic touches of dingy ochre.

When Moishe lost steam and flew off to attack someone else, I shuffled straight-faced back to my place at the counter and clicked at the computer keys, double-checking my work, keeping everything meticulous and spit-spot. Then, twenty minutes later, it developed that the invoice had been found—in the men's room! Behind a toilet-paper roll! Stuffed there like a dirty sock! This I learned because Moishe had switched to English. It was evidently not my fault after all. Although I didn't see why this exonerated me, I accepted my release from ignominy and resigned myself again, as I did every hour of every day, to the mystery of this place. I accepted the now-tainted scrap of paper, smoothed it, and stowed it in the pile of the accounts payable du jour. For the rest of the morning, I did my work and kept my pencils sharpened.

At noon, Yanti and I ate our lunches together at the end of the street that dead-ended at the water by the lumberyard lot, sitting on a resin-smelling, felled telephone pole. We'd each brought our food from home. Yanti had chicken and dumplings and beet salad left over from the night before, cooked by his boss's wife, which he washed down with a plastic bottle of sweet, wholesome homemade iced tea. I was jealous of his lunch, so neatly tucked by a woman's hands into plastic bowls with airtight lids. I had made my usual bachelor lunch, cold and fatty and not nearly as nourishing as it should have been: a baloney and packaged cheese-slice sandwich on generic wheat bread, a small bag of corn chips, a package of powdered-sugar mini-doughnuts, and a carton of orange juice. Yanti snorted with pleasure and smacked his lips and burped. I looked across the glittering water at the dull brown projects of the Lower East Side and finished my sad sandwich.

"When Luz went to work every day, I used to stay home all

morning and then go out for lunch," I said. "One slice of plain cheese pizza from a little storefront place on Manhattan Avenue, and that was all. And a small soda. Money was tight but I needed to get out of the house once a day. Then in nice weather I would walk over to the park and sit on a bench and watch the drunks and pigeons and dog owners. It was like going to the circus."

"And what about on bad days? I mean in bad weather?"

"On bad days I would go up to the public library." I squinted, remembering. "It smelled like dust in there. But it was always spotless. I never checked out books. I read them standing up in the stacks. I had a serious crush on one of the librarians, maybe that's why I never brought books home, I felt too guilty. But I didn't flirt with her, I was all business coming and going, hello, good-bye. I can't flirt with a librarian no matter what the cliché is about them taking their hair down and their glasses off. This one's hair was already down, anyway."

We considered together a motorboat churning up a healthy wake until it powered away under the bridge.

"I used to tell my wife I was going to the grocery store and instead I would walk all over the place," said Yanti. "For hours sometimes. I made sure to buy a lemon or a bottle of seltzer to take home. No one was fooled."

"Why?"

"Why what?"

"Why the lemon? If no one was fooled."

"We needed a lemon."

I laughed. Our lunch break was over, but neither of us moved. It was the kind of day when eleven-year-old boys played hooky, when young lovers necked the day away in the grass, when old men nodded in the sweet sunshine recalling the days when they'd done both. I guessed I was approaching the latter category now. I brushed crumbs off my lap.

"I hate this place," said Yanti.

"It's okay," I said.

"Moishe," he said. "I live in his house. I work under him. I'm half a man."

Yanti had been deteriorating fast these past months. His skin was gray. His eyes were rheumy and dull. He was fat as a hippo, and he breathed hard and smelled like a homeless person. I worried about my friend, but he was a stubborn old addict who would listen to no one. As long as he still had a job and a place to sleep, things weren't so bad, and for years now, he'd managed himself so he was in no imminent danger of losing either. He'd die first, literally.

"I understand," I said. "But I think it's not that horrible. I feel lucky to be here."

"Eh," he said. "Yah."

We crumpled our lunch bags and heaved ourselves up and went back to work. Later, the midafternoon sun disappeared behind thick, heaving clouds and then it started to rain. I could smell the warm water as it hit the concrete outside and bounced in puddles of oil and wood dust. My work seemed impossible suddenly, as if I were in a nightmare in which I was expected to carry out duties that made no sense, and my livelihood depended on it. But it wasn't a dream. I felt as if I were underwater. The Yiddish all around me sounded like the most alien tongue on earth. Business was off because of the recession; every penny counted, even more than usual. Those of us who worked in Accounts Payable were under a constant low-pressure awareness that we could not screw up. This morning's lost invoice haunted me. Who had put it there? Shoulder to shoulder, I worked with Yanti and Levi in our corner of the office. Was it one of the other two? I knew I hadn't done it; Levi was a stolid, doughty young man with eyes rimmed in pink like a bunny's. He possessed not one spark of mischief or rebellion. So, Yanti? I refused to suspect him of any wrongdoing. He was my compadre, and I was his. It must have been a dybbuk.

At five o'clock, I unlocked my bicycle and set off slowly back along Kent Avenue, wobbling a little at first until I got the knack of it all over again. The streets gleamed with rain. The river was milky, the wind warm and noxious, all traces of the morning's splendor crushed by diesel fumes and commerce. It happened every single spring day in Brooklyn: awaken to fresh glory, fall asleep to blight and ruin. I began pumping the pedals. Riding a bike made me feel kidlike again—not young, or even youthful, but it gave me the illusion of being somewhat irresponsible and free in a way that walking did not.

Instead of going straight back to my empty little studio apartment, I turned right onto Calyer and slid off my bicycle in front of Marlene's. Karina had called me at work that afternoon and asked if we could meet when I finished, so I told her to come to Marlene's, not wanting to expose her to the dump I lived in now. It would only make her worry. I locked the bike to a scraggly little tree and plunged from the bright haze of late afternoon into the smoky indoor gloom and plunked myself down at the nearest end of the bar, by the window.

George emerged from the dimness like a fish swimming up out of nowhere in an aquarium tank, slow and expressionless.

"Whiskey, beer back," I said. "How are you, George?"

"Never better, you?"

"Never better. I just got off work." I tried to sound casual when I said this. I hadn't been in a position to say this for most of my adult life, since writing and the occasional teaching gig hardly qualified as work in a place like Marlene's.

George tossed two coasters in front of me, flipping them so they landed with a little puff of air and a slight bounce. "How was work?"

I tried not to take pride in the fact that he asked this without skepticism or scorn, as if he accepted me unquestioningly as the sort of man who went to a regular job at a lumberyard. "Work is work," I said.

"I hear ya," he said, pouring a scant dram of amber liquid into a squat glass. "I hear ya," he repeated as he pulled beer from the tap into a small iced mug.

Chesty, emphysemic laughter erupted nearby, one cackle, one guffaw, and one titter. My old eyes adjusted enough to make out the gaggle of female regulars perched on their stools, the magpies, the crows, Mary and Sue and Cindy, but today not Jenny, a matching set of peroxide shag haircuts, glittering hollow eyes, beaky noses.

"Hey!" said George, delivering my drinks. "What's so funny about the unemployment rate?"

"Ha," said Cindy, her sharp eyes snapping at him, "there's always something to complain about, you have to go to work, you can't get work, you lose your job, you hate your boss, it doesn't pay enough . . ."

"I haven't worked in twelve years," said Mary, who was the zaftig, mousy version of her bony, slutty sister, Sue. "I'm on disability. Can't complain about that."

"But her knee always hurts," said Sue. "Anyway, Harry, we won't bore you with our female issues. How ya been? Where ya working these days?"

"The big lumberyard on the waterfront, on the south side," I said, this time almost entirely managing to stifle my pride.

"How'd you get work there? I thought they only hired other Hasidics."

"I have a friend who works there," I said. "He's Hasidic, he owed me some favors, he pulled some strings."

"That's how you get a job, these days," said George. "You should have come into Acme, I would have hooked you up."

"I dropped off an application a couple of months ago when I was looking for work," I said. "Are there openings there now? It's closer to home than the lumberyard."

"Eh, you're better off at the lumberyard," said George. "Acme's got its dark side."

"Everything has its dark side," said Sue. She winked at me so hard her whole face seemed to shift to the left.

Sue was an aggressive flirt who, if a man didn't keep tabs on his proximity to her carefully enough, might end up with her tongue shoved down his throat. She moved fast; she pounced. The presence of other people was no deterrent. She wasn't picky or interested in reciprocity. All of this, I knew from experience. I slid my eyes away from hers, hoping it wasn't too late.

"We all do," Sue added as a suggestive lure meant to tempt me back to the fishhook of her gaze.

"Not me," I said, swimming away. "Do you, George?"

"Do I what? Have a dark side? Hell, no. I keep to myself."

"That's what I mean," said Sue, but she had lost her amorous energy. George and I were a couple of bottom-feeding trash fish, I could feel her thinking, not worth the bait. "The things you don't tell anyone. Right, Mary?"

Mary tittered and waved her away.

"All right, another round here," said Cindy, lighting up a cigarette.

Even though I didn't normally smoke, I liked it that Marlene had found a way around the antismoking laws by calling the place a social club and charging everyone who came in twenty bucks a year to join. That way, it wasn't a bar. It was a private establishment, for members only. A lot of cops from the nearby precinct belonged, so it was even sanctioned by the local law enforcers. I had my membership card in my wallet, a laminated piece of cardboard with my name printed on it by none other than George himself.

George got busy.

"What's Acme's dark side?" I asked him.

"Certain of my co-workers," he said with a meaningful gleam at whose import I was left to grasp.

"Rough trade?"

"You could say that." He set fresh beers in front of the ladies, who were yakking and chortling amongst themselves again. "You could say that. You writing any more of that poetry these days?"

"Not really," I said with an involuntary inward convulsion of psychic weepiness. Thinking about writing poetry felt like crushing shards of glass into my brain. "I can't seem to get anywhere with it," I added.

"Sorry to hear it," said George. "Are you living around here? I haven't seen you in quite some time."

"You know I was living in Bushwick for a couple of months, taking care of dogs for room and board?"

"I didn't know," George said, smoothing his lank, colorless quiff against his scalp with the flat of one hand, his eyes hollow ciphers.

"I lived in the basement of a fine upstanding woman named Zeldah Speck," I said. "She's a hairdresser by trade, but in her spare time she collects wayward dogs and finds them homes."

"Don't know about that," said George. "There's too many dogs already. I see nothing wrong with putting them all down."

"I walked them twice a day. At night, I sat upstairs with a book after dinner while Zeldah read her Bible."

"No TV? Couldn't afford one?"

"She had cable," I said. "All the channels."

"You didn't watch?" His voice cracked with puzzled agitation.

"We watched the news," I said, which seemed to soothe him. "We got along well. Not like that. She was a Girl Scout leader kind of woman."

"Always liked Girl Scout cookies," said George.

"Me, too," I said.

"So you're a long way from Bushwick, coming by here."

"I don't live there anymore," I said. "Her daughter came back a couple weeks ago, and Zeldah felt it was better for everyone if I moved along."

"Because of the daughter," said George, as if he understood everything.

"So guess where I live now? The Astral. Right downstairs from my wife. She's on the top floor, I'm on the second floor. I never see her, but I know she's there."

"Men living alone," said George. "Happiest people in the world."

"Not necessarily."

Karina came in on a gust of warm early evening. Before the door shut behind her, I could see outside that the air was glowing the pale peach-gold of almost sunset. I caught a whiff of tree blossoms from somewhere, then the door sealed us all off from anything natural or salubrious.

"Hello, sweetheart," I said as she alighted on the stool next to me. She wore jeans and a blue sweatshirt. Her red hair was newly cut in a pixie; she looked very young and fresh faced. "You look very pretty."

"Is that your daughter?" Mary cooed. "Isn't she cute."

"Karina," I said, "meet the ladies. Mary, Sue, Cindy."

"Nice to meet you, darling," said Cindy.

Karina waved at them all and turned to me. "I just saw Mom." She paused, as if she was mulling over how to tell me something that would upset me.

"Spit it out," I said. "She met someone else?"

Karina shook her head, but she kept her eyes straight ahead.

"Which means yes," I said, "but you're too kind to tell me."

"I don't know, actually," she said. "No, it's something else."

"Tell me," I said.

"I brought you a phone," she told me. She held out a cell phone and shook it at me insistently, willing me to accept it. "I paid for a month of calls for you, and then you're on your own. I got you a good plan. Please take it, Dad. Don't be such a Luddite."

I ignored the phone, too distraught to acknowledge her generosity and thoughtfulness. "What is it, about your mother?"

She set the phone on the bar next to my glass. "First of all," she said, "I found some people who can tell us about this cult Hector's in and help us get him out. I told Mom exactly what I'm about to tell you: we have to do this as a family. It's the only way it will work, that's what they told me. She agreed to go to a meeting with them even though I said you had to be there, too. She said to tell you she won't look at you or speak to you, but she'll go. She'll do anything for Hector, no matter how mad at him she is. They live in Queens. I'll pick you up tomorrow night at seven. She'll take the bus from work and meet us there."

I could hardly hear when she was saying. "Tell me the rest," I said.

She sighed. "She's losing her job."

"What? She's been there for more than thirty years!"

"The hospital's closing. They've gone bankrupt or something. Everyone has to go."

I clicked my tongue against the roof of my mouth, trying not to hyperventilate with alarm. "That job is everything to her. She loves it there, it's her second home."

"Dad, she'll find another job, she's a nurse. But you're right, she's not doing well at all. This is the last thing she needs."

"She must be having a nervous breakdown about the hospital!" I said.

"She's heartbroken," said Karina.

I couldn't respond to this. There was nothing I could say.

Karina gave me a sidelong look and asked, "What's going on with Marion these days?"

"I just saw her yesterday for the first time in two months. She's doing very well."

"Mom is totally obsessed with her. I mean obsessed."

"Jesus," I said. "Still?"

"As much as ever. Maybe more. She's started mentally going over all her memories of dinners and parties and other times where you were all together, through the years. She's analyzing all these memories for clues, for things she feels she ignored or missed at the time. And guess what? She's decided you guys got involved about fifteen years ago and were having an affair all this time."

"What?"

"She is absolutely sure of it. Positive. She can hardly function."

"I can see why, if it means questioning fifteen years of a seemingly happy marriage. What makes her think this? What got her onto this?"

"Well," said Karina, "at one point, about three weeks ago, Mom was almost ready to believe you."

"No," I said. I almost couldn't bear to hear this. "No."

"I've encouraged her in this direction all along. I've always said I don't think you two were ever involved. I think she started to listen to me. I told Mom I really believe that you love her."

"I do," I said on a wave of irrational, childish hope that this story would have a better ending than the brutal one I knew was coming. "I love her. I always have, I always will."

"She went to Helen, her therapist, and said that she had found a letter Marion wrote to you when she was in France, right after Ike died, saying how glad she was that you were such a good friend to her and how glad she was to have a close male friend who had always been like a brother to her, like family. She actually wrote that she was glad there had never been any romance between you."

"I remember that letter!" I said. "Oh God, she found it?"

"She called me and read it to me and I said, 'Sounds like they're telling the truth, Mom.' She agreed."

I almost levitated in my seat with terrified joy. "And?"

"She went in and told Helen about it and Helen said, 'What if they planted that letter to throw you off?' Helen is sure you two are having an affair and have been for a long time. She told Mom to proceed on that assumption, that to think otherwise is naïve and irrational."

"Are you serious?"

"Mom likes her. She thinks she's dark. A maverick."

"Dark mavericks make great bookies," I said. "Palm readers, magicians. Not therapists! Never!"

"I'm afraid when she loses her job she'll go over the edge."

I couldn't speak for a moment. Then I said, "Does she know I'm living right downstairs from her?"

"She does now. She thought you and Marion were still living together. She almost didn't believe me when I told her about Zeldah. I swore it. And also swore that you're back in the Astral. She thinks it's a trick, she thinks you're up to something. She asked if you and Zeldah were lovers. I swear to God, Dad, she's losing it."

"I would say she needed therapy," I said, talking lightly although I was distressed and shattered. "But therapy seems to be her undoing. Thank you, George, bless you, in fact," I added as he set a fresh round in front of me. "'The stars are not wanted now: put out every one; / Pack up the moon and dismantle the sun; / Pour away the ocean and sweep up the wood. / For nothing now can ever come to any good.'"

"Did you write that?" Karina asked. I couldn't tell whether she was impressed or put off.

"I wish I had," I said. "Karina, Karina, I don't know what to do. God, I miss your mother. I saw her yesterday morning, and she wouldn't speak to me."

"I know she misses you, too," said Karina. Her face looked pinched and wizened. "I know she does, it's just her pride, and the things Helen tells her, that won't let her admit she's wrong."

"I wish I could sue that crazy quack," I said. "There should be laws against this sort of therapist. Why aren't there laws?"

"I'm sorry to be the one to tell you," said Karina. "I didn't want to. It's hard to be the go-between."

"How is it that this woman is given such power over other people's lives? She's a sociopath! She's dangerous!"

"Dad, stop, calm down."

"Please tell your mother Helen's wrong. It's all imaginary, and this crazy shrink is reinforcing all her paranoia." I balled my hands into fists and socked my own thighs. "I can't stand this."

"Dad, Dad," said Karina.

"I have to do something."

"You can't do anything."

"She was ready to forgive me? She believed me? Do you think she would have taken me back?"

"I don't know, Dad," said Karina. Her voice sounded cracked.

Finally, it dawned on me that I was upsetting my daughter. "I'm sorry," I said.

A few yards down, George leaned against the bar, his arms folded as he listened to the magpies twitter and caw, his face a mask of ashen solitude that admitted neither passion nor yearning. I envied him with all I had.

Chapter Fourteen

Using my new cell phone, I called Helen's office number the next morning and told her voice mail I needed to see her as soon as possible. She called back within the hour and gave me an appointment that same day, at five o'clock. On the phone, her voice sounded businesslike enough, revealing nothing.

I arranged to leave the lumberyard early and spent the day rehearsing what I would say to her. My plan was to spend the entire fifty minutes putting her on trial and convicting her of her unbelievable heinousness. At the end, I would inform her that I wasn't going to pay her for the time because she owed it to me; it was the least she could do after ruining my life and my marriage and my wife's life. Then I would walk out, my job done.

Her office was in the West Village. I walked through the small marble lobby and rode the little jewel box of an elevator up to the sixth floor. I found the door marked "Helen Vollmann, M.S.W." and went in and sat in one of the armchairs in her tiny waiting room. I was five minutes early. While I waited, I examined the framed *New Yorker* covers on the wall, touched the potted succulent, and determined that it was artificial, and turned off the noise machine in order to eavesdrop on whichever client was in with her. I couldn't hear anything, so I turned it back on. I yawned and scratched my earlobe and stared hard at the most odiously whimsical of the *New Yorker* covers, a pigtailed little girl on roller skates gliding through the Metropolitan Museum, gazing up at an empty suit of armor.

I was well aware of the fact that every one of Helen's clients saw her voluntarily, knowing full well that everyone else they knew was seeing her, too. This didn't excuse anything, it just made me even more wary of her. My friends were not stupid or naïve people. Any harm Helen caused couldn't have come about if they hadn't all given her so much power. And these many crimes I wanted to accuse her of were no doubt justified, as far as she was concerned, by the fact that her self-romanticizing professional unconventionality put her beyond the normal ethical boundaries of therapy, such as they were, and allowed her to do whatever the hell she wanted. This must have been the thing they all liked so much about her.

But, naïve as it may have been to feel this way, it truly shocked me that Helen had commanded Luz to disregard irrefutable evidence to the contrary and to persist in believing that Marion and I were sleeping together. And it had always shocked me that Helen had agreed to see an entire group of friends, including several sets of married couples, as well as people they'd been involved with before they got married and others who had had affairs with members of these couples. Obviously, she was a bat out of hell, and someone had to stop her.

When Helen's door opened and she came out and introduced herself and shook my hand, I was flustered and surprised. I wasn't sure what I had expected her to look like, maybe Morticia Addams crossed with Joan Crawford with a dash of Lizzie Borden; whatever I'd expected, this was decidedly not it. She turned out to be an ordinary-looking woman with a helmet of coiffed blond hair, neither stout nor thin, a plain, pleasantly shrewd face, about my own age, but better preserved than I was. She wore a white blouse under a black suit whose skirt reached her knees, a turquoise bracelet, and gold earrings. Her shoes were plain black pumps. So far, she was an exact replica of more than half the therapists within a five-mile radius. No doubt this was one way she inspired confidence: she looked like a therapist, she decorated like a therapist, therefore . . .

"Have a seat, Harry," she said, indicating the black leather couch across from the ergonomic chair with padded headrest into which she slid. I eased myself onto the couch, which gave a little gasp as I displaced a pocket of air beneath my rump.

The showdown was at hand.

"So," she said, leaning forward to look intently at me and clasping her hands around her kneecaps, "what brings you here today?" I noticed a furrow between her eyes, slight dewlaps around her mouth, and was comforted.

"Where do I begin?" I said. "I hardly know."

"Most people who first come to see me do so because of a crisis," she said with businesslike concern. "Maybe this is true of you."

"You know who I am," I said. "And you know what crisis happened in my life recently."

Her face took on a skeptical, disapproving, mildly kvetchy expression. "So you have indeed experienced a crisis."

"Cut the crap, Helen. My wife sees you, half my friends see you, my ex-lover sees you. You know exactly who I am."

She looked at me. The sour expression deepened. I didn't give a fuck. I wasn't here to impress her. I stared back at her with equally sour disapproval on my own face.

When it became apparent that she wasn't going to say anything, something detonated in my head. My skull pulsed with my heartbeat. The silence lengthened. It ballooned, expanded, grew tipsy, and collapsed in on itself.

"What brings me here today," I said, "is the need to take your turkey neck between my two hands and twist it till you fall limp as a rag doll."

Her nostrils stretched themselves wide, but except for that, she didn't move or react.

"'Limp as a rag doll' is a cliché," I said, my eyes white-hot, my heart beating too hard. "I apologize for that. How tedious of me."

"Clichés can be useful," she said, reaching with casual slowness for the cordless phone on the table. "That one is particularly vivid."

My left arm morphed into a serpent and slithered to the phone and wrapped itself around it, retracted it, and shoved it down my shirt. "No, you don't," I said. "You're going to answer for what you've done."

"You are out of control," she said. "Please leave my office."

"What you've done," I said, "is not answerable, so I'm not sure how this will go. The rag doll comes to mind again."

She had not reacted to me or shifted in her chair or even changed her expression very much. I strongly suspected that she perceived me as an unfortunate consequence of the kind of therapeutic work she did as a dark, edgy maverick, nothing more. Through her eyes, I saw myself: deranged, unhinged, someone to be coolly managed and turned over to the authorities.

"I can feel how angry you are," she said.

"Wow, you must be a genius," I said.

"And threatening me isn't going to help you. Hurting or killing me isn't going to help you, because you'd have to suffer the consequences."

I almost laughed, but kept myself in check because once I started, I wasn't sure I could stop. "Consequences?" I said. "I'd happily get ass-raped for forty years in a maximum-security prison as a reward for strangling you till you squawk. It's not a deterrent, believe me."

"Ah, yes, ass-raping," she said. "Let's talk about your happiness at the idea. Some people crave it, more than you would think. Some people secretly want it so badly, they're willing to do anything at all so they can finally surrender to it. Whether it's a cock, a dildo, or a vegetable, they want something shoved up their ass, if only they could bring themselves to ask someone to do it to them. Most middle-aged, heterosexual married men feel this way, Harry, it's not abnormal at all. It's a craving for domination, variety, for someone else to wield the cock for a change. It's something that happens in midlife . . . men become more feminine, they get in touch with their animas. I think what you're doing here might have everything to do with your desire to explore your deep, unconscious need to get ass-raped. It has nothing to do with me, or your wife. I think it could be very rewarding for you to explore this here. I could help you uncover the urges and unfulfilled needs that brought you here."

"So this is how you work," I said. We were talking in conversational tones, with something that resembled gentleness and civility but wasn't either of those things. "My need to have a dildo shoved up my ass! Yes! That must be exactly why I'm here. Never mind the fact that you wrecked my already damaged marriage and pushed my poor wife even further over the edge. I need a good sodomizing! I can see why everyone's so enthralled by you. You're dark and irreverent and original. I am impressed."

"Are you?" she said. "I don't think so."

"Absolutely brilliant. Avant-garde. I'm waiting for you to offer to whip out a dildo and therapeutically shove it up my ass."

"Yes," she said. "Interesting. I wonder where this hostility toward women comes from."

"Not women," I said. "Just you."

"Your mother was probably undemonstrative, withholding. But she was powerful, too. She kept you in a state of always wanting more. You most likely have never forgiven her for it."

She had scored a bull's-eye. I knew she could tell. But so what? Luz had probably told her all this.

"And now it's your turn," I said. "And it's harder for me to read you, because I don't have your friends and your wife as my clients, so I don't know anything about you except what I can see for myself. And you know what? I can see plenty. You are fucked-up sexually and otherwise. Maybe someone molested you, but I doubt it, you're more twisted than that. It has to be more complicated. I think your mother trapped you in a psychosexual spiderweb. She damaged you with her neediness and her guilt-trips, as you shrinks call them. You have never entirely gotten free of her, even though she's very likely dead by now, since you're no spring chicken yourself."

She had nothing to say to any of this; I paused, just in case.

"Also," I went on, "judging by the dry, lonely look around your mouth, I have a feeling that you wanted kids of your own and couldn't have them and were too narcissistic and stubborn to adopt. You've been unlucky in love, too. You choose losers and snakes. And you give yourself to them, become their slaves, and they cheat on you. All of them. You have it in for cheaters, you think everyone cheats as a matter of course just because you're always betrayed. And you probably get dumped by them all, too, and don't see it coming, even now after all these years. And you'll fall for another shithead, maybe on a singles cruise next fall, maybe you'll pick him up in a bar, maybe you'll find him through online dating; you'll never give up and you'll never learn. I think you're lonely and hard up and full of bitterness and pain and regret, but what do I know? I'm just a layman, I'm no maverick. So I don't really care. What I do care about is the fact that you work out your unfulfilled needs on your clients and derive a sense of power from their dependence on you and get off on it when you're alone at night. You probably masturbate to images of your clients. James Lee? You wanted him bad. You couldn't believe it when he had an affair with Marion Delahunt instead of taking you up on your offer to fuck him. You've been punishing her ever since in any way you can. And me. Who knows why, but you've got it in for me, too. I'm probably a stand-in in your head for all those men who treated you so badly."

I was right on target with almost all of it, I could see it in her eyes, which were hooded and opaque, but that didn't fool me.

She sniffed. "Say more. This seems very cathartic for you."

"You don't give a fuck about me or anyone else," I said. "Don't pretend with me. Then there's the matter of Samantha Green."

She continued to look at me.

"Oh," I explained. "How quickly you forget. I had an affair with her twelve years ago. I'm sure Luz talks about her quite often in here. And she was a client of yours, and maybe still is."

"Samantha," said Helen. "I know who she is."

"How can you justify seeing both the mistress and the wife as clients? How can you possibly think you're objective about anything?" I paused, breathing hard. "Is it true that you told Luz to ignore any evidence that I'm not having an affair with Marion?"

"My work with Luz stays between us," she said. "I have strict professional boundaries."

"You are a liar. You have no boundaries whatsoever, professional or otherwise." I stood up. The phone fell out of my shirt. I kicked it under the couch, and then I began to pace back and forth over the rug, which was a woven modern Rorschach-like pattern. If anyone had asked me, I would have said that it resembled a smashed beetle. What this said about my psyche, I didn't care.

"Luz is in danger of losing her marriage because of you," I said. "Because of you, she is unable to do what she really wants to do, which is to forgive me and take me back. She knows in her heart that I'm faithful to her. She can't admit it without help. Her pride won't let her, and you're capitalizing on that. You're keeping her helpless and making her unstable. You crave other people's dependence on you. You couldn't have kids, and men always leave you, but at least your clients need and respect you."

I engaged Helen in a staredown. She didn't blink or look away. Some hurt creature deep in the underground pools of her sky-blue eyes quivered and wept, but her face was adamantine, her expression controlled.

"You're driving my wife crazy," I said. "She is having a nervous breakdown, and it's being exacerbated if not outright caused by you, the person she pays to help her, the professional she came to in dire pain. You're making it worse. You're trying to wreck her life. But how will she pay you if you drive her into extreme, bottomless despair and she kills herself?"

I stopped pacing and stood directly over her, my fists clenched, my voice implacable. "You are evil," I said. She flinched slightly. I took pleasure in this but didn't let it slow me down. "Evil. I don't use the word lightly. You are encouraging my wife to believe a lie about the husband who dearly loves her, and whom she dearly loves, out of your own perverse need to portray me as a cruel bastard. You're inflicting your own twisted history onto her. Because why should anyone else's story have a happy ending when yours never does?" I breathed. In, out, in, out. "I am not having an affair with Marion or anyone. Is that clear?"

Helen did not respond to this.

"Unfortunately," I said, "there doesn't seem to be any sort of system in place for prosecuting evil therapists. Add to that the fact that I will do anything to save my marriage. And factor in as well the fact that I'm innocent. Luz is innocent. Marion is innocent. You're the one who's guilty."

"Sit down, please," said Helen.

"Is it clear to you now what I'm doing here?"

"Sit down, please."

"I will sit down," I said, "because we aren't finished talking. You haven't apologized yet. That's the first thing you have to do."

I backed away from her and sat down on the couch, but my fists were still balled up.

"Okay," she said, "I would like to establish that it may have been necessary for you to say those things to me, but it was extremely inappropriate. Extremely, Harry. Inappropriate and out of control. The therapeutic process as I practice it is not ever threatening, on either side. You may not threaten me again. Is that clear?"

"What's clear," I said, "is that this conversation is not over yet. And you're not in control here."

She leaned back in her chair and crossed her legs and gave me a glinting smile. "There's plenty of time left in our session," she said. "Let's talk about why you're really here. Let's examine your fear of taking charge, your passivity, and your inability to tolerate any reality but the one you've decided is the only true one. Let's talk about your marriage and the real reasons Luz ended it. We can delve as deeply as we have time for into how terrified you are of living without your wife, the person you've been completely dependent on for decades. This little posture of threatening violence you've just performed was very instructive for me; it gave me a real window into your psyche that will be very helpful in our work together." She gave that same glinting smile again. "We can use ass-raping as a point of entry, if it makes it easier for you."

"That's never been a particular fantasy of mine," I said, "but if it gives you a thrill, I'm willing to go with it."

Helen's phone rang, so I reached under the couch, fished it out, and checked the caller ID screen to see who was calling.

"It'll go to voice mail," she said. "I don't answer calls during sessions. I meant to turn the ringer off, but you snatched it away from me."

"It's Lisa," I said. I hit the talk button. "Lisa," I said. "It's Harry. I'm in Helen's office. Can she call you back when we're done talking?"

"It's me, actually," said Lisa's husband, my old friend James Lee, the guy Marion had had an affair with all those years ago. He had told me, around the time of the affair, that when he'd complained to Helen that Lisa, who was also Helen's client, didn't want to have sex with him anymore, Helen had urged him to hire a prostitute, and then she'd offered—jokingly, according to James—to have sex with him herself. "Can you tell Helen I won't be in for my session tomorrow? Celeste has the flu. I'll call back to reschedule, but I just wanted her to know."

"Sure," I said. "Good to hear your voice, it's been a while. We should have a drink."

"Anytime," said James. "That would be great."

"How about tonight? Marlene's?"

"Marlene's?" said James, as if I'd suggested meeting at a gas station or a school cafeteria. "No, come over. Lisa will be out, so I have to stay home with Celeste and Ethan. Come for dinner, actually. Can you come straight from Helen's office?"

"I'll come straight from here," I said, and rang off. "James won't be in tomorrow," I told Helen. "He'll call back to reschedule."

She shook her head. "I asked you not to pick that up," she said.

"It's okay," I said. I was trembling. My rage was still, even now, continuing to mount; apparently according to my body, I had not even begun to vent it. I hoped I wouldn't really strangle Helen, but at that moment, I understood that I actually had enough built-up rage to provoke me to act violently, something I had never done before.

"No," she said, "it really wasn't okay."

"I answer the phone at my job," I said. "I like to think I have a kind of rough charm. Anyway, where were we?"

"I was offering to help you examine the real causes of the end of your marriage." She seemed so controlled, so unperturbed. But a few minutes ago, I had struck a nerve. I had been right about her love life, at least; that much, I knew. I could see it in her face, a webby desiccated disappointment around her lips and eyes, a papery, powdery lonesomeness in her cheeks. No adequately loved woman kept her hair in that smooth helmet of shining, artificial blondness. Adored well-fucked women allowed their hair to be mussed, to tousle and even curl a bit. I had never thought about this, but now that it occurred to me, I couldn't fathom why I hadn't observed it before.

"What we were doing," I said, "was waiting for an apology from you for wrecking my marriage."

"Well," Helen said. "Your wife asked you to move out. She has no interest in reconciling with you. She's made it clear she doesn't want to see you or have anything to do with you. This is her decision. I have no influence over her. All I can do is to help her better articulate and understand her feelings. That is all."

I stared back at her so hard my eyeballs vibrated in their sockets. "Liar. You told her to assume that Marion and I are sleeping together, even though we're not, even though she found real evidence that we're not and never have been."

Helen shook her head and made a dismissive clucking sound with her tongue on the roof of her mouth. "I suggested that, given the fact that she wants to end the marriage, it doesn't matter. Who cares what you did or didn't do? She doesn't want you back. It doesn't matter anymore."

"She does want me back," I said.

"Do you know what she thinks of you? Do you know what she says about what it was like being married to you? I do, because I listen to her."

"She's hurt and angry," I said. "And she has no reason to be."

"She married you because she thought you were a genius. She worked her ass off for years to support you and your writing. She thought you were the next Shakespeare. The truth began to dawn on her years ago but she tried to shake it off. Finally she couldn't anymore. She thinks you're a rotten writer. She destroyed those poems because they were bad. She kicked you out because she was through with you."

"I never said they were great," I said. "They were works in progress. And she told me all that when she threw me out, and I did listen."

"Your marriage is over."

"No," I said. "It's not. You'll see."

"As long as you remain deluded and in denial to this extent, you'll be stuck. You can't move forward until you accept the truth. She wants a divorce."

"As long as you keep controlling her and lying to her, this breakdown she's having will get worse. She'll go off the edge."

"In my own marriage," said Helen with pointed deliberation, "I often find that my husband won't listen to me until I repeat something eighty times. My children," she added with even more pointedness, "call it 'dadtardation.' Harry, you are exhibiting dadtardation. That's my professional diagnosis. You've got to listen to your wife."

"I do listen," I said. "She won't speak to me, but she told our daughter, just yesterday, that this whole question of my affair with Marion is driving her crazy, and it's getting worse. She's started fabricating incidents and rewriting memories of our marriage."

Helen cocked her head and didn't answer. She appeared to be waiting for me to say something more.

I inhaled through my nose, hard. "Forget the fact that she wants a divorce. Causing her to call the entire marriage into question is wrong. It makes her believe things that hurt her and aren't true. It causes unnecessary pain. It does matter, what I did or didn't do. It matters more than anything else to her. At least let her have the truth, at least let her rest."

"No, you let her rest, Harry. Give it up, let her go. She's finally done what she wanted to do for so many years. Don't make it harder for her than it already is to get free of you. You say you love her. If you really do love her, which I'm finding very hard to believe, then accept that she's through with you."

"Why is it hard for you to believe that I love my wife?"

"Because you're invasive and controlling. You won't listen. You moved back into her building, for God's sake! She told me in our session this morning that she feels stalked and spied on. And now you've threatened her therapist. You're the one who's out of control; you're the one who's going over the edge. You're losing your grip on reality."

"Luz has no grip on reality! All I want is for her to believe the truth and decide accordingly!"

"She's considering a restraining order," said Helen. "She's about to serve you with divorce papers."

I gazed at Helen through a sickening cloud of disbelief. She gazed back at me with no expression on her face at all.

"You know, Harry," she said, no doubt marking and enjoying my distress, "she told me she'd come home from a day at work and find you in the exact same place she'd left you in. She cooked dinner, she helped the kids with their homework. She said it was worse than living alone. She told me it was an ongoing heartbreak to live night after night with someone who wasn't really there. Now that you're gone, she can breathe."

"I washed the dishes," I said. "I was there! I was home. I didn't go out. I didn't run around. I slept right next to her every night. I didn't hog the covers."

When the session was over, I told Helen with weak defiance that I wasn't going to pay her; she owed me.

"Well then." She smiled without any apparent concern. "I'll address the bill to you and send it care of Luz's address."

Horrified at the thought of Luz opening a bill for my session with her own therapist, I paid Helen in cash and walked out. Not only had I not punished her, I'd had to pay her for my failure.

Chapter Fifteen

The defeated feeling lasted two blocks, and then I was enraged again. That fucking lying bitch of a stuck-up stone-faced shamanistic manipulator, so that was how she did it—she said whatever it took to maintain her control over her clients. She tapped into their deepest, most private, irrational, ancient fears, confirmed those fears as real in one massive terrible landslide of diagnostic flimflammery, and then pretended to offer them a shovel to dig themselves out from under the avalanche she'd caused, but as the client shoveled and shoveled and shoveled, she kept heaping more dirt on until they were buried alive. I didn't give a fuck that this metaphor was overblown and overextended, I could do whatever the hell I wanted in the privacy of my own head; that was one of the only good things about being alive. And then, when they were well and truly buried, she kept them there, mummified in their fear and weakness, and bled them dry of a hundred and fifty bucks a session. It was a good racket, like dealing heroin. I could see exactly how she did it, but somehow I was immune to her tricks. Maybe I wasn't invested enough in optimistic self-improvement. Or more likely, I was so calcified in my own self-generated cocoon of skepticism, I was impervious to anyone else's influence.

But that was a big steaming load of manure, what she'd said about Luz. Helen was egging her on to think those things about me and our marriage, and Luz was susceptible to authority, unlike me. And unlike Marion, for that matter. Luz wasn't a practicing freethinker, as Marion and I had called ourselves with broad, winking self-mockery when we were younger. Luz needed structure, craved dogma. Knowing her as well as I did confirmed my long-held suspicion that people who espoused religions and belief systems did so because they were inherently spineless. They lacked a moral compass and ethical core, and therefore, they didn't know how to live correctly, how to answer to their failings and trespasses, without some external prod. I'd always felt superior to my wife because of her need for confession and prayer. She was weak because of that. I was always determined to muddle through on my own, fucking up and apologizing and learning from my mistakes and moving on. That was what grown-ups did; that was the responsible way to go about things.

Luz was a child, a simpleton, a Boleslaw. She couldn't fathom human complexity: everyone had to be either all good or all bad. She herself was complex, but she didn't know it. She was blind to herself, and therefore blind to everything and everyone, especially me. She was both simplistically moralistic and mulishly stubborn: a fatal combination. Forgiveness was conditional. Learning from past mistakes was apparently not something she could imagine anyone doing, because she was incapable of such a thing herself. She lacked imagination. Marion was right. That was her fatal flaw.

And that was why she needed me, the primary reason. From me, Luz had derived a vicarious sense of what it was like to live according to your own damn ideas. She needed the artificial life support of religion and authority herself, but she loved watching me operate, she got off on my ability to breathe on my own, like a little polio patient in an iron lung watching a healthy kid playing in the fresh air outside the sanatorium window.

Here I was, going around in these same circles again with no way out.

I wish there were a god to blame,
Some hard-fisted, furrow-browed jehovah

I could impugn in clotted voice with pointed finger.
Or better yet, a slippery and sycophantic satan—
I could take my pick of those, but what's the use?
There's no one to blame for our shared
Privation and loneliness, each of us stuck here
In our husks of flesh, unable to sleep
Without the other's body to lie beside
After the easy grace of habitual sex,
Back when every night was a rehearsal
For the grave, or so I thought.

Goddamn her. And goddamn that self-righteous bitch of a shrink. She was causing Luz to suffer even more under her so-called treatment than she'd been suffering alone. Helen was as bad as the Catholic Church, inventing sin where none organically existed, positing a higher authority to strip away autonomy and internal bearings, creating a stringent but illusory system of self-castigation and expiation, and making people pay, pay, pay. Therapy wasn't the problem. I wasn't that naïve. A true, dedicated therapist might have helped her recognize her own crippled state and offered her a temporary crutch, moral exercises, a genuine, painstaking means to self-understanding and eventual self-reliance. Helen had to be killed. Or maybe she needed something a little more figurative than that.

Because she had this power over my wife and so many of my friends, Helen had no doubt thought she could suck me in and make me believe her version of reality, too. But she had underestimated me. I knew what I knew, and no one could tell me otherwise. My own experiences were the highest authority I had. A hard-won, cumulative knowledge of what was real and what wasn't was one of the other only good things about being alive.

I'm the boss of myself, I muttered, as Karina might have when she was four or five.

All of this transpired in my brain as I rode my bike down to Delancey, over the bridge, and along the waterfront to Greenpoint. By the time I got to Noble Street, I had wrestled my mood into some sort of shape for socializing, but it took some doing. I climbed the steps of James and Lisa's house and rang the bell, realizing too late that I had come empty-handed.

"Come on in," said James, his slight, soft body encased in a big butcher's apron smeared with what looked like, and turned out to be, blood.

"Are you performing surgeries?"

"On dead rabbits."

In the big, tracklit, gleaming, technically tricked-out kitchen, he handed me a glass of wine that tasted fine and was, I knew, ridiculously expensive. James always had to have the best of everything, whether it was a car, an upright bass, a pair of shoes, or something for his kitchen. Or a mistress. In all our discussions about his long-ago affair with Marion, I always had got the slightly creepy feeling that she had been another of his superior acquisitions. James was pragmatically cold, deep down, for all his seeming generosity and caring. That was how he stayed married to Lisa: he required no genuine connection. He was very comfortable hating his wife, defying her in invisible but profound ways while appearing to kowtow and accommodate.

James and Lisa had started their own business straight out of Wesleyan, where they'd met as freshmen, both scholarship students, in the early 1970s. Back then, they had been promising musicians; James was a fantastic upright bass player and Lisa was a trumpet virtuoso and singer. With three other college friends they'd had an avant-garde cabaret-rock band that was allegedly on the verge of being signed to a major label. Whatever might have happened with that, they would likely have gone on to become rock stars, but Lisa abruptly decided that she and James should get married and become wealthy burghers, and all that potential glamorous superstardom went out the window.

Lisa was a redheaded thunderbolt, hard-nosed and funny, moody and insecure, pragmatic and full of inchoate fears. She made all the major decisions, and James, who was dreamy, earnest, and meek on the outside and a volcano of frustrated creative energy on the inside, agreed to anything to keep the peace with his wife. They were both native New Yorkers, both the children of poor immigrants. James's Chinese parents had run a shoe repair shop on the Lower East Side. Lisa's German political dissident father had escaped from the Nazis in 1939 and barely supported his Romanian wife and their two kids by translating scientific and technical tracts. James and Lisa therefore had no illusions, either of them, about the romance of struggling. Lisa's decision to invest their collective marital talents in a solid business instead of a mercurial, risky music career had paid off in exactly the way she'd hoped it would. Custom Case, their instrument-case design and repair shop, was housed on an entire floor of a lovely old warehouse in Red Hook. They designed and built cases for classical-music icons, rock stars, and ordinary kids who wanted cool cases for their trumpets and guitars and violins. Consequently, Lisa and James were now millionaires with a beautifully renovated brownstone on Noble Street; their oldest son worked for them and would no doubt take over Custom Case someday, their second son was becoming the rock star his parents had failed to become, and their two youngest kids, both adopted when the older ones went off to college and Lisa freaked out and informed James that they needed more kids, lived at home.

All appearances to the contrary, their sexless, detached, bloodless marriage gave both of them exactly what they most deeply needed and desired. It worked because each had a sphere of power in which the other never interfered. The whole thing rested on a precisely calibrated fulcrum of control. He ran the business, she ran their lives; they observed the outward forms of proper married etiquette. James's affair with Marion had caused some brutal repercussions, the most obvious of which was that the two couples, formerly friends, no longer spoke; Lisa viciously bad-mouthed Marion to anyone who would listen, injecting our whole group of friends with her venom. James, in his guilt, then gave Lisa carte blanche to control his time, his freedom, and his expenditures even more stringently, but this, I suspected, was what he had unconsciously wanted all along. James and Lisa had one of the most successful marriages I'd ever seen.

On a butcher-block cutting board, James had laid out two skinned bunnies, which looked like the naked, hunched carcasses of miniature human children, Hansel and Gretel maybe. Something was cooking in a pot on a burner of the huge state-of-the-art chef's stove. Above James's head dangled a cluster of copper pots and cast-iron skillets suspended from hooks in a stainless-steel grate. His knives were arrayed on a magnetic strip in a cruel-looking row. The counters were made of some kind of extra-sparkly granite, fool's-gold flecks, maybe. The floors were buffed oak planks that had absorbed who knew what manner of grisly splatters and spillages. It was a medieval torture chamber of a room, aggressively culinary, not cozy or peaceful at all.

"How are you, Harry?" James asked in his dulcet voice. His head was the shape of a chickpea, round with a pointed chin. He had short, thick black hair, skin the color of green tea, and black-almond eyes. His expression was often innocently merry and sweet. Marion had told me that she'd fallen for him because of his appearance of openness and enthusiasm, which had been as refreshing to her as cool water to a parched desert crawler. Her own husband had been tough-minded, crusty, and skittish, and during that era, he and Marion had catapulted themselves into distant orbits from each other in that usually temporary but often terrifying way of most long-married couples. Compared to her distracted, always-working husband, James had seemed so completely present to Marion. She had only later become aware of his real qualities. Affairs were like that, of course. I knew all too well how dazzlingly perfect the secret lover seemed compared to the dull and obligatory spouse. This delusion was a species of insanity, but no one ever realized it except in hindsight. Knowing now what I knew about Samantha, it was clear to me how unsuited to each other we had been. Whether or not I should regret learning this, I didn't know. Maybe I'd needed to make such a colossal mistake to avoid making other, even worse ones in the future.

"I'm all right," I said, perching on a stool at the island in the middle of the room. I swilled some wine. "Been better. You've heard all the gossip, I'm sure."

We were dancing around my presumed affair with Marion.

"How was your session with Helen?" James asked. "I didn't know you saw her. But I'm not surprised. Are you seeing her individually, or with Luz?"

"This was a one-shot thing," I said. "I went in to tell her to stop manipulating Luz. I told her she was ruining Luz's life. I think I threatened to kill her at one point."

James stopped deboning bunnies and looked up at me, laughing. "I bet she loved that. She's always up for a challenge."

"She didn't seem to love it," I said. "Not especially."

James kept his eyes on me. He was still smiling. "You might have misread her."

"James," I said. "The woman is the devil incarnate, to use the term very loosely. Why do you people all keep going to her? How much money do you think you've given her through the years? You see her alone every week, and you go to group twice a month, and you and Lisa see her together once a month, and Lisa sees her. Have you sent your kids to her yet?"

James turned back to his carcasses. "She's worth it. I'm going to keep seeing her until she retires or I die, whichever comes first."

"Did you ever take her up on her offer to fuck you?"

James laughed like a promising but unseasoned actor who was practicing his guffaw. This was his normal laugh. "Ho, ho, ho," he chortled. "I told you she said that? She was joking. It's her humor."

"She joked about ass fucking. With me. If she was really joking."

"Helen's a provocateur. She likes to verbally goose her clients, make us react, get us thinking in different directions. She's very open. There's nowhere she won't go. She's a genius."

"If you call brainwashing genius."

James gave a modified, lesser rendition of his trademark laugh. "Brainwashing?"

"She's convincing Luz that our marriage was a mistake. She's encouraging her to think heinous things of me. You know how easily influenced Luz is. She loves cockamamie theories that let her avoid reality. Helen is full of those theories. The two of them together are like gasoline and a match, and I'm the pile of trash they're igniting."

James knit his boyish brow in an approximation of empathetic concern. "I know you're in a lot of pain," he said. "I know this is a terrible time for you, and I apologize for not asking you to have dinner sooner. But the truth is . . ." He studied the neat parcels of rabbit meat he was excising.

"It's Marion," I said. "Right? Lisa thinks I'm involved with her, and she wants nothing to do with me now."

He widened his eyes at me, which I took as involuntary assent, then he got back to work.

Squinting with outrage, I finished my glass of wine and set the glass carefully on the granite top of the island. "How is it that you actually did have an affair with Marion, yet here you still are in your big nice house, marriage intact, and no one says boo to you about anything? Meanwhile, I didn't sleep with her, not even close, and here I am, in this ridiculous mix-up. What's your secret, James?"

"Lisa couldn't afford to throw me out," he said, refilling my glass. "And Luz can afford to throw you out."

We both laughed. It was true. The tension that had been there since I'd arrived dissolved, or maybe I was imagining this. You never knew with James. He was a slippery little bugger. But even so, I relaxed on my stool, which was buffed stainless steel and no doubt the best one could buy at any price, and said, "She can't afford not to. According to Helen, I'm nothing but dead weight."

"We're all dead weight."

"You're not, if she can't afford to throw you out."

"Only financially. Emotionally, I'm a tire-shaped rock around her neck. That's all we are, anymore, we husbands, isn't it?"

I declined to agree with this in the eager manner of self-loathing men everywhere these days. I no longer had the luxury of laughing at my own haplessness. I had lost my sense of humor about it. "Did you hear, I got a full-time job," I said. "At the Hasidic lumberyard, working in Accounts Payable. I moved back into the Astral."

"Well, well, well," said James, who had obviously already been in possession of both these pieces of information. "Are you writing?"

"Barely. Does anyone care? Are you playing music?"

"Obsessively," said James. "Does anyone care?"

He wheeled around his bristling kitchen in his tightly wrapped apron, all trim and comfy. James reminded me of a contented caged bird who pretended to try to escape, for show, whenever the door was accidentally left open, but always made sure he was caught and put back again.

"Once again, James, I have to ask, financial considerations aside," I said in a voice reedy with insuppressable feeling. "What do you know that I don't? How is it that you're still here? Does this mean I'm guiltier than you are, even though I didn't do anything wrong?"

He cocked his head at me, blinking, his busy chef's hands momentarily stilled as he thought.

"Maybe it doesn't matter what we do or don't do," I went on. "Maybe all that matters is what punishment the world sees fit to give us. Innocent people have been burned at the stake and shot by firing squads. Innocent husbands have been thrown out. And evildoers everywhere live in comfort and ease. Cheating husbands are forgiven."

"What are you trying to say?" James asked, still watching me.

"Could it be that the crime is irrelevant? How's your conscience, James?"

"Clear," he said. "I sleep well at night. I don't think I'm any better or worse than the average man. Well, probably worse, but so is Lisa. We're even."

"Has she ever had an affair?"

"Harry," he said. "You're really not sleeping with Marion?"

"If you knew how many times I've been asked that. Actually, I should have been asked that more. Actually, I'm tired of saying I'm not."

"A long time ago," said James, "a couple of years before my affair with Marion, Lisa fell in love with someone. A woman." James twinkled his eyes at me; I took this to mean that he found this sexy. I was unable to twinkle my eyes back at him. The idea of Luz with a woman did absolutely nothing for me, probably because I was only half a man at that point. But the idea of Luz with a woman had never done anything for me. Luz would have no sooner slept with a woman than she would have stabbed and boiled and eaten one. Therefore, the two ideas were roughly concomitant in my simple brain.

"Her name was Sherry. Sherry fell in love with Lisa, too. Finally, she demanded that Lisa leave me. Lisa wouldn't do it. Sherry threatened to tell me, so Lisa had to come to me and confess everything. That was one of the hardest moments of her life, poor girl."

James's protectiveness of his wife amused me. Under an ostentatious display of neurotically sensitive vulnerability, Lisa was as hard as a railroad bed. James had always seemed perversely aroused by this disparity in his wife's character; he seemed to enjoy colluding in the idea that she was fragile, even as she pushed him around and manipulated him. Come to think of it, maybe he was the one who wanted to be ass-fucked; maybe that was where Helen got her weird ideas about middle-aged husbands.

But no matter. I wanted something from James, information, not just chitchat. Irrationally, childishly, I felt he owed me.

"What are people saying about Luz and me?" I asked. "Our friends. Like Phil and Suzie. I haven't seen anyone."

James went to the refrigerator and pulled some things out. I watched, waiting for him to answer, biding my time, while he chopped mushrooms and shallots and sautéed them in butter, added white wine and some fresh-chopped herbs, stirred, tasted, added black pepper, stirred, added cream, tasted, assembling his sauce with the grotesque levity of a leprechaun in a science lab.

James and Lisa's adopted daughter, Celeste, wandered in, red faced, wearing pajamas, her blond hair in a tangle. She saw me and ignored me. "Do we have any fresh-squeezed OJ, Dad?"

"In the door compartment in a pitcher."

"When did you make it?"

"Three hours ago."

"It's old!"

"Says my Appalachian orphan," said James, "rescued from a life in the coal mines by her loving parents."

"I wouldn't have worked in a coal mine," said Celeste. "I would have run away and been a child movie star, but now I can't."

"Why not?" I asked.

Continuing to ignore me, she reached into the fridge, sniffed the juice, poured herself a glassful, left the pitcher on the counter, and wandered out.

James put the juice back into the refrigerator, then went to the stove and tasted his sauce, added a little more cream, tasted it again. Finally he said, "Who am I to judge you, Harry? Who is anyone to judge you?"

"That's what I'd like to know."

"The truth is, we all judge you."

"What do you mean?"

James fetched a package wrapped in butcher's paper, unwrapped a stack of bacon, and began separating the slices. "We all talk about what happened, we pick it apart and choose sides, we say Luz is insane or Marion is predatory or you're a fool or you're a bastard or Luz is a rock of strength or Marion is an innocent bystander in a marital psychodrama." He wrapped a chunk of raw rabbit in a piece of raw bacon and set it aside. "And you know what? We have no fucking clue, but talking about it is more fun than anything else that's going on around here." He smiled at me.

I laughed. It came out sounding a little forced. I was trying not to show how upset I was, how urgently I wanted him to stop treating this like an exercise in social fun. I didn't want James to sense any weakness in me, which was of course ludicrous. He wasn't a mean man. He would have understood. But my male pride prohibited a plea for sympathy or pity. "Do you want to know what's really going on?"

"No!" he said, his lips pursing with adamant emphasis. "That would ruin everything. I love thinking about you two together. Let me at least just keep that bit of excitement." He wrapped another rabbit chunk in another piece of bacon, and another. "Please just grant me the fantasy of you two together."

"Marion and I have been lovers since the day we met," I said in a voice so sarcastic, I didn't see how he could do anything but laugh. "The night I met her, when we were both twenty-two, and I say this so you picture her at twenty-two, not me, we got drunk and then I took her to the bathroom of the Pyramid Club and lifted up her dress and had her against the sink."

"Thank you," James breathed, massaging his little pile of bacon and rabbit, staring hard at it.

I looked at him with unconcealed loathing, but he was concentrating on his cooking and so didn't see the dangerous glint that must have been in at least one of my eyes. The knives were out of my reach, luckily.

"I'm kidding," he added without looking up. "Easy there."

"What the hell are you making?"

"Not sure. Inventing as I go. Improvisational cooking with maximum fat content. I have to say, Harry, I think you've become overly obsessed. You went to see Helen and you threatened her. You've moved back into the Astral. You think about Luz so much, your brain is short-circuiting. You can't stop mentally arguing with her about what happened with Marion, or didn't. But let me tell you something honestly, no one else is thinking about it or talking about it. It happened a while ago. There's a whole new fresh scandal now." He paused. "Did you hear about Debra MacDougal?"

"Whatever happened to her? I was just thinking about her."

"She tried to commit suicide three weeks ago. She caught her husband and her twin brother in bed together."

"She got married? Who did she marry? Or do I mean whom?"

"This guy she met online. They had only been married a year, maybe even less. Her twin brother," he repeated, looking at me with earnest significance.

"So that's your new fantasy," I said. "Her husband and brother in bed together."

Immediately his seriousness cracked. "You and Marion were starting to pall a bit."

"I can imagine," I said. "Is she still speaking to her twin brother?"

"I don't know," he said. "She overdosed on Dilaudid. She almost died. She just got out of the hospital."

"Where did she get enough Dilaudid to overdose on?"

"I wondered the same thing."

"Which hospital?"

"Why does that matter?"

"I'm just trying to show I can think about something besides my own mess of a life."

"Bellevue," he said.

"Did she leave her husband?"

"She kicked him out. So now you're both single. You should give her a call."

"I am not single," I said.

He looked at me again with even more earnest significance than before, something I had not imagined to be possible. "Harry, Luz was just here last week, talking to Lisa, and based on what she said, if I were you, I would move on. Accept that your marriage is over."

"Is Luz . . ." My mouth was so dry I had to take a sip of wine to ask the question. "Is she with someone else now?"

"A boyfriend? Luz? Right now she hates our entire sex. She's bitter, Harry. She hasn't softened or mellowed toward you or Marion at all. Not one molecule. She's thermonuclearly angry. Lisa is worried about her."

"I can just imagine the two of them, chewing on Marion together."

"Apparently it didn't help matters, according to Lisa," said James. "She ended up inadvertently fueling Luz's fire. She said Luz . . . she's bent on vengeance, in a 'hell hath no fury' kind of way. She's as obsessed as you are, come to think of it."

I laughed, sort of.

"I know," said James. "It's tough."

"No, you don't know," I said. My mounting envy of James Lee was something I wanted no part of. Since I had walked into his house, I had been doing my best to laugh at it, disavow it, sidestep it, throw it from me like a stifling cloak. "Try to imagine for one minute that you've been sent packing. You're living in a crappy apartment and Lisa's not speaking to you. In fact, she hates you."

"I'd be free," he said instantly, with raw yearning I didn't buy for a millisecond. "It's ironic, isn't it. Your wife made you go, and you want to go back. Mine won't release her death grip on me; I would love to be thrown out."

"You could leave her."

"Lisa? She would slaughter me in the divorce. She fights dirty."

"So you always say. With some glee, I have to add. I thought she couldn't afford to throw you out."

He ignored this last comment. "No glee when I'm the victim of it. She would take me for everything. Keep the house, kids, money, my underwear, although God knows what she'd do with it."

"But you'd be free. And you could make enough money for her and you both."

"That's what I know how to do," he said with vague assent, seemingly unaware of the fact that he was contradicting what he'd said earlier. He stirred his sauce, which smelled alchemically inspired. "I make it, she appropriates it. Not very catchy, but tragically accurate."

"I think you like being controlled by her. Some kind of kinky power thing." A small bleating noise came from my pants pocket. I fished around in there and pulled out the cell phone Karina had given me. "Hello?"

"Dad, where are you?"

"James and Lisa's," I said.

"Stay there, it's just a few blocks." She hung up.

"Damn," I said to James. "No fat rabbit in fancy sauce for me. I forgot, I have a meeting about this cult Hector's in. And Luz is going to be there. No wonder I put it straight out of my mind. Karina will be here in three minutes."

"You and Luz in the same room," said James with a big grin. "Wish I could be a fly . . . anyway, that's too bad. I have something else I wanted to talk to you about."

"You mean there's another topic in the universe that isn't my marriage?"

He laughed. "I want to offer you a job."

"I have a job."

"Well, I want to offer you a better job."

"Doing what?"

"Working for me."

"Doing what?" I repeated with leery caution. James had once bragged to me how cheaply he got his mostly foreign-born labor. I had no desire to become another one of his underpaid Mexicans.

"Accounts Payable, same as you're doing at the lumberyard, but for more money." He named a salary that was considerably more than I made at the lumberyard. "That's enough for you to get out of the Astral and get a real apartment for yourself."

"I smell a condition," I said. "Did Luz put you up to this to get rid of me?"

He looked at the ceiling, then at his hands, then at me. "I just thought of it now."

"The answer is no, but thanks." I stood up.

James hugged me at the front door, a manly hug in spite of his silly apron. It felt genuine if slightly theatrical. "Come back again when you can stay and eat," he said.

"Some night when Lisa isn't home?" I said. It galled me. It was my right to dislike Lisa, but she had no right to dislike me.

Chapter Sixteen

I can't believe you forgot!" said Karina as I got into her car. "They asked if we could be sure to be there on time because they have another meeting scheduled at nine."

"They'd better be good. James was making rabbit with bacon and some kind of cream sauce."

"Yes, they're good, they're cult-exit specialists. They know all about Christa. They helped get three other people out last year. They used to be in another cult she was the leader of."

"I am not looking forward to seeing your mother."

"Good, because she won't be there."

"What?"

"She refuses to be in the same room with you. I said you're willing to be in the same room with her, and this is for Hector, and she doesn't have to talk to you or even look at you. She said she'll meet with them on her own if she has to, she will not be in a room that also contains you."

"This, from the woman who supposedly loves Hector above all other living things?"

"She's not exactly speaking to him these days." Karina made a sour, half-amused face. "And she wouldn't listen to me."

"She never listens to anyone. Your mother is like a bug caught in its own excretions."

"Hey, I'm not taking sides," said Karina. "Just reporting the facts."

Karina and I had made another pilgrimage out to Long Island in late April to visit Hector and his group, who were now calling themselves the Children of Hashem. On this second visit, things were all very different. The atmosphere was more intense. Since our first visit, they had, Hector told us, amped up their prayers for the Rapture and the return of Yashua. Hector was somehow at the center of all this activity, but it was unclear how or why. Karina pressed him for information as much as she could, but the more she poked him, the more he clammed up. Christa was nowhere to be seen, and the group members were apparently no longer under orders to try to convey the impression of being frankly forthcoming with us. Instead, they were edgily detached and aggressively evasive. The men's ponytails seemed tighter, their beards looked more biblical. The women seemed altogether more severe and puritanical and much less pretty. Karina thought their changed manner toward us was due to the fact that they suspected that we knew they were a cult and maybe had even caught a whiff of the fact that we were thinking about trying to yank Hector out of there, but I wasn't so sure. In fact, I seriously doubted they thought about us much at all. They showed no sign of curiosity or interest in anything but their own internal schemes and goings-on.

Since that visit, Hector was rarely available to come to the phone and never returned my calls, which I now made several times a week. The two times I did manage to get him on the phone, he'd sounded manic and full of himself. In all the years since he had learned to speak, I had never heard him sound either of those things. Hector had always been the most unassuming, humble person I had ever known. This sudden change in my almost pathologically heartfelt son alarmed me far more than the odd behavior of his cohorts, people I didn't care a fig about and who frankly gave me the creeps, at least en masse.

In Forest Hills, Karina parked on a leafy little side street lined with narrow semidetached houses, early-twentieth-century mock Tudor. We rang the doorbell of one of these identical houses and waited for several seconds, and then the door swung wide open and a voice issued from behind it: "Come in! You must be Karina and Harry."

Karina went first. The hallway was too narrow for two people to stand side by side, and it was dark. We followed the dim person into the living room, which was brightly lit. "I'm June," she said in a high, quick voice, turning to smile at us, "and this is Emery. Sit down, please. Would you like tea? It's already made. And I put out a plate of sandwiches, in case anyone's hungry."

"How kind of you," I said. "I didn't have time to eat."

June was a tiny, anxious-looking blonde with flyaway hair. Her accent was perkily, earnestly midwestern. She wore a pink sweater and high-waisted jeans. Emery was a massive, swarthy man with muttonchop sideburns and a unibrow. He wore a flannel plaid shirt and work pants, and he took up most of the couch. June and Emery's living room, with its crocheted lace antimacassars and chintz curtains, could have been in a farmhouse in Iowa in 1956, which is to say, it was identical to many of my neighbors' houses when I was growing up. In fact, I thought I recognized the needlepointed cushion of the footstool by the whatnot as the same flowered pattern that had been in Mrs. Jones's living room.

Karina perched with unusually reticent politeness on an armchair. I did the same, but more comfortably. I felt right at home here. I took a sandwich and bit into it and almost smiled with happiness. It was ham and Velveeta on white.

"We're glad you could come," said June, handing out teacups.

"We're glad you exist," said Karina. "We're so worried about Hector."

"Well, let's get right down to it, then," said June. She hopped onto the couch next to her husband. The juxtaposition was comic and sinister at the same time. They looked like a backwoods axe murderer and his sweet little victim. "Back in Taos, when we knew

Christa, this is like ten years ago, she was calling herself Isis, and she was a healer and a shaman and all sorts of things, but mostly she was a thief and a liar."

"Her real name is Kirsty McDevitt," said Emery. He spoke much more slowly than his wife and an octave or two lower, and his dry drawl came from much farther west than hers, I would have guessed Idaho or eastern Washington State. Talking to them was like listening to alternate archival recordings on two different speeds. "She's forty-eight years old now. She's from Salt Lake City. She grew up Mormon."

"She rejected all that for a while and went off to be a stripper," said June, wide-eyed with the effort to sound nonjudgmental about this. "She did pretty well at it, I guess. She'd been working the casino shows in Vegas before she came down to Taos. For all we know she was also a prostitute, but we never did prove that and she would never admit it, for all her big talk about her dark sinful past. She had this whole story about her revelation of her powers and her life change and her link to the spirit world and how we could all do the same if we followed her example and unleashed our magical powers." June rolled her eyes. "We fell for it."

"Isis rooked a whole bunch of people, including us," said Emery, slinging one huge hammy leg over the other and rubbing his belly with a hand the size of a small meat loaf. "She's a scam artist. She ran off with everyone's money. We went after her. We took her to court."

"You can read all about it if you Google it," said June. "It was quite a trial. She claimed it was a witch hunt and we were persecuting her."

"We won," said Emery. "She did five years in prison and got out. Now she's up here, starting all over again."

"Is she violating parole by being here?" Karina asked.

"She's not out on parole," said June. "She did her time fair and square and she can move to China if she wants. I wish she would."

"This new group," said Emery, "your son's group, this is something more serious. She's talking about end times again, but now it's Jesus and the Apocalypse and the lake of fire, not spirit animals and sweat lodges and the Mayan calendar's 2012 prophecy. She's really gunning for something. She owns that fancy beach house legally. And she's socking away money, apparently. One of the ex-members of this group was her financial planner, you'll meet him. He says she's got almost a million bucks salted away. She just recruited a Getty and he's signed over his whole wad to the group."

"She wants to marry Hector!" said Karina.

"We know," said June. "We know. He's a virgin. He's pure of spirit. He'll make her look good by association, if and when her past comes to light. Supposedly, according to Jennifer, the most recent member we helped get out, Christa has announced that among her followers, he has the power, whatever that is. They're being made to think of Hector as some kind of messianic figure. It sounds like they're toying with the idea that he's the second coming of Yashua, but he has to pass three tests first. That's all we know."

"Tests," I said. "That doesn't sound good."

"I agree," said Emery.

"Yeah," said Karina. "That sounds completely fucked up and dangerous. What are the tests, do you think?"

"Whatever they are," I said, "Hector won't be able to resist them." I tossed my tea back with a few big gulps and set the cup on a coaster on the table next to me. "The chance to be the second coming of Jesus is not something most people could or would pass up."

"Does Hector's mother know what's been going on with him?" asked June. "I had thought she would be here tonight."

Karina looked at me, clearly waiting for me to field this one. Having no desire to do so, I looked back at her silently until she said with prickly defiance, "She says to tell you she's very sorry, she couldn't make it."

"That's too bad," said June.

I disagreed; I could easily imagine how different this meeting would have been with Luz present. I pictured her sitting in ice-hot, tragic self-righteousness, the heartbroken mother, the wronged wife. She would have silently judged June and Emery, found fault with them for being too New Agey or too bossy, something. She would not have looked at me once the entire time, but her hatred would have smoldered in my direction. I was passionately glad that she wasn't there. I took a handful of potato chips. Midwestern women always knew the best ones to buy. These chips were my madeleines; I was back in Muscatine, and it was almost fifty years ago, and I was about to go down to the river and fish for some crappies. I wriggled my feet with nostalgic contentment.

"My parents are estranged at this point," said Karina, "having nothing to do with Hector. And my mother's not doing well these days, emotionally, so we haven't fully filled her in. So we'll see what happens tonight, what we learn, before we involve her more completely."

"Are she and Hector close?" asked June.

"You could say that," I said.

"She's not speaking to him since he joined the group," said Karina, "but they've always been very close."

June shook her head as if this made her even more anxious than she already was. "Then she's got to become involved in the intervention. Also any of his friends he's close to. The more people we have, the better."

"Don't get ahead of yourself, June," said Emery. June smiled at him as if nothing could have pleased her more than being told by her husband to stifle it. "We have a lot of ground to cover before we start planning anything." He uncrossed his legs and leaned back even farther into the couch cushions. The couch's bones creaked, but its integrity held. "Did you two read the book I recommended?"

"I did," said Karina, "but I doubt my father has."

"I've read about half of it," I said, shooting her a look. "It's fascinating. I'll read the rest of it this week."

"So you know quite a lot about mind control, then," said Emery. He sounded like he might have been challenging me to prove it. "That's good."

"Yes," I said, bristling at the blatant skepticism in the room concerning my claim to have done my homework. I decided to unleash some of it on them. It served them right for doubting me. "I was interested to learn," I said, trying not to sound aggrieved, "that the typical cult recruitment tactics are love bombing, a warm bath of total acceptance, and the illusion of a welcoming utopian community. Anyone can be susceptible under the right circumstances, but on the whole, most people who join cults are like Hector: bright, somewhat lost young people who feel out of place in mainstream culture and are hungry for something better, a communal, spiritually committed way of life. How am I doing so far?"

"Dad," said Karina. "You read the book?"

I didn't answer; I was imagining Hector going to a seemingly random place, a café or music festival or one of the other places he liked to go to find other earnestly searching kids to talk to, and there, two or three unnaturally upbeat, highly articulate people his own age had approached him and struck up a conversation. They described their lives in such glowing, idealized, bright hyperbole, Hector couldn't be anything but intrigued. They invited him out to Long Island to see the place and meet the other members and spend a night. And when he went, he was embraced, complimented on being special, one of them, spiritually awake, made to feel part of things, tempted to stay longer. Instead of the blighted streets of Greenpoint, the sordid chaos of the Astral, instead of combating the hidebound Catholicism of his mother and numbing atheism of his father, he had found a calm, bright, ordered place where all his questions were answered and all the dishes matched and the sea grasses blew in the morning breeze.

"And then, once the person joins," said June, "this love bombing goes away. Little by little the new cult member experiences isolation from the world, sleep deprivation, lack of solitude, overwork. He has to keep up with constantly changing rules. His personality is broken down, and a new cult self takes its place. Most times, they get new names, too."

"Hector's is Bard," I said. "Which is interesting, considering that he dropped out of Bard College and his father is a poet."

"Oh," said June, "you're a poet? Wow. I love poetry. Anyway, where were we? Oh right, the cult self. He feels exhaustion, fear, confusion. That's what happened to us, and that's what's happening to Hector now. Anytime his real old self wakes up and starts to ask questions and feel doubts, his new cult self snaps into action and stifles it. It's a closed system, mind control. Cult members feel like they have to act like everything's fantastic, in order to quiet troublesome thoughts and keep other members from ratting them out. This happy-smiley act makes other people buy into the whole thing and join the group. And it convinces outsiders that people in cults are perfectly happy there, that it's a valid belief system and way of life. But this smiling, happy mask actually hides fear and horrible self-hatred. I know, I was that person."

"Cults are mostly about power," said Emery. I adjusted my ears to the sudden drop in vocal timbre and conversational speed. "They might start with all good intentions, but like they say, power corrupts, absolute power corrupts absolutely, whether it's Hitler or the pope or Kirsty McDevitt from Salt Lake City. Now she's gone into hyperdrive. Her followers are a means to an end for her, and the end has no limit. And also, of course, it's about money. The leader or leaders get rich off their followers while preaching poverty and humility. And this is where Hector is now, working fourteen-hour days that begin and end with two-hour prayer meetings."

"I remember those from when we were in her last group," said June. "They're horrible! We were called upon to expose anyone who'd expressed doubts or failed to uphold doctrine. The punishment was harsh. You had to repent and confess over and over until you were purged. You'd think everyone would just leave, but they're scared to. It's drummed into your head that terrible things will happen to deserters. Things like being hit by a truck or going insane or dying of cancer or turning homosexual. People really believe this."

It sounded a bit like my marriage, I thought with mordant humor. It had operated along the lines of a two-person version of this group dynamic. It had started with love bombing, the promise of utopia; once I'd convinced her to marry me, Luz had flat-out adored me. She told me I was a genius, cooked for me, praised my work, supported me during the years when I wasn't bringing in my share of the money, which was most years. And I was complicit in this mollycoddling. I turned passive, defenseless, soft. My identity became fused with my wife's. Without even realizing it, little by little, I gave up my free will, my autonomy, my ability to act without considering what she wanted and needed.

When I really fucked up, after my peccadillo with Samantha, Luz knocked me off my pedestal and turned the klieg lights of her ice-cold gaze onto every bit of evidence, any minuscule contradiction or microscopic disparity she could uncover, building her case to prove that I was a lying, cheating worm. Of course, anyone might look like a worm if an obsessed, hell-bent prosecutor lifted up enough rocks. But no matter, Luz had split me open with her fascistic scimitar, then she'd flayed me with the wet noodles of my own guilt. James had suffered the same fate from Lisa. That was marriage, sometimes. Wives got their husbands under control and kept them there. That was how they operated, these possessive, manipulative, needy, controlling women, they pretended to be soft and vulnerable, sweet and loving, and we, big dumb dogs that we were, fell for their cooing flattery and breasty softness, tried to be the heroes they wanted us to be, to live up to their expectations. And when we failed and our wives lashed out, we skulked around, tails between legs, hangdog and furtive, doing their bidding until they forgave us, if they did. Now it was happening to my son. Christa was calling him the new Messiah, worshipping his purity of spirit, bending him to her will with flattery, seduction, and praise. But the instant he crossed her, she would destroy him.

But not all women were like that—Marion was something of a dog herself. But alas, I was not in love with Marion and never had been.

"We were among the first members of the Taos cult," Emery was saying, "so we were in the inner circle. We saw and heard things the others didn't know, the hidden doctrines."

"That's right," June said. "Hidden doctrines, those are important. That's the main way that cults differ from religions."

"That's what I was saying, Dad," Karina said. "Remember?"

"With religions," said June, "you know what you're getting into from the get-go, it's all laid out. Even a lot of fringe fundamentalist groups, like say Mormons or Hasidism, they tell you up front what they're about. With cults, they only show you what they want you to see until you're sucked in and under mind control, and then they reveal the rest of it on a need-to-know basis to keep you on your toes, as a means of wielding power. Hidden doctrines. That's Kirsty's stock in trade."

"And now here she is again," said Emery, "up to her same old tricks."

"I just don't like the sound of these three messiah tests Hector has to pass," said Karina. "What the hell are they? Do you know? It sounds so kooky and stupid, like some kids' game."

June set her teacup on the coaster on the lace doily on the table at her elbow. That arrangement—coaster, doily—brought back my mother's homemade crocheted lace cloths, which she'd draped over everything, tables and the arms and backs of chairs and couches, and you had to use a coaster or a napkin on top of them or you'd spoil them. I hadn't seen a crocheted doily, runner, or antimacassar in so long, I had forgotten all about them. They were a gladsome sight to me now. They soothed and buoyed me.

"The ex-member we just rescued, Jennifer," June was saying, "told us they were devising these tests when she left the group. This was a couple of weeks ago. She said she wasn't sure, but one of them might involve walking on water."

"Oh well then," I said, going for jocularity to quell a rising sense of alarm for my son. "He's not the Messiah. He can't even swim."

"How did you help Jennifer get out?" Karina asked. "How do you plan to get Hector out?"

"An intervention," said Emery, "isn't kidnapping and reprogramming anymore. Those old tactics just replaced one form of mind control with another. Nowadays, cult interventions are entirely voluntary. What happens is, we have to manage to get Hector to a safe place. Somewhere isolated and self-contained, where he can't easily leave. Like a cabin in the mountains, say you invite him on a family camping trip. Members are still permitted to leave for short visits with their families. We could also use a place here in the city, but that's much trickier, because when things get gnarly, which they always do in these situations, he's got to stick with it through the hard part, when he starts to realize the truth about this group and himself and what he's been going through there."

"Emery means," said June, "that it's for his own protection to isolate him with us. Now, it all happens with his full cooperation, so there's no coercion or trickery whatsoever. You sit him down, Harry, and say, 'Son, we've heard some things about Christa's group that are really scaring us, and we're very concerned about you. We would love for you to hear these things from the people who told us. Then you can reassure us, if they're not true, so we can stop worrying about you. Would you be willing to have this conversation?' If he says yes, then Emery and I and Jennifer and the other two ex-members, Toby and Sylvia, come into the room and sit down and the intervention begins."

"What if he says no?" I asked. "Knowing Hector, he very well might."

"Then you keep at him," said June. "Don't be afraid to be persistent. Rephrase the question. Ask him what he has to lose. Tell him you've heard that Christa used to be a stripper or even a prostitute, for example, and that she's been in prison for embezzlement, and that you've heard her group is a cult. Tell him those things and show him how much concern this causes you because you love him so much. Eventually, even if it's just out of a need to prove he's right, it's likely he'll agree to talk to us."

"And then what?"

"And then we tell him about our experiences with Christa when she was Isis. The whole story. Show him the news clippings, give him some transcripts from the trial. We'll explain how mind control works, how we all got sucked in, and how we got out, and what we know now. It generally takes many hours of intense talking. Interventions can last a couple, three days. They can be powerfully emotional for everyone involved. Often, all sorts of things come out within families. But the important thing is to stay connected, stay with him, not to give up at any point, to keep telling him the truth until he's really heard it, until he can't deny it anymore. And then, once he has all the information, he can make his own decision."

"Maybe he'll decide to stay anyway," I said.

"Some people do return to the group after an intervention," said Emery, "but their conscious, real selves remember everything they've heard. Hearing what we have to say sets up something called cognitive dissonance that causes the two selves to be at war, the cult self and the true self, in a way that's not sustainable for long. We'll just have to be patient if he goes back and trust that eventually he won't be able to reconcile what he knows with what he's forced to do there."

Ah, I thought. My old friend cognitive dissonance, the discomfort caused by trying to hold two contradictory ideas in the brain simultaneously; I knew it well. In fanatical thinking, in my son's belief system, one self had to be squelched at all times; there was no reconciliation or even tolerable coexistence for the two. One of them had to die: cult self or real self, Bard or Hector, believer or doubter. He was caught in this unwinnable battle to kill half of himself, paralyzed by failure. "Without contraries there is no progression," Blake wrote in *The Marriage of Heaven and Hell.* I would have added that without contraries there was no poetry. Writing was the only place I had ever found where my two disparate selves could coexist, where I was afforded the illusion of being integrated, where the part of me that wanted to be a good, decent, responsible man and the part of me that was hell-bent on selfish immersion in mindless animal pleasure met and shimmered in dissonant grace together on the page. I could fuck other women and be faithful to my wife. My horndog self could possess their thighs, their tangy folds and clefts, their pillowy buttocks, all day, and then my good self could lie in near-perfect monogamous slumber next to my wedded spouse all night. I had thought I could get away with this, have my cake and almost eat it, too. I had also believed that my wife truly loved me. I had been as happy trying to balance these simultaneous, irreconcilable poetic and domestic illusions as I had ever been in my life.

"Let's hope Hector's real self is strong enough to vanquish the dubious honor of being Bard the Messiah," I said. "And the charms of Kirsty McDevitt."

"Those charms wear off eventually, don't worry," said Emery.

I gave him a shrewd look. He looked back at me, his face full of the rest of the story, the part he hadn't told us.

"God," said Karina. "This whole thing is so sad, but I'm kind of annoyed. I'm like, I can't believe Hector fell for this floozy and her bullshit!" No one said anything. "Sorry," she said. "I didn't mean—"

"It's okay," said June. "We can't believe we fell for it either. But people do. Even very smart ones."

"It's just that this seems like it's going to be so hard," Karina said. "It's going to take so much time and energy and money, and everyone in my family works hard, and we don't have a lot to spare. It just pisses me off that Hector is making us do this, that's all."

"It's all right to be angry," said June.

Karina slitted her eyes and subsided.

"Where are you from?" I asked June.

"Originally? Coralville, Iowa, then I moved to Seattle after college, and that's where I met Emery."

"I'm from Muscatine," I said.

"Go, Hawkeyes!" June said. I wanted to hug her.

In the car on the way back to Brooklyn, Karina said, "I frankly don't believe that anyone can get sucked into a cult. You never would, I never would, and nothing can convince me otherwise. Those people are freaks, June and Emery. Hector's a freak, they all are. This whole thing gives me a stomachache. I'm so pissed at Hector."

"I understand," I said.

"It just sucks," she said. "I love him, he's my brother, I want to help him, but there is so much else I could be doing, if I didn't have to. And what about Mom? Will she help us if it means having to be in the same room with you? This family is such a fucking mess. You're all idiots."

"Hector's not your responsibility," I said. "Neither am I, and neither is your mother. Stop trying to take care of everyone. Why don't you forget about the intervention? I can take it from here. I'll talk to your mother."

We turned onto the Pulaski Bridge just as the drawbridge began to rise. While we sat and waited for the boat to pass below, I rubbed Karina's shoulder blades exactly as I had done when she was a little girl and had one of her sobbing fits. When the drawbridge was down again, she gave me a wet smile, put the car in gear, and followed the line of traffic over the bridge. As we came onto McGuinness Boulevard, back into Brooklyn, she said, "I'll be okay. I just needed to have a meltdown. I can't let Hector get all the attention."

"Sibling rivalry never dies, does it."

"You wouldn't know; you're an only child."

We turned onto India Street. When we were a block away from the Astral, for a split second I remembered sitting in my old chair by the window with a pen and a pad of paper, sunlight or streetlight streaming in, everything cozy and quiet, Luz cooking and calling out an occasional question or comment, the clink of spatula against frying pan, the opening and closing of the oven. How lucky I had felt, all those years, to have that life. But now, in this idealized memory, for the first time, I noticed the clamp on my brain, the tamping-down of myself I had willingly undergone in order to give Luz what she wanted. I saw how castrated I had been, sitting in that chair, how meek, how boneless I had become, trying to reassure her, to convince her of my fealty. And I had failed, and she didn't want me anymore. I couldn't tell her anything, couldn't argue. She already knew everything about me there was to know. There was nothing to argue against. It didn't matter, really, whether I was innocent or guilty, true or adulterous, a genius or a retard. Nothing I could say or do would change her mind, because for once, her mind hadn't made the decision, her heart had, and that was beyond argument. The marriage was over.

Karina pulled up in front of the Astral and waited for me to get out so she could drive herself back to Crown Heights. She looked like a wizened, careworn little elf.

"Are you all right, alone in that house all the way out there in Zululand?" I asked her.

"Dad!" she said. I loved to tease my politically correct daughter by pretending to be a clueless schmuck; she was used to it by now. "That's so racist! Yes, I'm fine."

"Would you like it if I moved into your spare room? Maybe you could use some company out there. And help with your finances. I'll pay the going rate for rent."

"You're leaving the Astral?"

"Let's talk about it," I said. "For now, go home and do something fun."

"Like cleaning out my fridge?"

"Emphatically not."

"That's what's on the agenda. Can't be helped."

"Kids these days," I said, kissing her and getting out of the car. "Whatever happened to sex and drugs and vandalism?"

She laughed and drove off.

I let myself into the building, went up the one flight to my apartment, unlocked the door, turned on the lights, puttered around for a while, took a shower, and got into bed just before ten o'clock. I lay on my futon listening to people on the stairs, in the apartment above me, outside on the sidewalk.

For the first time, I wasn't entirely sure that I would have wanted to go back to Luz anymore, even if she had had a complete reversal of heart and had thrown herself at me, pleading, in tears. Nothing would change if I went back. I was tired of trying to prove to her that all men weren't like her charming, lying, unreliable, long-vanished, now-dead father; I had never asked her or anyone to undo my equally dead mother's long-ago damage. And I was deeply tired of her unpredictable oscillations between abject devotion and irrational psychodrama. Devotion was nothing but control in sheep's clothing, and psychodrama was a means of avoiding a true internal reckoning with one's own self. I was exhausted by her self-blindness, her toxic rage. She had worn me down with her shredding cruelty. This last inquisition had almost done me in. She had spied on and misread and tried to destroy my friendship with Marion, my oldest friend, someone who had never asked a thing of me beyond my company. She had spied on and misread and destroyed my new book, those silly, innocent poems written to keep me true to her, written out of a sense of freedom and playfulness and love. She could not understand either thing, and those were the things that mattered most to me, besides my marriage and family. And she had ejected me from my home, the place where my kids had grown up, where I had lived for most of my adult life. She had wrecked everything I loved with her furious, desperate, insecure need to control my thoughts, my mind, my heart, my body, like a one-woman fascistic government.

Why, exactly, had I been fighting so hard to go back to that? I felt as if I'd been like a dog going after an unattainable but rotten bone. I had been chasing after her primarily because I couldn't have her, and because, like a dog, I wanted the familiar, the comfortable, the known. But our marriage hadn't been any good for either one of us, not for a long time, maybe not ever. Living with me, her dreamy, self-absorbed, once-unfaithful husband, Luz had been in a constant state of suspicion and frustration, loneliness and anger. I had tried to squash myself to fit her expectations, shrink myself down to a safe and manageable size so she wouldn't feel threatened by my brash curiosity, my appetites and lusts, my energetic spleen. I'd tried, but I had failed. She was a tame little thing. She wanted, above all else, reliability, stability, safety, and attention. I was a wild animal who'd been trying to live in a cage, to behave, to domesticate myself. I scared her, and she bored me. Well, I was free now. She'd forced me out, of course, but now, for the first time, I was choosing to be out, and that made all the difference.

I lay awake for a very long time, feeling tender and a bit wobbly inside. Saving my marriage had obsessed me for so long, I had shaped myself around the battle. My sudden, unforeseen capitulation had knocked me backward, and I had nothing to hold on to. My internal weather was eerily calm, as if in a tornado's aftermath, birdsong, sunshine, supersaturated colors, wreckage all around, and myself, dazed and limping.

Part THREE

Chapter Seventeen

Karina had bought her house right after college. She had swashbuckled out to Crown Heights on a tip from someone who knew of a nineteenth-century row house that was allegedly in foreclosure and available "for nothing." The house itself had turned out to be full of trash and scarily decrepit inside, but underneath the ugly fixtures and wallpaper, it had original moldings and French doors, a backyard, a working fireplace, and, according to the engineer Karina hired, decent structural integrity. Karina plunked down all the money she'd socked away over the course of a short but frugal and very hardworking lifetime, which, along with help from Luz's savings and a midsized inheritance from my father, was enough to buy the place outright.

Immediately after the closing, Karina moved into the place with her college girlfriend, Maureen, a sullen, chubby, multi-pierced, barely verbal girl with dead-white skin and a jet-black crew cut who, despite her lack of any other discernible charms, happened to be in possession of contracting skills and uncanny physical strength. She lived with Karina rent-free in return for doing much of the renovation. Karina acted as gofer and assistant before and after her daily job, a low-paid internship at a news website. It was amazing, watching them go at it. After demolishing cheesy paneling, drop ceilings, bad partitions, linoleum, and shag rugs, and digging the backyard out of a two-foot-high pile of trash and rocks, they spent months rewiring, replumbing, replastering, drywalling, painting, and refinishing the oak floors. These two young girls, with some help from me, Hector, and a handful of college friends, refinished the basement to turn it into a rental apartment, built a kitchen from scratch in a former first-story bedroom, and knocked down a wall to make the upstairs bathroom big enough for a claw-foot tub and a washer and dryer. They found all their building supplies, fixtures, appliances, and fittings for nearly nothing at an outer-borough warehouse full of donated and recycled construction materials. They planted a lawn and flower beds out back with turf and seedlings they got from a hinterland Long Island nursery that was going out of business, poured a concrete patio and found a piece of corrugated fiberglass for the roof. They furnished the place by "curb-shopping," as they called it. They found kitchenware, linens, gardening tools, and planters on various freegan websites. Suddenly, Karina's crappy, ugly house had been rejiggered into an oasis in a blighted ghetto with a rental-income basement apartment and a nice yard for cookouts on hot nights. The *Times* real estate section got wind of it and asked to do a story; Karina, with characteristic fuck-you mistrust of unwanted publicity, turned them down flat.

Conveniently, when the bulk of the renovation was pretty much completed, they broke up and Maureen moved out, and that was the end of her, as far as I could tell. I couldn't pretend to be anything but relieved. Despite her prodigious handiness, Maureen had seemed entirely unsuitable for my lovely, bright daughter, not nearly worthy, but what father ever thought anyone was good enough for his girl? Karina had lived in her house alone ever since, except for her downstairs tenant, a quiet middle-aged black man named Dewey who worked odd hours as a livery cabdriver and rarely made a peep when he was home. Dewey's rent covered Karina's car expenses, utilities, and taxes; she Dumpster-dove for as much food as possible and all her clothes and household goods. She worked freelance temp jobs when she had to. Her life as a "power freegan," as she jokingly called herself, was passionately committed but pragmatically nondidactic. "Most people could never do this," she had said when I'd asked her about the philosophy behind it all. "I think it's right, and it's nice to live so cheaply when there's so much free good stuff out there, but I know it's not for everyone, I know it's extreme." She had been interviewed a few times, as one of the movement's more articulate, low-key, nonrabid spokespeople, on radio talk shows on the likes of WBAI and WFUV. She helped run one of the better-trafficked freegan websites and held meetings in her living room. One of these meetings was in full swing on the last day of May, the night I arrived with my belongings to take up residence in the spare upstairs bedroom as a rent-paying tenant.

I came up out of the IRT station at the Utica Avenue stop with my suitcase and bag. I walked through Crown Heights feeling a kind of dazed anticipation I hadn't felt since I was a young man, before I was married. I was amazed by the euphoric relief I felt, getting out of Greenpoint, coming here, away from the Astral and the people Luz and I knew in common.

It took me a while to identify the cause of this newfound happiness, but about a block away from Karina's house, as I checked out the saucy, tight-jeans-clad ass of the woman walking ahead of me, it hit me that, for the first time in all these years, all these decades, I was free to fuck someone besides Luz, aboveboard, no sneaking around, free and clear. This realization was as fizzy and exciting as a drug or a blast of cold air on a scorching day. Tempering it slightly was the fact that moving in with my daughter might cramp my style just a bit, but I wasn't in a hurry. Just knowing I was allowed to seemed like enough for now.

The night was hot and loud, humid and full of smoke from sidewalk oil drum barbecues, joints and cigarettes, diesel exhaust pipes, fast-food air vents. It was Memorial Day. A hip-hop-pumping Escalade with spinning rims stopped at a red light, bouncing from the force of the bass line. Three male Hasids rushed past me in full summer regalia, white kneesocks, lightweight hats like fur discs on their heads. The fried chicken place on the corner was lit up with fluorescent cheer, crammed full of kids, all black. I wanted to tell them to disperse, they were just feeding into racial stereotypes, but the chicken smelled great. I almost went in and got some. I could understand why they were all there.

"Dad," said Karina as she let me into her house, "do you want to go up and get settled, or do you want to meet these people? Up to you."

"I apologize for the brusqueness of this question," I said. "Do you have any food?"

"Why are you always so hungry?"

"I don't know. I forget to eat. It's a rather complicated—"

"I made chili," she said. "But I warn you, all of the ingredients are freeganized."

I stowed my things upstairs and went down to the kitchen, where I filled a ceramic bowl with vegetarian chili. It looked and smelled delicious, and I had no qualms about eating it, because I knew that Karina didn't literally pull food out of Dumpsters. She went around to grocery stores and restaurants and picked up unwanted, still good food before it went out with the garbage. This chili, the beans and vegetables and spices, was no doubt made from ingredients past their expiration dates but still perfectly edible, collected by Karina as she made her rounds in her car. It was almost as if she had bought groceries from a supermarket, except that it had been free.

I joined the group of trash-divers in the living room. Everyone was standing around talking, a farrago of races and ages and types and physiques, the common denominator of which was evidently a great deal of what they used to call "good energy" back when I was Karina's age. I sat in my chair, which Karina had salvaged from a closing restaurant along with seven others just like it, and watched everyone as I shoveled the food into my mouth. As my blood sugar rose to acceptable levels, I noticed that one of the women present seemed to be in love with my daughter. She was a tall, broad-shouldered brunette who must have been forty at least, although I was a bad judge of anyone's age. She was clean-cut, athletic looking, and "handsome," as old-timey novelists used to describe the kind of woman who wasn't born conventionally pretty but became better looking as she aged. She leaned against the mantel out of the fray and didn't say much, but she listened to everything Karina said with the shiny-eyed raptness of someone in the grip of ardent admiration. I also noticed, as I swabbed my empty bowl with corn bread and washed the last savory mouthfuls down with beer, that Karina hardly noticed this attractive older woman. She was too busy arguing with a gray-dreadlocked man about the ethics of veganism, which he espoused and Karina did not, necessarily. "If perfectly good milk and cheese are there for the taking," she pointed out, "why not use them?"

"Where do you draw the line?" said Dreadlocks. "It's a slippery slope from dairy products to Perdue chicken and downer hamburger meat."

"No, it's not," said Karina. Her manner was easygoing, but her face was fierce. "I can make those distinctions. What am I, a two-year-old?"

"The important thing," said Karina's dark-haired admirer, "is not to support the consumerist, cruelty-based economy. We can all decide where we fall within those parameters. There's a lot of room for differences."

"What would you do without that economy, though?" I asked. I held up my empty bowl. "If it weren't for all the abundant wastefulness, what would you eat? Would you forage for edible weeds in Prospect Park?"

Karina gave a small snort. "Dad," she said, "come on. Of course we would. Or we'd grow it ourselves. A lot of people here do that already."

I subsided into humble silence. As the meeting ended and people dispersed, Karina's admirer approached me and sat in the empty chair beside me. "I'm Diane," she said. Her handshake was surprisingly gentle and feminine. "You're Karina's dad?"

"Yes," I said. "My name is Harry."

She leaned back in the chair and crossed her legs and gave me a direct, engaging smile. She had a strong, squarish face, ice-blue eyes, and a small, full-lipped mouth. Her hair was cut in a kind of bob so it fell in a silky swath around her cheekbones. She looked Nordic and semi-famous, like a former Olympic ski champion. It occurred to me that she might have been flirting with me, and that maybe I'd misread both her sexual orientation and her feelings toward my daughter.

"Did you come to learn more about us?" she was asking.

"To be honest, no," I said. "I just moved into Karina's spare room, so I thought I'd be sociable."

"Well," she said with another charming smile, clasping both her hands in front of her. "She'll have your head in a Dumpster in no time."

"I wouldn't be surprised," I said.

Karina, having bid good night to the last of the freegans, pulled a chair over so we made a cozy triangle in front of the unlit fireplace.

"Paul gets a little intense for me," she said to Diane. "I never know whether he's completely serious or not."

"He needs to cut off those damn dreadlocks," said Diane.

Karina laughed. I got up and went into the kitchen and fetched fresh cold bottles of beer and brought them out to the ladies.

"Dreadlocks on white people are ridiculous," Karina was saying. "Okay, if you're twenty-three, it's possibly cute. But he's got to be what? My dad's age?"

I whistled in shock that anyone besides me could be so old. We all laughed and then took swigs of beer, in unison.

"So Dad," said Karina. "I'm really glad you're here. But last time I saw you, like, four days ago, you were living in the Astral . . . I'm just wondering, did something happen? With Mom?"

I squinted at her. "No," I said. "Nothing happened."

"Sorry," Karina said to Diane. "This is my first chance to ask, I've been wondering all night. My parents are not on good terms."

"I'm sorry to hear that," said Diane to Karina. "Well, I'll be off then, and let you two catch up."

"No, no," I said before she could get up. "It's all right, I haven't got anything to say that I can't say in front of you." I looked at Karina. "To put it simply, and then we can move on to more interesting topics, I realized that I wasn't getting anywhere with your mother, being there, and that I might as well be paying rent where it could make a difference for you. I'd give you money outright if I had it to spare, but at least this way, we both win. And I think it's good for me to be out of the Astral for a while."

"Oh," said Karina. I watched her wrestle with the temptation to quiz me further, and win. "Well, I'm glad you're here."

I had decided not to tell her the whole truth, not right away, because she was right, all of this seemed extremely abrupt, out of the blue even, and Karina disliked sudden change. And this was not the time, of course, to tell her that Luz and I were filing for divorce. The day after the cult-intervention meeting with June and Emery, I had left a message on Luz's cell phone letting her know that I was ready. "Luz, it's Harry. I've been thinking a lot these past weeks, and I've come to accept that our marriage is really over. I'm ready to end it. I'd like to do it as amicably as possible." I had said it without inflection or emotion. I had not asked her to call me back; I'd given her my address, as if she didn't already know it, and as if she couldn't just walk downstairs and hand the papers to me in person. She had mailed them immediately, without a note. So this was where things stood. I had the divorce papers upstairs. I hadn't signed them yet, but I wasn't planning to wait much longer. It was good to have things clear and definite.

"Wow," said Diane. "Most daughters wouldn't feel that way. I would never want my father to move in with me in a million years. I love the guy, but he would drive me nuts."

"I hope I won't drive you nuts, Karina," I said.

"If you do, I'll kick you out."

We all laughed. Diane was gorgeous, I thought in my beer-glowing, full-bellied haze. Maybe she wasn't after either me or my daughter; maybe she was happily married to a devoted, handsome, sexually adept man with a huge bank account.

"What do you do, Diane?" I asked her. "Where do you live?"

"I'm a schoolteacher. I live in Kensington. I teach junior high English at a private school in Park Slope." She swept her swaths of hair off her face with both hands at once. It all fell right back again, silky, glossy. "Those kids are the most vulnerable, sweet, earnest things I've ever seen. They get such a bad reputation, twelve- and thirteen-year-olds, but really they're babies, they want attention and love and respect, and if they get it, they're easy to deal with. Well, I'm free for the summer at the moment, so of course I'm all rosy about it. Ask me how I feel next February when it's cold and everyone's sleep deprived and cranky and no one's done their homework."

"What do kids learn in English these days?" I asked. "Does anyone diagram sentences anymore? Do kids read poetry? Or is it all standardized testing?"

"It's a lot of standardized testing, but I sneak in the occasional goodie if we get ahead of schedule and have twenty minutes to spare. Creative writing, grammar game-show-style competitions, we manage to have some fun a few times a semester."

I was so smitten, I almost fell off my chair. "I wish I'd had you as my English teacher," I said. "I had an old crone named Mrs. Morneau who was obsessed with Armageddon. She scared the bejeezus out of me."

"I had Sister Mary-Bernadette," said Karina. "I worshipped her.

She was my first crush. The day she read my essay aloud to the class, I almost passed out."

"You went to Catholic school?" Diane asked, laughing. "You sent her there?" she said to me.

"Her mother did," I said. "I had no say in the matter."

"I liked Northside," said Karina. "It was all girls, which was great for me, being a dyke. And we wore uniforms, so I never had to worry about clothes, and the teachers were weird and sexually pent up, but so were all us kids, so we all had that in common. And if you were smart and did your homework, they loved you."

"What do you do, Harry?" Diane asked. "Where are you from?"

I launched into a monologue about being a poet, growing up in Iowa, and a bit about my current situation, keeping the details of my marital schism sketchy but making it as clear as I could without upsetting Karina that I was single and available, just in case that was the direction in which Diane's antennae were waving. While I talked, I watched Diane respond to me, all my senses alert as I tried to parse out this intake of breath, that wide-eyed nod, that encouraging laugh, that throat-clearing invitation to continue. I was woefully out of practice. She was probably just being friendly, and she was this engaged and warm with everyone on the planet.

The three of us drank more beer, and then we went out with more bottles of beer to sit on the stoop and enjoy the warm night and watch the kids walking by in loud clumps, all drifting somewhere. After an amicable, contented silence, we all three stretched and yawned at the same time. Karina yawned again. "Bedtime for me," she said. "Don't move, you two, just promise me you'll lock up, Dad. Diane, it's late and I know you have a ways to go, so please feel free to crash on the couch, it's pretty comfy."

"Oh," said Diane. "What time is it? I wasn't keeping track."

"I'll put out a shirt for you," said Karina. "I might have a spare toothbrush somewhere, too."

"A Dumpster toothbrush?" I asked.

"I draw the line at personal hygiene items," said Karina.

She left us there on the stoop. Diane put her head back and gave me a sidelong smile. "I think I drank too much," she said. "I need to get out more, I've been such a good citizen."

"How do you reconcile the freegan lifestyle with teaching school?" I asked her. "Seems like a full-time job wouldn't leave much time for foraging."

"Oh," she said, laughing a little, "I'm not a full-on freegan, I just really like the principles, and I respect them all a lot. I do what I can, I come to the meetings, I think they're absolutely right in their ideals, but I can't commit as fully to it as they have, obviously."

"So," I said, teasing her, "you're like one of those straight women who think lesbians have the right idea, and hang out with them, and support their politics, but sleep with men."

"I am exactly like that."

"I actually did think you were a lesbian," I said. "When I first saw you, I thought you were in love with Karina because of the way you were looking at her. And I must say, I approved of you as a daughter-in-law, based on initial impressions."

She threw her head back and laughed. "I'm probably no more than five years younger than you!"

"I'm fifty-seven," I said.

"I'm forty-nine," she said. "And I'm as straight as a die. I just think Karina is the most fantastic young woman. By the way, I love how you're such good friends with your daughter. I've always imagined that she had great parents."

"I tried," I said. "But to be honest, she was born that way. We didn't have to do much. Do you have kids?"

"Only my students," she said. "They're enough for me. I love to go home and be completely alone."

So she lived alone. We kept talking, idly, easily, leaning into each other with warm relaxation. Her lips were moist, because she kept licking them. Her eyes sparkled in the streetlamp with diamonds of promised sex. I had no further doubts now as to the object of her interest.

I stood up. "I'd better get to bed," I said. "It's been a real pleasure talking to you."

She followed me inside and waited near me as I locked the door. We were in the dark foyer, at the foot of the stairs, I turned toward her, intending to say good night, to be polite, to shake her hand, and the next thing I knew, we were kissing. I was certain I hadn't done anything to provoke this, but if that was true, it meant that Diane had single-handedly caused us to go from standing separately to full-blown making out, which couldn't possibly have been the case, because I had felt no coercion; it took two, of course, to tango.

Her body was softer and cuddlier than I had expected. Her mouth tasted of beer and her own native sweetness. She smelled so good I wanted to inhale her right up my nose. It had been so long since I had touched a woman, so long since I had been touched by one, I felt dizzy, almost nauseous, from the unaccustomed contact. Her hands pressed under my shirt at the small of my back. My hand cupped the nape of her neck. My other hand had boldly found her breast. Her nipple was erect. So was every part of me.

But my brain was ticking away. I looked down the barrel of consequence and saw nothing good. I remembered the psychopathic lout Boleslaw, beating me up out of the blue for flirting with a doughnut girl, those hours in a holding cell with a broken nose and bleeding mouth. I saw Zeldah Speck's pained, proud, apologetic face as she asked me to leave her house, all because of my unacted-upon crush on her precious daughter. Then I recalled my prescient, uncharacteristic intelligence in cutting my losses and running away from the Mullet at the threat of the approach of Lexy Levy's starstruck, no doubt thermonuclearly hot friend, my alleged fan. How wise that had been; how unwise it had been those other two times to allow myself to experience attraction. I had been punished, swiftly and well, both times, although I'd technically done nothing, ironic echoes of being thrown out by Luz. And the one time I'd exercised restraint, I'd been rewarded with a glorious nap, no hangover, and the offer of a job at the lumberyard.

Diane was making a purring sound in the back of her throat.

I said with my mouth on hers, "No, no," and tried to break free.

"Let's go lie on the couch," she whispered, and softened against me even more. "This feels so good."

We started kissing again, maybe because I stupidly felt this might forestall the thing I knew I couldn't do, the thing she so clearly wanted. Or, really, we both wanted the same thing, but we weren't in her daughter's house, so she was freer than I was. Her mouth was open and hot and wet. Nothing on earth in my entire life had ever, it seemed, felt as good as her face mashed openmouthed into my face, the smell of her breath and the silkiness of her hair and her hard nipple under my eager hand and the amazing knowledge that she wanted me to fuck her.

The intelligent, self-protective, infuriatingly sane part of my brain projected against my skull's internal screen the dream I'd had during my nap after running away from the Mullet: myself alone floating in a rowboat on a still, clear lake, mountains looming, shaggy old New England forests all around, suspended there with a feeling of happy, boyish, innocent freedom.

This was my daughter's house. I was here on my first night as her tenant. She had gone up to bed easily, naturally, without any apparent warning, which meant that, despite everything, she still thought I was worthy of her trust. Her good opinion of me would be devastating to lose, beyond recovery, tragic, the emotional equivalent of the Gulf oil spill. And I knew now that such things could happen. I was immune to nothing. What was the opposite of a fairy godmother? That's what I had.

"We'd better not, it's my daughter's house," I said as quietly as I could, aware that Karina's bedroom was directly above us, and this place echoed because it had no rugs or curtains. "Can I call you? Can I take you to dinner? I'd love to see you again."

"Okay, yes, good night," she said on a long, regretful exhale.

"Sleep well," I said. Then I was safe, alone, upstairs in my new room. Karina had made up the bed, opened the windows, put some flowers from her yard in a jar on the bureau. I brushed my teeth and crawled chastely between the clean sheets in T-shirt and briefs and lay awake with a drunken buzzing head, feeling as if I'd narrowly escaped a situation I craved more than anything. Outside, things were just revving up; it wasn't even midnight yet. I heard yelling, music, thumping bass lines, engines revving, the whole world out there alive and awake, and my body couldn't calm itself down until almost dawn, when the world turned cool, quiet, the sharp-edged streetlamps blinked off, and the light became gentle and pink and soft.

Chapter Eighteen

I pried myself out of bed the next morning before anyone else was awake. I put on some clothes and tiptoed down to the foyer, trying not to make a sound on the rickety old stairs, which were as creaky and fragile as an osteoporotic grandmother's spine. I let myself out without disturbing Diane, whose sleeping form I glimpsed out of the corner of my eye with a jolt of remembered lust as I passed the French doors that led to the living room.

It was a warm, heavy, overcast morning. The street was so quiet I could hear my shoes on the pavement. I had rushed from Karina's house in a fever to be gone, and had therefore neither urinated nor drunk any coffee; my bladder was full, my head aching from beer and lack of sleep. I had left my bike locked outside the Astral, so I headed to Church and Utica. Getting to the lumberyard from Crown Heights was easy enough, a straight forty-five-minute shot north on the B46. I sat on the jouncing, almost-empty bus, squeezing my thighs together, clenching my teeth, apologizing to my bladder, and jonesing for caffeine. This had the advantageous effect of consuming all my attention so I didn't have to consider what had happened, or almost happened, with Diane. But the thought of calling her and arranging another meeting away from Karina's house was so tantalizingly sweet, I could taste it on my tongue, counteracting the stale beer and morning mouth.

I got off the bus and walked down Broadway, almost goose-stepping with the pressure in my bladder. Luckily, the pretentiously overpriced coffee place near Berry Street was open, so I went in, peed a steady, foamy, gaspingly joyful stream for what felt like five minutes into the vintage toilet in the artful bathroom, bought a four-dollar coffee, dumped as much milk and sugar into it as it would hold in lieu of breakfast, and walked down to the lumberyard gulping it as fast as I could.

At the lumberyard, something dastardly had evidently occurred. More papers were missing from Accounts Payable. Moishe was in a dark temper. I stood by the desk and sipped a coffee from the office machine, cringing at the acrid taste of overcooked bad grounds, nondairy creamer, and artificial sweetener (all the Hasids seemed to be diabetic; real sugar was in short supply here) after that organic French roast, farm-fresh half-and-half, and raw turbinado sugar from the hipster place. My stomach roiled with empty postbeer sleep-deprived tension as Moishe scrabbled through the office, muttering, opening drawers, and breathing hard through his nose like a maddened beast.

Yanti hadn't arrived yet. Levi and I exchanged worried looks as Moishe's rage crescendoed toward some sort of climax, we knew not what. Levi and I had never established any sort of camaraderie during the months I'd been at the lumberyard; he was so colorless and bland and almost invisible, and for my part, I was a non-Hasid, and worse, Yanti's friend. I had gathered that he and Yanti were mortal enemies. This had something to do with Moishe's patronage of Yanti, the overboss's favoritism for the naughty crackhead black sheep while the quiet labors of Levi, pink-eyed rabbit diligent unobtrusive Levi, went unnoticed.

I gave a fuck about exactly none of this internecine competition. All I cared about was my own livelihood. Someone in Accounts Payable was apparently sabotaging someone else in Accounts Payable. There were only three of us: I hoped I was neither of these people, but I could only be sure of one end of the equation. I knew I was good at this job. It was very surprisingly easy for me, a dreamy poet, to move financial numbers around quickly and without error. But it stood to reason that maybe someone wanted me out. I was the new guy here; business was off along with the whole country's economy. And, according to rumor, the lumberyard had just been sold to developers and was going to be supplanted by a twenty-two-story high-rise condo building, but I had decided to believe that when it happened.

Moishe grilled Levi in Yiddish for a while, gesturing to the files, to the computer, to me, to the floor, to what I guessed was either Hashem or the ceiling tiles. Levi answered in a voice so tragically circumspect, his manner so insanely cowed, I thought he might bust out a machine gun in the manner of downtrodden, clinically enraged, finally-exploding underlings everywhere and mow Moishe down. But by some miracle, he did not. Nor did I once hear the name Yanti mentioned with outraged, defensive, finger-pointing blame, which suggested to me that Levi was either delirious with altruism, guilty as charged, or aware of something going on that I had no clue about.

Then it was my turn: Moishe interrogated me in his thick-tongued, condescending English, making it clear that he was naturally angry at our entire department for fucking up but even more so at whoever had spawned and raised me, thereby forcing him to wrap his superior lips around this lowly, common tongue spoken by Puerto Ricans, as a second language, of course, but even so, he hated it.

And then things moved with blurry speed. Moishe's interrogation of me turned out to be no interrogation after all, but a dramatic monologue in the tradition of various dramatis personae, Hamlet among them, in which the speaker determines by means of a lengthy soliloquy that he is being had and will shed the offender's blood in retribution. Back when the missing invoice turned up in the men's room, Moishe had given me the grudging benefit of the considerable doubt. There had been a couple of other instances when it was to everyone's advantage to chalk things up to human error and forget about it, but apparently I had been under suspicion for quite some time. This was the first I'd known about my apparent culpability in these matters, but of course, I didn't speak Yiddish, so I had missed most of what went on around here.

Once Moishe had ultimately decided, with exhaustive Shakespearean incisiveness, that it was my fault, all of it, I was invited to collect my things and beat it. Then he disappeared in a puff of black, sulfurous smoke.

"If you cut me, do I not bleed? Does a goy fall in the forest?" I said, feigning insouciance to mask my shame and worry. I threw away my coffee cup and looked around the office to make sure none of my few belongings were here. "Something is rotten in the state of Yidmark. If I were a skidmark, I would beedle deedle beedle dreidl doodle on skid row—"

"It was Yanti," said Levi at my elbow. "He screwed you. They were gonna cut one of us. He was afraid it would be him."

"Thanks for speaking up on my behalf," I said.

"I'm telling you," he said, his nose twitching. "It was Yanti."

We exchanged a level look.

"It's all right, Levi, I know you take care of your own even when they're crackheads you can't stand. It's a tribal thing. I was lucky to have this job at all."

"He's no friend to you," said Levi, and then he crept back down his rabbit hole and vanished.

I left the lumberyard laughing grimly. As I wended my way on foot along Kent Avenue to Franklin and thus to the Astral to collect my bicycle, I parsed out this latest setback in a life that seemed increasingly to be made up of little else. The childish sense that I was being punished suggested the existence of a punisher, and I believed in no such thing; therefore, these negative occurrences, as I had decided to euphemistically refer to them from now on to myself, were merely the natural social consequences of my own actions, nothing personal. They were just ironic tropes, and my entire life was a catastrophic little essay.

It was too early to go to Marlene's. I rode my bicycle up Calyer then turned right on Guernsey, a sordid, narrow canyon that ran for several blocks between two facing sheer high walls of claustrophobia-inducing attached apartment buildings. The malevolent tops of tall trees met overhead in sinister patterns of spindly branches. The people who lived on this street always seemed to me like troglodytes in their caves, or mythic nocturnal beasts, pale, spooky wraiths dashing along the dark sidewalk, afraid to make eye contact, haunted by their own ghosts. On this summery morning, the street was chill and shadowy and smelled of stale urine.

I emerged into the light of day again and rode my bicycle into McCarren Park. Every Saturday morning in good weather, the Greenmarket took over an entire corner of the park, where happy, healthy neighbors pawed through heirloom squash, homemade jams, and organic lettuces while their children frolicked in the grass. That corner was empty today, but even so, I could feel the subatomic waves of didactic gourmandise that emanated from the very pavement now. I avoided that little swath of hell and wheeled between the scruffy baseball diamonds, then crossed Driggs and rode past the dog run, filled with maladjusted mutts and their neurotic, self-righteous owners. I dismounted and locked my bike to a fence, then moseyed over to the running track that ringed the soccer field. I sat on a bench in a patch of hot, diffuse sunlight and watched people running around and around on the springy red rubber track. Each runner's body and running style were completely different from all the others: a skinny old man who ran with a sidewinding, shoulder-hunched lurch; a fat little Latina in swishy shorts who trotted and trundled; a willowy girl whose blond ponytail swept side to side between her shoulder blades as she loped along; a massive, muscular black guy whose thighs were so hugely developed, he had to mince in a pigeon-toed, prissy hop. People were the landscape in the city, and the weather, and the wildlife. I hadn't sat and watched the locals in a long time, I realized. It felt odd not to be at work, odd to be unemployed again. I missed Luz, but I batted that feeling away, knowing it was just a bad old habit, and it was only coming back now because I was forlorn.

Walking toward me along the path next to the track was Marion. She wore a sleeveless sundress and sandals. Her hair blew around her face, golden brown now, no gray at all. She looked tanned, happy, and carefree. An arm was slung across her shoulders. It belonged to a young, dark-haired, gypsyish man. He was strikingly good-looking. I studied him. He probably provoked interest wherever he went, I thought with mild envy, and he probably knew how to handle it. He had that look about him. Marion was looking up at his face, saying something to him, laughing. He smiled at her, pulled her closer, kissed her on the mouth, and then they separated. He headed back toward Lorimer; she continued along the path toward me, smiling, preoccupied. She would very likely have walked right by me if I hadn't said, "Hello there!"

She turned and saw me. "Harry," she said, and stopped walking, idled there in front of me, smiling. "How have you been?"

I gestured with vague, all-encompassing, noncommittal limpness. "Fine," I said. I stood up. "Where are you headed?"

We set off for the other side of the park.

I said, "So that's why you look so good."

"I won't pretend I don't know what you mean. Or that I'm not flattered to hear it."

"How old is he?"

"He just turned thirty-three."

"He's almost twenty-five years younger than we are!" I tried to sound amused, but there was a well of unease in the pit of my gut. It felt like a betrayal. I would never have admitted this out loud in a million years, but I was threatened on some primal and of course wholly irrational level by Marion's affair with this kid. We were supposed to stay in our own age group. Or rather, women were. What the hell did that snot-nosed postadolescent have to offer a woman of her experience and intelligence? What did he know about anything yet? Did he have the slightest clue what to do in bed?

"I know," she said. She sounded amused and ebullient. "He was born in the late seventies. Can you fathom it?"

"When you and I first met, as adults, he wasn't even born yet."

She looked sideways at me, shaking her head. "How old was Samantha? You didn't seem to mind."

"I was embarrassed by her age," I said. "I knew she was too young for me."

"Bullshit," said Marion. "You were no such thing, you just pretended to be. You loved that she was so young, it made you feel like a stud. Having a double standard about this is just idiotic. Age has nothing to do with anything. Anyway, his name is Adrian, and he's amazing."

His name was Adrian. Of course it was. It perfectly suited that quasi-Euro look he had, his feline slinkiness, the slight pouf in his black Mediterranean hair.

"I'm sure he is," I said. "I'm happy for you." I meant it, halfway.

We continued on, past benches full of people with dogs on leashes, self-conscious-looking picnickers on blankets in the grass, and a nonstop advancing phalanx of people walking toward us, most of them young. Marion and I knew each other too well to have this conversation without allowing some shakeout of static electricity to avoid escalation into some odd sort of conflict. We allowed the silence between us to grow until we were both comfortable together again. This was one of the graceful prerogatives of longtime friendship. I was so happy to feel it assert itself now, when I needed it most.

"Anyway," she said, "what's going on with you? Have you got a new girlfriend yet?"

"What?" I said, affecting outrage, but secretly flattered. "Last time I talked to you, I was still trying to save my marriage. As far as you know now, I'm still married."

She laughed. "Last time I talked to you, you were in masochistic thrall to a raving psycho bitch who wanted us both dead. I don't believe you still want her back, after everything she did and said."

"We're getting a divorce," I said.

She stopped and turned to me, amazed. "You're kidding. Since when?"

"Since a few days ago. I have the papers."

"Good lord," she said. "What changed your mind? Did something happen?"

I told her about everything that had happened since I'd seen her the week before, my session with Helen, my conversation with James, the meeting with the cult exit counselors. "And then it hit me," I said, all inflamed with a need for her to know, that feverish intensity that can set in when a person talks for an unnaturally long time without being interrupted in the presence of a good listener. "Sitting there in their living room talking about the mechanisms of mind control, I was reminded of my marriage, and afterward I realized that I couldn't go back even if she wanted me to, which she doesn't."

Marion was silent for an instant, her gaze on the ground in front of us, her expression inscrutable. "Talking about cult mind control made you think of your marriage?"

"That's right," I said. "I've never told anyone that." We walked several paces. "It sounds crazy, doesn't it."

Marion laughed. "Harry. You think Luz brainwashed you?"

"Well," I said, feeling a little sheepish.

Her clever, quick face contracted with sympathetic laughter.

"Please. You can't compare your marriage to cult indoctrination. You were not under mind control, you were just part of a marriage. That's the way it always works."

We had been walking around the park through the throngs, talking as if all the other people were props. Now, as if we'd made a conscious agreement to do so, we approached an empty bench and sat down. Two small leashed dogs truffle-pigged under the bench for scraps. A few more idled nearby on leashes while their owners talked. Behind us, across Driggs, the dog run was full of canine yaps, barks, and shrieks.

"So many dogs," I said. "This neighborhood never used to have so many dogs."

"I almost adopted one," said Marion. "A huge silver pit bull, a female named Xanadu."

"Named what?"

"I know," she said. "The people at the shelter named her. They're borderline psychotic. Especially the guy who runs it, this fat, bug-eyed misanthrope named Sal who's violently rude to you if you show signs of being unworthy of adopting one of his dogs. His shelter is just awful, it smells of piss, the animals are crammed together in an echo chamber, they feed them the cheapest food . . . The people there are the ones who really need help. They all seem damaged and out of their minds, and they hate people and are rabidly protective of these poor animals. Did all their parents molest them? Were they tortured as babies?"

"Maybe they're just garden-variety crazy," I said.

"Or maybe they're right. The older I get, the less I want to have anything to do with any people at all. I'm thinking of selling my house and moving to Maine. I mean it, Harry. It's all going to shit anyway." She trailed off. "Anyway, poor Xanadu found another home right after I changed my mind."

"Why didn't you adopt her?"

"Because I decided I didn't like her. She was beautiful, but so stupid and mulish. When I told them, at the shelter, they looked at me as if I'd committed bestiality. I went in a week later to ask about a different dog, and they froze up and wouldn't meet my eye till I walked out in something like disgrace. Jesus!"

I laughed and leaned back against the sun-warmed bench and took a lungful of humid, grass-smelling air. "I just got fired this morning," I said. "From the lumberyard. My crackhead friend Yanti screwed me over because he was afraid that otherwise it would have been him."

"Really?" she said. "Jesus, I'm sorry. What are you going to do?"

The topic of James had long been a delicate one for Marion. I understood. The navigation of the aftermath of an extramarital affair was fraught and uncharted, especially when the participants all lived in proximity to one another. But Marion always wanted the truth, no mollycoddling or euphemisms.

"James offered me a job at their company," I said.

Her expression hardly changed, just a slight flinch in the corner of her left eye; I chalked this up to the healing powers of Adrian. "That's good," she said.

"Also, I just moved in with Karina. She needs a roommate, and I need to get away from Luz. For now, I'm living in Crown Heights. It's good to get out of this neighborhood. I'm surprised at how good it feels. I have so much history here, I can't walk down any street without thinking of a thousand things that happened on it, without seeing someone I recognize. It's been so long. Decades of accrued stuff. I had started to think I was grafted onto this part of town. I didn't realize it was possible just to up and leave it. Crown Heights is only a few miles away, but it could be a whole new country, as far as I'm concerned. I feel so much better all of a sudden. Here I just got fired from my job, and I'm almost happy because it means I won't have to spend any more time in this part of the world."

"I can imagine," said Marion. "Adrian lives in the South Slope. I love visiting him in his little bare-bones apartment. My house is full of so many years of accumulated emotion, good and bad, but so much of it painful. My marriage, my affair, all the work troubles I've had, the fallouts with gallery owners and the competition with other photographers and drunken parties . . . going to Adrian's is like taking a vacation."

"So," I said, trying to sound merely curious, not at all judgmental, "how did you and Adrian meet? He was the guy in the bar who kept calling you, right?"

"No, believe it or not, he's yet another much-younger man." She laughed. "We were set up by a mutual friend of his aunt's and mine, my friend Laura. On a blind date. She said, 'My friend's nephew is perfect for you. I just know it. He's young, but don't let that stop you, give him a chance.' The only reason I went was that he was so young, I figured nothing could come of it, so I was safe. That was a week ago. The joke's apparently on me." She stretched and yawned and rubbed her hands together. "Anyway, I'm so happy you're finally getting free of Luz. So glad, I can't even tell you."

"So am I, and I mean that. You were absolutely right about her." I cleared my throat. "I met a woman last night. A schoolteacher. She was at Karina's for dinner; they're friends, but she's almost as old as we are."

"What do I care about how old she is? What's she like?"

"Beautiful and smart," I said. "I like her. She likes me. I can't believe I'm allowed to . . . you know."

"Fuck her?"

I laughed. "I was going to say 'ask her out.' But yes, now that you mention it."

"Isn't that the best part of having a marriage end? You're suddenly allowed to sleep with other people, and no one can say boo to you about it."

"I was just thinking that last night," I said.

"After Ike died, I cried so much I thought I would never stop. I got an eye infection from crying. Our marriage was complicated and difficult, but I would always have chosen it over not having it. I thought I'd never get over the loss. We've been through hell this year, you and I. We both lost our spouses. So good for us, here we both are."

"Good for us," I said.

We settled into a daydreamy silence, two old friends basking in the sun, letting the war wounds heal, or so I liked to think of us right then.

Chapter Nineteen

The upside to being fired, the only upside, was that now I didn't have to go off to work every day; my time was my own to spend as I wished.

Downstairs in the kitchen, Karina had just made a pot of coffee and was scrambling eggs. We sat over breakfast at her table and made a plan for the day: we would drive out to Long Island that afternoon and surprise Hector, swoop in on him unannounced and try to get him to come to dinner with us somewhere nearby. Failing that, we'd try to cadge an invitation to dinner at his house, but it would be better to get him alone. "Divide and conquer," said Karina.

"Karina," I said. "Can I ask you something?"

"You frequently do."

"You were there, you saw it all happen. In your opinion, was I a terrible husband to your mother?"

"You were my father," she said, looking straight at me. "She was my mother. You both seemed like good people to me from a very early age. Maybe sometimes she wanted you to pay attention to her more than you did, but in my opinion, Mom is pretty demanding, and you were busy."

I couldn't help laughing. "I love how nonmelodramatic you are. Such a straight shooter."

"I'm no romantic, am I. Since this whole thing blew up between you, spending time with both of you, I have to say, I've started seeing you more objectively as separate individuals, and knowing you both as well as I do, I find it amazing that your marriage lasted as long as it did. Like, fundamentally, chemically, you seem like you come from different tribes of people. I don't mean because she's Mexican and you're . . . whatever you are, Iowan. I mean your makeups are foreign to each other somehow. Does that make sense?"

I cupped my coffee mug in both hands and looked right back at my daughter. "Yes," I said. We smiled at each other, but the air between us was tinged with blue sadness and regret.

After I'd done the dishes, I went upstairs to make a call. James picked up on the second ring. "Custom Case," he said. "Oh shit, sorry, this is my cell. Hello?"

"James, it's Harry."

"Harry! Hello, good to hear your voice."

"I'll get right to the point: I got shitcanned from the lumberyard yesterday."

"What happened?"

"As far as I can tell," I said, "I was framed by a fearful crack-head who thought it was either him or me. He hid some invoices, and being the odd man out, I took the fall. Is your offer still open? I assure you, I'm very good at this sort of work."

"I have no doubt," he said. "When can you start? Monday? On the terms I mentioned the other night?"

"It's a deal. Do I come to the Red Hook building?"

"That's right, you know where it is. Come to my office at nine, and I'll show you around."

Just like that, I had another job. It was good to have friends in this world.

Karina and I set out in her car after lunch. It was a cool, clear, blazingly bright day. The breeze blew through the open windows and circulated in the car, making everything feel exciting and full of possibility. Being in Karina's car with her driving along always freed me somehow to say the things I couldn't quite say when we were inside, stationary. "I liked your friend Diane a lot," I said, almost shouting to be heard over the rushing wind and the roar and hiss of trucks.

Karina looked sideways at me. "You two were flirting like teenagers."

"We were," I said. "It's true. Karina, I have to tell you something very serious about your mother and me."

"What?" she said.

"We're not going to get back together," I said. "We're going to get a divorce."

It was a relief to tell her, and much easier to yell it in a moving car than to have to say it facing her at a quiet breakfast table.

"Really?" She whipped around to look at me, her hands on the wheel, not slowing down. Her expression was stricken and shocked. The car swerved slightly. She jerked her head back to look at the road.

"Yes," I said. "I have to accept that it's over."

"Are you sure? Did you talk to her?"

"If I could have talked to her," I said into the hullabaloo of traffic, "believe me, I would have. The last thing she said to me was that she wanted a divorce, and that was a long, long time ago. She isn't going to take me back. I have to stop trying to convince myself otherwise and get on with things."

"'Things' meaning Diane?"

I mulled this over for a few minutes.

"Hello, Dad?"

"Maybe," I said. "I know she's your friend. I know this is probably really weird."

"Probably!" she said. "Yes! Very weird!"

We drove without speaking for a number of miles, came to a knot of traffic, slowed down, crawled along, and didn't look at each other.

"Did you sleep with her the other night? In my house?" Karina asked.

"Of course not!" I said. My relief at my ability to be emphatically honest about this was so intense, I felt a little light-headed. "I would never do that."

"I'm not your mother," she said. "Just—you know."

The traffic cleared; we sped up again.

"Listen," I said, feeling nervous but determined. "I'd like to ask her out to dinner. I promise never to bring her to your house if you'd rather I didn't. I also promise I am not betraying your mother here. She doesn't give a damn what I do anymore."

Karina was tapping her thumbs on the steering wheel in a probably entirely unconscious imitation of Luz. "You're a grown man, Dad. I'm not your keeper. I guess, to be perfectly honest, I have to admit that you have every right to do whatever you want and I really appreciate that you told me all this." She stopped chattering for an instant. "I won't be a brat about this. I love Diane. She's been through a bad breakup. She could use a distraction right now. It's okay, really, I swear."

I reached over and rubbed the spot between her shoulder blades. "Easy there," I said.

"I'm trying here," she said.

"I know," I said. "So am I, believe me. It may not seem like it, but I am."

"This is all just kind of weird."

"It is weird. Your father is asking permission to date your friend. And on top of that, he lives in your house like some role-reversal kid."

"As long as you're home by ten." She tried to smile and almost succeeded. "And use a condom."

We drove into the driveway of Hector's house just before three and parked in the shade of a grove of scrubby ocean-side trees. It was chilly out here on the Island and much windier than it had been in the city. Karina had wisely brought a sweatshirt, which she put on now; I had unwisely ignored her advice to bring a jacket, and so had no recourse but to grit my teeth and get out of the car in my short-sleeved cotton shirt. We walked toward the house on the oyster-shell drive, our crunching footsteps the only sound besides the wind in the sand dunes and treetops. The house looked deserted. The windows were blue mirrors reflecting empty sky. No one was on the porch or lawn.

We climbed the steps and rang the bell. It vibrated in the hollow interior of the house.

"Maybe they're all out somewhere," said Karina, just as the door opened. "Oh!" she said.

The young woman's face showed no signs of recognition. Maybe she was a new member, or maybe she had been trained to pretend not to know outsiders, or maybe she had forgotten all about us. She looked identical to all the other young women we'd met when we were here before, fresh faced and neat and primly dressed, so it was impossible to know.

"We're here to visit Hector," I said. "I mean Bard. Is he around?"

The cult clone didn't budge. "He's being prepared right now. I'm sorry, please come another day."

"Prepared for what?" Karina asked.

She smiled and began to close the door.

Karina stuck her foot out and stopped it, but not as if she'd meant to; she did it as if her foot had involuntarily jerked that way.

"I'm Bard's little sister, and this is our dad," she said in her sweetest voice, ducking her head so a lock of red hair fell against her pale, freckled cheek, looking up through her lashes. "We were in the neighborhood and were hoping he could come for a walk maybe, and to dinner with us tonight. We miss him so much. Could you please just tell him we're here?"

The girl's blank expression hardly flickered. "Wait here," she said and closed the door.

Karina and I sat in some chairs on the porch around the side of the house and looked out at the ocean, which was corrugated and foamy from the wind. I shivered in my summer shirt.

"Do you think they'll let him come out?" Karina asked.

"I wonder whether they'll let us go in," I said.

"You're freezing! Want my sweatshirt?"

"I'm fine," I said.

We were almost whispering, as if what we were saying would reveal our true reason for being here if they overheard us. Karina looked as uneasy and guilty as I felt. "See him as much as you can," June and Emery had told us. "Reassure him of your love, give him news of people he knows, keep reminding him of his real self. The more contact you have, the better, and the more he trusts you, the better." At the moment, I felt as if we were betraying him, and I was afraid that he would know this instinctively. Our presence here felt false and manipulative, as if we were on a top-secret spy mission against our own son and brother, even though it was out of concern for him and a real desire to help him.

The cult maiden stuck her head around the corner of the house. "Come on in," she said. "He'll see you."

Karina and I exchanged a look; she sounded as if she were talking about an emperor in state on his gold throne, a pasha being fanned by eunuchs. We followed her through the front door and up the curved staircase to a big, austerely clean bedroom on the second floor. The room held four bunk beds with white coverlets, a number of plain wooden bureaus, and a straight-backed chair at a small table. Hector lay on one of the lower bunks. He was barefoot and his hair was wet, and he wore white cotton trousers and a white cotton shirt. He was smiling, his eyes closed. I was shocked to see how fat he'd become. His stomach was soft and wobbly under the thin cotton. His jaw had grown little baby-fat jowls.

"I told Lake to bring you upstairs," he said, still smiling, not opening his eyes. His voice was urgent with sincerity. "I must lie here for a while, but I can visit with you both as I do so."

I stifled a derisive cough. He sounded like a minor character in a grade-B sci-fi movie, where everyone used the same old-fashioned, stilted locution, as if human verbal communication were going to regress to faux courtly speech instead of becoming slangier and more modern the way it usually did.

"Please sit down," he added as if he had become accustomed to being obeyed.

I sat on the lower bunk nearest Hector's; Karina took the chair.

"How are you, Hector?" I asked. "Are you sick?"

He laughed, but he didn't sound amused. It was the laughter of someone who'd been asked a stupid, simpleminded question. "No," he said. "Not sick at all. I've never felt better in my life. I am extremely well."

Karina and I looked at each other. She started to say something, then caught herself, and we waited for him to go on. June had told us to do this when we wanted more information instead of asking direct questions, on the theory that if we left a space of silence, he would fill it. This whole dynamic felt so uneasily false, and this place gave me such willies, I could hardly stand it here another minute. I reminded myself that my son's life might be in danger, figuratively and maybe even literally. I had to do this, and I had to do it right. No matter how deceptive I felt, there was no better way to help him. I could see, on Karina's blunt little face, the same struggle to reconcile what we'd learned with her strong native instincts to tell the truth and be direct. I was glad Hector's eyes were closed; he would almost certainly have seen it too, in both of us.

Lake reappeared in the doorway. "Bard," she said, "can I offer your family some refreshments downstairs?"

"I'd like to talk to my father while I rest and prepare. Maybe my sister can help you all down in the kitchen."

Karina stood up. "I'd love to," she said. I could follow her reasoning as easily as if she were speaking aloud: It would be much easier to deal with strangers than her own brother, and she could ask the women as many questions as she wanted in the guise of honest curiosity. And she could do something with her hands.

Lake held the door for Karina, and they both disappeared.

Alone with my son, without Karina there to witness and share my perfidy, I felt a bit easier. I leaned back against the pillows on the bed and looked out at the sky and ocean, opposing blue expanses punctuated by whitecaps and tiny clouds, stitched together by diving gulls. Through the wavy old glass panes, it all looked unreal and pristine; I imagined that it was very easy to forget, living here, what was going on in most of the rest of the world. I imagined it was easy to forget everything. In the few minutes I'd been in this house, I'd begun to feel swayed by the collective influence of this weird group, or cult, whatever they were, felt my behavior influenced by theirs, even my thoughts. It was uncomfortable for me to admit this, even to myself, but once I'd realized it, I began to resist it. They were all exhausted, lost and paranoid and afraid, I reminded myself. They seemed happy, they seemed to have all the answers, and they seemed serenely content with whatever pecking order existed here, but that was all an illusion. Underneath, their real selves were seething, stifled. Any power this place had was derived from the squelching of authenticity and freedom. Historically, of course, I knew that this means of controlling people never worked for long. La la la, and so forth.

Hector was wriggling his hips a little, rocking them from side to side, his feet crossed at the ankles, his toes rubbing together. He'd always done this as a kid when he felt safe and cozy. It was the most genuine thing about him at the moment, that gesture, and I trusted it. I decided to cut the cult-intervention bullshit and just talk to him straight.

"You seem happy," I said.

"I am very happy," he said.

"What's going on today? Where is everyone?"

"The other men are at the job site, working on a house renovation. Some of the women are working in the gardens and others are cooking and others are cleaning. The women are all over the place." He laughed. This time, his laugh sounded almost like his real one.

"Where's Christa?"

"She's gone to the city on business. She'll be back tonight for the ceremony."

I did my best not to sound worried. "What ceremony?"

"Dad," he said, his voice cracking a little on the old name, which, now that he was a grown man, felt like both a formality and an endearment, "I'm being tested tonight. The handmaidens are preparing me to meet the challenge of Hashem's will for me, anointing my head with oil, washing my feet, blessing me, and praying over me. I'm gathering my strength and powers. I must rest today, for tonight will bring the truth."

"What are the tests?" I asked my plump, supine, oily headed, clean-footed, prayed-over son with a slowly thudding heart.

"The ones Yashua passed, in our first incarnation, when he walked the earth," said Hector without a flicker of awareness of how insane this sounded. "I must perform three miracles."

"What miracles?"

"I must walk on water, change tap water into wine, and heal my sick sister Lake with the laying-on of my hands."

"Lake is sick?"

"She has lupus," said Hector.

"Do you know how to cure lupus?" I asked.

"Christa has faith that I can and will. And I have faith in her." Under its new rim of fat, his jaw tightened, so slightly that if I hadn't been watching him with all my attention, I might not have noticed.

"I hope she's right," I said. "You can't swim, Hector."

"I will have no need of swimming. My feet will not penetrate the water's surface."

"Ah," I said. "I see." I wanted to laugh out loud at the ridiculousness of it all, the sheer clichéd unimaginativeness of the three miracles, which were like a kids' game, and at the way my son, born and bred in Brooklyn, was now talking, flattening his vowels with a twang; it occurred to me that he was imitating Christa's western accent and fake-biblical diction. What a protoplasmic puppy my son was, lying there so self-importantly with his lips pursed, with fresh young handmaidens to oil him up and a former stripper hot-tamale girlfriend to convince him he was the Second Coming of Christ and entice him with promises of matrimonial, God-approved sex. We'd never get him out of here at this rate unless a better offer came along, but what could possibly be better than this?

"You have no faith," Hector said with his ancient, lifelong impatience with me. "Therefore you cannot imagine what can be accomplished by those who possess it. 'Blessed is the man who trusts in the Lord and who has made the Lord his hope and confidence.' 'It is done unto you as you believe.' 'If you can believe, all things are possible to him who believeth.' The Bible is the truth, Dad. It's the only truth."

"I disagree vehemently, as always," I said, "my dearest son." I could see him start to tense up and begin to marshal a biting rebuttal. "But," I added with unctuous disingenuousness intended to soothe and placate, "I respect your beliefs, although they're completely different from mine. Can you say the same?"

"No," he said. "I would be lying if I said I thought your belief, or lack of belief, was a fraction as valid or true as my faith. This is absolute truth, Dad, not relative or comparative. You either believe or you don't. You're either right or wrong. There is no middle ground. And you do not believe, and so I fear for your mortal soul. I fear for your future, after the Rapture, burning in the lake of fire for all eternity. I wish I could save your soul, but only you can do that, by accepting Yashua as your lord and savior."

"That will never happen," I said. "I'm just not made that way. Hector, your mother is worried about you. Will you please phone her? Soon? Tomorrow?"

"Why should I?" He sounded slightly hurt. "She wouldn't speak to me if I did."

"She might," I said. "Things are very hard for her lately. The hospital closed. And we're getting a divorce."

He opened his eyes and stared at me. "Are you having another affair?"

I gave an angry bark of laughter. I deserved it, I supposed, but given the circumstances, the question irked and dismayed me. Then, seeing how serious Hector looked, I stifled my hotheadedness and became appropriately solemn. "She thinks I am, but I swear to you on whatever you hold sacred that I am not. Anyway, whether I am or not turns out not to be the point. She's through with me. She's just using that as an excuse to get rid of me."

Hector closed his eyes again, but his expression was no longer beatific.

"I'm sorry to spring this on you like this, on such a big day for you," I said. "I came out here today expressly to tell you, and I know the timing is bad, but you should know that this is going on."

"Sure," he said. "Of course. And I will call her."

"Thank you," I said.

"I'm not doing it for you," he said. "I'm doing it for her."

"Even so. I'm glad. She will be so happy to hear from you."

"If you say so," he said with heavy skepticism. He looked painfully young and vulnerable to me. Maybe he always would, no matter how old he got. I couldn't imagine a time when I wouldn't feel this mix of fatherly tenderness for and exasperation with my son. He was so maddeningly didactic and condescending, and so endearing, admirable, intelligent. "Do you still love her?" he asked.

"I'll always love her," I said. "She's been my wife since before you were born. But she's through with me, Hector. I tried everything I could to convince her that I wasn't sleeping with Marion—"

"She thought you were sleeping with Marion?" He laughed. "Well. That's a new one. And you weren't?"

Something had shifted. I could feel Hector fully present with me, his old, real self, not his new, weird, messianic self. We were lying parallel to each other, separated only by a few feet of air, both of us on our backs.

"Of course I wasn't sleeping with Marion."

"You're still not?"

"I'm not sleeping with anyone, Hector. And Marion's got a new boyfriend who's barely older than you are."

"Seems to be going around," he said. "Christa's forty-eight. Did you tell Mom you and Marion weren't having an affair?"

"I told her till I was blue in the face, and she still wouldn't believe me. But it doesn't matter, in the end. She wants a divorce, and I'm giving her one. You know her. You can't get her to do anything she doesn't want to do. She never admits she's wrong, either."

"I think she might have, once," Hector said. "Like ten years ago, when she lost a bet we made about something, I can't remember what. But even then, she claimed that she wasn't completely wrong, she just didn't have all the facts beforehand. She tried to paint it as a misunderstanding. I was like, no way, Mom, pay up. I could tell it almost killed her to give me that dollar."

We both laughed. "It's good to see you," I said, turning my head to look at him. "I've missed you, Hector. So has your sister. I wish we could see more of you."

"I'm right here," he said.

"I know, geographically you're not far away. This new group seems like something you've wanted to find for a long time. I'm happy you've found it, but you know, I'm your dad. I'm a little worried about some things, a few aspects of your life here that don't quite add up."

"You think we're a cult," he said, sounding amused. "You think we're all brainwashed, right?"

I put my hands behind my head. "It had crossed my mind."

Hector exhaled through his nose vehemently, but it wasn't an angry sound. "I am deeply happy," he said, sounding like his new self again, as if the word "cult," as he spoke it, had triggered a mechanism, defensive or otherwise, whereby he phased back into the persona of Bard and stuffed Hector back into squashed submission, like a sleeping bag in its sack. "This is the place I've been seeking all of my life. I was a soul in the wilderness, crying out, and now I've found my true home."

"And you're really going to marry this . . . Christa?"

"It has been foreordained. We are soul mates."

"How much do you know about her?"

"Everything," he said. "We have no secrets, she and I."

"You know about her past?"

"She was a stripper," he said. "She's been in prison for embezzlement. She has repented deeply of her sins. She has come through it all and is purified, reborn in Yashua."

"And this test tonight . . . I know I sound like an overprotective old hen, but how are you going to walk on water? That sounds at best impossible and at worst dangerous."

"I'll walk into the pond," he said, "and the soles of my feet will be held up by my faith in God alone, acting upon the waves and changing their nature."

"What pond? Is it deep?"

"It is pretty deep." He laughed in his new, superior manner. "I'm not going to drown. I promise."

"You swear?"

We were looking straight into each other's eyes. Mine had worry and judgment in them, his nothing but unshakable conviction.

"I swear," he said, mocking my fear, and I had no choice but to believe him.

Chapter Twenty

When Lake came upstairs, Hector told her that Karina and I were staying for the ceremony tonight.

"Have Birch give them a tour," he told her. His voice was impersonal, smooth. His earlier intimate, frank manner had completely changed with the presence of Lake. "Father, I'll see you at dinner."

He had never called me Father before in his entire life. I apparently had a new name now, too.

I followed Lake downstairs. She looked perfectly healthy to me, but then, how did I know what a person with lupus was supposed to look like? To my knowledge, I'd never met one before.

"I'd love to show them around," said Birch when Lake found her folding clean napkins in the dining room and informed her of Hector's instructions. I followed them both into the kitchen, where Karina and two other women were sitting at a worktable, picking through an enormous pile of mussels. A heap of fish lay on the sideboard.

"You don't catch your own fish?" Karina was asking.

"Not always," said one of the women, yet another fresh-faced girl with nut-brown hair in a bun and bright blue eyes. Someone in central casting was due for a raise. "Sometimes we do. But we always get our own clams and mussels."

"So are you self-sustaining here?" Karina asked.

"No," she said, sounding slightly defensive. "But we're becoming more and more so all the time. The end times are upon us. The earth is going to erupt in famine and disease. Until we're taken to Hashem's eternal shining kingdom, we will be safe here."

"I'm Birch," said Birch to Karina. "Your brother asked me to give you and your father a tour of the place." She added to Lake, "I will of course be back for my kitchen duties."

"No, women's prayer is before that," Lake said.

"Yes," said Birch. "Of course!"

"She's a new member," said Lake. "It takes a while."

Birch's face was stony. I could tell she was mentally knifing herself in the gut for forgetting. Something had darkened here since our first visit, when they had been so festive and welcoming. The air felt bluer and heavier; everyone looked tense. Well, today was a strange day for them, portentous, high stakes, and Karina and I had shown up unexpectedly, uninvited. It had been up to Hector, apparently, whether or not he would see us. And it had been at his directive alone that we'd been allowed to stay. No one seemed to question his authority. His standing here had obviously skyrocketed since last time. It made sense—he was probably the Messiah, after all, and he was about to marry their leader and guru. It occurred to me that maybe what I was feeling from these women wasn't censure or dislike but shyness mixed with apprehensiveness.

"There's a lot to remember here," I said, feeling sorry for them, knowing what I knew about their lives here. "I would imagine, anyway. You work so hard and have so many responsibilities."

Birch said with eager alacrity, "My life here is so joyous! I am thankful for every task I perform in his name. Every moment here is full of the presence of Hashem. We don't want to sleep, even, for fear of missing a conscious moment in his grace."

"That's for sure," said Lake. "I pinch myself at night in bed to stay awake!"

"Sometimes I slap my own cheeks."

"I take off the covers so the cold keeps me awake."

"Sleep is good for you," said Karina. "I get eight hours a night, and if I don't, I'm a raving bitch."

The women looked at her with smiling pity.

Birch led us out the mudroom door onto a recently built screened-in porch whose beams were still green with newness and that smelled equally of fresh wood and animal droppings. One wall was lined with metal cages. In each an enormous, immobile rabbit sat humped and quiet. Sodden bits of lettuce littered the wooden floor. "These are the bunnies," she said. "We are their stewards, and they reward us with meat."

She led us outside and showed us a huge wooden bin with a hinged lid. "The compost," she said, opening the lid to emit a rich, vegetal stench. "Everything organic goes in here, returning earth to the earth."

"You should get some worms," said Karina.

"I know," said Birch. "I'm working on it. I can't wait to get some red wigglers in there."

Outside, away from the group, Birch had dropped some of her stiffness. I could begin to see the person she had been before she'd turned into a Hashem freak: earnest, slightly overbearing, easily excited. I couldn't tell much about her figure in that long skirt and loose-fitting smock, but she seemed to be built like one of the ripe-breasted, strong-limbed country lasses I'd tumbled around with as a teenager. She was pretty in a moonfaced, bright-eyed way that I could imagine might have had a lot of allure for some men if she hadn't been under mind control. Actually, come to think of it, a woman under mind control might be a turn-on for the type of man who liked moonfaced, bright-eyed nature girls. I could imagine my old nemesis Dan Levy blowing a lot of hot smoke in her direction, for example.

"You joined this group recently?" I asked as she led us to a small, neat outbuilding beyond the sheds.

"About a month ago," she said. "Everyone is so thankful for our brother Bard. We trust that he is our lord, come back to lead us."

She'd only been here a month, and she was already talking like this with a completely straight face.

"But what if he isn't?" Karina said. "What if he fails the tests?"

Birch's face went joyfully blank. I could see a door slamming shut in her brain at the very suggestion. "Oh, he won't," she said. "Christa has foreseen it."

"I've known Hector all my life," said Karina. "He's my brother, he's a great guy, but the Messiah? I think not."

Birch looked at her as if she might have argued with this, once upon a time. Something kept her from it; maybe she realized how futile it was, maybe she thought Karina and I weren't worth engaging in this discussion, because we obviously weren't likely new members.

"These are our girls," she said, opening the door to the chicken coop. A soft explosion of tiny pinfeathers erupted from the doorway. I heard rustling and a broody, throaty noise within. "Cluck cluck, little sweeties! Oh look, eggs."

We dutifully regarded a flock of large, golden chickens, then trooped off to a nearby greenhouse to admire burgeoning lettuces and tomato plants. Karina began to ask a lot of pointed, half-didactic eco-freegan questions about pesticides, planting cycles, and chicken feed. Birch answered them with apparent openness: no, they used no chemical pesticides, only natural repellents; yes, they mixed their own chicken feed and it was all organic; no, they didn't plant by the moon's phases, they didn't believe in that.

"This is a great setup you have out here," said Karina. "I wish I could do the same, but I live in Brooklyn."

"You should move out here," said Birch.

Karina smiled. Their gaze held for a second longer than necessary.

Were they flirting? Aha! I would have bet that lesbianism wasn't accepted here at Hashem House. So she was either closeted, in denial, or determined to overcome it.

"Are you married, Birch?" I asked her.

"Not yet," she said with a wide smile. "I am praying that Hashem leads me to my soul mate very soon."

"Is everyone married here?"

"Oh, not yet," she said. "We have been blessed by four unions, and now three of my sisters are pregnant. Hashem is revealing to us in the fullness of time the paths we might take together in married unions. The union of husband and wife is the mirror of the perfect blissful union of the soul with Hashem. Not until we're married are we truly one with him."

"I see," I said with an odd, entirely unexpected pang for my wife. The strangeness of not being with her anymore hit me in the gut out of nowhere. I couldn't remember for a moment why we were apart.

"And now, the gardens! Over here," she said. We followed her up a path through some scrubby trees into a cultivated field ringed with chicken wire, mirrors winking everywhere, a finely crafted scarecrow in the middle looking very much like a man being punished for some socially deviant crime, dressed in idiot's clothing and hoisted up on a stake. Inch-high plants grew in neat rows. The field glittered and shone with different shades and shapes of green, rows of ruffled, pointed, or broad leaves in emerald green, dark green, pale green.

"Wow," Karina said. "This is just fantastic. Did you do this? You've only been here a month!"

"They started before I came, of course, and Lake and I and two other sisters have been working very hard to get in a really good bunch of stuff," said Birch. "We work from dawn till dusk, practically." Something changed then; she slid back into her less authentic-seeming persona, the ecstatic, wide-eyed personality everyone around here seemed to imitate and affect. It seemed to me that this shift was usually triggered by a negative thought or a niggling doubt. "I just love this life," she was saying. "I am so happy here." She opened her arms to indicate the gardens, the house, the ocean, the sky. "It's heaven on earth to live with my brothers and sisters in peace and harmony. I never dreamed this would be possible."

"Where are you from?" I asked.

"I grew up on a farm upstate, in Columbia County, near the Berkshires, which you'd think would be great, but I hated it there. My family was so decadent and atheistic. My parents smoked pot, they believed in social freedoms, but they had no moral basis. Then I moved to New York and worked in an office for three years and tried to save up enough to buy my own land. It was death, living death. Now I awaken with the sun and my hands are in the earth all day, growing things, and I pray with my best friends, my new family. What could be better?" She put the flats of her palms together under her chin, prayerful. "I love Christa so much. She's our spiritual mother, a true child of Hashem. Now I'll show you the orchard."

The orchard was a field of small, wind-gnarled apple, plum, and peach trees. "They don't look like much, but Lake tells me they produce enough fruit to keep us canning around the clock during the hottest days of the year." She laughed. "It might sound crazy, but I can't wait. Now I should get back for prayers. You two should feel free to walk or just sit on the porch, up to you."

Karina and I wandered off to the beach. I shivered. The wind was stiff and chilly and briny smelling.

"Oh my God," said Karina as we came over the dunes. "I feel like my head is going to explode from being in the kitchen with those women. They're so incredibly scared to say anything wrong. I asked them all these direct questions, and I felt it was like talking to a corporate customer-service person, the answers were all scripted and fake and programmed. How can Hector live here?"

"I think he loves it here," I said. "I feel like it's a dream come true for him. He gets better treatment than the rest of them. He's like their puppy or something. They take care of him. I'm much less worried about that aspect of things now. But while you were in the kitchen, he told me that tonight is the night he has to pass these Messiah tests. He has to walk on water. That, I'm a bit worried about. I'm glad we'll be here, just in case."

Karina hunched into her hoodie and shoved her hands into the pockets. "Maybe he'll fall in, and they'll laugh at him, and we can pull him out of the pond and take him back to Brooklyn."

"Best-case scenario, I guess," I said.

"But then, on the other hand, do you ever wonder what would become of him if he left this place? It's not like he had so much else going on before he joined. It's not like it's so great out there, either."

"I think about that a lot," I said, "and I keep reaching the same conclusion. It's better to be lost and floundering and in full possession of your own mind than to be controlled by fundamentalist belief. If I believe anything, it's that. And a few other things."

"I agree," said Karina, "but I have to keep reminding myself."

The damp beige sand was stippled with tire marks and footprints. Here and there, plastic bottles and tampon applicators had washed up to the high tide mark. We passed a dead seagull, a scraggy mass of dirty feathers. A transparent, shallow wave of seawater rushed up the beach and nipped at our shoes. The sunlight was watery and diffuse. I inhaled the air deeply through my nose and felt the atomized salt spray invigorate my lungs.

Into my mind came a few lines from García Lorca's hauntingly sinister "Malagueña": "*Y hay un olor a sal / y a sangre de hembra / en los nardos febriles / de la marina.*" Luz used to love to recite that poem to me in as close to a fiery, soulful trance as she ever got, postcoital, inhaling the smells our bodies made together: the salt smell of menstrual blood, the feverish spikenards . . . what were spikenards? I had always imagined they were some kind of slippery seaweed, waving underwater like a woman's long black hair. It was strange and hard, remembering Luz naked with flared nostrils in our bed, reciting Spanish poetry, to believe that our marriage was over. I kept catching myself thinking about her as if she were still my wife. I wondered now how long it took for a finished marriage to clear the synapses.

When Karina and I got back to the house, the kitchen was full of clattering pot lids, female voices, and the smells of roasting meat and baking fish. Hector was still upstairs preparing for the night's ordeal, I gathered; the men had returned from their construction job, sweaty and dirty, and were rushing around carrying things, building some sort of wood structure outside, bringing in wildflowers and flowering branches from some other garden we hadn't been shown by Birch; evidently the flower garden was not her province.

Karina and I sat on the porch in two Adirondack chairs while the men dragged the tables and chairs outside onto the freshly mown lawn, set them with the full formal regalia of tablecloths, cutlery, glasses, and china, set out vases full of flowers as centerpieces, and prepared a makeshift sideboard.

"Christa is back!" someone yelled, and there were cries of joy and excitement. Several of her followers gathered to greet her car as it pulled up. She emerged from the backseat holding bags and packages marked "Calypso" and "Anthropologie." When the driver got out, I thought I recognized him; he might have been one of the men we'd met last time, the blond, frat-boyish Wing, but he looked like all the other men in his beard and short ponytail, his plain cotton pants and shirt. He opened the trunk and took out more bags and parcels and followed Christa up the steps. She was wearing a long white dress that showed some cleavage and the kind of gold, strapped sandals that used to be popular with Greek goddesses. Her hair was so blond it was almost white. She looked artificial and sexy and shrewd. She smiled when she caught sight of Karina and me, but not before I'd registered a tiny flicker of something other than utter joy at our unexpected presence here. She disappeared into the house without a word to us.

Dinner was served at seven o'clock. We all gathered around the tables. Christa invited Karina and me to sit at her table and placed us near her and the empty chair I gathered was being saved for Hector. She was distant, abstracted, and said almost nothing to us. When we had all sat down and were helping ourselves to food, Hector came out onto the front porch. He wore a different, more formal set of white cotton pants and white cotton smock-type shirt. His feet were bare. His hair was still wet looking from the oil. He walked down the steps and joined Christa, Karina, and me at our table. There was silence as soon as he appeared. He sat down. He raised his wineglass and said, "Blessings to you all."

"Blessed be Yashua," everyone said, and we all started to eat.

Hector smiled at Christa. "My love," he said. "Welcome back. How was the city?"

"Intense," she said, looking into his eyes with her own dizzyingly blue ones, not breaking their gaze even to blink. Her diction was that particularly Californian mixture of surfer girl and guru. "The people all seemed so lost! So filled with fear and emptiness. Rushing around, trying to get from A to B to C, talking on their cell phones. It is a blessing to be back here where everything we do has purpose and meaning. Like coming home to paradise."

They were very obviously performing, probably for Karina and me and the others at the table with us, but just as likely for themselves. It was impossible to gauge the temperature or quality of their real feelings for each other. Their bond reminded me of an arranged marriage between those who used to be nobility and were now movie stars: it seemed largely overt, existing primarily to convince others of its authenticity for the purposes of what used to be power and was now publicity. In the case of Christa and Hector, it was both. Their fans were also their subjects; they were both the show and the people who ran it. Watching my son talk to this woman as if she were his equal, his consort, gave me the strong feeling that he was no longer mine in any sense of the word. However fraught and imperfect our bond had been since he was born, it had been deep, and now it was broken. I knew somehow that if he ever did decide to leave this group, his exodus wouldn't mean a return to his family. He might reestablish a connection with his mother, but that would be different.

Even more interesting to me was the fact that my virgin son seemed to be at least half in control in this relationship, whatever it may have been privately between them, with this much-older, very experienced, undeniably powerful woman. I wondered whether he could possibly love her, or whether he was too wrapped up in himself to pay attention to another human being. To be a fanatical believer of any kind required an enormous ego, or so it had always seemed to me: God was created in the image of his believers. Maybe Hector and Christa saw in each other complementary, opposite images of their own idealized selves. That struck me as a fairly legitimate reason to fall in love with and even marry someone. Luz and I had done something similar, and it had brought out the best in both of us, at least it had for a while, until the inevitable had set in.

I felt flummoxed and impressed by Hector's evident self-possession. Where had he learned that? Not from his father, surely. My own mother, that tall drink of correct, sharp-eyed, puritanical ice water, had led me to expect no warmth or sympathy from women even as she proclaimed me a boy wonder, her brightest light. Luz's half-withheld ardor, her squinting askance at me with low expectations even as she married me and bore my children and called me a poetic genius, had been much more in line with my youthful experiences than the wanton, unearned adoration of my high school and college girlfriends. Luz's bracingly skeptical attitude toward me had always made me feel safe and comfortable, knowing anciently as I did both the limitations and possibilities of this sort of love.

Maybe Luz's blind adoration of Hector had given him this

preternatural confidence in his dealings with women; I had never seen him with one before, so this was my first and perhaps only chance to find out.

Dinner ended, some sort of music began; there was a prayer circle during which everyone was vocally thankful for their brother Bard's existence and filled with hope and trust that he would receive from his father Hashem the ability to perform the three miracles tonight. Karina and I stood on the periphery. I had to repress a strong urge to let out a mocking howl of laughter. Somehow, I kept a respectful silence.

Finally it was time to traipse to the pond and watch Hector fall in and flail around trying not to drown. As we walked inland single file through grassy sand and scrub, past the gardens and orchard, to an edge of a still, midsized pond, I thought with no small measure of internal irony what a shame it was that his mother wasn't here to witness what was surely, to Hector, the most important event of his life. It was like missing his first steps, or his graduation from high school. Despite everything, I felt irrationally lucky to be here, and I missed Luz. What she would have made of this scenario, I could well imagine. She would not have been willing to hold her tongue the way Karina and I had. By now, after saying one too many cutting things to Hector about the ridiculousness of this outfit, she would have been told by him to stop being disrespectful, then have entered into an almost loverlike spat with him about doctrine and belief and observance and the truth, then been told to wait in the car, where she would simmer, in a towering rage, before exploding back into the house to fly at Hector again with her questions and her outraged objections to what he was doing.

I was relieved, in one sense, that she wasn't here, but picturing her engaging Hector's fruity beliefs head-on, directly challenging his statements about Jesus, not to mention his claim that he was the Messiah, gave me a strong pang, almost painful, of longing emptiness. Luz was a hotheaded, hot-hearted force. I was made of cooler, more temperate stuff, a cool fan of skepticism that had met the volcanic gusts of her absoluteness. We had been good for each other, she and I; she had enlivened me, amused me, warmed me, and I had steadied and challenged her. Without her tremendous, energetic narrow-mindedness to come up against, my need for nuance and shades of meaning felt slack, mealymouthed. Arguing with her had given my unbelief a strong backbone. Now it felt colorless and inert, lifeless and dull.

The whole group of us stood onshore as Hector was rowed out toward us from the opposite side of the pond, tracing the moon's rippling reflection as it rose behind him. He stood in the boat facing us like the iconic Founding Father painting while one of the bearded thankful men, as I had begun to think of them all in the aggregate, plied the oars. I could just make out the figure of Christa kneeling before him in the prow, her head tilted back and her hands clasped together, no doubt gazing at him in some kind of reverential adulation. The night was warm, humid, the only sounds the rhythmic bleat of crickets and the creak of the oars. I couldn't hear the ocean; this far inland, the sound of the surf was muffled by the dunes. The mood among the small crowd onshore was hushed, excited, and not, as far as I could tell, in the slightest bit nervous or doubtful. I found myself being carried away by this highly aestheticized tableau vivant, as if I'd been invited to watch a scene in a film shot on location and starring my son as Jesus.

When they had gone out about fifty feet from shore, the boat stopped and the oarsman stuck one of his paddles vertically into the pond to steady the boat and perhaps to show us all that it was at least two feet and not two inches deep. Christa reached into the water, running her hand along the side, stood in the boat, and dabbed some water on Hector's forehead. Then he turned and stepped from the boat onto the surface of the water. He did not sink. My eyes went dry from staring, unblinking, watching as his feet stayed on the surface of the pond. Karina, next to me, put her hand on my forearm and leaned against me. Some of the others nearby gasped in excited amazement. Hector put out one foot, then another, and glided over the water almost as if he were skating or dancing. He was like a balloon man, weightless and incorporeal. It might have been a hilariously magical sight, this chubby man on the moonlit pond's surface, all dressed in white. He raised his arms to what he clearly imagined were the heavens. I pictured a temporary wooden pier below him, holding him up.

"Thanks be to Hashem!" Christa called from the boat in a raw, raucous voice.

"Praise be to Bard!" everyone responded in an overwrought chorus.

Hector walked back over the pond, back to the boat, and stepped into it. I was almost waiting for someone to yell "Cut," but instead there was weeping in the crowd around me. The boat came toward us to land on shore. Hector stepped onto the bank and was embraced and kissed in a mood of wild hysteria. He accepted their adoration, beatific, quietly self-important.

Karina and I stood by, totally irrelevant to all of this. She was silent and consternated. I felt an odd sense of paternal pride mixed with a good dollop of disappointment; what, exactly, was I proud of my son for doing? Hoodwinking a crowd of mind-controlled cult members? There were so many other things he could have done. Again, I stifled a hyena-like laugh. Back when I was his age, kids were setting the world on fire, or so we'd thought. I watched as Hector was enfolded into his group's ecstatic hugs. He didn't seem even to remember that we were there.

"Come on," I said to Karina when I realized that Hector had no intention of coming over to us. We followed the crowd back up to the house, up the porch steps, and into the dining room.

With everyone standing at one end of the emptied room, Christa stood by a small table at the other end and lifted a glass pitcher of what looked like plain tap water and said, "By his faith in Hashem, Bard shall turn this water into the finest wine." She held it up for all of us to see, and handed it to Hector, who stood next to her. He poured some into a wineglass and stuck two babyish fingers into the water and began swirling them around slowly. Lo and behold, the liquid turned red as blood, or wine, or chemically altered tap water. There were cheers, and handmaidens began opening wine bottles and pouring wine for everyone, passing glasses around. Karina groaned audibly and held tight to me, turning away from the group and muttering into my ear, "I can't take it anymore. This is bullshit!" We were handed glasses of wine from someone as the whole group raised their glasses in the air and drank a toast to Bard and Hashem.

I watched as Hector lifted his own wine, or whatever it was, to his lips. He appeared to take a sip, but who knew, and then he set the glass on the table. His face was clear and blank; he looked comfortable and solemn. Christa, standing next to him, said, "Now Sister Lake, approach and be healed." Lake came forward; Hector put his hands on her head, looked into her eyes, held her head between his palms for a while, then kissed her forehead and said, "Go forth in good health, Sister Lake."

"Thank you," she said. She turned toward the crowd. Everyone waited. She touched her chest, her own arms, her face. "I feel wonderful," she said. "I am well! Praise Bard! Praise Yashua!"

"How the fuck does she know?" Karina said into my ear, her frustrated voice very quiet in the hubbub of congratulations and joy.

"The power of suggestion," I said.

"This whole thing is a pathetic trick. He knows it too. Jesus, Dad, he's totally in charge of this place, isn't he?"

I looked over at Hector, who looked back at me with a cold, distant, affectless expression, as if he hadn't meant to look at me at all or meet my gaze and had done so by accident. He looked away as if he hadn't seen me and walked arm in arm with Christa out of the room to join the celebration spilling out onto the back lawn. It might as well have been their wedding. We might as well have been crashing it.

"Let's get out of here," said Karina. Her head was resting on my biceps; she was too short to reach my shoulder. "I feel sick."

"Out we go," I said, and led her to the door.

We walked down the drive. Behind us, the huge house was lit up. On the lawn, a little band of accordion, guitar, and violin was playing. We heard shouts, laughter, singing.

"I'll be right back," I said. "Wait here, get in the car, I'm going to go and talk to Hector."

Before Karina had a chance to talk me out of anything, I headed for the back of the house, where they were all gathered.

Hector and Christa stood at the farthest edge of the lawn, toward the driveway. I approached them from the back and got there before they heard me coming.

When I touched Hector's elbow, he jumped and turned. Before he saw who was there, his expression was defensive, defenseless. Then he recognized me and relaxed. "Dad," he said.

"We have to talk, Hector," I said. "I need to ask you some questions."

"We're in the middle of a party," he said.

"Talk to your father," said Christa. "It's always good to help people understand what we're doing."

I gazed into her eyes. They were vacant and self-righteous, without fear or mercy, the eyes of a sociopath who would do anything to anyone without a qualm.

"Come for a walk with me, Hector," I said. "For five minutes."

I could feel how reluctantly Hector separated himself from Christa and walked with me around the edge of the lawn. The sandy path gleamed with dull luminescence.

"What is it, Dad?"

"You didn't perform any miracles," I said. "I can't believe those poor suckers fell for that. They're under mind control, of course; otherwise they would have laughed at you."

Hector was silent. I waited for him to respond, but he walked along behind me on the path without a word. I could hear him breathing, hear his soft footsteps, otherwise I might have thought he'd gone back to the party.

We came to the pond and stood together on the shore looking across the water.

"I want you to know something, Hector. I can understand why you'd want to live here. I understand why you'd want to live with these people, too. They all seem very idealistic and sincere, and very well intentioned. A nice bunch of kids. But Christa is not nice, and she's not sincere, and she's not well intentioned. She's a crook, and she's got you playing Bonnie to her Clyde. I can't stand by and watch you turn into a criminal."

"I'm not a criminal," said Hector. He was trying his hardest to sound calm and serene, but there was a microquiver in his voice. He was, even after all Christa's seductive instructions and flattering determinations, still the boy Luz and I had raised. He still had a conscience, and it wasn't perfectly clear at the moment. "What law have I broken?"

"Don't pull that shit with me," I said. "All these people have given every cent they have to Christa. They've given everything up. You've tricked them into believing a lie. And of course you know Christa's already gone to jail once."

"She has repented of that," he said. "She has come clean in the blood of—"

"There was a platform out there, under the water," I said. "You and Christa put it there."

Hector stared out at the water. A track of moonlight shimmered on the quiet waves. The air smelled piney and salty and fresh. I was shivering, but I wasn't quite ready to go home yet.

"I could row myself out there right now and find it," I said. "There's no use denying it."

"You wouldn't understand, Dad," said Hector.

"Understand what?"

"The need to use gentle deception to achieve a higher end. You wouldn't understand any of it. You have no faith; to you it's all one thing or another."

"To me, it's perfectly clear. You pretended to do something, and you actually did something else. You lied, in fact, three times tonight."

"In the service of Yashua, certain steps become necessary," he said. "To achieve the final victory, we need to share an absolute certainty together, this group. We have to live in solid and harmonious belief."

"You mean Christa needs total control, and she's using you to get it. She produced the Messiah; now everyone is doubly bound to her. Including you. Especially you. I hope you won't end up the lapdog of a con artist. I hope you'll eventually realize that it's not worth it. You're a true believer, Hector. As far as that goes, you're the real thing, and this is just lies and trickery. Christa's corrupting you with all this power and glory. And you'll never be able to stay true to what you really believe."

"Fine words, Dad. You have no idea what you're talking about. No idea at all. Let's go back now. I've let you have your say."

We walked back to the house. The party had gone on without us, and when Hector reappeared, there was a general shout of joy. He didn't say good-bye or good night to me; he disappeared into the crowd and was embraced as their savior.

I walked back down the drive, teeth chattering. Karina rolled down her window when she saw me coming. "How did it go?" she asked.

"He's not leaving anytime soon," I told her. "He's having too much fun."

"How am I going to tell Mom?" she said as I got into the car.

"You're not," I said. "I'm going to tell her. It has to be me."

She started the engine. "You promise?"

"Of course," I said.

"That place could be kind of great if they weren't so full of shit," said Karina, turning from the driveway onto the road. "Why do they have to be so full of shit?"

"I think that's the point."

We drove home in the moonlight. I felt nostalgic and embittered. What Karina felt, I didn't know, but I imagined it was something along those lines. Moonshine, I thought. Flimflammery, chicanery, humbuggery, quackery, hogwash.

Chapter Twenty-one

Diane had asked me to come at 7:00, but, fueled by eagerness, I made it to Kensington by 6:55, so I locked my bike to a lamppost down the block from her place and dawdled around her block and the next one until I was a correct, thoughtful ten minutes late. I climbed the steps of her building, a three-story brick row house that was architecturally identical to every other house on her block, and rang the doorbell. A yappy dog barked its fool head off somewhere in the house, but it didn't scare me away. I heard footsteps. Diane opened the door. She looked flushed and sparkly eyed, which was exactly how I felt, like a teenager on a date with his big crush. "Come in," she said, sounding a little breathless.

I followed her, unable to resist the temptation to notice how pretty her ass looked in the formfitting summer skirt she had on, up two flights to her apartment. The high-pitched barking grew louder as we passed the second-floor apartment, then subsided as we mounted, and trailed off into yips as we went into Diane's place and shut the door behind us. We were in a small kitchen; something was bubbling in a pot on the stove.

"Glad that's not your dog," I said.

"So," she said, smiling, turning to face me, "let's see, can I offer you a drink?"

I handed her the bottle of white Bordeaux I'd bought, chilled, at the wine store in Karina's neighborhood. "I think it's still pretty cold, but maybe a few minutes in the freezer—"

"Thank you for bringing that!" she said. "It looks great." She opened the bottle, struggling a bit with the cork while I stood by, hovering, thinking I should have done it myself. We took our glasses of wine into the bright, crowded living room and sat side by side on her couch. The knee-level plate on the coffee table in front of us held a round white cheese, a knife, and some round white crackers. Nervously, my adrenaline peaking and crashing, I cut a piece of cheese and put it on a cracker and stuck it into my mouth. "Nice place," I said with my mouth full.

She looked around her living room. "Do you think? I have so much stuff, it doesn't really fit in here. I keep meaning to get some freegans to come and haul half of it away."

"It's cozy," I said after I swallowed. I hadn't been on a first date in more than thirty years; Samantha didn't count. The other night, Karina had made us an instantly intimate threesome, we'd been drinking beer, it had all felt so easy. Now, at Diane's place, just the two of us, dinner on the stove, nothing to do after we ate but go to bed, a couple of obligatory hours to fill until then with conversation, the liquid ease between us had cooled and hardened. I felt a resurgence of the worry I'd felt as I toweled myself off post-shower just before biking over here. Because of all the bicycling and walking I'd been doing in recent months, I was in much better shape than I had been when Luz had thrown me out last winter and called me withered and washed up, but I was pushing fifty-eight, things were not what they had been and never would be again no matter what I did. Meanwhile, Diane looked so good, her face firm, her arm muscles lovely and bare in her sleeveless blouse, her calves full and supple. What did women do to keep themselves so youthful looking? I ate another piece of Brie, no cracker this time (they were a bit stale), hoping she wasn't disappointed by what she saw in the clear light of evening. I had shaved carefully, had dressed with great pains to look presentable in a fresh white shirt and clean summer-weight trousers, but I should have trimmed my shaggy white eyebrows, I realized now, should have got myself a new haircut.

"I got divorced a few years back," Diane was saying. She ran her palms down the fronts of her thighs as if she were drying them on her skirt. "I didn't want to pay to put all my things in storage, so I just sort of moved them in here temporarily right after we separated, thinking I'd get a bigger place when we sold our house and split the money. But I hate moving so much, and it was such a monumental pain to move into this apartment up two flights, you know, and to find it in the first place, then get settled, everything, I've just sort of . . . stayed here."

"Karina mentioned that you'd been through a bad breakup," I said.

"Oh!" She looked startled. "Oh, no, that was more recently . . . that was the, um, the guy I sort of left my husband for. It didn't work out. Well, it lasted three years, so it was hardly a flash in the pan. I sound defensive. I feel defensive." She was talking fast, looking straight ahead. "I stuck it out with Eric much too long, probably unconsciously just so my ex-husband, Alex, wouldn't be able to say 'I told you so.' My ex-husband is like a spiteful older brother at this point, waiting for my life to fuck up, hoping I'll fall flat on my face without him so he can feel vindicated somehow." She rubbed her palms together, rubbed them over her hair. "I'm talking too much. I'm nervous, to be honest. I've been looking forward to this evening so much. I haven't been on a date since Eric and I broke up." She lifted her wineglass and said, "A toast to this evening. I have a feeling it's been a while for you, too."

I clinked my glass against hers, we drank, and then I said, feeling insecure but trying to sound suave and confident, "How can you tell?"

"Karina told me," she said, and we both laughed, finally meeting each other's eyes.

I leaned back against the cushions and looked around the room, which was indeed crammed floor to ceiling, in piles, over every available spot of wall and floor: furniture, books, primitive-looking stringed instruments and drums, framed photos and paintings, plants, candles, painted wooden masks, woven hangings, needlepoint pillows, and vases. I could see why she'd want to keep it all; it was a fine accumulation of possessions, the accrual of a no doubt rich and interesting life. Still, it didn't fit comfortably into this room, didn't fit at all.

I reached over and put my hand on hers. I could feel its fine bones, her heartbeat. I let my hand rest there, a little too heavily, and she sighed and leaned against me.

"Diane," I said. "I've thought about you constantly since the other night."

"Have you? Me too." Her hair smelled like a fresh, fruity shampoo, strawberries or peaches; I could feel the rhythm of her breathing against my shoulder. "I have no idea what I made for dinner. I'm no cook, to be honest."

"I don't care," I said. I enfolded her sweet, skittish hand in mine and felt much better.

We sat there for a moment, not talking.

"Oh!" she said. "Damn. The pasta." She jumped up, ran into the kitchen, and made a commotion of clanging and rushing water. While she was gone, I studied the living room more closely. The place was truly packed with artifacts. It was like a museum storage room, with paths between stacks to navigate through, essentially a repository of the past, mostly her marriage; I could see that Diane and Alex had traveled to Mexico, Turkey, and China, had had friends who were painters and photographers, had more than a passing interest in musical instruments, even if only for display. Or maybe Alex had hated all this stuff, and she had foisted it onto him. Maybe he'd chafed at all this, and now that they were divorced, he lived in a bare, modern chrome-and-glass box.

I saw, through an arched doorway into another small room,

cardboard boxes stacked against the far wall, just as neatly, just as crowded together as everything in here, halfway up to the ceiling. Everything was so neatly placed, I could discern patterns and groupings; there was method to this obsessive-compulsiveness. If this apartment was viewed as a metaphor for Diane's mind, then she had a brain that was orderly and full, and she had an excellent memory, and she had trouble letting go of the past, of anything, for that matter. Or rather, she had no trouble letting go of things that she was finished with, but the things she treasured, she was tenacious about. She'd jettisoned a husband, a house, a whole life, for example, so obviously these objects were the things she cherished most, these memories in physical form.

How interesting but daunting this was, to start over so late. Luz and I had been so young when we met, we'd had nothing much about our pasts to tell each other. With Diane, I felt a certain reluctance to open the subject of the past. Once we started, we'd have to talk nonstop for months to catch each other up on all that we'd missed. So much catch-up for so little time left to spend together. The math seemed lopsided, although I suspected we'd discover some sort of shorthand, since we were almost the same age.

Diane came back and sat next to me again, but not as close as she'd been before. "A little overdone, but still edible," she said, gesturing, not looking at me. It seemed she'd become shy again during her stint in the kitchen. "The thing about cooking, for me, is that it seems like everyone else always makes such a big deal out of it. You know, buying the right ingredients, having the new recipe no one else knows about. For some reason, it's always annoyed me, this obsessive snobbery about food, so I resisted the trend. I feel like I don't want to be like that about food, it's just *food,* for Pete's sake, we all eat it, so I went in the opposite direction. Dinner tonight will definitely reflect this."

I laughed. "Do you believe in God?" I asked.

She laughed too, and seemed to feel more at ease. "What an odd question. Is it apropos of my being a bad cook, because I'll probably rot in hell?"

"No," I said. "In fact, I applaud your attitude toward food. No, it's something I've been thinking about recently."

"I don't *not* believe in God," she said. "I mean, it isn't something I think about very much, so I don't have a firm opinion one way or another. My family had no religion. I consider myself an ignorant agnostic. What about you?"

"I'm an evangelical, fundamentalist nonbeliever. I actively disbelieve in God. I'm thinking of going door-to-door."

She regarded me with curious amusement. "But how do you know there's no God? How can you be so sure?"

"I'm as sure that there isn't a God as my son Hector is sure there is one. We're equally mule headed and equally extreme. Like father, like son, I guess."

"Karina told me he's in some sort of religious group on Long Island?"

"He's the leader now, I think. He and their guru, Christa. And he's marrying her. I should be so proud of my boy, he's risen to the top of his company! He's the equivalent of the CEO, if Christa is the president, or maybe it's the other way around. She's more than twenty years older than he is, by the way, not that that matters."

Talking about Hector and his life in this jokey way loosened a vise around my brain. I hadn't told Luz yet, hadn't even tried to talk to her. I was deeply dreading my conversation with her because she would, in a manner of speaking, rend her garments and weep and pull out her hair when she heard what was going on with him. Meanwhile, Diane smiled, taking everything I said at face value, including my tone.

"Has Christa ever been married before?" she asked.

"I don't know, why?"

She grinned. "Middle-aged women used to leave their husbands for other middle-aged women. Now we leave them for much-younger men. My ex-boyfriend was twelve years younger than me. Things always happen in clumps. We're that kind of species."

"Who do middle-aged men leave their wives for?"

"Middle-aged men don't leave their wives."

"You seem very certain of all this." Our wineglasses were empty. My arm was draped over the back of the couch, the standard high-school movie-theater trick. I caressed her shoulder and drew her in closer so her head nestled into my shoulder. She bent her knees up to curl against me, resting her forearm on my thigh and holding my kneecap in her hand. Things were progressing rapidly and well.

"I've conducted a certain amount of research," she said, her breath warm against my neck, her forearm pleasantly weighty on my thigh. "Informal, of course, but no less accurate for that."

"Technically, I left my wife. She threw me out, but I left."

"But if she hadn't thrown you out, you'd still be there," she said. Her dark, silky hair rustled in my ear and released another sexy strawberry-scented cloud. I inhaled deeply, my nose against her head. "Right?"

"Okay," I said. "But what does it all mean? What conclusions do you draw?"

"Ah," she said. "I'll tell you that after dinner."

"I don't care about dinner," I said, sliding my free hand up her neck to cup her cheek, turning her face to mine. Our kiss started out gentle, hesitant, romantic, but it didn't stay that way for long. Soon our mouths were open and wet and mashed together, and we were breathing hard, and our hands were clutching at whatever parts of each other's body we could grab. It was a full-on gropefest, hotly adolescent, unabashedly horny. "Can we take off all our clothes now?" I said without taking my mouth from hers.

"I don't know," she said. "An atheist like you?"

"I believe in many things," I said. "Besides God. Does that count?"

She pulled back to look at me, laughing. "Like what?"

"I'm a poet," I said with my eyebrows raised to indicate how significant this was. "That means I'm soulful, romantic, and earnest."

"And mystical," she said.

"Very mystical," I said. My fingertips were bunched around her nipple, stroking it.

"You know who the real mystics are? Physicists. They're the ones with their thumbs on the throat of the universe or whatever the saying is."

"Yes!" I said. "Poetry is tame by comparison." I took her hand. "Let's go to bed," I said. "But you have to lead me, because I don't know the way to the bedroom."

"It's not really a bedroom," she said, and led me through the archway into the room with all the boxes. In the corner was an antique cast-iron bed, made up with a white coverlet.

"Then what is it?"

"It's a sleeping alcove, according to Realtor-speak," she said, stripping off her shirt. She had no bra on underneath. Her breasts were small, well shaped, and as appealing as the rest of her. Giddy and thrilled, I divested myself of trousers and briefs in one motion, swooping them over my erection and quickly down, out of legholes, and free. We fell naked onto the pristine bed. I lifted myself onto one elbow to look down at her. Her legs were strong and shapely, her hips full and divine. We both had slack little bellies, the slightly thickened waists and softened stomachs of otherwise thin people of a certain age. Hers was adorable and sexy, but I averted my eyes from my own damn self, knowing all too well what it looked like.

"You gorgeous thing," I said. I cradled her head in one hand and her hip in the other. Her body was more elegant than Luz's, longer and lankier. Her skin was creamy and fair; Luz's was olive, pigmented, roughened in places. No sooner had I realized that I was thinking along these lines than I banished all comparisons, all thoughts of my wife. I tried to think about nothing but Diane while I touched her and kissed her and made love to her, but there was a warm, dark, womblike tunnel my mind always got sucked into during sex, and here I was again in its compelling vortex, surrendering myself to its gravity, as always. But after it released me and I emerged out the other end back into light and life, Diane was as affectionate and cuddly with me as if she hadn't known I was gone. She wrapped her long legs around mine and rested her hand on my stomach and kissed my neck and shoulder and face until I was hard again. We stayed in that bed for a long time, hours, till well after dark. Finally we ran out of steam and slept for a little while, then woke up ravenous. We got out of bed and sat, naked, on the couch together. We drank more wine and ate big platefuls of room-temperature overcooked spaghetti with grated Parmesan and olive oil.

"This is the best meal I've ever had," I said.

"You poor thing," she said.

We grinned at each other, dazzled and light-headed. She looked wondrous, like a girl in a painting. I felt wondrous and didn't care how I looked.

"What's in all those boxes?" I asked.

"My secret papers."

"Really?"

"Well, lots of tax returns and files and records, but mostly books. I have so many damned books."

"You should hire someone to build shelves in here. It would look so nice, a wall of books in the sleeping alcove."

"I know," she said. She looked at me with no expression. "I should."

"I could . . ." I tried to think: did I know how to build bookshelves?

"No," she said. "Absolutely not, I just met you." She was still smiling, but something had shifted just now between us; the mood was not as easy as it had been ten seconds ago. "Harry . . ."

I finished my spaghetti and put my plate on the coffee table. It occurred to me that we were both sitting butt naked on her perfectly clean couch after hours of lovemaking. I shifted a bit, crossed my legs, hoped I wasn't getting bodily fluids and sweat on the upholstery. I missed the euphoric glow between us, that endorphin high that had just dimmed a bit because of what I'd stupidly said about those damned bookshelves. "What?"

"Just so you know, I have no expectations here. I know you just got out of a marriage. You're not even divorced yet."

"I have the papers," I said. "It's just a formality at this point. I'm a free and single agent. Really."

"Okay," she said, putting both hands up as if she were warding me off. "But nonetheless, I want to make it really clear that I'm not putting any kind of hold on you or anything, I'm not like that."

"I hesitated just now," I said, feeling my way into it, "because I wasn't sure whether or not I knew how to build bookshelves, not because I didn't want to. Sorry if that was awkward. I would hate to offer and then show up with boards and bungle around all afternoon and end up fucking up your entire wall. But if I knew how, I'd love to do it. It would be satisfying to empty most of those boxes. Does that make sense?"

"Sure," she said, relaxing again. "Want more wine? I have another bottle in the fridge."

"I would love some more wine," I said. "If only because that means I don't have to leave yet."

"You're welcome to stay over!" Something shifted in her face again. "Although again, if you'd rather go home, I understand. Some people prefer to sleep in their own beds."

Evidently, she thought I was some kind of wild animal reluctant to be trapped, a woodland creature she had to coax into her lair with treats and promises of freedom. I could see how nervous I made her, the possibility of what this might be, the tentative but headlong tumble we had just taken together. She was vulnerable; I understood that. So was I, but of course there was no way she could know that right away. She would learn it soon enough.

"Go home to my monklike single cot at my daughter's house rather than entangling my limbs all night with a gorgeous woman in her beautiful bed? Do you think I'm insane? Diane, I want to stay here for a solid week, are you kidding?"

She was laughing, not even trying to pretend she wasn't relieved. "I'll be right back."

She went into the kitchen and came back with an opened bottle of cold white wine and poured some into our glasses.

"And now," I said, "it's after dinner, so you have to tell me."

"About what?" she asked over the rim of her wineglass.

"About the fact that marriages only end now if a middle-aged wife falls in love with a twelve-year-old boy."

"Oh, that," she said. "Women want attention, we want closeness, whether we admit it or not. When our husbands start to ignore us, we find it elsewhere. It used to be with other women who wanted the same thing, and now it's with cute young lambs coming up all bright eyed and emotionally clued-in because they were raised by mothers who taught them to pay a lot of attention to women. And they're excited by us because we don't want babies, we're usually in no hurry to marry, and we're self-sufficient and experienced and sexually confident. Am I generalizing ridiculously? At least I'm not asking you if you believe in God."

"That was a bit sophomoric, wasn't it."

"Especially because you don't."

We laughed.

"But tell me," I said, going back to it like a terrier after a scent. "Women leave their husbands, or kick them out, because they feel like we're ignoring them?"

She looked closely at me for a moment, during which I reflected that maybe this question had revealed more about me and my state of mind vis-à-vis my marriage than was wise, given the fact that Diane and I were now . . . something to each other.

"Let's leave it," I said.

"No, it's okay," she said. "The real answer is that I can't possibly know why every woman leaves her husband, but it's in my nature to generalize, so I'll say a qualified yes, barring abuse, addiction, et cetera. Men take up so much room. You're humble and attentive until we marry you, and after the wedding you gradually realize we're not leaving. That gives you license to tune us out when we tell you what we want and spread your legs on subway seats and take over the bed snoring and blanket stealing and keep the TV on much too loud and just generally act like we're there only to be adjuncts to your gloriousness. It's a real difficulty, when you're a woman living with a man, to feel like you entirely exist. Even still, now, after all this so-called feminism and equality. Do I sound angry?"

"No," I said. "For some reason, you don't."

"That's because I'm not angry, I'm amused. At my age, anger is pretty hard to sustain. I love living alone. I'm in no hurry to get married again. The second I do, I'll be back in the same place as before, whether I marry you, the postman, the boy next door, or Brad Pitt."

"I heatedly and entirely but respectfully disagree," I said. "I don't think I ever ignored my wife. I'm sure I did other terrible things, but not that."

"Maybe your wife had a different reason, then," she said. "But if I asked her over a cup of tea, I'm sure she'd tell me some things that would surprise you."

The thought of Luz and Diane having tea and discussing me pleased me greatly, of course, but I couldn't admit this, of course. "I'm trembling with fear, imagining the two of you dissecting me over tea," I said.

"No you're not," said Diane, rolling her eyes. "You're thrilled."

"And if I married you, if I were lucky enough ever to do such a thing, I would never ignore you. Never. I would worship and treasure you to the end."

She rolled her eyes again, but this time she was laughing, and I could see that she had melted toward me again. She wanted to be proved wrong, and I wanted to prove her wrong. The problem was that she was very likely right, if only because she was more intelligent than I in these matters. Luckily, we didn't have to contend with that yet or possibly ever or at any rate for a long time. For now, we could finish our glasses of wine and go back to bed. We made love again, more tenderly than before, with knowing, fond smiles into each other's eyes. Afterward, I curled my body around Diane's and held her close while she slept.

Her mattress was firm, the air in the room warm enough not to need a cover but not too warm for comfort, and I couldn't believe my luck to be lying here naked with such a woman. But I lay awake, thinking. I had to admit to myself, in the dark of night with no one watching, that it made me feel extremely sheepish to be doing this at my age, getting involved with a woman like Diane as if I were the kind of man a woman like Diane would want to get involved with. The fact that she was so wonderful made me feel worse. She had been partially right, in what she'd said about men taking up too much space, but she'd missed the point, the real reason we behaved the way we did toward our wives, toward any woman we were involved with. By middle age, most of us, the smart ones, anyway, had lost faith in our own charms and prospects. We saw ourselves for the hairy-eared, buffoonish, cantankerous things we had become, and we couldn't muster the self-love necessary to undergird our outward affections. We subsided into snoring, opinionated, passive fortresses encircled by alligator-infested moats. We let our wives slip away because we hated ourselves, not because we didn't love them. Those young frisky boys in their twenties and early thirties still had the audacity and confidence we older men had lost through simple attrition. Eventually, the world taught us that we weren't nearly as great as our egos had once caused us to believe. But this knowledge came to us not in the form of self-pity or self-centeredness or self-anything; it was quite the opposite, it was accompanied by a loss of self. When I'd watched Hector walk over the pond, his feet skimming the water's surface, for the instant before I'd dismissed it as ridiculous trumped-up bunk, it had struck me as a pretty good metaphor for being a certain kind of young man.

Chapter Twenty-two

Riding my bike to James's factory building on Monday morning was pleasurable and entertaining. The route from Crown Heights to Red Hook was short and direct, but it ran through a mishmash of different villages and zones. Karina's neighborhood, wide avenues lined with brownstones and trees, gave onto a chaotic many-laned thoroughfare of chain stores and zooming traffic I eventually left for a street of cavernous, bullet-riddled industrial buildings that turned just as abruptly into winding, rather sweet lanes of row houses, then just as suddenly I was dodging truck traffic and pedaling under the catastrophically loud BQE on the nondescript boulevard that led into the serene, anarchic maritime backwater known as Red Hook, that flat round curve of land jutting into the water like a polyp on Brooklyn's side, beautiful and mysterious with its wharfs and old warehouses and detached wooden frame houses and little family-run stores and restaurants. Except for the vast IKEA store and a gigantic supermarket on the waterfront, the place felt untouched, preserved. No subways ran here, and only limited bus service. It felt like the kind of place people didn't leave or visit, a self-contained little time capsule of waterfront Brooklyn life whose quietude was rare and undisturbed.

As I pedaled along, a realization arrived in the forefront of my mind, thumping all of a piece on its porch like a delivered newspaper: Diane was probably as much of a piece of work as Luz, but of a different variety. She might be just as needy and demanding, but in a softer, quieter way. She might require as much attention as Luz had, and would be just as hurt when I failed to give it. But somehow I sensed that she wouldn't obsess or accuse. She wouldn't spy on or persecute me for thought crimes with relentless, cold intent. She might crumple a bit, retreat into a den to lick her wounds and keen to herself, and I would have to go in after her and bring her out; otherwise, she might stay there. I could feel between us already the potential for tangles of misunderstandings, hurt feelings, and perceived neglect. I knew myself, knew I had it in me to appear to be a bastard when I was distracted and writing and living in my head. Things wouldn't change just because I was with a different woman. I wouldn't become better suddenly; Diane wasn't necessarily better than Luz. But I preferred her softness and quietness to Luz's outrage and hardness.

We were all crazy, that was a given. Maybe, though, I could choose someone whose vulnerabilities and reactions I could actually live with, whose brand of craziness jibed with my own. I wouldn't mind going after Diane when she retreated; I would prefer that to being attacked by Luz. It was worth a shot. Nothing was perfect, but this might be more comfortable somehow than my marriage had been. Maybe I was a better man for Diane than I had been for Luz, maybe I wasn't an asshole, I just hadn't been able to act correctly in the face of Luz's adamantine, irrational, fearsome lack of faith in me.

James's company was housed in the Beard Street Warehouse, an old, beautiful, restored group of factory buildings on the waterfront. After I was buzzed in, I rode up to the fourth floor in a creaking freight elevator. James was waiting in the elevator bay, looking dapper and freshly shaven and, as always, unnaturally well rested.

"Welcome to Custom Case, Harry," he said with a half-ironic smile. He gave me the usual warm hug that went on a fraction of a second too long, not homosexually, but socially maladroitly. He led me through a steel door down a creaking, blond-wood hallway to his office, an enormous, high-ceilinged, mostly empty grotto. This was where James spent most of his waking hours, running his small empire, writing songs, surfing the Internet, and doing God knew what else. It was the kind of private, luxurious retreat most men would have given their left nut for. There was a double bass and music stand in a corner next to a huge leather couch, an expensive stereo system with mounted speakers on a high shelf, a swivel chair and stainless-steel desk in the middle of the space with nothing on it but a gigantic flat-screen monitor, and beyond that, a worktable covered in wood and cloth samples and a couple of instrument cases I assumed were prototypes. Huge scrim-covered windows looked straight out into New York Harbor. Off in the distance, through the filmy scrims, the Statue of Liberty held her torch high, looking as militant and masculine and implacable as ever. Across the water were the low, ugly banks of Jersey, softened, Photoshopped by the gauze.

"Cup of coffee?" he asked, going over to a long table that held a mini-fridge, coffeemaker, and microwave. "Milk and sugar, right?"

I drank my coffee sitting in a straight-backed chair James pulled from a hidden corner while he rapidly went through a few e-mails and answered a phone call, something to do with a case for a harpist who needed it by that afternoon. He soothed her and got rid of her without promising anything, then turned to me with a bright grin.

"Glad you're here," he said. "It's good to have a friend around the place."

"Well, you're saving my ass," I said, "so I'm glad it's good rather than obligatory and awkward."

He swung his feet up on top of his desk. "How are you, these days?"

"Much better."

"Have you called Debra MacDougal yet?" he asked with sidelong mischief. "Now that her husband ran off with her brother and she's available?"

"I haven't called her, no," I said. "I think you're the one who wants to, frankly."

He laughed but didn't otherwise respond to this.

"Anyway," I said. "I'm living with Karina. I accepted Luz's demand for a divorce. Time to move on, let go, all that sort of thing."

"Yes," he said. "I had heard you'd left the Astral and that the divorce was moving forward."

"From Luz?"

"Not directly. She talks to Lisa, not me."

"And I talk to you," I said. "So anything I tell you now will get back to Luz through Lisa, because there is no code of secrecy among spouses."

We exchanged a long, level look. I could tell he was dying to know whatever it was I didn't want him to tell Lisa.

"I promise," James said. "If you specifically ask me not to tell Lisa something, if you tell me it's being said in strict confidence . . ."

"I met a woman," I said. "You might have observed my rosy glow."

James was genuinely surprised by this, although he made a visible effort to hide it. "Where did you meet her?" he asked, as if he could prove by demonstrating my lack of opportunities to meet women that my doing so was impossible, and therefore could not have happened, or, if it had, he could undo it by Socratic questioning.

"At a freegan meeting at my daughter's house the night I arrived. We hit it off. I asked her to have dinner, she invited me over, I went, I spent the night."

His upper face went into paroxysms of attempted comprehension. "You're . . . sleeping with her?"

"Slept, singular," I said. "Once. But I likely will again, I hope, if I'm lucky. I like her. Her name is Diane. She teaches junior-high English. She couldn't be more different from Luz, which is refreshing for me. She's got no psychodramatic tendencies or moralistic limitations that I can see. An oasis of calm and gentleness. Sweetness and light, that's what she gives me."

"Wow," he said. He waggled his eyebrows again and blinked a few times rapidly, as if he were trying to massage into his brain the idea that I was actually, really, truly involved with someone besides Luz, sleeping with another woman besides my wife, and that I was now allowed to do so openly, without cheating or sneaking around. I could see how hard it was for him to grasp such a thought, how deeply it threatened the most closely hewed-to strictures and stringently imposed prohibitions of his own life. I waited until he shook his head one more time and said, "That is amazing news, man. Good for you."

"It is good for me," I said. "Diane is not someone to treat lightly. She's a rare person . . ."

"You're falling in love with her?" His voice squeaked a little. His brow was still wrinkled up into knots of computations and internal adjustments. My friendship with James had always made me think of Pete Dyer, the best friend I'd had as a kid, a short tough kid whose company I had initially fallen into in third grade by virtue of enforced proximity—he moved in next door, sat next to me in class, and our parents were becoming friends. Pete had been unable to contain his mounting disbelief, when we both turned fourteen, that I was now allowed to date girls and he wasn't. "That can't be true," he'd said when I told him, "that *can't* be true," as if by insisting on the fact's impossibility, over and over, he could undo it, thereby restoring us to parity and shared datelessness. Instead, I squired Annabelle Morrissey to the movies on the following Friday night, and Pete Dyer sat with our third-wheel fallback friend, Moe Harris, a few rows behind Annabelle and me.

As with Pete, I had been thrust into James's company, and he into mine, since we were part of the same circle of friends, and our wives had become close friends. That we'd genuinely liked each other had been sheer luck, as it had been with Pete Dyer. And now, similarly, I could feel James trying and failing to overcome his preference for my company when I was rejected, cast out, wifeless, and frankly envying him, as I had been the last time I'd seen him. He'd been anticipating, and who could blame him, welcoming me to my new job with coffee and a sympathetic shoulder, offering comfort in the form of both a paycheck and marital advice from the double-barreled security of his incorporated kingdom and his secure married state. Instead, he had just learned that I, as a newly freed agent, was doing exactly the thing he secretly most wished he were allowed to do, and doing it with someone worthy and interesting and sexually available.

"No, no, not falling in love," I was saying, my tone conciliatory. "I like her, I'm attracted to her, but it's too soon to think about anything more serious than that. I'm still married, technically. I mean, I still feel married."

"When does that wear off, I wonder?" he said with genuine curiosity.

"I don't know," I said. "I think I'll always feel married to Luz, somehow. I can't erase all those years. I feel like I'm going on without her in one way, the most literal way, obviously, but not really. Not internally."

James looked mellower, more comfortable, now that we were on the subject of my recent troubles. "If Luz asked you to come back, would you?" he asked, leaning forward, his nose twitching as if he were trying to sniff the answer before I gave it. I could see that he was certain the answer was yes, and that extracting this from me would reassuringly vindicate his own circumscribed life.

"I ran into Marion the other day," I said, to distract him, and also, I had to admit, as a kind of payback for his self-serving question just now. "She has a new boyfriend. I saw them together in the park. It gave me a bit of a shock."

I sat back and watched his brain shift gears, saw him reluctantly let go of the topic of Luz and me, momentarily hang in conversational limbo while he replayed what I'd just said, and then engage just as avidly, and more intensely, with the question of Marion's new boyfriend.

"Why?" he asked.

"Because the guy is hardly older than Hector," I said. "And he looks like an Italian movie star. I have to admit, I was a bit flummoxed at first. I asked her about it. She says she's happy. I believe her."

James was gently hyperventilating, staring at me so intently his eyes seemed to bulge. "Well," he said. "Wow."

"She looked gorgeous," I added, cruelly, but also honestly. "Radiant, even."

"Oh," he said. "She must be happy, then."

"She seemed a little defensive about it. But maybe that was just because she could tell I was . . ."

"Jealous?"

"God, no! I'm not that way about her, James, you know that. I was going to say disapproving. In a brotherly sense. I just felt at first that she should be with someone more . . . okay, a guy more like us, our age, someone who has more stature. You know. Ike was a solid guy, a grown-up. Whatever their problems were, they were equals. My first thought when I saw her with this guy, Adrian his name is, was that he was too young and too pretty and would take her for a ride. Anyway, after I talked to her, I felt differently about it. She's happy, and that's all I care about. And she's no fool."

"Maybe she's filling her loneliness," said James. He was recovering his equanimity. Analyzing the vulnerabilities, insecurities, and potential pitfalls behind choices he secretly envied made by the people he was close to never failed to perk James up. "She never had kids. Without Ike she's all alone. This beautiful young guy must fill a big void for her."

"Like getting a pet?" I said.

James had the good grace to laugh at this.

"She's really happy," I said, pressing it home out of loyalty to Marion. I wanted James to know this, wanted him to have to face it. As Marion had pointed out to me the other day, we had both overcome the loss of our spouses. I wanted, I suddenly realized, to make James know that this was possible. But James had no real desire to leave Lisa, so obviously I wasn't telling him this in order to give him courage and hope. I was forced to admit to myself that by saying all this, I was trying to prove to him that his life wasn't better than mine or Marion's just because he had things that she and I lacked. True, she'd never had kids and she'd lost her husband, but now she had Adrian. And true, I'd lost Luz and been cast out of my home, but now I'd found Diane and a home with my daughter. I didn't want James's pity.

But as my brain went along this track, it led me to the obvious conclusion that empathetically pitying and fretting about those he secretly envied was James's way of maintaining control over his own most repressed emotions, his primary recourse against his most self-serving, strongly quelled urges. And why would I want to deprive him of that? I was his friend.

"In the end," I said, "Marion and I ended up acknowledging how hard it's been this year. It's been the most difficult time either of us has ever had. So it's nice that we've both found a bit of comfort, in the aftermath of so much suffering."

I knew James so well; I could see him inflate and pinken in the warm internal wind of compassion. I'd hit him in the solar plexus with a sweet-spot massage. "I'm happy for you both," he said, and I could tell that he was even happier that he could say that and mean it without any imminent threat to his sense of well-being. "And you probably haven't heard, but Luz has found another job, as a private full-time nurse for a rich old man on the Upper East Side. She shares the twenty-four-hour day with two other nurses, in shifts, and he pays them all a fortune. She seems to like it. She told Lisa that after St. Vincent's, taking care of one old man in a plush apartment is like being at a spa."

James's phone rang; he answered it, dealt with whoever it was, and hung up.

"Should I get to work?" I asked.

"Nah," he said. "Not yet. More coffee?"

"Sure," I said. "You make a great cup of coffee, I have to say."

"All it takes is the best machine and the best fresh-ground coffee and the best water and perfect proportions," he said, pouring and stirring. "Nothing to it."

"Thanks," I said, taking the fresh cup from him. "How's Lisa these days? I haven't seen her in months."

"The same," he said, beaming with amusement. "In her mind, we're on the verge of bankruptcy, the kids seem troubled and depressed, she thinks she has melanoma. She's so charmingly catastrophic during the best of times, I'd worry if she suddenly thought everything was okay. Then I'd know we were in trouble. Speaking of trouble, how is Hector doing in the group?"

"Karina and I were just out there. He's immersed in this cult, he's marrying the leader, and they think he's the Messiah." I told him about the trials, the aftermath. "Luz is going to have another nervous breakdown when I tell her, but she has to know."

"Yes," said James. "Should I have Lisa run interference for you? She could tell Luz you need to talk to her about Hector."

"I'll call her myself, thanks," I said. Then I reconsidered; Lisa would pave the way for me, act as an interstitial spur for Luz, who generally needed goading, arm-twisting even, to do anything she didn't want to do. "On second thought, maybe it would be better if Lisa said something first."

"Consider it done," said James with a lordly, husbandly magnanimity I decided to accept as his fee for services rendered. He leapt up and danced across the blond-wood floor of his domain like a caffeinated Chinese pixie, over to the far corner, where he curled himself around his instrument, a polished antique he'd nicknamed Jezebel, and began plucking with vigor at its two lower strings in that funny, ham-fisted way of upright bass playing. "Are you writing these days?"

"I seem to have quit," I said to the accompaniment of the bass's *plunk-plunk-plunk.*

He put the bass aside and leaned one hip on his worktable. "What do you mean, quit?"

"I started a new book this spring," I said, "but it's fizzled out." I paused. A feeling was swelling in me, one I hadn't acknowledged to myself yet, something that had been lurking in my depths and was just now showing itself to me for the first time. "I've become unspeakably, pun intended, bored by the sound and sight of my own poetic voice. I feel like I've gone as far as I can. I've said everything I have to say. When Luz wrecked my last book, I think she de-balled me."

"Impossible!" said James. "There's always more."

"No," I said. The dark, creaturelike feeling in me emerged further from the depths and showed me more of itself. As I spoke, I made it manifest, held it up and looked at it. "I've lost the egomaniacal steam that powered the whole enterprise. Without that juice, my subjects have dried up and blown away."

James bunched his lips together and let out a thoughtful puff of air. "It seems to me you should be starting your elegiac phase. What about yearning and loss? Meditations on mortality, the scope of the years, the decay of the body, that sort of thing."

"I've been bushwhacking in that direction for months now." I laughed.

"I'd love to see what you're doing," he said with an endearingly earnest expression. He picked up a piece of what looked like raw silk and ran it through his hands. "Why are you having so much trouble with such a worthy subject?"

"It seems," I said, "I've hit a brick wall head-on and sustained a concussion. Pardon the metaphor. I can't avoid it. Speaking of metaphor. That's the crux of it. Nothing has objective value; the only realities I've acknowledged are perception and experience, and they're subjective and shifting and up for grabs. There is no sun, so to speak, there is no ultimate, verifiable, central truth. Therefore, anything can be anything else if you juxtapose them on the page.

That's how my mind works. That's been my source of power really, but it's a form of egomania, it's a kind of swagger that doesn't age well, it can't weather the temporal equations of midlife. When I was younger, which is to say until a few months ago, I put all my faith in tropes. I believed only in the magic of verbal transformation. I sidestepped lyricism and went for irony. I thought I was so smart. I thought I was avoiding the sand traps other poets fell into, the loopy flights of faith, the leaps and curlicues of religion, the whole goddamned God thing. I thought I was better than they were. I wrote in formal verse, I hewed to the traditional structures, but I did not accept the common notion that poetry has to involve transcendence. I avoided transcendence. I deliberately denied its possibility. I kept my work in the world, bound up in what can be seen and felt. But now . . ."

James was nodding with slow head bobs of encouragement at this outrush, but whether or not he had a clue what I was talking about, I couldn't tell. No one loved empathizing with others' troubles, artistic and otherwise, more than he did. His emotionally vampiric nature thrived on this sort of bloodletting. I waited for his response; he liked to cogitate at length during shared moments of silence in the course of conversations. He fondled the piece of silk, put it down, picked up a small square of laminate and ran his fingertip over its gloss until he had clouded it with skin oils.

"Why not use that as your subject?" he said after a lot of consternated eyebrow twitching. "Write about this need for some sort of faith in order to keep on writing. The search for transcendence after a deliberately faithless life. This could be an epic poem. A masterwork."

I laughed; he did not.

"I'm quite serious," he said. "I think you're bored with your own cleverness. You need something else to get caught up in. A challenge. And this is nothing if not a challenge for someone like you—to admit that your own experience is limited and your perceptions are circumscribed and there are wild mysteries out there that only honesty, curiosity, and humility can penetrate. I would be excited to read poetry like that by Harry Quirk. A lot of people would."

"I'd better get to work now," I said, setting my empty coffee cup on the edge of his desk. "Accounts Payable is where I belong these days."

"Accounts Payable," said James, his shining black hair catching the gleam of the floor. "Accounts Payable. There's your next book's title . . ."

"Thank you, James," I said as I followed him out of his palatial office, down the hall to a much smaller, windowless office with three desks in it. "I'll think about that."

"Welcome to your new office," he said. "I'll send Maureen over to show you what's what. And let's have lunch later. I want to talk more about this. Come back at twelve thirty, we'll go out."

"All right," I said, and then he was gone. I located the desk that didn't seem to be inhabited, the one with no personal effects on it, and sat down and awaited the arrival of Maureen, whoever she was.

Chapter Twenty-three

It felt strange to let myself into the Astral again with my old key, strange to climb the old stairs and knock on my own apartment door, and stranger still to be let into my old home by my hard-faced, silent wife without a kiss or any warmth whatsoever.

She led me into the kitchen. I sat down at our old chrome-and-Formica table, in the same chair I'd sat in for decades. I rested my left fingertips on the familiarly comforting, rusty patch on the chair's underside.

Luz had agreed to see me only because Lisa had told her I had urgent news about our son that I had to tell her in person, and she had refused to meet somewhere neutral. We had both just put in long days at work, and I could see how tired she was. She looked older, paler, smaller somehow than she had the last time I'd seen her. That she had found a good new job was a source of no small relief for me; that I had a job at all was, I could only surmise but strongly suspected, of similar relief to her.

Luz put the kettle on without asking what I wanted to drink. Of course, she thought she knew that I wanted coffee, even though, given the choice, I would have asked for tea. Karina had been giving me a cup of strong black tea with honey and lemon when I came home from work, and I'd started to look forward to it with Pavlovian anticipation as I biked back to Crown Heights from Red Hook. Tea, at least the way my daughter made it, tasted so much better than coffee, I was considering switching in the mornings, too. I watched Luz measure scoops of coffee into a filter and didn't say a word about this or anything else.

I had come armored with the allure of my new life, my recent resolutions and revelations, last week's and last night's conversation and exciting sex with Diane, and, of course, the signed divorce papers in my pocket. I couldn't shake the persistent, extreme unreality of the juxtaposition of my present circumstances with being back here. The silence between us felt consensually prolonged, genuinely fraught, and equally painful to us both. While the water in the kettle heated, Luz stood against the counter with her arms folded, not looking at me. I could tell that she was making this coffee for me not out of generosity or kindness, but because she wanted something to do. Evening sunlight came through the window in an oblong splotch of brightness that lay flat against the butter-yellow wall and the laminated cabinet doors.

Finally, she set a cup of coffee in front of me, sugared and creamed exactly to my ancient liking. She sat down across from me and finally looked directly at me with her hands around her own mug of coffee. Our gaze held.

"So tell me," she said. Her voice was as cool and flat as her face. Between us, the tabletop gleamed with decades of wiping.

"First," I said, taking the papers from my pocket and unfolding them and smoothing them. "I signed these. Here. They're all yours." I slid them across the table toward her. They came to rest at her cup, right side up so she could see for herself. But she didn't even glance at them. She was clearly waiting for me to say what I'd come to say, drink my coffee, and then leave this place, probably forever.

Although I had expected nothing more or less than what I was getting from her, this enraged me. After all these years together, she couldn't even bother to look at the papers I'd signed or acknowledge the fact that we were now as good as divorced. Of course she had walled herself behind a thick pane of glass to obscure her emotions and refract the sight of me into something tolerably negligible, but it pissed me off anyway.

"Hector is marrying his cult leader," I said, spitting the words like hard little pebbles at the glass. "They've decided he's the second coming of Christ. We have no hope whatsoever of getting him out of there, because he's in charge, he's not a victim—"

"I know," said Luz. "He told me."

"When?"

"He called last week. We talked for a long time."

"And you didn't go right out there to try to rescue him?"

"What's the point?" she said. She looked exhausted and pinched, but much too remote and removed for compassion. "You just said it yourself. He's not leaving. He's getting married. There's nothing we can do."

"Then what the hell am I doing here?"

"What do you mean?"

"You agreed to talk to me because Lisa told you I had something to say about Hector."

"How was I supposed to know it was what I already knew? I haven't slept much since I talked to Hector, but really, I don't know what I can say to you about it."

I knew exactly what she meant: we weren't in this together, so she would suffer through the loss of Hector alone, without me, and I would have to do the same.

My rage doubled in size. To hell with that. "Karina and I just went out there, and I have to say, it's not a bad place, all in all. But we saw those so-called Messiah tests. We saw him walk on water and turn water into wine and heal a girl with lupus."

I waited. She said nothing, but I had her attention.

"That is what our son is doing with his life. And this Christa person is sleazy and corrupt. I was thinking about how you would have stormed in there and gone all Catholic on him."

"I don't 'go all Catholic,' Harry." The side of her mouth twitched in a half smile.

"Yes, you certainly do."

There was an uncomfortable moment of almost-warmth between us, which Luz deftly sandbagged by sighing and saying with that same cold, sour detachment, "Well, anyway, on the phone I couldn't say much. I just listened. He could tell I was upset. I asked if I can go to his wedding, and he said outsiders aren't invited, it's a private ceremony. Outsiders. That's who I am now. You can imagine how that feels."

I finished my coffee and set the cup on the table in exactly the same spot I had always set my empty coffee cup: near the middle of the table, situated to cover a small, comma-shaped burn mark in the Formica. I had done it unthinkingly, like a dog who pees in the same spot every day.

"And lupus?" Luz said.

Her voice had always had a nasal edge, a mosquito-like, breathy whine I'd once found poignant and sometimes sexy and often hilarious, when she was meanly making fun of someone or laughing at something. But now it was provoking in me an itchy, restless need to stand up and pace around. I pushed my chair back and went to the sink and got a glass of water and stood with my back to the counter, turning the glass in my hands so it sweated into my palms.

"It's an autoimmune disorder," she was saying. "It's incurable and progressive. Her symptoms won't go away, and then what?"

"And then they'll throw her out for her lack of faith," I said, "and she'll have to go home and live with her parents, and Hector will be untouched."

"Hector's the only one I'm concerned about here."

"Of course," I said; her maddening, willful myopia would never go away. "But everyone there is someone's kid, and Hector is running the show, so your concern can take a little breather for a while. He's got a new persona, I think he got it from you. Can that be considered a calling? Cult leader? That's his career. That's his dream job. You should be very proud of your son."

"It's not funny," she said with icy calm.

"I'm not laughing," I said.

"You think this is *my* fault?"

"Is that what I said?"

"It's obviously what you think."

I took a gulp from my glass of water. It tasted as if it had someone else's sweat and blood in it, like some intimate, disgusting thing. I turned and spat into the sink and poured out the rest of the glass. "Has the water here always tasted this foul?"

"The water is fine," she said. She sat very still, her back straight. She was sitting in the chair that had always been Hector's, the one with its back against the wall, facing into the room. "It's always been fine."

"Then the problem must be me," I said with a sharp edge I was unable to mitigate into humor.

Luz let this one go, and I suddenly ran out of fuel to feed the flames. We were vacillating between being too tired to let our anger at each other get out of control and being too angry to let our tiredness stop us. Ten years ago, we might have been trying to strangle each other at this juncture. Thank God for advancing age; it was good for keeping some measure of civil peace, at least.

"I heard you slept with someone," said Luz. The mosquito whine in her voice was intensified by the judgmental, belittling tone I knew well.

So she hadn't been too tired to fight, she'd been conserving her venom like a coiled snake, and now she was striking.

"But James said—"

She gleamed with cold triumph. "Of course he told Lisa. What did you expect? Everyone knows, Harry, they're all talking, and it doesn't sound good. It's vulgar and insulting to me."

"It has nothing whatsoever to do with you," I said in as hard a voice as I was capable of mustering. "I slept with someone, and I'm going to sleep with her again. In case you forgot, you threw me out and told me it was over. And we're getting divorced. What do you care what I do now?"

We stared at each other.

"And by the way," I went on, "it wasn't Marion. Not ever. Not even close. Not that you give a shit about that or anything anymore, and not that I owe you one fucking word of explanation ever again. I've got to go."

I put my glass in the sink and headed for the door, dying to get down the stairs and outside, where I could vent my rage by stomping to Marlene's for a drink.

"Harry," she said to my retreating back. "What made you change your mind?"

I halted with irascible reluctance and looked back over my shoulder at her. "About what?"

"The divorce."

I turned in the doorway, my hands balled up. "I realized that I didn't want to come back."

"Yeah, I got that. But what made you realize that?"

"I finally got it through my head that you're a controlling, closed-off, lethally angry bitch, and nothing I do is ever going to please you. Then I had an image of coming back to you, after I realized that about you, and I felt like I was going to choke, like I was going back into a cage. I decided I would never do that." I grimaced at her. "Answer your question?"

"No," she said. "Keep going. I want to hear this."

"Why?"

"Because," she said.

"Is this some manipulative idea of Helen's?"

"I stopped going to her."

"You realized she's a crock of shit?"

"I was finished with therapy."

I scratched my head. "I have nothing more to say, frankly. I'm through. You've caused me enough pain and suffering already."

"*I've* caused you!" She gave a gasping intake of breath that sounded like a half laugh. "I've caused *you*!"

"Yes, you caused me," I said, my words clipped and brisk and matter-of-fact, because once I was finished saying all this, I was gone from here. "I couldn't win. Either I was too distant and adulterous, or I was always underfoot and in your way. I was your genius in a box, but I wouldn't stay where you wanted me, wouldn't act the way you thought I should. You always had the moral upper hand. I was always in the wrong. You'd go off to church and come back feeling straight and narrow and good with God to find me sitting in my chair all loutish and scurrilous and atheistic, and you'd look at me with the most scathing . . . yes, exactly the way you're looking at me now. Judgmental and superior and smoldering with anger. Your church can't help you with that anger. It's poisoning you, and no amount of genuflecting or holy water will get it out. It poisoned me, for years. No wonder I had to write poems about other women."

Her toe was tapping against the rung of her chair. Her lips were pressed together so hard they were white. "Keep going," she said when I stopped.

"Being with Diane is so easy. She likes me, I like her. She talks to me like one person to another person. When is the last time you did that? I can't remember."

"What?" she whispered. "You're crazy. That is not how it was. We loved each other, Harry, it wasn't all me criticizing you." She began to weep with a guttural, deep hacking in her chest. "It wasn't," she said, her mouth stretching oddly around the words.

"You wanted me to say all this," I said. "I'm explaining why I signed the papers. You convinced me. It's over. You win. But so do I, it turns out."

"We both lose." She cried for a moment, grimacing with the

effort to stop and get her words out. "You gave up, Harry." She seemed about to add something else, then thought better of it.

"You were about to say, how typical. How like me that is, giving up. But I haven't given up. I've accepted reality. That's the thing I always do, I don't give up, I see what's there and act accordingly. I have no faith in the imperatives of any holy ghosts."

"Maybe you should try it."

I was still standing in the kitchen doorway with my hands clenched at my sides. "Maybe I will try it. But not with you!"

She looked at me, her face streaming with tears, her eyes swollen from crying.

"You want to think I'm a passive schlub who's all washed up and a hack of a writer? Knock yourself out, sit here and think that all fucking night long, for the rest of your fucking life. I don't care."

"I don't believe you," she said with a short, low moo of tears. "You wouldn't listen. You wouldn't look at me when I came home. You never saw me. If you had only—"

"Too late," I said, "too late. You asked me to come over here because Lisa told you about Diane. Right? You already knew about Hector, so that wasn't it. You heard I've got another woman and you summoned me here so you could find out about her firsthand and punish me all over again. Admit it. When I was begging you to let me come back, you wouldn't talk to me. Now, right, sure, now you're talking, now you're crying, now you're sad."

She stood and came toward me and put her arms around my neck and stood on tiptoe and put her head in the crook of my shoulder, as she had done thousands of times before, and wept into my shirt. My hands stayed at my sides as I stood there like a civic statue in a courthouse square. I inched my torso away from hers.

"Nope," I said. I reached up and removed her arms and pushed her away, not too hard. "Stop it, Luz, I have to go."

She stood looking up at me, her face wet. "I know you do. But let me say what I have to say first."

"Okay," I said. I folded my arms and waited.

"When I went to see Helen, she told me right away that the problem was simple, you didn't love me anymore, and there was nothing I could do about it but ask for a divorce. I didn't believe her at first. I wanted to believe you still loved me, and I wanted you to win me back. I wanted you to save our marriage."

"Could have fooled me," I said. "It seemed to me it was completely over when you threw me out. You wouldn't give me a chance to save it."

Luz made a gesture telling me to shut up, it was her turn. "But you know what? She was right, I finally realized. You didn't love me anymore. It happened gradually for years. My heart broke over and over and over. I was in love with you to the very end, Harry. You can argue with me all you want, but I know how I felt. You couldn't save our marriage because you didn't love me anymore."

"I couldn't save our marriage because you refused to speak to me," I said with weary, mordant amusement. "Seems to me that's the minimum requirement."

She wasn't listening to me. "And I was so heartbroken, you hurt me so badly, I wanted to hurt you back. Helen helped me understand that too. I needed to cause you a fraction of the pain you caused me. It was so hard to get your attention. I had no power. Well, that got your attention."

I laughed, a bark of angry expostulation. I couldn't help it. "Yes," I said. "I think spying on my correspondence and tearing up my book and throwing me out of our house and vilifying me and my best friend to the entire neighborhood with a trumped-up lie got my attention. Scalding my face with acid would have worked, too. Cutting off one of my balls would have been very effective as well. So I hope it made you feel better, Luz, because that would be the one good thing that might have come out of this entire terrible time that you single-handedly caused."

"No," she said. "I don't feel better at all. But I had to hurt you back. It was all I had. You were off with another woman, I was left alone, I wanted to cause you pain. Don't you see? It was the only thing I could do."

"Leaving the ludicrous notion of 'other women' aside for the moment," I said, "what you're saying is, you cooked up this whole destructive psychodrama instead of just telling me how you felt. You wanted to condemn and execute me instead of figuring out what was really going on and trying to fix it. That's what you're saying?"

"I tried to figure it out with you for ten years."

"Where was I when you were doing this supposed figuring out?"

"Standing right there with your arms folded, like that. Waiting for me to be quiet so you could go away again." Tears ran down her cheeks, but she didn't sob.

"You are so good at playing the victim," I said. "You're a genius at it. You kept me enthralled for years with all your needs and rages and vulnerabilities. You were the most fascinating, beautiful thing I ever met."

"And then what happened?" she said. "Tell me. I want to know. What changed? How did I lose you?"

"I think we'll never agree on what happened, and that's the problem right there," I said. "We can stand here talking until we're ninety and gaga, and we won't agree on what happened for those years we lived here together. Maybe that's the problem, maybe that's what happened. We spent thirty years under this roof together, and we have totally different ideas about that entire time we called a marriage."

I stared at her. My hands were clenched. Neither of us took our eyes off the other's face while we thought about this.

"Maybe," she said.

My hands unclenched. "Well, we agree on that," I said.

"Finally," she said with a bleak, pale, small smile.

"I really loved you," I said. "More than I've ever loved anyone else."

"Me, too," she said.

We were quiet again, looking at each other without expression. Something ballooned between us, a rich, heavy, immense bubble. It grew until it couldn't sustain its own weight, and then it collapsed into empty air.

"I have to go," I said.

"I know," she said. "Good-bye, Harry."

I left her standing there. I walked out of our apartment, closing the door firmly behind me, down the stairs, and out to the sidewalk, where the humid, sunny evening air jolted me like a good shot of whiskey, which was exactly what I wanted right then. I stood on the sidewalk getting my bearings, taking stock of my internal state, until I came to a conclusion about where to go next.

Instead of unlocking my bicycle and wheeling it to Marlene's, I left it where it was and walked up the leafy tunnel of sidewalk along India Street to Manhattan Avenue. I turned left and headed toward the butt end, Newtown Creek, chuckling to myself, light of step, feeling nimble and hearty. I swashbuckled past a woman with a dog, a man with a hat, a kid with a scowl on his red, angry face. I caught sight of my own reflection in the window of the secondhand shop. I looked jaunty, like a free man.

As I passed the flophouse where I'd briefly lived all those months ago, I almost crumpled to my knees as an attack of terrible sadness engulfed and weakened me. Luz was alone back there in the Astral, up in the aerie where we'd lived as young lovers and then as parents and then alone together again, no longer young, or really lovers. She sat now by herself at our old table looking at my empty mug, crying, and it was more than I could bear, it made me feel so desolate I wanted to fall in a heap in front of this mattress-piled storefront window and howl with the unfairness of it.

Crippled by sadness, my shoulders hunched and my neck twisted, I scuttled on to the End of the World. I stood looking out through the chain-link fence at Hunters Point. The church spire glinted in the slanting sunlight, the warehouses were reflective, blinding white rectangles, the surface of Newtown Creek was a writhing skin of warm scum and oil.

On the other side of the fence, near me, on the sloping concrete jetty by the warehouse, two plump, brown, shirtless boys were dangling lines into the creek and peering into the water. A small cooler sat next to them on the concrete slab. Several bodies of indeterminate character writhed in a net sack next to the cooler.

"What are you fishing for?" I asked.

"Crabs," one of them said.

"You eat those?"

"Yeah," said the other one with enthusiasm. "They good."

"What's in the cooler?"

"Chicken. It's for bait."

"Why not just eat the chicken and save the trouble of catching crabs?"

They laughed and didn't answer.

"You swim in there?" I asked.

"Sometimes," said the first one. They were obviously brothers, close in age. They looked like good boys, reckless and merry, occasionally pranksters or sneaks, but on the whole, solid citizens in the making.

"Have you grown another head yet?" I asked.

They laughed and kept crab baiting.

"There's a lot of really nasty chemicals and poisons in there," I said, but they weren't listening to me anymore, they'd caught another crab and were busy securing it and stowing it with the others.

ABOUT THE AUTHOR

Kate Christensen is the author of five previous novels, including *In the Drink*, *Jeremy Thrane*, *The Epicure's Lament*, and *Trouble*. *The Great Man* won the 2008 PEN/Faulkner Award. She has written reviews and essays for numerous publications, most recently the *New York Times Book Review*, *Bookforum*, *Tin House*, and *Elle*.